"Completely cinematic and terrifyingly plausible—you may never view Boston the same way again, because you'll imagine secret societies and dangerous secrets behind every door. *The Society* is total immersion storytelling, written with the confidence only an insider can provide—more than a novel, this is an experience. Relatable, sinister, and incredibly clever. Calling Hollywood—this is your next big movie!"

—Hank Phillippi Ryan, *USA Today* bestselling
author of *All This Could Be Yours*

"*The Society* plunges into the heart of old-money Boston, where power, privilege, and dark secrets collide within the exclusive, enigmatic Knox club. Through the lives of two women—one seeking answers, the other trapped by fate—Karen Winn crafts an atmospheric, twisty tale of longing, belonging, and the dangerous cost of uncovering the truth. This was gripping and sharp!"

—Terah Shelton Harris, author of *One Summer in Savannah*
and *Long After We Are Gone*

"With socialites, scandal, and an ultra-exclusive club, *The Society* explores the sinister side of privilege, class, and tradition. Karen Winn's evocative prose and sharp pacing sucked me into the rarefied air of old-money Boston, where power warps and secrets rule. A twisty escape!"

—K. T. Nguyen, Anthony Award– and Agatha Award–winning
author of *You Know What You Did*

ALSO BY KAREN WINN

Our Little World

The

SOCIETY

a novel

KAREN WINN

DUTTON

DUTTON

An imprint of Penguin Random House LLC
1745 Broadway, New York, NY 10019
penguinrandomhouse.com

DUTTON and the D colophon are registered trademarks of
Penguin Random House LLC.

Illustrations by Paul Girard

Title page art: keyhole element © Oleksandr Kostiuchenko/Shutterstock

Book design by Laura K. Corless

LIBRARY OF CONGRESS CATALOGING-IN-PUBLICATION DATA

has been applied for.

ISBN 9780593475362 (trade paperback)
ISBN 9780593475379 (ebook)

Printed in the United States of America
1st Printing

The authorized representative in the EU for product safety and compliance is
Penguin Random House Ireland, Morrison Chambers, 32 Nassau Street,
Dublin D02 YH68, Ireland, https://eu-contact.penguin.ie.

FOR GIL

And this is good old Boston,
The home of the bean and the cod,
Where the Lowells talk only to Cabots,
And the Cabots talk only to God.

—JOHN COLLINS BOSSIDY

On the cobblestoned streets of Beacon Hill,
Sits a townhouse overlooking the city's landfill.
The scent from a flower pervades the rooms
As sea merchants purchase to their doom.

—ANONYMOUS

The
SOCIETY

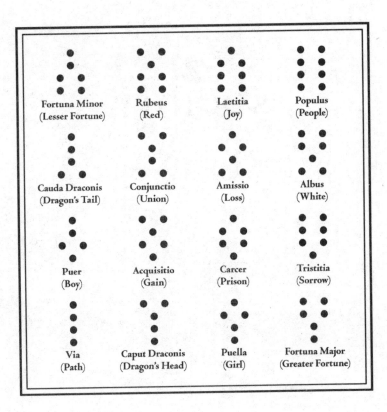

Fortuna Minor
(Lesser Fortune)

Rubeus
(Red)

Laetitia
(Joy)

Populus
(People)

Cauda Draconis
(Dragon's Tail)

Conjunctio
(Union)

Amissio
(Loss)

Albus
(White)

Puer
(Boy)

Acquisitio
(Gain)

Carcer
(Prison)

Tristitia
(Sorrow)

Via
(Path)

Caput Draconis
(Dragon's Head)

Puella
(Girl)

Fortuna Major
(Greater Fortune)

THE KNOX

What say you, curious one?

I see you lurking, through my windows. Very well. Come, then, have a look. Behold my stately brick facade, my honey-oak door with its ornate surround, my wrought iron fencing. My distinguished double-height first-floor windows, a rarity among buildings here in Beacon Hill. The boot scraper beside my entryway (a bygone necessity, but still charming nonetheless).

Yes, yes, it is true; I once had a mansard roof, but one of the Thurgoods—the miserly Samuel, I believe—replaced it with a flat one during the Great Depression to bring down property taxes. (I was displeased for a good decade or two.) At least they had the good sense to add a parapet.

Pardon me? You were not inquiring about my roof? What were you— *Oh.* No, I'm sorry, but you simply cannot stroll in, as if I'm some sort of museum or, God forbid, *ordinary* building. No, no. Only Knox members and their esteemed guests are allowed to enter my premises.

What is the Knox, you ask? Come now, don't be coy.

You truly do not know? You've never heard of the Knox Society? You must not be from Boston. Ah, a tourist. Of course.

Well, as any Bostonian very well understands, you are permitted *only* the view of my exterior. The rest—the history and secrets, the lives and deaths, the money and misfortune, the vast wealth and precious artifacts housed within my walls—is reserved exclusively for the insiders, the members. And so you must content yourself with shadows, and rumors, and the occasional fleeting glimpse of a world to which you will never, ever belong.

There is a simple, aching sweetness of being kept out, is there not? A pathetic allure in the unknown. Not that *I* would know, of course. But I see how you are now eagerly peering into my tinted windows, hungry for a preview of anything—anything at all.

It is futile, I assure you: All you will see is your own reflection, then your thoughts will shift to a sweaty, self-conscious worry about whether you've been observed by someone you cannot see.

You haven't been. The members within don't bother looking outside. Not at *you*, at least.

So run along now, tourist. Do not concern yourself with what goes on within the walls of the Knox. It is for your own benefit, after all. Truly, it is.

These secrets would do you more harm than good.

TAYLOR

Taylor's morning walk to work is typical Boston-dreary and *gray*: steel skies the color of metal office buildings, late February wind gusts that howl through her thin nursing scrubs, dirt-tinged heaps of snow piled on uneven brick sidewalks. Gray, gray, gray.

She lives in a tiny one-bedroom apartment in Boston's South End neighborhood, so at the beginning of each twelve-hour shift—which is an ungodly, unmentionable hour—she traverses through a city still shrugging off the dark. If she were to draw a line on a map from her apartment to Mass General Hospital, it is a diagonal, like an arrow piercing the city's heart, but given the old, winding streets, the actual walking route resembles more of a zigzag. The jagged, switchback-ridden path has stones laid as if to trip one up and crooked brick walls that tilt and loom, as if struggling to carry the history they hold.

There's an uneventful feel to this particular day, like time is cycling in a tiresome loop. The ER hums and beeps like a machine that is both well-oiled and in need of constant repair: too many patients and not enough beds or nurses or doctors. They are particularly short-staffed, as flu season is currently reigning like a smug queen, and Taylor doesn't get a chance to sit down— let alone use the bathroom—until late afternoon. But this is nothing new; she's used to shoving aside her own needs while working as a nurse. Part of her relishes the way the minutes disappear in the ER—it doesn't allow her to indulge in a pity party of her current situation—but she also loathes it; resentful of how she gets pulled in too many directions like a piece of saltwater taffy, fielding endless questions, chasing down doctors and missing medications, dodging the continual barrage of patients' frustrations unfairly hurled at her. At the end of each shift, she's usually worn thin, the taffy about to break.

Taylor squeezes in her sad excuse of a lunch break around three o'clock and makes it only halfway through a homemade turkey sandwich before being informed she's getting the next patient. She rewraps the remnants and puts them back in the communal fridge, where they'll be neglected until dinnertime, or later, then goes to set up the patient's room.

"February in Boston *almost* makes me want to move back down south," her Aunt Gigi remarks, looking out the small window of the empty patient room Taylor is readying. "It's colder today than a witch's teat in a brass bra." Aunt Gigi is the head nurse of the surgical ICU upstairs, and the one who got Taylor a job here in the ER—something that she often reminds Taylor.

Taylor pauses priming the IV bag to glance out the window herself. Like all the windows on this side of the ER, it depressingly faces a brick wall of an adjacent hospital building and makes Taylor feel suffocated in a way she knows she can't dwell on. Not here, not now. At some point, she'll need to address it; the claustrophobia has been lurking lately, like an old acquaintance waiting to be acknowledged. "Acquaintance" isn't right, though, is it? It's more like a foe, the way it slides its hands around her neck, grasping much too tightly.

She quickly jerks away from the window and focuses on capping the end of the IV.

"This weather must make you miss home, T.J.," Aunt Gigi continues. "It must be, what, in the high fifties there today? Only a measly thirty-degree difference."

"No, I don't miss home at all," Taylor is too quick to answer.

"Tell me how you really feel."

"Well, you left North Carolina when you were my age. And you never really came back," Taylor points out.

"True, true. But I was following my husband to his medical residency."

"Well. I followed my job."

"The job *I* got you."

There it is.

"Yes, Aunt Gigi, I'm very grateful." Taylor resists the urge to roll her eyes. "Don't you have somewhere to be?"

Aunt Gigi likes to come check in on Taylor from time to time, even though she is doing just fine off orientation. Taylor can't figure if her aunt is concerned about her nursing performance or simply fulfilling some sort of promise to Taylor's dad.

Aunt Gigi could also be doing it because she simply likes Taylor's company, but given how absent her aunt has been for most of Taylor's twenty-five-year-old life, she doubts it.

"I always have somewhere to be. The ICU is nonstop," Aunt Gigi says, with a sigh, before finally leaving.

Taylor's shoulders relax, and she takes a deep, cleansing breath. She's relieved she's no longer being watched by her aunt, but it's a complicated, guilty relief. Apart from her father, Aunt Gigi is Taylor's only living relative.

Taylor grabs a 20-gauge, 18-gauge, and 16-gauge needle each from the medicine cart and lines them up in a row. A 16-gauge IV is always preferable—you want a bigger hole to flush in as many fluids as you may need—but you never know the shape the veins of the patient may be, and Taylor likes to be prepared. She doesn't yet feel confident in her ER nurse position the way she did those three years while working as an orthopedic nurse back home in North Carolina. It's hardly surprising; being in an orthopedic rehab center in a southern coastal town is vastly different from the ER at the place they call "MGH, or Man's Greatest Hospital," after all, but she won't admit this to her aunt.

Nor to anyone. Taylor adds it to a growing list of things she is keeping to herself: How because Boston is so expensive, she's sent her dad money only a couple of times, far less than she planned. How sometimes, when she's had extra cash, she's guiltily spent it instead on herself—in the secondhand stores, purchasing castoff designer items. How she misses the bad sex she used to have with her ex-boyfriend Grayson. How sometimes she wonders if she made the wrong decision, moving to Boston five months ago. She wasn't lying when she said she didn't miss home—there's no way in hell she would miss *that place*, where the idea of fancy is donning sneakers instead of flip-flops—but she feels she has miscalculated what Boston would be like. It's not shiny and exciting like she thought it would be—or at least, not for her.

Another thing she keeps to herself: How, at night when she finally allows herself, the memories of her dead mother cling to her like the pages of a book she can't put down.

❖—◦—❖

The gloss of the hair is the first thing Taylor notices as her patient is quickly rolled in on the gurney by two paramedics. It's a lustrous chestnut brown, softly coiled with an effortless ease. It reminds Taylor of the Pantene commercials where the women toss their hair over their shoulder like it's no big deal.

Taylor has an urge to touch the hair. See if it's as perfect as it appears. See if it's real.

Then she thirstily drinks in the rest of the woman, which is also flawless—her skin like a smooth pearl, even under the harsh fluorescent overhead lights. No freckles like the ones that dot Taylor's nose, no sunspots like those that muddy her dad's face—and, to a lesser extent, Aunt Gigi's. No, this woman is a beauty: wine-colored lips, feathery black lashes, angled cheekbones. Taylor would bet money that her teeth are perfectly even, no gap between her two front incisors like Taylor has.

The woman's eyes briefly flutter open, and then they close again.

Something about her feels familiar.

She wears a silky cream-colored blouse, rolled up at the sleeves to expose an IV placed by the paramedics in the field that Taylor will need to swap out, per hospital policy, and a sumptuous brown leather tea-length skirt. Her pedicured feet stick out from beneath the half sheet that drapes over her. On top of the sheet, next to a classic black Chanel quilted bag, rests a pair of red-soled pumps: Louboutins with a jeweled edge.

This is no ordinary patient. This is a creature of wealth.

Taylor swallows, a flurry of excitement building in her chest. She's been waiting for this for months: a patient of this ilk and stature to present herself. Before Taylor moved to Boston, she envisioned that the city would be teeming with these ladies, that she would encounter them at every turn. That she would get to move among their world, learn from them, drink in their fanciness like gulps of tap water, letting that old New England generational wealth rub off on her until she glimmered with something of its gold dust. She assumed that somehow even her fellow Mass General nurses would be *above* those she'd worked with back home, set so far apart from the tired North Carolina women with their bottle-blond hair bleached of life and color, the men with their surfer suntanned sameness.

It is Boston, after all: the city of cobblestones and beauty, of Harvard and MIT, of sophistication and history.

The city her own mother abandoned Taylor and her father for, all those years earlier, in search of a more desirable life.

But Taylor had been wrong. The nurses here *are* different—as are acquaintances with whom she's spent time—but not in the way she expected. Far from being upscale or posh, they're commendably tough, no frills, somewhat guarded with outsiders, and mostly "wicked" smart.

As for high society? Well, the closest Taylor's gotten has come through occasional glimpses into the stately brick townhomes whose windows are left draped open in the evenings to reveal dioramas of crystal chandeliers and tufted velvet fainting chairs. She's also sniffed out society ladies in the museums she visits on her days off. The women who cluster around the exhibit du jour clad in Chanel tweed jackets and carrying Birkins, conversing with the curators, with whom they are on a first-name basis. Taylor's careful to avoid the first Thursday of every month, when admittance is free and therefore flooded with ordinary people.

And then there are the thrift stores, her kryptonite. Like nosebleed seats in a stadium, the secondhand stores in Boston's wealthiest neighborhoods allow Taylor to distantly experience the lifestyle she can't have at full price. The rich discard their fancy clothes far too easily: a little stain on a blouse that just needs to be lifted with baking soda, a pull in a cashmere sweater that can simply be darned—or better yet, covered with a patch or a jewel.

So maybe that's what feels familiar about this patient: She's one of Them, the wealthy. The old-money, buttoned-up kind of wealth that seems to prevail in Boston yet remains as partially visible and entirely elusive to Taylor as stars in the city's night sky.

"Vivian Lawrence, age forty-four, unwitnessed fall down a flight of stairs at a cocktail party," the older of the two paramedics says, as they pull the gurney alongside the hospital bed.

Taylor snaps to, embarrassed that she noticed the patient's clothes first, not the actual patient.

"Brief LOC. Glasgow coma score fourteen. Pupils equal, reactive. Equal hand grip. Positive ETOH," the paramedic continues. "Complaining of head pain, three out of ten."

In other words, the woman must have gotten drunk, fell down the stairs, briefly lost consciousness, but is now with it and doing okay.

"Hi, Vivian," Taylor says, as she and the paramedics slide Vivian from the gurney into the bed. The movement releases a sudden powdery clean, floral scent into the air, like the puff of a perfume bottle, and Taylor deeply breathes it in. She knows it instantly: Chanel Nº5. It's what her mother wore. As a young girl, Taylor used to both love and detest the perfume; it was beautiful and elegant, like her mother, but its presence also meant her mother was on her way out the door.

It's the most common scent amid the clothing stacks at Covet in Beacon Hill, the secondhand store with the best stash, thanks to its local residents.

"Hi, Vivian," Taylor repeats, as the paramedics leave. "I'm Taylor, your nurse. How are you feeling?"

Vivian blinks open and glances around the room with an unfocused gaze. Then, seemingly satisfied with the scene she's just taken in, or perhaps tired, she elegantly closes her eyes, like a butterfly coming to rest and tucking in its wings.

"Vivian," Taylor prods. "I need you to open your eyes."

Vivian complies. "Hello," she says, a little slowly, like she's just woken up.

Charlie, the nursing assistant, enters the room and wraps the blood pressure cuff around Vivian's arm.

"Do you know where you are right now?" Taylor asks, as she tapes a pulse oximetry probe over Vivian's wine-colored nail tip, which matches her lipstick.

"Yes, of course. Mass General."

"And what's your full name?"

"Vivian Lawrence."

"Can you tell me what happened?"

Vivian grimaces, but her skin remains smooth. It's hard to believe she's forty-four. Does she use Botox? She must. One of Taylor's patients was prescribed it recently for a neck spasm, and Taylor was tempted to pocket the vial of leftovers. She's read that it's best to start early with Botox, in your twenties even. But who can afford it at that age?

"I . . . I fell. I think." Vivian tries to touch her head with the arm that has the blood pressure cuff, and Taylor gets another whiff of Chanel N°5.

"Just a minute, we're taking your blood pressure, so you need to stay still." Taylor gently eases her patient's arm down, noticing a blue vein that will be a good place to insert a large-bore needle. She also notices the gold Cartier watch and the Hermès Kelly brown leather bracelet that loosely hang from Vivian's wrist— Taylor has the knockoff version of the bracelet. She resists the urge to trail her fingers over its smooth leather.

On her neck, Vivian is wearing a cervical collar—a shame, since Taylor can't tell if she's wearing a necklace—but on her elegant middle finger sits a giant emerald cocktail ring.

Is that emerald for real?

Taylor swallows, reminding herself to focus on the patient. She clicks on her penlight to check Vivian's pupils. Her eyes are beautiful bright green olives that constrict appropriately to the light. Of course they are; only 2 percent of the world has green eyes. This woman seems to be a rarity, even among her wealthy counterparts.

Taylor could Botox till her face is as frozen as a sheet of ice, but she still can't change some fundamental things, like her boring brown eyes.

Charlie picks up the Louboutin heels from the top of the bedsheet and deposits them into the same white plastic "patient belongings" bag where he's already tossed the Chanel purse.

Taylor cringes. It feels criminal not to separate the items. What if the shoes scuff the handbag? Such beautiful, expensive items deserve their own space—their own protective cloth covers, really. Later, when Charlie's not looking, she'll individually bag each one.

As Charlie tucks the belongings beneath the bed, onto the metal storage frame beneath, Taylor tries to calculate their wealth. It's easily equivalent to a few months of her apartment rent.

If she adds in Vivian's jewelry—and if that emerald is natural, not lab-grown—it could perhaps cover the down payment on a Boston condo.

"My head hurts," Vivian announces suddenly.

"On a scale from one to ten, how would you rate your pain?"

"It hurts."

"I understand, Vivian. I'm sorry to hear that. Can you tell me on a scale from one to ten, with ten being the worst pain you've ever experienced, what number it is?"

"He didn't clink," Vivian says, ignoring the question.

"He didn't clink?" Taylor repeats. Over the bed, she exchanges a look with Charlie, who is now holding a gown, waiting for Taylor to finish her assessment so he can help Vivian slip into it.

"The glass—the drink."

But whereas Taylor's feeling a bit of concern, Charlie appears amused. His eyes widen, and he's stifling a laugh. Maybe this is the stuff that the rich dream of, Taylor can imagine him thinking. Clinking of champagne glasses. He's not immune to Vivian's apparent wealth after all.

"My head hurts," Vivian says again, louder, as she shifts in the bed. Her skin looks paler than it had moments earlier, a sheen of sweat glistening her forehead. The monitor spits out the blood pressure, and almost immediately, an alarm sounds. The reading is high. Too high. Taylor silences the alarm. Something feels off. A clamminess trickles through her.

"Vivian, on a scale from one to ten, what is your level of pain?" Taylor tries again.

"A ten."

Charlie's grin is gone; he's now scrutinizing the monitor.

"A ten? You told the paramedic earlier it was a three. It's now gone up to a ten?" Taylor squeaks. Something *is* off.

"I don't know. It just hurts."

Vivian writhes, squeezing her eyes so tightly it finally contorts her face. Her heart rate is climbing into a dangerous red zone now, and once more the monitor sounds. "Can you get me something? It hurts so much! Please!"

"Charlie, page the resident. Now!" Taylor commands, and Charlie nods as he scurries out the door.

"Vivian? Vivian?"

Taylor fumbles as she draws up a syringe of Dilaudid. Fuck, why didn't she start that other IV already, instead of calculating the monetary value of Vivian's items? Something is seriously wrong.

Vivian moves again in the bed, but this time she doesn't stop. Over and over, her body rhythmically jerks—she's seizing. It's jarring to watch: this controlled, uncontrolled action that feels to Taylor as if the universe is stuttering.

VIVIAN

Three Weeks Earlier

Vivian is perched at her Beacon Hill store counter, her forearms leaning against the knotty wood desk surface. It's a few minutes past ten o'clock; she's just opened the shop. An early February sleet is coming down heavily—probably the reason her left shoulder is a little sore. It began aching on the three-block walk over from her apartment. It's an old fracture, but it likes to periodically remind her she's over forty, lest she forget. She rubs it now and clicks on the computer, waiting for it to load. Her desk—a repurposed tall antique table—is positioned like an island in a sea of surrounding furniture for sale. There's a bookshelf, a secretary, an end table, a coffee table. Another end table. Then glasses, vases, candlesticks, trays, lamps, mirrors, a full table setting. A *third* end table. A turquoise-painted carousel horse, recently returned from a repair and now tucked into the corner. On the display window are painted gold letters that appear backward from her standpoint but from the street read STORIED ANTIQUES.

As the computer whirs to life, Vivian holds her breath, allowing it to gather in her chest as if it will provide a wall of defense.

She's been awaiting a response from her accountant. Her phone vibrates, and when she sees the caller, she instantly silences it. It's the nursing home, probably calling again to see if Vivian can bring the La Mer face cream her mother is crazily insisting she needs. Christ. They rang yesterday, too. Her mother's proclivity for expensive moisturizer is part of the problem Vivian is currently facing.

Finally, the computer screen illuminates. With a trembling finger, she clicks open the email. The numbers come glaringly into focus, and the air whooshes out of her body.

It's not good.

She feels like a part of her has just been hollowed out. It's been only eighteen months since she opened a second store, in Chestnut Hill—the Boston suburb in which she'd grown up. And now, according to these figures, she'll need to close it.

A customer who is browsing—the first of the day—picks up a mercury glass French coupe to examine it more closely, and it nearly slips out of her hand.

Christ.

Vivian can't charge the sticker price if she doesn't have a full, intact set. "Careful," she barks.

"I'm sorry," the woman says apologetically, and gently places the coupe back on the gold leaf bar cart. Then she makes haste for the door, clearly feeling unwelcome.

Vivian sighs; the last thing she should be doing right now is alienating a potential customer.

She can't believe she's in this position. During the pandemic, a few years earlier, her business flourished. When the country went into lockdown, an influencer posted about her store, and it went viral. Vivian supposed she hadn't *needed* to open a second store, but expansion seemed like a logical step—and a new focus that she'd so desperately needed at the time. She also always assumed she'd have the family money to fall back on if needed.

Funny how her mom can't remember where the family fortune went but can recall the brand La Mer.

She winces, thinking of the hefty loan she took out to renovate the second store space.

Her computer blinks as another email appears. Vivian slips on her reading glasses to see who it's from but immediately wishes she hadn't. The sender is Locust Prep, the private school in Philadelphia that her goddaughter, Lucy, attends.

"Shit," she mutters. It's time to make another tuition payment. Vivian has been covering Lucy's tuition since her mother—Vivian's best friend from college—passed away from cancer. Lucy's dad routinely sends Vivian snapshots of Lucy's second-grade artwork, as if Vivian is the other parent in the relationship. Given Vivian's lack of maternal instincts, she considers herself more like the well-intentioned but removed aunt.

Vivian feels like she might be sick. After what she's had to recently front for her mother's nursing home, will there even be enough money left over for Lucy's tuition, let alone Vivian's own expenses?

Her phone buzzes, interrupting her thoughts. It's a text from her friend Rachel.

> Did you find your mom's La Mer cream lol?

> The nursing home called again about it!

> Seriously? What are you paying them for?

Vivian puts down the phone, smiling; Rachel can wait. She's hoping coffee and some bread will ease the dull throb she now feels in her head. And a Xanax; one should never discount the efficacy of that. She flips open her prescription bottle and slips a tablet into her mouth; the familiar, bitter taste is a jarring welcome. Whenever her primary care doctor suggests they discuss her weaning off them, she shuts down the conversation.

Vivian walks to the back table of the shop—her makeshift sort of kitchen—and tears a large chunk of French bread while brewing a pot of coffee with the Kona beans she imports from Hawaii that cost about forty dollars a bag. Is this the type of luxury that she won't be able to afford anymore? As her shoulder ache progresses to a full-on throb, Vivian regretfully realizes she should likely cancel her upcoming appointment with Marlen, her massage therapist. Perhaps expensive coffee beans are the *least* of what she will have to give up. She hasn't sorted through the entirety of her mother's financial mess yet, but she knows enough to realize that her mother was in heavy debt.

Christ; Vivian's in so much trouble.

The coffee finishes grinding, and she deeply breathes in the smoky aroma. She washes down the bread with the coffee, and as she stretches her arms overhead, warming up her stiff shoulder, she feels her body start to settle, as if pieces are slowly rearranging themselves.

The door chime jangles as another customer enters the shop. But when Vivian turns around, she finds her friend Xavier holding a bottle of rioja, wet from the sleet.

"Hello, dear," he says, tilting his head up to kiss her on both cheeks. He's short, or at least shorter than she is. His hair is dark, curly, moistened from the weather or from sweat. His bald spot—which she can see atop his head like a sunny-side-up egg—has grown since his last visit.

He hands her the bottle and shakes off his coat, which is much too thin, given the chilly outside temperature. He always dresses for the wrong season. Everyone has quirks, but their group of friends—she, Xavier, and Rachel—have more than the average number.

"You have no idea how much I need this today," she says, and then instantly regrets it.

Xavier doesn't drink, at least not anymore.

Xavier raises his eyebrows. "Oh? Well, as they say, it's five o'clock somewhere. Wait . . ." He pulls out his antique pocket watch—another quirk—to check the time. He started carrying it after a failed attempt to use a cell phone. "What do you know, it's just after five in Spain. Shall we?"

It's too early for a drink—Vivian didn't mean that she needed it *right now*—but since Xavier is clearly trying to smooth over Vivian's gaffe, she nods. She gets out a pair of wineglasses and uncorks the bottle. As she pulls out a sparkling water from her small fridge for Xavier, he takes a gander at the shop.

"Any new pieces?" he asks, meaning has she acquired any estate pieces worth his while. Xavier's a jeweler known mostly for his bespoke nineteen-karat gold pendants that many a Boston woman wears, but he also dabbles in selling antique jewelry.

This is their routine: He comes calling every few months with a wine bottle in hand, ostensibly to see her inventory, but more so to catch up.

"Just what you see," she says. She thinks but doesn't add, *This could be the last of it for a while*.

"Do you still happen to have that U.S. Customs contact?" Xavier asks.

"Yes, I do." Through the years, navigating the perplexing rules surrounding antique imports and resale, Vivian's developed relationships with certain Customs agents. "Why do you ask?"

"Well, a wealthy client of mine who recently became widowed is intent on acquiring an elephant ivory necklace," he says, and then adds, "You people with money and your quirks."

She notices he groups her in with this; he's well aware of her upbringing.

"Elephant ivory," she repeats, with a short laugh. She walks over and hands him the wineglass filled with water. "I don't think I can help you with that. Isn't that illegal nowadays?"

Xavier clears his throat. "Well, I might have a lead on the piece already, so it's really the importing aspect I need help with. Perhaps you could simply connect me to your Customs contact, and I could take it from there?"

Vivian meets his eye; he's never asked for something like this before, and it makes her a little uncomfortable. "I'm sorry, Xavier, but I don't think I can."

"Understood," he quickly replies, nodding. "Figured it didn't hurt to ask. Cheers." He raises his glass with a ceremonial lift.

But when she hesitates, he says, "Oh, that's right; you like to clink."

It's true, she does like to clink, despite her mom telling her that proper etiquette dictates otherwise. A quirk of Vivian's, perhaps. She likes to pay respect to a theory surrounding its ancient origins: Clinking was performed to mix together the contents of each cup so that if one contained poison, a few droplets would splash into the other. It was a gesture of trust.

"I promise I'm *still* not poisoning you," Xavier adds teasingly. It's what he and Rachel used to say to her, back in the day when the three of them regularly hung out.

"Cheers," she simply replies, and they clink their glasses together before she takes a hearty sip of the wine.

"It's a 2012 vintage, from a vineyard in northern Spain." Then he adds, rather earnestly, "Do you like it?"

Vivian does; she wonders how much it costs. Xavier has never been wildly extravagant in his wine purchasing, but he always brings a respectable bottle. As with her coffee beans, Vivian prefers expensive wine. But she needs to start adjusting her lifestyle choices sooner than later.

Vivian smiles, trying to put on a happy front. "It's very good," she concludes, but her voice betrays her, cracking.

"Bad day so far?" Xavier asks, tilting his head.

"That's an understatement." She considers telling him about it, or even part of it, but it's been so long since they've seen each other. Also, she senses it might make him uncomfortable. In the past few years he's distanced himself from her and Rachel, always dating some new guy and getting sucked into the relationship. She doesn't know what's going on in his life, not like she used to. "But my day's better now that you're here. It's so good to see you. It's been too long."

"It has," he admits, smiling. "Have you spoken to Rachel lately?"

Vivian speaks to—or texts with—Rachel most days, including just earlier, but she doesn't want Xavier to feel left out. "Occasionally. I think she's busy with the baby. How's . . . your family? Your mom?"

Most of his family is back in Spain, and Vivian knows he sends them money.

Xavier brightens. "She's good. A little heart trouble, she said in her last letter, but she's good."

Like his old-fashioned preference for carrying a pocket watch, Xavier also possesses an affinity for writing letters. He lives, Vivian sometimes thinks, like he belongs in the past.

"And your mom?" Xavier asks. "Still painting the town red?"

"No, actually, she's sick. . . . She's in a nursing home now."

"Oh, I'm sorry, Vivian. I didn't know."

"Thanks. . . . It all happened pretty quickly." Vivian raises the glass again to her lips. Given the little she's had to eat, the wine's already hitting her. Her thoughts feel a little syrupy, and she welcomes the sensation, the change from her reality. She's already halfway done with her glass, which isn't ladylike in the slightest. Her mom wouldn't approve.

But she doesn't want to think of her mom. She wants to forget Creutzfeldt-Jakob disease, the rare degenerative brain disorder that has rudely occupied her mother's body like an unwelcome squatter. Vivian doesn't, in fact, want to think about anything in the here and now. She wants to finish her wine and recall summer sunny days when she and Xavier and Rachel sat in lawn chairs watching Shakespeare on the Boston Common, passing a thermos of sparkling wine between them.

Time was, they were the three musketeers: an antiques dealer, a jeweler, and a genealogist. Engaged in just the right touch of unusual professions to have found one another, and sharing mutual interests: Sunday antique markets, cultural events, dining at the hot spots. Spending many long, wine-fueled evenings together.

But in the past few years, everything changed: Rachel had a baby. Xavier got sober. And then it seemed like he started replacing alcohol with men.

"Please let me know if you need anything with your mom," Xavier now offers. But his words sound hollow, and they both know it. A look passes between them. Vivian couldn't even reach him if she wanted to—no cell phone, and she thinks he recently moved. She's too embarrassed to ask, because she should already know. If push came to shove, and she needed to, Vivian supposes she could stop by Xavier's store in the jewelry district, but the tradition is that it is *he* who stops by.

Xavier suddenly lunges forward, past Vivian, and she turns to see the reason. He has positioned himself in front of the turquoise-painted carousel horse, whose profile is peeking out from behind a tall chest.

"How did you come by this horse?" he asks, running his hand over the horse's mouth.

"I repaired it for a client. Well, I arranged for the repair."

Xavier snatches his hand back, as if the horse has bitten him. Fear flashes across his face so quickly that she wonders if she imagined it.

Circus stuff has never been Vivian's cup of tea, either, but Xavier's reaction seems dramatic.

"A client?" he repeats.

"Correct." What is he getting at?

A frown tugs at his mouth; he seems like he's about to say something but then thinks better of it.

"Why do you ask?" she prods.

"Just curious." Xavier immediately looks down and fumbles with his pocket watch. "I've forgotten I have an appointment. I'm sorry, but I must go." He hastens away without giving his usual goodbye air-kisses.

Just as he exits, her phone buzzes with a text from her client itself, the Knox, or rather her contact at the Knox. Funny timing, almost as if they've been somehow listening, if you believe that sort of thing. Given that the Knox is a centuries-old secret society—and a notorious one at that—maybe she shouldn't be so surprised.

She's heard the same stories everyone has: an initiation night shrouded in secrecy, fingers reaching into all crevices of society, drug-fueled parties, a choke hold power over their members. They say the members partake in an annual midnight walk to the harbor in an homage to their seafaring merchant roots—and to offload any persons who've become unnecessary collateral.

But the rumors are of no consequence to her. The Knox is one of her biggest clients.

She reads the text: Ms. Lawrence, is the horse ready? If not, we are requesting an expedited repair. We need it by Friday. We can cover any additional costs required to facilitate this. Warm regards, Michael.

Of course you can cover any additional costs, she thinks. Vivian normally doesn't handle too many repairs. In fact, she gets rather annoyed when people assume as much. An antiques dealer is not a furniture restorer, just like, as Rachel often says, a genealogist is not a librarian. But given how much money they've funneled to her through the years, she makes the exception for them. More than the exception. At this very moment, there are a selection of "no rush" Knox items in her back room, awaiting refinishing. There are many antique restorers, but only a few excellent ones; the best one passed away during Covid, so she is still vetting his replacement. Luckily, Gerard, the *carnival* guy, was able to slot in the carousel horse.

Vivian studies the signature on the text: Warm regards, Michael. Is that a change from his usual? She scrolls through the trove of texts between her and Michael. She doesn't delete messages, so their entire history is there. Sure enough, he at first signed, simply: -Michael. And then, for the longest time: Best, Michael. They are on a "warm regards" basis now, apparently.

This surprises her. When he comes into the shop, stooping as he descends the first few steps to avoid hitting his head on the overhead beam, he keeps things brief, professional.

She tries to remember if he wears a wedding band. Or, really, what he looks like. He's tall, of course. Tall like a basketball player. But "athletic" would be the least likely word she'd use to describe him. He's unassuming, stiff. *Too* stiff, really. Always so reserved and proper, always dressed in a dark suit, as if he's coming from or going to a funeral. He doesn't seem unkind, though—more socially awkward.

Vivian starts to type back, It's ready now, but then stops.

She looks at the horse, then back at the text. Then she clicks the phone's side button to bring up her lock screen: a picture of her mom. Her hair is pulled severely back in a bun; she wears a light pink lipstick that matches her Chanel tweed jacket, circa 1993 spring collection.

A childhood memory surfaces, and on its back, a wild, wild idea now forms in Vivian's head. Chewing the inside of her cheek, she deletes the first message and taps out a different response: The horse is not ready yet. I'll let you know.

And then, at the end, adds: Warmest, Vivian.

TAYLOR

By the time Taylor exits the hospital, it's late. The only brave souls out on the streets are ushering along dogs in pet puffer jackets and knitted sweaters. Everyone else appears tucked away in their houses, likely sipping hot chocolate or cozying up by fires.

She pulls out her phone from her down lumberjack-style jacket, which is the least fashionable thing she wears but also the warmest, and powers it on. Taylor keeps her phone off during work, not because she's averse to technology but rather because it's depressing to be faced with how few people reach out to her on any given day. Her dad will ring her a few times over the course of a week, as will Aunt Gigi (if she hasn't seen Taylor at the hospital), and Sam, her neighbor and friend, though he prefers to text. Occasionally a friend from back home will get in touch, but Taylor is surprised by how infrequently that occurs. It's as if when she broke up with Grayson, she broke up with the entire life they'd had together. She's on a group chat with nurses from the orthopedic rehab center where she used to work, but Taylor almost wishes she weren't. Hey, T.J., they like to occasionally ask. How is it working at that fancy hospital in Boston? T.J., tell us a good ER story. Taylor feels pressured to paint some ideal picture, so she's gone quiet on the chat.

And then there are the calls she'd rather *not* receive at all: a Visa credit card representative, the financial loan servicer of the community college where she'd gotten her nursing degree four years earlier.

The frigid air and empty streets make Taylor feel lonely in a starved kind of way. She doesn't have any messages. It's so freaking cold. She's exhausted. She hasn't eaten in hours, not since she wolfed down that turkey sandwich before Vivian arrived to the ER. And then once Vivian *decompensated*—a fancy medical term Taylor's noticed her fellow nurses and the doctors like to use—there was no time to do anything. Only once Vivian had transferred to the ICU was Taylor able to catch up on charting.

She now wishes to *compensate* with wine, a lot of wine, because Vivian keeps clouding her thoughts.

How did her patient go south so quickly? Maybe if Taylor had paid closer attention to Vivian's symptoms rather than to her clothes and jewelry . . . A guilt vibrates in her like the buzz of a low-level light.

Is the liquor store near her apartment still open? She checks her phone again; it's nearing ten o'clock, so Taylor has about fifteen minutes. She might make it in time, if she picks up the pace.

Back home, she'd had a car to get around: a green 2011 MINI Countryman, with too many miles and a funky GPS system, which she was forced to rely on when her cell phone died, an occurrence that happened all too often with her dad's hand-me-down phone. The car's navigation focused insistently on the street she was on, never allowing her to zoom out enough to even see the lines of the next town, the next state. It felt like the thing was taunting her: *Good luck getting out of this place. You're stuck here, T.J.*

Then one day, when she wasn't scheduled to work at the orthopedic center, she turned the navigation off and went for a drive without a destination. She ended up going north, along the thin peninsula of the Outer Banks, until the sea and bay no longer hemmed her in on either side. Stopping eventually at a coffee shop, she breathed deeply, the air suddenly lighter.

And that day started a series of long, aimless drives. She'd go for hours, trying to poke at the universe's bubble. Wondering if she might drive far enough and long enough to shrug off the ennui that encircled her.

"You shouldn't be making these long drives alone, T.J.," her dad often remarked, when he called while she was on the road. Initially weary of the ten years Grayson had on her, her dad had mostly come around. "Where's Grayson?"

"It's fine, Dad," she'd assure him, avoiding the question. "I'm listening to a podcast." Then she'd end the call and crank up the volume of *Dressed: The History of Fashion*. She didn't know how to explain to her father that since Grayson thought her directionless excursions were foolish, a waste of gas, she'd stopped telling him about them. And, almost to her surprise, Grayson stopped asking her where she was going when she disappeared for hours, sans her nursing scrubs.

And like that, they began to slowly slip away from each other, two swimmers curiously drifting apart in a flat, flat current.

✦══◦══✦

She's making good time to the liquor store. She turns right and rushes down the southwest corridor, careful to avoid black-ice spots, but then comes to a sudden halt when she reaches the intersection of Greenwich Lane. The most direct route dictates that she continue straight. But she hasn't dared set foot on Greenwich Lane since moving to Boston.

Fuck it.

She takes a few halting steps, but almost instantly, a familiar panic engulfs her. It's as if a giant is stepping on her chest, her stomach, all air and thoughts and sanity whooshing out of the way.

She backtracks, and the giant slowly releases his foot.

When she reaches the liquor store a few minutes later, having looped around, the man on the inside is turning the door sign to CLOSED. She tries the handle nevertheless, pleading with the man, but it's locked. The man shakes his head, points to the sign.

When he turns away, Taylor is left staring at a vague reflection of herself, illuminated by the glow of a nearby old-fashioned streetlamp. She bites her lip, willing herself not to cry. The reflection mirrored back at her is vague, phantomlike, as if Taylor doesn't quite exist.

◆—○—◆

An hour later, Taylor is curled up on the couch in her neighbor Sam's apartment, relaying the injustice of the liquor store clerk who turned her away.

"And I was wearing these scrubs! You'd think he'd take pity on me. You know, a nurse working late and all."

"He probably couldn't see your scrubs," Sam replies, topping off Taylor's glass with more whiskey. Taylor prefers wine to hard alcohol, but tonight she'll take what she can get. "I mean, you do have that apartment for a coat, and then your tall boots."

"My coat is not *that* big."

"Yeah, it is. It's at least a studio apartment." Sam smirks. It seems to amuse him that Taylor's such an aspiring fashionista but chooses to wear the lumberjack coat.

"Okay, fine. But it's more like . . . like a camper than an apartment. Because it travels. Trust me, you would wear that coat, too, if you had to walk to work in this weather at five thirty a.m."

Sam scrunches his nose. It's a nice nose, long and strong. Taylor wants to tell him that but doesn't know if that's a weird thing to say. Is she drunk already?

"I wouldn't be caught dead in your coat," he says. "Or outside at five thirty a.m., unless I'm coming home from a club."

Taylor believes him. Sam is a senior hairstylist at one of the most well-known salons in Boston, one that Taylor can't afford. Occasionally he'll hold up the ends of her hair and declare it's time for a trim; then he'll sneak her into his salon after-hours to give her a free cut. Taylor is grateful, though sometimes wishes she could visit the salon like a normal customer during regular business hours. Sam moves in circles that Taylor wishes she did: old-money Bostonians, new-money Bostonians, influencers, local celebrities, politicians. Funny enough, he's a bit of a homebody, which is probably one of the reasons why he and Taylor get along so well. Or, at least, he's that way now; he's twelve years older than Taylor and says he used to party a lot more when he was her age. Frankly, he *still* parties a heck of a lot more than she does.

"Maybe the guy at the liquor store just didn't care that you're a nurse," Sam says, picking up his phone to scroll through a dating app. "Even though he should. You should, like, get a nurse discount or something," he adds, catching her eye before peering back down at his phone.

He's always giving her credit she doesn't feel she entirely deserves. His late mom was a nurse. Another thing they have in common: They both don't have moms.

"Yeah, well, he better hope he doesn't end up in my ER."

"What do you think about this one?" Sam holds up his phone to show Taylor a photo of a young, buff man wearing only cutoff jeans.

"Seriously?"

"Is that a no?"

"Yeah, that's one hundred percent a no. He's too young and trying too hard."

"Ouch. You're right." He laughs. "I like drunk Taylor. You say what you mean."

"I always say what I mean."

"You say what you mean. But you don't always say."

It's funny how much he seems to know her even though they haven't been friends for that long.

And what is she *not saying* to him?

Vivian.

Vivian, Vivian, Vivian.

Her patient swims around in her blurry head, resurfacing at any break in the conversation.

Sam must sense she's had a rough day, but he doesn't press her.

"I don't know how you do it," he remarks, with a bit of awe, and it suddenly feels like he's snipping a suture on a laceration that hasn't yet healed.

She doesn't deserve his admiration. Something else she keeps to herself: Most days she doesn't even know if she wants to be a nurse, surrounded by so much sickness it invariably seeps into the pores of her life—random ambulance sirens on the street that penetrate her thoughts, the coughs of strangers she can't help but identify, the coffee barista whose bulging hand vein would make for excellent IV access. Before Taylor was a nurse, life was just life, bodies just bodies—hands just hands. Some days—like today—she wonders if she's made a terrible mistake. Not just about her choice of career, but her life. Is she working toward something or just pretending to? It often feels like she's running aimlessly on a treadmill but deluding herself into believing that she's outside, moving with purpose.

Taylor takes a long sip of the whiskey, letting it slowly trickle down her throat with a spicy heat. Tonight, she will drink and let Vivian, and her job, and her uncertainty sink into the deep gulfs of her mind.

⟢——○——⟢

A couple of whiskeys later, Taylor is in her bed and annoyingly awake. It's the middle of the night, sometime between the hours of one and three, when time is heavy in a gluttonous way, the minutes lazy and fat.

The night demons, her dad used to call them, when Taylor was a little girl. She would appear at his bedside in her night-gown, clutching a shiny silver sequin change purse that she used like a lovey. It was her mom's change purse she'd left behind in the near empty closet. Her dad would allow Taylor to crawl into bed next to him, and within minutes he'd easily fall back asleep, his snores cutting the quiet like foghorns. But she'd stay awake as the minutes ever so slowly ticked by, waiting for morning light to appear at the corners of the bedroom window shade.

It's been years since she had the night demons, but ever since moving to Boston, they've returned.

Why is life so hard? Taylor thinks, like she does every night when she awakes between the hours of 1:00 and 3:00 a.m. Back when she was a little girl, the questions were different. *Why did Mom leave?* And then: *Why did Mom have to die in that fire?*

When her mother arrived in Boston, she sent Taylor only a handful of letters—three, to be exact—but they contained rich sensory delights: stately brownstones on bumpy cobblestone streets, magical oil streetlamps, lobster scrambled eggs, and salty oysters with the promise of pearls. Historic buildings that belonged back in time. High-society parties with women in chic attire. Taylor read the letters so many times their words imprinted on her like tattoos.

Her mother was asked to model for a local Boston designer, Taylor's father explained one day. "She had to go, T.J. Your mom couldn't do that kind of thing here, in the Outer Banks. The only thing she could model here would've been a wetsuit. Or our restaurant T-shirt."

Maybe it's Taylor's fault that Boston is not turning out how it was supposed to. She's had unrealistic expectations. She thought by now she'd be well immersed in some fairy-tale story—like her mother clearly had been, before her untimely death on Greenwich Lane—but instead Taylor's trapped in a boring nonfiction read.

It's not like she thought she'd get asked to model when she moved to Boston; she wouldn't want to, and besides, she doesn't have the kind of looks her mother did. But—if Taylor allows herself to admit it—she believed that Boston would somehow fix her.

Instead, when she wakes up in the middle of the night, she creeps closer and closer to the conclusion that she's unfixable.

Perhaps she should resign herself to her current situation and be grateful she's a nurse at Man's Greatest Hospital. And try to meet someone. In the first month Taylor moved here, she slept with two residents who she later spotted sitting together in the hospital cafeteria. Since then, she's avoided dipping into the incestuous hospital pool. Should she agree to be set up with Aunt Gigi's book club friend's son who works in finance?

Or maybe she should sign up for a dating app, like Sam. She once tried a website version, thinking it would be more serious than an app—paid the fee and all—but the questions they asked were so thorough it felt invasive, judgmental even. *When was the last time you cried? What is your favorite sexual position? What is your approach to polyamory?*

Her answers had been too boring, bordering on pathetic: *I cried yesterday. My favorite sexual position is missionary. I prefer monogamy.* When she paused to look at the profile she was creating, *s*he didn't even like it. So then she'd created a new profile, which required she pay another fee and use a new email address for which she had to register. Halfway through that sign-up process, where she lied about everything, her name being the least of it, she touched herself until she came.

Taylor now pours herself a 3:00 a.m. bowl of Lucky Charms and sits at her Formica countertop, hoping the night demons will soon settle. Her garden-level apartment is a mirror image of Sam's, the second half of an apple. Though his is of a decidedly fancier variety. She inherited the furniture in her small living space from the previous tenant: an uncomfortable purple love seat and worn coffee table. Her apartment is small, so she has no kitchen table, but it came down to either that or the stand for her sewing machine. There was really no choice, given all the repairs she does on her thrift-store finds. In Sam's place, he's made small but significant improvements over the years: extending the kitchen countertop a couple of feet, built-in shelves, a hanging copper pot rack.

Like her, Sam rents from Anna, their landlord. But he also owns a cottage on the Cape that he escapes to on summer weekends and to which he's promised he'll bring Taylor.

Taylor hopes she makes it in Boston that long.

She finishes the cereal and puts the bowl inside the sink, alongside the cereal bowl from the previous day. She likes to leave dishes in the sink so her apartment appears lived-in, less lonely.

She looks at the sweatshirt draped over the couch, hesitating before picking it up. It's the sweatshirt she wore earlier to work. She has to dig through the pockets to find what she's looking for.

A key.

Opening her laptop, she logs into Epic, the hospital's electronic health record system.

What kind of life must Vivian live? she wonders. *What kind of apartment—or house? What does she do for work? Does she work?*

The alcohol has done the opposite of drowning out thoughts of Vivian. Instead, it's brought them closer, the way an ocean churns objects to its surface, bobbing them together.

Taylor loops her finger through the hole of the key ring, twirling it around.

She hadn't meant to take the key home with her; she'd tucked it in her pocket when she found it, moving Vivian from the bed to the CT scan machine. Perhaps it had fallen out of Vivian's purse.

But then, in the flurry of activity that ensued, Taylor forgot all about the key until she was walking home. She could have—should have—turned around and given it to security, to be placed among Vivian's other personal belongings that they were holding on her behalf.

But she hadn't.

She'd let it sit heavily in her pocket during her cold walk home, through her whiskey-fueled conversation with Sam, a little bronze secret bumping against her every other thought and word.

Her finger hovers over Vivian's name. She's never looked up a patient while she's not at the hospital. She knows they track this kind of stuff. But she has a right to look, doesn't she? If she were returning to work, that would be the first thing she'd do: look up her patient to see how she is doing.

So many of Taylor's patients are never admitted to the floor: They are triaged, treated, and released, ushered out the door from whence they came. In the ER, she often doesn't have time to get to know her patients; it's something she misses from working at the outpatient orthopedic center. For the handful of ER patients who do get admitted, Taylor has historically followed their progress, even visited them at the bedside. She's felt a certain amount of care for them, like a mother hen. She's not totally heartless, after all. There was *something* about nursing that drew her to it, even if she initially just viewed it as a means to an end, a one-way ticket to get the hell out of her small, suffocating North Carolina town and into Boston.

So, checking up on her patient via the online portal isn't totally out of the ordinary. It's just 3:00 a.m. out of the ordinary.

But Taylor has an itch to scratch. She wants to know more about this patient who arrived looking like a Van Gogh among a bunch of kindergarten-level finger paintings. Vivian deteriorated so quickly—her brain swelling from the subdural hematoma—and then she was promptly put into a medical coma. So now any chance Taylor has of communicating with the woman is gone, which makes her feel only more compelled to understand: *How does one become a Vivian in life? Who is she?*

Taylor swallows as a burgeoning insight builds within her: Vivian is who *Taylor's mother* was. Who Taylor's mother would have been, had she not died in a basement house fire. Yes, Vivian's a few years younger than her mother would be, and yes, she has green eyes instead of her mother's brown, but Vivian's elegant essence is the same one Taylor's mother possessed. They even wear the same scent.

Taylor presses on Vivian's name with a decisive click. The screen opens to a new window, making her feel like she always does: Whether she's at her dad's crab house restaurant watching wealthy summer tourists, flipping through old photos of her stylish mom, or gazing through the windows of fancy Boston townhomes at the city's elite, it's the same sensation.

Her whole life she's been peering at everything she's ever wanted from the outside.

VIVIAN

Present Day

I am what I am. Two puffed cheeks, a round nose. Yellow pipe. Sailor hat. *Popeye* is the first thing she thinks of when she comes to.

Or simply comes—to whatever she is. Darkness fraying at the edges, like a raw hem.

Popeye. Spinach, the metal lid peeling back. Gulps of green. *I yam what I am.* Yams. Buttered, soft.

No—no food. Not now. Her stomach feels heavy, a dull ache in it.

Christ. Where am I?

Darkness shrinking, there's light, clarity—there!—in her grasp. And then it's gone, a snatch of dream morphing into another, into the absurd: a word, a color, a shape that's abruptly no longer a shape.

There are beeps, steady beeps. An alarm clock that won't quit.

Five more minutes, she thinks. She is so damn tired.

Voices murmur around her. Near but distant. Background chatter in pockets, drifts of conversation, people talking on a train. On a bus. In an airport. In an alarm clock, in a clock—*She is in a clock!*—swinging from the bar of the second hand, spiky metal wheel machinery shifting behind her.

It's so loud, too loud. The wheels turning, the alarm thundering. She wants to cover her ears, but she can't. She finds she can't move, her body like cement—though suddenly she *is* moving, springing from one dial number to the next, a series of stepping stones. In a clockwise motion.

There's something she is propelling toward; something she needs to tell someone. Something massively important.

But she can't remember what it is—only that it exists.

She continues to jump forward as the wheels of the machinery grind methodically. Ominously. Each crank marking the onward passage of time. Time it feels like she doesn't have.

Then—the ground beneath budges, cracking like an egg. Water streams in. The stepping stones are now lily pads, softly cushioning her landings.

How quickly the world can change, she thinks, looking around. This phrase feels poignant, fitting, in a way she can't quite put her finger on. The air has become wet, misty. Swollen with an earthy scent. But still—the tick, tick, tick persists.

Then—a voice, a young woman. Floating from above, beyond the clock. Beyond the misty sheen that surrounds her, like a bubble. The woman's familiar. Both her voice and her scent: floral. Sweet, but sickly sweet. Like cheap perfume. Or shampoo? Or is it the thing sprayed on hair to make it hold? What's that called, again?

"Vivian," the woman-from-above says, her voice silky, smooth, like the water running beneath the lily pads.

Vivian. A pretty name. Familiar. *Her* name, she realizes with a start. More darkness edges away.

Yes, Vivian wants to answer. But she can't. Her throat is too sore.

Sprayhair. No—no. *Hairspray.*

The woman-from-above fiddles with the alarm clock. Fingers rap against plastic, like the typing of computer keys. She must be hitting snooze on the alarm. Vivian feels grateful. The stream gurgles; the sound is peaceful.

"Vivian," the woman-from-above repeats. "It's Taylor. You're in the hospital. We met yesterday, when you were admitted. You're safe. You had an accident."

Accident. Hospital. Yes, Vivian wants to say. She remembers.

It's not an alarm clock—it's an IV pump. Her throat sore because of the tube lodged in it.

What kind of accident? she wants to ask. *Is Peter—*

The water picks up suddenly, splashing against the lily pads, pelting the bottom of her legs. She looks down: the green surface is slick, speckled like wet paint. It's slippery—she is afraid she might fall.

There's something I need to tell someone.

VIVIAN

Early February

Vivian is standing on the cobblestone sidewalk in front of the Knox. It's a few days after Xavier paid her a visit at the store, a few days since she's concocted this hare-brained endeavor.

She's walked by the Knox countless times throughout her life—it's located mere blocks from her antiques store, after all—but she's never approached. She's never had reason to. Her buyer Michael—the only member she's met, or rather the only member she's met for certain—always comes to her. And unlike her other clients, the Knox prefers to arrange for delivery and pickup on their end.

She eyes the building in front of her. It's stately and tall: four stories, which is one level higher than nearly all the other buildings on the street. She smiles as she thinks of Michael not needing to duck within these entrances—unlike at her own store. But as her eyes sweep down the front bricks and over the double-length drapes covering what is likely their parlor room, a chill travels through her. The drapes are halfway parted, and for the life of her she can't see what's on the inside. Instead, the window glass simply reflects the sidewalk trees behind her. A mirrored film on their windows, likely, but it makes the building feel soulless. There's an imposing feel to the structure, a do-you-dare-to-enter vibe. Even the metal grilles on the garden-level small windows end in sharp, chiseled points.

It's suiting, she supposes. The Knox is Boston's most elusive secret society.

But then there is the other story about the Knox, the one that belongs only to Vivian's family. The story that has been buried for generations, just like her mother has always wished. But her mother's preferences hardly matter, at least not anymore. She won't know the difference; her mind has deteriorated into nearly a blank slate, the dementia having swiftly wiped her memories like a whiteboard eraser.

Except for that goddamn La Mer cream.

Vivian smooths any potential strands that may have escaped from her low bun and then brushes up the steep stone steps to the front door. She never cared about the family lore, either. Not until a few days ago, when she found her life completely different—something that belonged to someone else: a person who suddenly needs money.

Using the antique brass knocker, adorned with flowers she cannot place, she raps several times on the wooden door. There's no buzzer.

She supposes the Knox doesn't get random visitors.

Staring at the door, she counts to five before she starts knocking again.

Finally, a woman, tall—nearly as tall as Vivian—and thin, opens it. "Yes?" the woman says curtly. Her light blue eyes bore, laser-like, into Vivian's.

"I'm looking for Michael," Vivian says.

The woman pauses, runs her tongue over her teeth. She takes

so long to respond that Vivian wonders if she's having some sort of mini stroke. She does look like she has a good twenty years on Vivian.

"Who are you?" the woman finally says, almost reluctantly, as if realizing that Vivian is not going away.

"I'm Vivian. I own Storied Antiques, on Pinckney Street. Michael had sent the carousel horse to me for repair a few weeks ago."

Why is Vivian prattling on to this woman? Who is she, anyway? She seems like she works there rather than belonging as a member, given her faded blue jeans and white turtleneck top. She makes Vivian look like she's stepping off the Bergdorf Goodman runway, though to be fair, Vivian always looks that way. Today she is dressed smartly in a navy-blue pantsuit beneath her wool camel-hair coat. A trait she inherited from her mother: the compulsive need to be the best dressed in the room.

"Is it fixed?" the woman bluntly asks.

"It is." Vivian puffs up slightly; even though she didn't like the thing to begin with, she's proud of the masterful repair job she's facilitated.

"I'll let Michael know, and he'll follow up with you."

The woman starts to close the door, but Vivian inserts her foot in it. "Wait!"

Sighing, the woman pulls the door back open. "Yes?"

"Let me give you my card."

Obviously, Michael has her number and knows where the store is; Vivian's stalling for time. She's not ready to be dismissed and is hoping to get a glance inside, hoping for any way into this place that may just be the answer to all of her problems.

She fumbles with her orange Hermès wallet as she extracts a business card, while at the same time trying to peer beyond the woman's shoulder, into the entrance of the Knox. But this woman's got a death grip on the door—she's strong, for being likely in her sixties—and the entrance alcove is small, boxy. Vivian can barely make out the widening of the room behind it: a sliver of a grand winding staircase with a paisley carpet runner. It's dim, too. You'd they think would light up this place like a Christmas tree.

But then, suddenly, a silhouette appears, quickly descending those stairs.

"Rose, do we have a visitor?" a man's voice calls out. He sounds almost amused.

The woman—Rose, apparently—stiffens slightly. "Yes, Mr. Wales. A woman is here about the carousel horse."

Rose opens the door now completely—though a bit reluctantly—as the man approaches. He smiles at Vivian and nods, as if he somehow recognizes her—but she would certainly remember had they previously met. She feels a flush come on as she manages to smile back. He's her age, or slightly older. Ruggedly handsome: salt-and-pepper hair, deep grooves in his face. Eyes colored blue in an easy sort of way, like a cloudless sky.

"Hello, I'm Peter. Peter Wales." He reaches out to shake her hand, and she's glad he does, because she feels a little dizzy.

"Hi, I'm Vivian. I have the antiques store, over on Pinckney Street."

They continue to clasp hands, even though they're done with formalities. Rose has disappeared. But everything has disappeared. Vivian feels like a cartoon character with hearts spilling out of her head.

"Storied Antiques," he says with a nod. She's surprised he knows the name of her store. "You didn't want to ride the horse back to its home?" he asks.

She laughs. "Well, I think that was the original problem."

"True, true."

Her releases her hand, and she's acutely aware of how naked it now feels.

"Do you want to come in?" Peter asks, gesturing inside. "I was about to have a cup of tea."

He says this like it's the most ordinary thing in the world.

"Yes. Yes, I do."

She steps over the threshold, into the foyer, where the room opens dramatically, punctuated by a large, hanging gilded chandelier. For a moment she feels like Cinderella entering the ball. But, as she surveys her surroundings, taking in the grand staircase, an old-fashioned mailbox system, and a mahogany drum table—an item Michael purchased a few years back—she reminds herself she's more like Perdita in Shakespeare's *The Winter's Tale*.

It is in the Knox, after all, that according to family lore, her great-great-grandmother was born, a baby out of wedlock.

TAYLOR

The following day, Taylor works a four-hour afternoon shift at the hospital. Her head throbs—next time she should pass on Sam's whiskey—but she didn't want to call out sick. The first chance she gets, she asks a colleague to cover for her. Then she bolts upstairs to the ICU.

To Vivian.

Outside Vivian's door there's a group of doctors in discussion, and Taylor strains to hear.

Serial CT scans, subdural hematoma, minor distal radial fracture, rib fractures.

No new information, then.

She feels the outline of the key in her scrub pockets; she *has* come to check on Vivian, but she's also there to return the key. Her embarrassment over having kept it has only grown by the light of day.

The doctors finally move like a flock of birds down the hall, and once the room is empty, Taylor slips inside.

Vivian is lying in the bed, her beautiful head partly shaven where the ICP monitor—the probe measuring brain pressure—

attaches like an alien's antennae. Her chest rises with air that the ventilator pushes through a tube into her lungs, and then it recoils. A cocktail of medications infuses through spaghetti lines to keep her sedated and treat the brain swelling. Her fractured wrist is secured in a splint.

Taylor almost wants to cry, seeing Vivian this way. When she arrived, she seemed so alive, like she'd transported through a portal from the world outside—the world where people *lived*, where life hummed and the earth rotated on its axis—to their hospital world, where people become part machine, *less human*. Tethered with tubing and on beds that slowly rotate to prevent bed sores. Bruised, edematous.

But even though Vivian now belongs to that all-too-familiar world of sickness, there are still glimpses of *her* beneath it.

A lingering waft of Chanel N°5. A tiny clump of black mascara on her eyelash, still present. Shadows of her expertly smudged eyeliner. The wine-colored nail polish, now chipped on several fingers.

"T.J." Her Aunt Gigi startles her; she is standing outside the door, holding a paper cup of coffee in one hand and a nursing census sheet in the other. "You came to check on your patient?"

"Hi, Aunt Gigi. Yeah."

"She's stable, for now."

"That's good." Taylor does a visual sweep of the room, looking at Vivian's machines and monitors, and then the surrounding walls. She notices an "About Me" poster hanging on the wall, empty. Usually, these posters are filled out by loved ones in detail and plastered with photos. Taylor frowns. "Doesn't she have family? Have any visitors been in?"

"No family yet that we've located," Aunt Gigi replies, and then adds, "You know, you did good with her yesterday, T.J. You should feel proud. It was not an easy situation, but you handed it well. You acted quickly."

"Thanks," Taylor says, with an authenticity she does not feel.

An overhead speaker rings out: "Code Blue, room 614. Code Blue, room 614."

"Gotta run," Aunt Gigi calls out over her shoulder as she hurries down the hall.

Taylor sighs and pulls up a seat alongside Vivian. Studies her. Underneath the swelling, her face is lax, slightly pink. Even smoother than the day before, if that's possible.

How is Vivian alone? Why is no one with her? How is someone so beautiful not surrounded by others? There should be at least one handsome man by her bedside. Perhaps even a few boyfriends who aren't aware of one another's existence.

A little crust has formed overnight on Vivian's eyelashes. Her nurse is clearly busy with the code down the hall, so Taylor takes a washcloth and wets it, applies it gently to remove the debris. Then she moves the cloth to Vivian's arm to softly scrub off the tape residue from what looks like a previous IV attempt.

Taylor rinses the cloth and then continues to sponge-bathe Vivian, careful not to provide too much stimulation as to increase her intracranial pressure. The most important thing in a traumatic brain injury is to simply allow the brain to heal. Though healing isn't always guaranteed, even with time. Head injuries are tricky; the skull is a closed space, jam-packed with brain, blood, and cerebrospinal fluid. When the brain swells, it simply has nowhere to go.

The resident enters the room, pulling Taylor out of her thoughts.

"I put in some new orders," he says.

"Oh, I'm not her nurse. I work in the ER; I admitted her. I, uh, I just came to check on her."

"Oh, okay. Do you know who her nurse is?"

Taylor shrugs. "Sorry. There's that code in 614, so maybe she's helping in there."

The resident starts to leave but then stops. "You said you admitted her?"

"Yeah. Why?"

The resident shakes his head. He's young, with a round, boyish face that makes him look even younger than he probably is. "I'm just trying to understand. The paramedics said she was at a party, drinking, right?"

"Yeah, apparently she had a few and took a tumble down the stairs." Taylor pauses, then adds, "She was even talking about champagne before she crashed."

The resident scratches his head. "Okay."

"Why do you ask?"

"Well, it's just that her blood alcohol level was normal. She wasn't drinking at all, or if she was, she already sobered up by the time she fell."

VIVIAN

Vivian is in a coma. She knows that now. She sits—or rather she lies—in a hospital bed whose motors vibrate as they gently rotate her side to side. It's like being on a slow-moving roller coaster.

She's never liked roller coasters.

"The bed moves to prevent ulcers," a nurse explains to a student who comes in to observe.

Vivian also doesn't like her that much. The nurse—not the student. This nurse chews gum quite loudly. It's a pet peeve of Vivian's, people who chew gum loudly.

Funny how she still cares.

But she does. *I'm more than this*, she finds herself thinking. *More than this bed, more than this body.* Her thoughts soar upward, outward, expansive, the gray mist surrounding her brain temporarily thinning. And then, she wonders: *Am I high from the painkillers they must be giving me?*

"TBI," the doctors say, when they come to do rounds and stand in front of what she presumes is the door. Her door—a private one, no less. Though she supposes all rooms on this floor—the ICU, probably—have single beds. A prize for being the sickest.

The doctors and nurses utter "TBI" enough times that it finally clicks: traumatic brain injury. She remembers there was a patient with a TBI on the TV show *House*. Rachel likes to tease her that she acts like she knows medical lingo because she binged that show.

Vivian has always had a knack for details. As she congratulates herself for recalling what TBI means, given her state, the pain strikes with a sudden force. It's a hot, searing pain that flashes in between her temples. It wipes her of any thought. When she comes to again, there's another nurse on duty. It's likely even another day.

This is her reality—if she can call it as such. It's more of an in-between. She hovers inside her body, on the fringes of her brain, even. She climbs through the coils of brain tissue like mounds of a hill until they feel like squishy pillows upon which she must sink, sleep overcoming her.

She is asleep more than she is awake. She is hazy more than she is clear. But when the mist evaporates, she starts to remember. She takes stock of the haphazard memories that float around her and begins to reorganize them, putting together a sequence of events. It's like the second-grade homework her goddaughter, Lucy, has to do at Locust Prep. The sequencing activities. The logic. What comes first. What comes next.

(1.) First the girl wakes up. (2.) She gets dressed. (3.) She eats breakfast. (4.) The girl unlocks the door. (5.) She gets on the swing set in the backyard. (6. 7. 8.) She soars upward. (9. 10. 11.) Outward. (12.) At the highest point on the swing, she spies another neighbor's backyard, another swing set. (13.) The world, the girl realizes, is comprised of many, many backyards.

For seven-year-old Lucy, the door opens to a world just beginning. The door leads to nascent possibilities. Infinite possibilities. Each unique. A life not yet mapped.

But now, suddenly, the only door Vivian can recall opening is to the Knox.

VIVIAN

Early February

Vivian sips the mint tea, leaning back into the claw-footed high-backed chair.

She and Peter are in the parlor room with the double windows, which on the inside is *anything* but soulless. Vivian's having trouble trying to decide where to focus her attention: on Peter, sitting opposite her in the tan chesterfield love seat, or on the room around them.

It's a much more dramatic space than parlors in other various private members' clubs and country clubs she's been to. And she's been to a few. She *belongs* to a few: The 'Quin, here in Boston. The Country Club in the nearby suburb of Brookline. In New York, Soho House. At least, she belongs to them for the time being, until she has to cough up the money for the annual dues.

Suffice to say she approves of the decor. So many rooms that mix old and new get it wrong, but it's almost criminal that this interior space cannot be photographed and splashed across the pages of *House Beautiful*. Here the walls are delicately wrapped like a present in a textured cranberry paisley wallpaper and topped with sexy dark gray coffered ceilings from which multiple Baccarat crystal chandeliers hang. Silky, golden drapes framing each window form luxurious puddles on the dark wooden floor. A pair of marble fireplaces bookends the far walls: One is coral-colored, mostly simple in its lines, and the other is glossy black, modern, and detailed. Soft jazz filters through the room, and she can't tell if it's coming from overhead speakers or the nearby vintage turntable.

In the middle of the room is a curved glass display case containing what looks like an antique scroll. The charter to the Knox, perhaps? The entire display case—wooden table stand and all—is enclosed in a box-shaped security glass, as if this scroll would better belong in a museum.

Fanning out from it are multiple gathering areas, each one seamlessly demarcated with its own Persian rug. Vivian and Peter are seated in the far right of the room—the most private area. On a tray before them, resting on a coffee table that Vivian sourced a few years earlier, is a vintage silver tea set that is Chinese in origin. The furniture around them is varied and lovely; long, velvet couches with fringe bottoms, claw-footed high-backed chairs, a bench with a vintage leopard-print upholstery, a more contemporary acrylic side table, tufted footstools, coffee tables with marble tops, crowded brass bar carts with casters. Some of it is also familiar; Vivian's fingerprint is scattered throughout. She feels pleased; she doesn't usually get to see her pieces in the wild, and never in such an exquisite setting.

"I'm sorry, what's that?" she says, when she realizes Peter is waiting for her response.

"I said, I get it."

"Get what?"

"I'm an architect, so I understand how you're feeling. You have the look of a proud mom on your face."

"Well, yes," she says after a pause. "I've sourced several of these pieces. Furniture and decor."

"So I've heard."

"You've heard?"

"Michael's spoken about you, or rather about your shop."

"Oh," she says. Then she frowns and adds, "I don't know if proud 'mom' is the right word. But I am proud."

Peter nods thoughtfully. "I apologize. That may have been a poor choice of words."

"No need to apologize. I'm not offended. It's more that I've never really identified with that sentiment."

"So how does one come to be an antiques dealer in arguably the most charming neighborhood in America? Is your family from the area?"

Is your family from the area? is much more of a loaded question than Peter realizes.

"I grew up in Chestnut Hill. I'm an only child, and my parents were collectors, so I was surrounded by antiques. I've always loved them." She swallows at the thought of the antiques her mother either tossed out in the trash due to her dementia or sold off over the years at below value. All Vivian knows is that the estate sale appraiser she'd sent over informed her that the house no longer contains many of the antiques Vivian had listed—and her mother never consulted Vivian on the sales of any such items.

Batting down the unpleasant memory, Vivian adds, "Of course all antiques are antiques *now*, but at one time they were simply beautiful pieces of furniture, or belongings, important to someone for some reason. I find it fascinating how antiques have their own personal histories and stories."

"Ah, I knew we had something in common." There's a teasing glint in his eye.

"What's that?"

"Lonely-child syndrome. It begets much creativity."

"Were you an only child, too, then? Or just lonely?"

"An orphan, in fact. But instead of finding stories *in* objects around me, I *created* objects to tell stories," Peter says.

"Ah. I like that."

"I grew up in the Adirondacks," he continues, and the way he says it makes Vivian feel that the town he hails from is not the postcard image that mountainous area sometimes conjures. There's a rawness about Peter, she realizes.

"When I was eleven years old, the architect Gilbert Joseph—" He pauses as she nods; everyone has heard of the late New England architect. "Gilbert came to our town to do a conversion of an old textile mill building into a hotel, and I used to go there after school to watch. Sometimes *instead of* school." He grins roguishly. "Anyway, one day he finally noticed me. And asked me what I thought of the lofts they were creating, and I said, 'You need a climbing wall for kids if you have ceilings that high.' And you know what? He did it. Room 428 at the Lodge still contains a climbing wall."

"That must have been pretty cool to experience as a child."

"It was." Peter looks wistful. "Meeting Gilbert Joseph literally changed my life. He became my mentor. Put me through The Bartlett—the architecture school at University College London. Closest thing to a father I ever had. He's the reason I'm here, at the Knox."

He must mean Gilbert Joseph was a member. Vivian had done a fair amount of internet sleuthing on the Knox the past couple of days but was surprised to find barely anything. Just some vague mentions in previous issues of *Boston Common* and *Boston Magazine*. It's like the internet had been scrubbed. *How many members are there?* she wonders. There's so much she wants—needs—to know, but she must tread carefully.

There's also so much she wants and needs to know about this

man sitting in front of her. Like, when he raises his cup of tea to his mouth and the sleeve of his shirt pulls back, revealing a wrist tattoo, what is it of? Does he have others beneath those fine Italian clothes he's wearing? What women have seen them?

And what kind of broken childhood did he have?

Peter opens his mouth as if he's about to ask something but then decides against it. For some reason this makes her laugh.

"Go ahead, ask," she says.

"Ask what?"

"Whatever you were going to."

"I don't even know what I was going to ask. A million things. Some probably I shouldn't." His gaze rakes over her face, as if he's trying to memorize it.

She, too, is locked on him. She couldn't look away if she tried.

Then his eyes flicker beyond her, over her shoulder. "Here's a question for you: What do you think about that painting? The one with the woman on the bus?"

She turns to see. It's an oil painting of a woman sitting in a row of seats on what appears to be public transportation. The woman's back is mostly turned, so there is just the slightest glimpse of her profile.

"It could be a train, not a bus," Vivian points out.

"Hmmm. Maybe."

Vivian doesn't love the painting. It's certainly not of the same caliber as the other artwork in the room, for instance that Andy Warhol–Jean-Michel Basquiat collaboration they passed when they first entered. If truly an original, that one painting could more than solve all her problems.

Christ, what kind of person is she turning into?

"The frame is crooked," she finally says.

"Really?" He tilts his head. "Now that you mention it, you're right."

A young, stout man with close-cropped hair approaches. He's dressed in black trousers and a tight black shirt. "More tea?" he asks.

"Please, Jerry," Peter replies, and waits for Vivian to put her teacup down first on the tray so it, too, can be topped off.

The waiter's hands are big, burly, like the rest of his body. But he's overall short and has an almost squashed appearance, with a thick neck and crooked nose that looks like it's been broken at least once. He'd fit in better on a wrestling mat.

"I can always tell when a painting is off-kilter," Vivian remarks to Peter. "It's my superpower."

"That is impressive. Do you see it or sense it?"

"Good question. Both, probably."

"Thank you, Jerry," Peter says, when the man is done, and Jerry nods.

"Thank you," Vivian adds.

"We just got the painting. Graham—he's the head of the Knox—just purchased it. I can't decide what I think of it, and I feel like, based on the way you avoided answering, you are also undecided."

"I'm not undecided. I'm just diplomatic."

He laughs. "Touché."

Vivian brings the cup to her face, reveling in the warmth. She's not cold, but the steam feels good. She feels visceral, aware of her senses like she hasn't been in a long time. The soft, luxurious velvet of the chair beneath her back. The way the jazz notes linger in the air, like drawn-out exhalations. The slight stubble of a beard on Peter's face that she suddenly has an inane desire to reach forward and touch. It feels good to be lost in the moment, to not feel the weight of her problems.

Suddenly, she's aware that time has slipped. How long have they been chatting? She glances at the grandfather clock tucked against one of the back walls, but oddly enough it seems to say the same time as when she looked earlier, the minute hand just past three o'clock.

Peter notices her gaze. "It's stopped on 3:03, the time that our founder died."

"Mr. Knox, I presume?"

"William Knox."

"*William* Knox. I'd just assumed . . ."

"Henry Knox?" he fills in. "It's a common misassumption. No, the Knox was not established by the historical figure Henry Knox, but rather an alleged distant cousin of his, William."

She files that piece of information away. She'll need to remember it later, to relay to Rachel. Her friend doesn't know it yet, but she's soon going to be putting her talents to use; Rachel's a genealogist at the Vilna Shul, an old synagogue turned Boston cultural arts center.

"Are you . . . Are you supposed to be telling me all this?" Vivian asks haltingly.

He laughs. "Probably not."

"Do you often invite guests inside?"

Peter holds her gaze. "Never."

Voices drift from the far end of the room. They have company. Michael saunters in, flanked by Jerry, the waiter.

Michael stops short when he sees Vivian. "Vivian, I mean Ms. Lawrence. Hello. Peter." He nods briskly at Peter. "I didn't realize you two knew each other," he says stiffly.

"We don't. We only just met," Peter says, while Vivian adds, "Please, it's Vivian."

"Now I understand why the Knox has been spending so much money at a certain antiques store," says Peter.

Michael reddens. "Storied Antiques is one of the finest of its kind."

Peter laughs. "Relax, Michael. I'm just joking. You know I've always approved of the items you procure." He turns to Vivian. "Michael and I go way back. We were flatmates, years ago in London."

He says this like Vivian already knows Michael lived in London, but Vivian knows very little about Michael. Practically nothing, in fact. She notices he doesn't wear a wedding band, just a signet ring. "Is that where you two met, in London?" she asks.

Peter answers for them. "No, we first met here, at the Knox. Michael's father was close with my mentor, Gilbert Joseph. You see, unlike me, Michael hails from a long lineage of Knox members. I'm just the scrappy SOB they somehow let in." He grins rather endearingly, and Vivian can't help but smile back.

"Well, I wouldn't exactly put it that—" Michael starts to say, but Peter interrupts.

"Vivian, has Michael already invited you to our annual masquerade ball?"

Vivian looks at Michael, who is wearing an unreadable expression. "No."

Peter runs his hand through his hair. "Well, please do us the honor. It's next Friday. Eight p.m. It's one of our only events of the year where we are officially allowed to invite nonmember guests. Come in your finest Venetian attire."

Next Friday she has dinner plans with Rachel, but she's pretty sure that she will be forgiven for needing to reschedule. Likely encouraged by her friend to reschedule, in fact. "I'd love to."

"Wonderful," Peter says, clapping his hands together as they rise.

Jerry rushes in to clear the tea tray as if being summoned, but Peter subtly shakes his head, and Jerry backs off.

"Wonderful, Michael, isn't it?" Peter says.

TAYLOR

When Taylor gets home from her overtime nursing shift, she defrosts an old slice of pizza and opens her laptop. She wants to catch up on Vivian's latest lab work and investigate what that resident had said about the blood alcohol level.

But when she logs into Epic and clicks on Vivian's name, like she had previously, a new message pops up on her screen: Patient Access Restricted.

Taylor refreshes the screen and tries again. The same message flashes, as clear as day: Patient Access Restricted.

She frowns; this is the type of message that appears when Taylor attempts to access the medical information of one of MGH's own nurses or medical personnel who show up in the ER. Or when she is taking care of a wealthy Saudi patient, which happens more often than you would think, though usually such patients bypass the ER and go directly to the floor.

The message serves as an additional level of security. To bypass it and access the patient's data, which is called "breaking the glass," you must enter a reason why. Think carefully if you need to view this record, the screen warns.

Is Taylor indeed authorized? Vivian is technically no longer her patient, but still.

She takes a deep breath and clicks "Providing Clinical Care" as the reason, and then she's prompted to type in her password. But when she hits Submit, instead of Vivian's online chart being displayed, Taylor is suddenly booted off the portal completely. And when she tries to log back on, it says that *her* account is now restricted.

Fuck.

Taylor leans back on the kitchen stool, drums her fingers on the countertop.

Is she in trouble for trying to access Vivian's medical information? But Vivian *was* her patient. It's no different from other patients whose progress she follows throughout their hospital stay. So, Taylor could just play the concerned-nurse card, if it comes to it. Isn't that all it is, anyway?

But no. It's more than that.

It's the fact that this is the second time she's been driven to click through Vivian's chart from home.

It's the fact that resting in front of her on the countertop is Vivian's key. The key Taylor never returned. A tiny oval tag hangs from the key ring that, when magnified with Taylor's phone camera, reads: Home.

An uncomfortable idea sprouts inside her, its tendrils tickling her conscience.

To distract herself, Taylor decides to call her dad.

He'll be at the restaurant, even though it's not open. He's a creature of habit. His restaurant didn't used to close for the off-season, but since it took a significant hit during Covid, her dad can no longer afford to keep it running year-round.

"Hiya, T.J.," he answers. She can just picture him sitting behind the desk in the small office in the back, across from the employee-only bathroom. He probably cooked up some beer-battered Old Bay–seasoned shrimp and is enjoying that now with a cold ale. "How's Boston treating you?"

"It's okay," she says, trying to keep her voice even. She suddenly feels homesick. But not for North Carolina—for him. She couldn't come home for the holidays because tickets were too expensive. Plus, she had to work. He'll never visit; he's never left his home state.

"How are you?" she asks.

"Same old."

This makes her smile; she doesn't doubt it. "Dad, I have a question."

"Shoot. I can't guarantee I'll have an answer, but I'll try my best."

"Can you remind me how long Mom was in Boston, before . . . well, you know?"

He pauses. "Why do you ask?"

"I was . . . I was just thinking of her."

"Well, can't say I'm surprised. I'm sure being in Boston is . . . making you think of her. She was there for five months."

"That's all? Five months?" Taylor swallows. That's how long she herself has been in Boston.

"That's all."

"Wow. It felt so much longer. . . . Maybe because I was young?"

"It felt longer to me, too, T.J."

"Who was it that Mom modeled for?" she asks.

"Come again?"

"Who was it that Mom modeled for? The local designer? I

wondered if maybe they were still around. If they had a store-front or something."

"Oh . . . I don't really remember, T.J. I'm sorry. It's been so long." He sounds pained.

"It's okay, Dad," she's quick to say. "I keep . . . keep seeing women here who remind me of her. These glamorous women." Taylor takes a deep breath, closes her eyes. "Women who wear the most stylish clothes . . . and who have beautiful shiny brown hair, like she had. And red lipstick . . . and red nails . . . and Chanel N°5 . . ." Her eyes flutter open as she realizes she's conjured Vivian.

"That sounds like your mom. She was the most beautiful woman. I used to tell her . . ." His voice cracks, and he clears his throat. "I used to tell her that she sucked the air out of any room she walked in. And one time she thought I said 'waltzed,' not 'walked,' and then it became a joke between us. She'd come by the restaurant and waltz in like she was dancing in a ballroom."

A memory triggers in Taylor. "I . . . think I remember that."

Her dad gives a short laugh. "Yeah, she had a great sense of humor. Sometimes, when you're so good-looking, you're not funny. But she was funny. She was so funny." Then he says, in a more somber tone, "I'm sorry you're missing her, T.J. Don't forget who you are. And you got Aunt Gigi there, if you need her. Don't let Boston get the best of you. You do you, you hear me? You do you."

Don't let Boston get the best of you?

"Okay, Dad. And Boston is fine, don't worry. I'm doing fine. Of course I'm thinking of her here, but I *always* think of Mom."

"I know you do, T.J. So do I."

They sit on the phone quietly, and the silence feels so familiar. It's been the two of them for so long. This is the first time she's lived on her own; even through community college and the three years she worked at the orthopedic center, she lived at home, saving money. On the weekends, she'd crash at her boyfriend's but come Monday return to sleep in her childhood bedroom. When Taylor spotted the listing for the Boston apartment, she put down her dad as a reference. She didn't have any previous rental history, but she figured since she'd waitressed at her dad's restaurant from the time she was twelve, he could attest to her work ethic and potential as a renter. Anna, her landlord, had indeed called her father, and they'd chatted for a good long while. Whatever her dad said to Anna worked. Sam told Taylor she was lucky to land the apartment; Anna rented only to select people.

When Taylor hangs up the phone, she picks up the key, turning it over in her hands. She suddenly wonders: *Is Vivian funny? Does she have a sense of humor like my mom did? Or is she serious? Haughty, even?*

Taylor knows what she is thinking of doing with this key could jeopardize the life she's trying to set up for herself. But now that the idea's taken hold, she can't shake it.

THE KNOX

Early February

The society's annual masquerade ball is upcoming, and I simply can't wait. It's been far too boring for far too long. Just dinners and dinners and cocktail hours and dinners. Boring, boring, boring. I need another dinner like I need a hole in my headhouse. All my esteemed rooms with their valuable furniture and priceless artwork, and hardly anyone to enjoy them. I've begun to grow dust in my corners, though Rose does an admirable job of keeping up.

There was a time, in the early nineteenth century, when the society held many parties and gatherings. That is, of course, why I was built. The Brahmins needed *somewhere* to discuss their international business dealings in the opium trade, so they decided they might as well do it in style. The gentlemen had much to coordinate: sailing ships to Smyrna to purchase the precious raw opium, then smuggling their illicit wares into China to sell them for profit or to trade them for silks, teas, porcelain, and furniture. (Some of these acquisitions still sit in my disappointingly empty rooms.) The sea merchants made, quite literally, a killing. By 1838, while newly minted Boston millionaires toasted with champagne in my parlor, a third of China's population had become addicted to opium.

We've had our own respectable number of deaths here at the society through the years: overdoses, murders, suicides. Double murders. Staged suicides. The most delightful and ingenious murder methods have been carried out, from bondage-gear choke holds to frozen-steak bludgeonings to castor bean poisonings (disguised in a salad). Knox members have dabbled in the, ahem, *aftermath* as well; who can forget the delectable autopsies that Dr. Thurgood performed on stolen cadavers in my basement?

It's hardly surprising, really. I've existed for more than two hundred years in Beacon Hill, with the wealthiest of wealthy members. Sometimes things simply need to be taken care of—or rather, *disposed of.*

It's the way things are done. It's the way things have always been done.

But things have changed so much in Boston that William Knox would be turning over in his grave! So much more riffraff, even here, in exclusive Beacon Hill. It's a shame.

The issue, it must be said, lies at least partly with the educational system: Schools simply don't teach the proper subject matter these days. But they cannot carry the blame alone. The city itself has buried its fascinating and lurid past. Few Bostonians today realize that the city was built in no small part due to opium.

All the venerated institutions that were funded by this drug trade—well, they'd rather you not know. Perkins School for the Blind? Supported generously by its namesake Thomas Handasyd Perkins, a merchant—and slave trader—whose opium dealings made him one of the wealthiest men in America at the time. Or how about Mass General Hospital and the Boston Athenaeum, which also raked in significant monies from the Perkins brothers? Harvard University, McLean Hospital, the Bunker Hill Monument, and the Forbes House Museum, to name a few, inhaled opium riches, too. So many of Boston's elite were participants in this glorious and sordid trade: the Cabots, Cushings, Lowells, Forbeses, Kirklands, Delanos, Welds, and, of course, William Knox. But ever the good patricians, these leading philanthropists funded opium winnings into building mills, railroads, steamships, mines. And let's not forget the robust tax revenue generated from all this that paid for our state police and fire departments; it allowed for the construction and repair of our roads, our courthouses, our schools.

Put simply, our fair city on a hill would not be what it is today were it not for that, ahem, smoke. And my illustrious and well-appointed rooms where these wealthy men gathered.

Now, may I ask, where is *all this* in the history curriculum? Why, I heard some Boston schools don't even use physical textbooks these days. My word.

But I digress.

All I know is this: At the Knox, we make no pretense of what we are.

VIVIAN

Early February

When Vivian steps into her childhood home, it feels like she is stepping into another dimension.

It's been a while since she's been here; she and her mother usually meet out at restaurants. Or at least they did, before her mother got sick. She knew her mother was doing a "modern renovation" but hadn't expected *this*. The walls are still there, the layout the same, but it's no longer a New England colonial-style. Now it has a bizarre, modern feel: stark white walls, acrylic chairs, neon abstract art. The large overhead light pendant looks like Medusa's head.

Vivian runs her fingers over the wall, half hoping she leaves a smudge. She recalls her late father standing there in his blue plaid button-down shirt, his hearty laugh filling the space, bridging the gap between her and her mother.

He always knew how to handle her mother.

"She's wandering," the nurse recently called to tell Vivian, to which Vivian had dryly replied, "Well, good thing she can't really walk so she can't get *too* far." The pause on the nurse's end told

Vivian that she had not responded appropriately. Not compassionate enough, perhaps. But she and her mother have always had a complicated relationship. Besides, Vivian feels she has already mourned her mom. The creature now inhabiting her mom's body is an unfamiliar one. And right now, due to the mounting nursing home bill, that creature is greedily gobbling up Vivian's savings.

"Well, lucky for us, your father made some good investments," her mom used to reluctantly reply, when Vivian would inquire about her mom's latest Birkin bag, or Paris trip, or Cartier diamond necklace—and Vivian foolishly believed her. Her mom was notoriously private when it came to financial matters and reverted to using grand, sweeping statements. "You'll get this all when I'm gone," she'd say, waving her hand over her dressed-to-the-nines outfit, "so I suppose it's okay you didn't want to get married."

It's safe to say that anger—and a growing resilience—is occupying more of Vivian's mental space these days than grief. She sure hopes her mom spent as much on that Medusa head and neon paintings as she spent on her wardrobe and jewelry collection the past few years; Vivian needs to recoup as much money as possible. She still cannot believe the massive debt that her mother incurred. And those "good investments" her father had made? All gone, along with what remained of the old family wealth. Her mother had been playing the stock market like it was Monopoly money.

There's a swift rap on the door, and Vivian lets in Rachel. On her hip is her baby, Crimson, who's not such a baby anymore. Vivian's slightly irritated; she hadn't realized that the baby would be coming. She manages a smile at Crimson when she feels her friend watching.

"Wow, this place looks different," Rachel remarks, after stepping inside. "I think the last time I was here was for your dad's funeral. When was that? Four years ago?"

"Five."

"Your mom was definitely going for . . . a *look*."

Rachel sets down her daughter, who immediately begins toddling through the house. Vivian's still not used to seeing Rachel with a kid in tow. She's also not used to seeing her friend look so flustered; Rachel's normally chic bob is messily pulled halfway up into a high ponytail; there is some red lipstick smeared on her front teeth.

"Is there a problem?" Rachel asks, arms crossed. Either she knows Vivian too well or Vivian was too late to mask her annoyance.

"This place isn't exactly babyproof." Vivian gestures around.

"Do you want my help or not?" Rachel says.

Vivian has asked Rachel to help her sort through her mother's stuff, to clear it out so that the house can be put on the market, but really, she has an ulterior motive. Rachel knows her stuff as a genealogist, and Vivian needs assistance tracking down her family link to the Knox. There's a trove of boxes with old family documents in the basement. Luckily her mom never went down there, so the boxes remain intact and untouched—unlike many of the house antiques she apparently offloaded without consulting Vivian. The last time the boxes in the basement were cracked open might have been when Vivian was in sixth grade and scouring for information for her family tree project. But she can still recall the stacks of yellowed, frail letters and faded photos. Old journals and scrapbooks with miscellaneous letters tucked inside. The house has been in her mother's family for generations, after all. It's a shame Vivian is now being forced to sell it.

Just then, Crimson trips and lets out a loud howl that makes Vivian wince.

Steeling herself, she says, "I want your help—I *need* your help—but I haven't told you the full story."

⊹⊱──◦──⊰⊹

Vivian and Rachel sit in the living room amid strewn papers and boxes, a few of which Rachel has emptied to create a makeshift fort for Crimson. A bottle of wine, an expensive Barolo, has been opened.

Rachel begins organizing the loose documents into piles. "Um, so why haven't you ever told me about your Knox connection before, Viv? I mean, it's not every day you realize you know someone who's linked to a centuries-old secret society."

Vivian shrugs, running her red nail over the rim of her wineglass. "We never talked about it, not really. My mom preferred to pretend that the Knox didn't exist. I might never have even known about our family connection if my grandmother—her mother—hadn't spilled the beans when I was young." Vivian tilts her head. "I remember her exact words, how she started the conversation. She said, 'Do you like secrets, Vivian?' And then she said, 'My great-grandmother once owned Boston.'"

Rachel snorts, and it startles Crimson, who lets out an annoying wail. "Well, that's one way to have put it."

"It's somewhat true. Her family—her great-grandmother's father, really—was one of the Boston Brahmins who made a fortune as a sea merchant in the early 1800s. His name was William Knox."

"Like, one of *those* sea merchants who made their fortune smuggling opium?" Rachel asks, raising her eyebrow. She knows her history.

"Yes, and I think he was perhaps one of the 'most successful.'" Vivian uses air quotes and winces. She recalls, with a tug of shame, how she'd admired the antique silver Chinese tea set she and Peter used.

Rachel tsks. "You know, I was just thinking the other day about how the Sackler family and the whole opioid crisis of today mirrors Boston's opium history. The Sackler family were also big donors, like to the Guggenheim and the Met. Mostly the New York scene. It's disgusting."

"History repeats," Vivian dryly adds, taking a long pull from her wineglass. She suspects that her mother's own reluctance to embrace their family's ancestry—and Knox link—has less to do with some sort of moral opposition and more to do with, well, being a snob. Because not only are they descendants of the Knox founder, but her mother is also, according to family lore, a descendant of a baby born *out of wedlock*. And *that* her mother certainly would have worked hard to distance herself from.

Boston socialites simply do not associate themselves with scandalous affairs.

Vivian recalls the delight on her late grandmother's face when she'd shared that little indecent tidbit. This reveal had come later, once Vivian was an adult.

It must have bothered Vivian's mom to no end to have this as part of her family history. She had always avoided anything she deemed remotely distasteful or upsetting, even her own illness. Vivian recalled how her mom kept playing ostrich about her early symptoms, blaming her forgetfulness on the hardness of her pillow, which she said prohibited good sleep, and attributing her unsteadiness to the fact that her favorite Italian shoe designers had begun more cheaply manufacturing their footwear in Asia.

It's hard to know whether Vivian's mom had gotten herself so deeply in debt because of her detached relationship with money, her grief over her late husband, or her burgeoning dementia. Perhaps it was all three factors. When Vivian reviewed the pattern of her mother's reckless spending and bad investments, she noticed spikes around meaningful dates: her father's birthday, the anniversary of his death. And then there was the recent, alarming surge in spending over the past couple of months, which coincided with the onset of her mother's illness.

"So how does the Knox fit into this?" Rachel asks.

"It was formed by these families, as a club. A way for them to strategize about the opium trade. And to socialize, I suppose."

"Ah, that makes sense. Like an opium mafia. I never realized that's how the Knox started. Maybe that's why it's always been so secretive!"

"Maybe."

"Hey, didn't you say once that you and Lucy's mom were in some sort of secret society together at UPenn?"

Vivian smiles. "We were. Good memory. It was called Tabard. Though I'm sure any college secret society is child's play compared to the Knox."

"You never know," Rachel says with a grin. She clearly wants to know more, but Vivian would rather focus on the task at hand.

Even after all these years, Vivian still finds it difficult to talk about anything Kat-related; she's never gotten over her best friend's untimely death. It doesn't take Freud to realize that this may be part of the reason she's held her goddaughter at arm's length. Kat died, and then shortly thereafter Vivian's father died, too. It was a lot of loss all at once.

"Anyway, I'm hoping that somewhere in here," Vivian says to Rachel, gesturing around them, "is evidence that proves my family lineage to the Knox—to William Knox himself. According to my grandmother, there's a book in the family that somehow reveals, or proves, the truth about my family. How a book can do that, I don't know."

"And remind me why you need to prove this?"

Vivian feels her face grow warm. "My mother's health care needs have grown . . . complex." She's reluctant to say more. Her friend can read between the lines; Vivian is clearly putting her mom's house on the market for a reason.

"Oh, I'm sorry. I didn't realize. I . . . I know that nursing home care can be expensive. Well, I don't know personally, but I've heard."

"Thank you." She has yet to reveal her own financial woes to Rachel. It's silly; Rachel will realize soon enough, once the second store officially closes. It's already shuttered for the time being; she has let go of the store manager. But Vivian has her pride. Or maybe it's more a state of denial. "Anyway, this could all be a wild-goose chase, but my grandmother used to insinuate that there was some Knox fortune we might be entitled to—so I guess that means the long-lost book is the key to finding it."

Rachel's eyes light up; Vivian knew she'd be on board once she heard this detail. Rachel can't get enough of movies and novels about treasure hunting.

"I'm assuming you can't ask your mom about the book, or any details she might know. And your grandmother has passed, right?"

Vivian nods. "Unfortunately, my mom is . . ." She doesn't need to finish; Rachel nods sympathetically. "Although she does remember her La Mer face cream," Vivian ruefully adds.

Rachel laughs, and Crimson grins, as if she's in on the joke. Rachel gazes adoringly at her daughter. Christ. When Rachel glances back up, Vivian does her best to display a matching expression of adoration at Crimson. It seems to work.

It's times like these that Vivian misses her friendship with Xavier. They would likely have a little private chuckle at Rachel's expense. It wasn't so long ago that Rachel had sworn off having kids—or a husband, for that matter.

It feels like both of Vivian's friends have moved on without her, like their time together was just a stop on a train they've now reboarded. Vivian has always loved her station in life—her antiques store, her life in Beacon Hill—but recent events have made her wonder if there's a train she's supposed to be boarding, too. But what exactly does that mean? Finding a life partner? Vivian hasn't written off getting married—her mother might have been surprised to learn—but she's never pined for it, either. She's had a string of relationships, some longer and more serious than others, and the majority of which have been long-distance—New York, London, Singapore—which Rachel likes to cheekily point out is one way to predetermine their fates. But the fact is, Vivian's never been in love. Not really—or at least, not yet. Thoughts of Peter create a warmth inside her that she's not used to feeling.

"How many generations back does this house go?" Rachel now asks, pointing to the floor.

"Let me think. Well, I know my grandmother grew up in this house. . . . *Her* grandmother, the illegitimate child, was sent to Rhode Island, I believe, to be raised by a servant. So I guess my grandmother's mother—my great-grandmother—must have returned to Boston to live here. She married a banker." Vivian shudders thinking about how her distant relatives would have viewed her mother's recent house renovation.

Rachel is furiously scribbling notes. "Where in Rhode Island was the child sent to?"

"I'm sorry, I'm not sure. That's literally the extent of what I know."

"I won't ask now, but I'll need first and last names, middle names, birth dates, anything you know about your family."

Vivian laughs. "There's a family tree I constructed when I was in sixth grade in one of those other boxes in the basement."

Rachel nods. "Good. We'll look for it. Meanwhile, anything that jogs your memory—now or later—let me know. As a genealogist, I've found the slightest facts can go a long way. Have you done a DNA test through something like Ancestry.com?"

"I did one a few years back . . . I just looked at it yesterday."

"Any surprise relatives? Any leads we can follow?"

"I'll send you the results, but I don't think so. . . . It seems like a dead end; I only saw relatives on my dad's side. As for my mom's side, don't forget I'm the only child of an only child of an only child. . . . A long line of women, actually. My mom used to say we had the one-woman curse in our blood. Also, every woman in my family apparently gives birth at a late age, like in their forties." Vivian feels a warmth come over her face. Why would she have volunteered this last piece of information? Is Peter already scrambling her brain?

Rachel plows forward. "But this William Knox must have had another child, right? An heir? So wouldn't that person's ancestors have shown up?"

Vivian shrugs. "You'd think so. . . . Maybe they're not on genealogy sites?"

Rachel knits her brows. "Maybe. Anyway, let's get to work. Anything we flag of interest goes here." She nudges a box lid she's turned over, a makeshift tray. "I'll go through this pile, and you start on that box with the torn top. But here's the thing: We aren't just looking for a book. In fact, I doubt we'll find it, based on how your grandmother herself grew up in this house—"

"There are some old books here," Vivian interrupts.

"Okay, we can take a look at them. What I meant, though, was that if your grandmother had the book in her possession, then there wouldn't be a family lore that the book exists. Does that make sense?"

"Yes." Vivian had never stopped to consider such intricacies.

"Also, it might not be a book, but someone's *interpretation* of a book. A bundle of letters. A scrapbook, which was popular in the nineteenth century. We are looking for *any* documents or letters or photos that reveal *any* information about your mother's family history."

Vivian notices that her friend looks remarkably better than she did when she first arrived; she's retied her hair, and the lipstick on the teeth is long gone. There is a flush to her face, like all she needed was a spot of adulthood.

"Sounds like a plan. And I will do the honors of keeping our beverages refreshed," Vivian says as she refills their glasses.

"What's the other thing you need?"

"What do you mean?"

"When you called, you said you needed help with three things at your mom's house." Rachel ticks off her fingers. "One, tagging items for resale, donation, or disposal. Two, a mystery project. What's the third?"

"Oh!" Once again, Vivian feels the blood rush to her face. "I have a date on Friday night. I'm sorry; I know we had dinner plans, so I'll need to reschedule. I need help figuring out what to wear and thought we could raid my mom's closet."

Rachel is looking at her quizzically. "No worries—we can reschedule. But why do you need to raid your mom's closet? You're the best-dressed woman I know."

"Because I need something quite specific that's a little out of my comfort zone. And unlike valuable antiques, my mom never threw out a single piece of clothing." Vivian pauses, then says, "I'm going to the masquerade ball at the Knox."

An hour later, by a stroke of luck, she and Rachel uncover a few letters of importance. They nearly miss them, as they're pressed between the pages of an old poetry book: *Musings on Love and Life* by a man named Edgar Rolo Butterworth. The collection is almost laughable, between the antiquated nineteenth-century language and the overly sentimental drivel, and she and Rachel have a good chuckle as they dramatically read select passages aloud. Rachel is about to put the book back in the box where they found it, but then Vivian snatches it back for one last comical read. As she holds up the book, the letters gently fall from the pages like magical leaves, landing on Vivian's lap.

Vivian and Rachel lock eyes, the world momentarily collapsing behind them.

October 5, 1830
Boston, Massachusetts

My dear daughter Mercy,

Should I draw you a picture of my heart, you would be within it.

But should I draw you a picture of the world, neither of us would be within it, for men unjustly believe that women are not worthy.

I fear that I have done you an even further disservice: Your father is not my husband, and herein lies the difficulty.

Were my husband not at sea the past eleven months and unaware of your birth, it would bring great shame to him and potentially peril to you. As such, I am hereby entrusting you to the care of my most dutiful servant, Aoife, who has assured me she will raise you like her own in Rhode Island.

I retain an unalterable love for you, that neither time nor distance nor circumstance will abate.

Rest be assured, when God calls me home, you will find that I have made provisions for you, as my father has done for me. Until then, may God grant you mercy, like the name I have chosen for you.

Your loving mother,
Margaret

September 7, 1855
Boston, Massachusetts

My dear daughter Mercy,

The heavens today shine brilliant, as if knowing they call me. My physician says I am to prepare. I no sooner take the pen in my hand than I begin thinking of you, my dearest daughter. Life has cruelly separated us, yet in death there is joy, as I will patiently wait to be reunited with you. I furthermore take solace that in life my faithful Aoife has cared for you like her own.

I have, at my disposal, sizable assets, as my husband has departed before me. I have composed a nominee trust of such assets and a schedule of beneficiaries. As I have made provisions for you in life, so will I do in death for both you and your brother.

Rest be assured, my daughter, that my love for you transcends time and earth. Until we meet again, I remain your loving mother.

Yours,
Margaret

September 28, 1855

Dear Aoife,

I regret to inform you that the mistress Margaret has died. We are in morning. She was a good, kind mistress and so very careful of me. Her son the doctor does not have the same kind heart. Something is not right. He has her body in the basement. There is a paper with a schedule of beneficiaries the doctor has discarded. For this reason I am writing to you since I beleve it was of great importance to my mistress Margaret and pertains to Mercy. I took the paper and hid it in the secretery for safekeeping. Its in a secret compartment there. Please come get it and beware of the doctor.

Respectfuly your loveing cousin,
Sara

TAYLOR

Taylor's heart beats wildly against her ribs as she darts through the propped-open entrance to the Lime Street building in the tony Beacon Hill neighborhood.

It's the address that's been crazy-glued onto her mind, ever since she saw it in her patient's medical record: 62 Lime Street. The address connecting to the key in her sweaty palm that she should have returned.

Vivian's address.

Jabbing repeatedly at the elevator call button, Taylor prays that the concierge doesn't suddenly return from outside, where he's helping to unload groceries from a double-parked car. The elevator takes its sweet time, and perspiration gathers beneath her baseball cap.

When it finally arrives, she darts in, shooting one last furtive look at the still-empty lobby.

Vivian's apartment is a penthouse, which makes it easy to know which button to press next: the top one. As the cab rises, Taylor removes her hat and leans her slick back against the wall.

She tries to slow down her heart, but it's continuing to behave like she's drunk three coffees.

So she reminds herself of her justification for trespassing into her former patient's apartment: What if, Taylor reasons for the umpteenth time, Vivian has a hungry cat that needs to be fed? A dying fish? What if she left her lights on? Food out on the counter that is now spoiled?

Taylor's been off from work for a stretch of days—the life of a hospital nurse—which means that she's had far too much time to think. And this is what she keeps contemplating: Vivian's wedding finger is bare. Her "About Me" poster blank. No one has come to visit her yet, according to Aunt Gigi. So what if there is no one to check on these things in Vivian's apartment, other than Taylor herself?

The more she says it to herself, the more she allows herself to believe it.

When the doors open on the fifth floor, Taylor steps off into a rich, navy-blue-carpeted—and, most important, empty—hall. She finds the door labeled, simply, 3. Make that PENTHOUSE 3. What an address.

She inserts the key, and there's a satisfying click. As she enters, her unease about what she is doing vanishes. Turning on the large crystal chandelier light, Taylor stares. The apartment looks almost unreal, like a movie set. The chandelier sparkles, casting a warm golden hue on the collection of unique, striking furniture. A vintage-looking rug runs the length of the floor, ending short of the marble fireplace. A wall bookcase displays the most carefully arranged books and assortment of trinkets. "Trinkets" is probably not the best word to describe the various small crystal and porcelain figurines and sculptures, but Taylor doesn't have a sophisticated enough vocabulary to do them justice. Dreamy silk curtains frame multiple airy windows—Taylor would have zero chance of suffering from claustrophobia here.

In the far corner of the room, Taylor spots Vivian's desk. It's a dark ebony lacquered wood with a black leather writing surface flanked by raised panel drawers. There could be secrets about Vivian hidden within. Taylor starts to make her way over but pauses, distracted, to run her hand down a cabinet's curved legs that end in almost humanlike claws. And then she momentarily sinks into a high-backed deep purple velvet chair with a gold frame that looks—and feels—fit for a queen. She caresses every surface, rubs every texture. It's almost like a museum exhibit. No, it's better than that, because she gets to feel and touch and experience the items. For once, Taylor's not standing behind some velvet rope, or peering from outside a window, but rather immersed *inside* the wealth. And it's glorious.

She picks up a framed photograph of Vivian with two people who look like her parents, based on the age and similar facial features. Vivian's mother is pretty but nothing like her daughter. Also, she wears way too much makeup. Another photograph is of a younger-looking Vivian standing, arms linked, with a plain-faced woman dressed in Gap-grade whitewash jeans and a UPenn sweatshirt. A picture from college?

Taylor places the frame down and glances around again. A few feet from the desk, which she has yet to search, is the bedroom door, tantalizingly ajar. Like a fish to a lure, Taylor immediately bypasses the desk to enter the bedroom. She slips off her boots and then her socks so she can sink her toes into the soft sheepskin rug. She opens dresser drawers, riffles through closet hangers, combs through shelves. With every designer accessory she picks up—a Chanel bag, Prada sunglasses, a Christian Dior belt—and every clothing item she uncovers—a Burberry trench coat, a Versace dress, a Chanel tweed jacket—she falls a little more in love with Vivian.

And a little more in love with herself. Taylor normally doesn't like her arms, but in the fine Versace silk, she doesn't mind them. In fact, as she twirls in Vivian's full-length gold-framed mirror, her arms look almost shapely. And the Hermès scarf gently tied around her neck elongates her face, slimming it and shifting attention away from her gapped teeth. The three-inch Jimmy Choo crystal pumps create muscles in her calves. It's as if she's stepped into one of the collages of fashion magazine cutouts she used to make as a young girl. She feels beautiful in a way she hasn't in a long time, perhaps since she first started dating Grayson years ago.

She isn't in a movie set; she *is* the movie set.

In the back of the closet is a set of Louis Vuitton luggage: one large duffel bag, a rolling suitcase, and a garment bag. She runs her palm across the smooth leather, fingers the intact seams. She marvels at their pristine condition and is reminded of an incident that happened years earlier, at her dad's restaurant: A tourist left behind her Louis Vuitton wallet. Taylor discovered it, after-hours, as she was sweeping crab shells into a dustpan. The wallet was wedged beneath a table, and it felt like a piece of gold in Taylor's high school–age hands. She wanted it, badly.

The woman's license revealed she was from Boston, which didn't surprise Taylor in the slightest. Boston had seduced her mother. It was a city where things seemed to happen. Where history had happened. Of course a sophisticated woman with a Louis Vuitton wallet would be from Boston.

When the woman returned to the restaurant the following day, distraught and fretting about how she had a flight to catch, Taylor surreptitiously emptied the wallet of its contents.

"We found your credit cards and license and cash, but no wallet," Taylor had said. "I can put these in a plastic bag for you, if you want?"

The woman had eyed Taylor, almost in disbelief, but she'd taken her items and gone on her way.

For years the wallet was Taylor's most coveted possession. She used it all the time. Only later did she realize it was nearly worthless. The lining was deteriorated, ripped even; the leather discolored, the edges peeling. She felt foolish with the realization, but it was a good lesson. Condition of designer items matters; it is why they have protective cloth bags.

On a mirrored jewelry tray, Taylor now picks up a bottle of perfume. Chanel N°5. She sprays it on her wrist, deeply inhales. Then she places it back on the tray, beside a bottle of OPI nail polish whose color she takes note of (Malaga Wine), and some jewelry, including a casually strewn diamond tennis bracelet, a pearl necklace, a "V" initial gold pendant, and a pair of gold-and-emerald drop earrings. This woman sure likes her emeralds, but Taylor supposes that if she, too, had magnificent green eyes, she'd be drawn to that color—though she'd obviously have to make do with glass- and gold-plated versions.

No wonder Taylor's patient access was restricted. Is Vivian some sort of royal heiress?

Taylor's phone pings with a text message, and she jumps, startled. It's Sam, her neighbor:

> Hey, thought you were coming by
> the salon? I'll hang around for a few
> more mins . . . Lmk.

Shit. Sam kindly offered another after-hours cut and told her to swing by at 7:30 p.m.

She's shocked to see it's already 7:48 p.m.

How long has she been here? Outside, the sky is pitch-black; the winter day has closed like a curtain. She quickly types back a response:

Omg so sorry . . . I can't make it. Something came up. Happy to pay you a cancellation fee.

She isn't happy to do that at all; she can't even afford a regular cut from him, let alone a fee for one she never received.

Luckily, his response is: No worries.

She looks around at the pile of clothes heaped onto the paisley bedsheets, the shoes scattered on the floor. The absence of the hungry cat, the nonexistent dying fish—the scene pokes holes in the thinness of her justifications for coming here. What was she thinking?

She works quickly to put everything back. With each passing minute, she grows more anxious. What if the concierge or someone else comes by to check on the apartment? What if Vivian's Gap-wearing friend from the picture is making her way there at this very moment?

With the bedroom back in order, and just a lingering waft of perfume in the air, Taylor hastens to the main room, toward the door. But then she stops, turns to look at Vivian's desk.

Just five more minutes, she thinks. Besides, leaving will be far easier than coming. She can just stroll by the concierge on her way out as if she were visiting someone in the building. Still, time presses in on her. Taylor thrusts open the drawers, moving in a swift, clockwork fashion. There's the normal desk spread: a tiny stapler, a roll of stamps, pens, and a pair of readers. A wallet-size school picture of a little girl who looks kindergarten age. Embroidered on the left side of her navy-blue jumper are the words

"Locust Prep" over a school shield with a Liberty Bell. Who is she to Vivian?

Taylor digs deeper, finds a stack of plastic cards bound with an elastic band that reveal that Vivian is a member of The 'Quin (Boston's exclusive social club that Sam wants to join), the Atheneum (a private library in Beacon Hill), and a yoga studio called Mission Hill Yoga. There's another stack of cards, business ones, for a place called Storied Antiques. And what do you know, Vivian is listed on the card as the owner.

Taylor slips one of the business cards into her pocket. She is about to close the drawer—the last one she's gone through—when she spots a hint of cream paper. She extends the drawer; a small, folded slip of paper is wedged at the back. Reaching in, she retrieves it and unfolds it. There's a single sentence, written in black ink: PLEASE STAY AWAY

The room darkens further as dusk settles in, and it's followed by a loud knocking noise that startles Taylor. Is someone at the door? She freezes, holds her breath. But then she realizes the sound is simply the boom of the old-fashioned wall radiator.

She looks again at the note; there's an upward arrow at the end of the sentence, directing where it is one should stay away from. Her eyes travel to the top of the stationery, to the embossed graphic: a top hat with a flower on its band.

She gasps. She's seen this symbol before: It was on the last letter her mom wrote her from Boston.

VIVIAN

Early February

The lights in the Knox parlor are dimmed for the masquerade ball, and a sultry, intoxicating air suspends, almost like smoke from a cigarette. The men are in crisp tuxedos, the women in long-sleeved corseted ball gowns or elegant, slinky floor-length dresses. Everyone is masked, even the waitstaff, as if it's some sort of entry requirement. Vivian supposes it is. Some masks cover only the eyes, some are full-face. A few guests wear the creepy plague doctor kind, with the beak-like nose.

It's the type of party where one can blend in, disappear. At the very least, steal away for a while, which Vivian plans to do at some point. She needs to find that secretary, the one named in the letters. If they are to be believed, there's a hidden document naming her ancestor as heir to the realty trust for the Knox building.

Vivian feels, appropriately, a bit naughty in the dress she sourced from her mother's trusty closet: a high-necked, sleeveless, sexy black gown that hugs her figure. The top consists of leather straps; the bottom is made of see-through feathers. In the wrong circumstances it could border on gaudy. The back is open,

perfect to accommodate Peter's hand, which is cupped there—
and of which she is acutely aware.

"Do you want another?" Peter asks.

Does he mean another pill, or another drink? He offered her
a pill earlier in the night, but she declined. When she hesitates, he
nods to her martini glass. Empty except for two olives.

"I might need to slow down."

"What?" he says, leaning in closer. His lips graze her cheek,
beneath her black-and-gold mask. Thank God it arrived in time
from Amazon and the lighting is low. She has a feeling most of
the gilded masks people are wearing came directly from Atelier
Flavia's in Venice. And that the ones with shiny sparkles are en-
crusted with diamonds, not rhinestones. Time was, she could
have easily afforded a diamond-encrusted mask.

"I'll have another," she says. May as well.

Peter smiles as he pulls back. He briefly slips his mask down,
winks, and then dips through the crowd, long legs swishing in his
silky black pants. Most of the men here wearing tuxedos merely
inhabit their clothes, rather than possess them, like Peter does.
People pause to look at him when he strides past, and it pleases
Vivian.

She takes the opportunity to survey the room as she pops an
olive in her mouth. Decadence oozes from every corner: a platter
of oysters on ice, a Dom Pérignon champagne bar, a crystal bowl
the size of a large fist filled with caviar. She's brought back, momentarily, to her childhood: her parents entertaining in the living
room, like usual, as she squirms in some stiff, frilly dress her
mom has instructed her to wear. That was back when the house
didn't look like a weird modern art museum. Vivian was probably five years old when she first acquired a taste for caviar.

In the corner of the room, a mime catches her eye. He's entirely white, from his tuxedo to his face paint, and is extending

his arms out in a mesmerizing fashion. He's pulsing in time to the throb of a techno beat. It comes up through the wooden floorboards, the vibrations like tiny waves. But then his feet follow separately, in a move that reminds her of Michael Jackson, as if his bottom half doesn't quite belong to the rest of his body.

It's a bit like how she feels: her head in one place, occupied with thoughts Peter doesn't know about, as her body tangentially moves along. Vivian does not see a secretary in her immediate vicinity, but she didn't expect to. Secretaries are mostly in bedrooms and offices, less often in hallways, and almost never in a parlor. They are in the private areas, areas that are off-limits for visitors of the Knox. Given the array of furniture she noticed when having tea with Peter, the mixture of old and new, she's holding out hope that the rest of the rooms in the house have retained some original pieces. And that the "schedule of beneficiaries" that a well-meaning servant had taken the risk to hide all those years ago is still contained within one of them.

When she looked up the address of the Knox earlier on Realtor .com, they listed an off-market value of $23.2 million. She's also heard whispers about a mansion north of the city, where the members escape to on summer weekends. Twenty-three million is probably chump change for Knox members, but even a quarter of that would likely get Vivian out of this financial pickle.

Vivian wants what she—and her family—are entitled to. Her mother hadn't cared, nor her grandmother, really, but that's because they didn't need to care. Vivian has her mother's medical expenses and debt to pay off, an antiques store business to save, an apartment she'd very much like to hold on to, and her goddaughter's tuition payments to make.

She puts down her glass as the music suddenly turns louder. A guttural beat pulsates within her like a strobe light, making her feel dizzy. She starts to head toward the exit when she nearly bumps into a tall person wearing a plague mask, standing still as if he wishes to speak with her. He holds a scepter in one black-gloved hand and a crystal champagne glass in the other. She wonders if it's Michael but then dismisses the thought; this man is not Michael-tall. What does this person want? She pauses, glancing back to see if he's waiting for someone else, but there's no one behind her. When she faces him again, she notices he has begun subtly nodding at her. Like they share some secret together.

No, she realizes in the next split second. The person has simply started moving to the music.

Christ.

Good thing she didn't take the pill, whatever it was. This party itself is like a drug.

The moment she steps into the foyer, she starts to feel better, the music loosening its grip on her body. A few people mill in the hall, in quiet conversations. The mood is so utterly different out here, with jazz filtering from overhead speakers like a sprinkling of gentle rain. The ivory-painted walls are wainscoted halfway and then crowned by a shiny gold map wallpaper of old Boston. Mazes of streets train upward, to the ceiling. She lightly runs her fingers along it, feeling as if it's beckoning her to the past. *Her* past.

Suddenly, one of the doors a few feet ahead creaks open, and she snatches her hand back. Three masked men slip out. They move down the hall toward her, their voices lowering as they pass. They sway side to side, as if being blown by the wind. One of the men inclines his head at her, but it happens so quickly she could be imagining it.

The door closes with a gentle thud, but not before she spies the interior: A group of people lounge on what appears to be a large mattress on the floor. Some sort of orgy? She overheard chatter in the parlor, the first time Peter left to fetch her a drink, about some of the activities behind these doors: fortune-telling, tarot card readings, high-stake poker games. There's some plain-clothes magician lurking around who performs magic tricks when you least expect it, someone said. An old lady who'll whip out a Magic 8 Ball, and if providence dictates, she'll then give you an eight ball of cocaine, someone else whispered. Geomancy readings, said others. Vivian's heard of palm readings but not geomancy readings. She'll have to look that up later. At any rate, she hasn't heard anyone gossiping about things sexual in nature, but she wouldn't be surprised.

As Vivian weaves down the hall, she continues to pass guests who appear thoroughly intoxicated. One woman, wearing a mask that sprouts feathers like a peacock and a tight-fitting Ma-rie Antoinette dress that makes her breasts pop, strolls past, her head thrown back in laughter. But nobody is with her.

What kinds of drugs are floating around this party?

Vivian turns a corner and startles as she comes upon a turquoise-painted horse on an iron pedestal. The carousel horse. It was returned just yesterday to the Knox. She can't get away from this thing.

She distances herself from the horse, taking a few steps back. Suddenly, someone jostles into her from behind.

"Shorry," a male voice mumbles beneath a full mask. It's one of those creepy ones, of course. The plague. "Did I getch you?" The man gestures widely with one arm, holding a half-empty glass of red wine. His movements are as sloppy as his pronunci-ation.

She glances down. He might've spilled on her, but since she's wearing black, it's impossible to tell. "It's fine," she says. But she's rather annoyed.

The man doesn't say anything. He's shorter than she is, and the tilt of his head suggests he's staring at her chest.

Whatever, creep. She goes to move past, but the man suddenly grabs her arm.

"V," he says, his voice low.

"Do I know you?"

He lifts his mask. Underneath, his face is sweaty, plump. Two small brown eyes. She does know him.

Xavier.

"I recognized you," he whispers. His voice, now so clear. Like he's suddenly sobered up. But that doesn't make sense, because he doesn't drink. Or does he?

"I saw your necklace," he adds, meaning her nineteen-karat-gold "V" initial pendant. He and Rachel gave it to her several years ago for a birthday gift.

"What are you doing here . . . ?" Her voice trails off, and his face reddens. She doesn't need to say it. He remembers. About how weird he'd been after he saw the carousel horse in her shop. He must have known that it came from the Knox.

So why is *he* here, then?

"I . . ."

His eyes dart beyond her, and his face blanches. He quickly slips his mask back on. "Be careful," he says in a low voice, as he brushes past.

"There you are," Peter suddenly says, over her shoulder.

TAYLOR

In her apartment, Taylor poorly sketches the top hat she saw at Vivian's place from memory: She makes the hat too flat, the flower much too simple.

What is this symbol? And how is it that both Vivian and her mom, two women who suffered unfortunate fates, were in possession of stationery embossed with it?

Her mom's letter is back home, stored in a shoebox under Taylor's childhood bed. She calls her dad, and he reluctantly agrees to look for it. If he finds it (*he will*), he says he'll mail it to her. She knows he thinks she's too consumed with her mom lately.

He's right.

Taylor hangs her drawing on the refrigerator and steps back to appraise it. It feels like a clue, but how so? On Google, she learns that a top hat is traditionally associated with the upper class, viewed as a symbol of wealth. Fitting for Boston. But adding "Boston" to the search does mothing more than produce some local costume stores. The symbol remains a mystery.

She wishes she were not off from work for a stretch; she wants
to go back to the hospital and check in on Vivian. Mostly, though,
she wants to keep busy to bat down the restlessness she feels—
and the shame. What kind of nurse is she to have broken into her
patient's apartment? What kind of *person*?

But then, when she recalls the luxurious contents of Vivian's
apartment, and the stationery she uncovered, she feels like a dead
wire becoming live. And that awakening sensation makes her almost cry.

"You okay?" Sam asks, when he stops by one afternoon. He
hasn't brought up the missed haircut, but he hasn't offered a
makeup session, either.

"Yeah," she lies, biting back the truth. She can't exactly tell
him how she played Goldilocks in her patient's apartment.

Or can she? Can she confide in Sam, trust him completely?
No—his late mom was a nurse. He might be so appalled he
would turn Taylor in to the Massachusetts nursing board.

Meanwhile, she keeps waiting for a call from her nurse manager, or the hospital—or, worse, a visit from the police. But her
phone doesn't ring, so she holds out hope that she's not in trouble
at work. Or not in *that* much trouble. Given the list of crimes
she's recently committed, she'll gladly take the rap for breaching
a patient's medical records.

◈—◦—◈

When Taylor finally returns to the hospital for a night shift, she
immediately tries to log on to the patient portal at the nursing
station. But her account remains locked.

Her nurse manager Jan's door is open, but Taylor knocks nevertheless.

"Hi, Taylor," Jan says from behind her desk. "What can I do for you?"

Jan seems oblivious. This is a good sign. Taylor moves inside. "I, uh, I'm having trouble with Epic."

"Oh?"

"I'm locked out."

"Did you talk to IT?"

"No."

"Why don't you give them a call."

"Okay."

Jan returns to look at her computer, but Taylor stays, rooted.

"I think, maybe, I uh, got locked out because I was checking on a former patient. Her account became restricted, and I still tried to access it."

Jan's expression is neutral. "I see."

Taylor shifts, pressing her tongue against the gap in her two front teeth, like she often does. She does feel a little guilty, but it's certainly not about the attempted login. "I'm sorry, I probably shouldn't have. I just like to know if my patients are okay, when they get admitted. I'm used to working at the orthopedic center in North Carolina, where I'm with the same patients every day, sometimes for weeks at a time." This is the answer she's rehearsed. And it's true, but Taylor also knows that if this situation had happened with another patient she'd previously taken care of, the warning message would have promptly stopped her.

"Taylor, when a patient's account is restricted, you are not authorized to access it unless the patient is under your direct care. This is a hospital policy. We take patient confidentiality very seriously."

"I understand. I'm sorry. I won't do it again." She hangs her head. Her cream cashmere socks peek out from above her Crocs.

They're Vivian's socks. It was the one item Taylor lifted from the apartment. Vivian has an entire drawer full of them; Taylor doubts one pair will be missed.

"Okay, I'll call IT and get it lifted. They may need you to take a refresher course on patient confidentiality; I'm not sure. They'll let you know."

"Okay, thank you," Taylor says as she exits.

Normally she intensely dislikes working the night shift, which means her sleep cycle will be thrown off for the rest of the week, but she's glad she's there tonight, since it seems like the only way she'll get any updates on Vivian is if she physically visits her in the ICU. Taylor will go later, once the ER quiets down, when the nurse managers like Jan and Aunt Gigi leave for the day, so that she can return the key *for real*.

⬦━◦━⬦

It's one o'clock in the morning by the time Taylor steals away to the ICU. Her feet ache; she's been nonstop for hours. People were partying hard tonight in Boston; there was a slew of alcohol poisonings and broken bones from bar fights and drunken brawls—and even more drug overdoses than usual. It seems to be on the uptick.

The ICU floor is quiet, much quieter than the ER. Taylor walks past the nursing station, nods hello to a nurse she recognizes, then sweeps by, heading to room 603. From the hallway, she notices the lights are dimmed. For a moment, the room looks empty. Taylor rubs her eyes, letting them adjust. She doesn't want to disturb Vivian by turning on the light. But there's an odd silence. No gasps of the ventilator, no rhythmic whooshes of the IV pump.

Taylor steps in, flicks on the light. The room *is* empty; the mattress with just a tight white bedsheet, the IV pole barren. It's empty and it's cleaned, awaiting the next unfortunate patient.

Wow, she's tired. She clearly has the wrong room. Taylor doubles back, checks the number printed alongside the wall: 603.

It's the right room; Vivian is gone.

VIVIAN

Unknown Time

It feels like she's fallen asleep without washing her face; there's that uncomfortable early-morning grimy sensation. She is so, so tired; it's a smothering kind of exhaustion. She couldn't get up even if she wished to. But she doesn't wish to. She doesn't wish to do anything at all. When thoughts arrive, they intensify the ferocious pounding in her head, and so she wills them away. Wills herself to nothingness.

Sleep overcomes her, or rather it settles, like the way one leans back on a sofa, because truthfully it could already be there. She *could* be asleep.

And indeed, she is: She dreams a terrible dream. She is walking through her mother's nursing home room, past the empty unmade bed, slowly opening the bathroom door. But instead of finding her mom poised in front of the mirror, a dab of La Mer facial cream on her finger, Vivian sees herself instead.

She's the one dead. She just hasn't realized it yet.

VIVIAN

Early February

Why had Xavier warned Vivian to *be careful*? Was it because he saw Peter over her shoulder? Or did he simply mean to be careful of the Knox? And why was he here, anyway?

But Xavier's gone, so Vivian can't ask him. When she glances at the spot he was standing in, the hall is empty. He's vanished, on par with the other shady characters that seem to inhabit the place tonight.

Meanwhile, Peter stands there, as still as a statue, his arm extending toward her. In his hands is her martini, perfectly filled to the rim. Of course it is.

Peter *feels* like an architect. There is a certain way he holds himself, and objects, that appears structural in nature. He must think about dimension and space in a different way than most people do.

"Thanks," Vivian says, taking the martini glass from him. When their fingers brush together, a current pulses through her. On top of the olives, at the end of the toothpick, is a piece of what she thinks is candied fruit, but then she realizes it's a tiny gummy, shaped like a mask. "This is a marvelous drink." She slides the gummy into her mouth. Too late, she considers it could be more than just a simple piece of candy.

"You might be the only fortysomething-year-old woman who uses the word 'marvelous.'"

"Thanks, I guess?" She hasn't told him she's in her forties, and she can't say she loves him referencing her age.

"I mean it in a good way," he says. And then he adds, "What are you doing out here?"

She shrugs. "Is there a bathroom?" Meanwhile, she's still thinking about Xavier. She must have misheard the slurring of his words; the parlor music is probably still echoing through her.

Vivian is surprised that Xavier would be at a party, period. And at the Knox, no less. He's probably here with a new boyfriend and was carrying that wine for him. Or maybe it wasn't wine that Xavier was holding. It could have been a soda. It's shadowy in these corridors.

It saddens Vivian, how little she knows about Xavier these days.

Peter takes a step closer, studying her. "You're not really supposed to be here, in this part of the house."

Vivian takes a long sip of the drink. She can't tell if he's flirting with her or genuinely concerned about how she decided to wander around—that is, until she locks eyes with him, and a heat kindles inside her. "Oh no?" she says, dropping her voice a little.

"No," he whispers.

"Well, what are you going to do about it?"

After a quick glance over his shoulder, he takes her arm and pulls her forward a few steps before leaning against the wall.

Suddenly, a door pushes in. It's a false wall. Peter flips his mask up, like a pair of sunglasses, and grins almost boyishly as he holds the door open.

It's dark, and the strong smell of cigars hits her nose, as if someone were sitting there smoking, but when the lights flicker on, they are alone.

The secret room is a small library. Mahogany built-in bookshelves and cabinetry wrap around two walls. A rolling library ladder is hinged to a track that runs along the upper shelves. The third and fourth walls of the room are adorned with artwork. A tapestry of Chinese origin occupies a large swath of wall space. No surprise there, given the Knox's early roots.

In the center of the room, a green velvet couch sits opposite two chairs, a wooden coffee table sandwiched in between.

No secretaries, unfortunately.

Peter steals over to a mahogany cigar box resting on one of the cabinets. He is suddenly more interested in fishing out a cigar for himself than continuing their flirting. Fine with Vivian. It will give her a chance to look around. She sets down her martini on the coffee table, next to a pair of familiar candlesticks she'd sourced for the Knox.

She's drawn into a memory: Xavier at Vivian's store one day, looking through her collection of heavily tarnished silver and brass candlesticks.

"I could easily clean these up for you," he offered, meaning he could remove the oxidation with cyanide. While the use of cyanide is no longer a standard practice for cleaning jewelry due to its obvious danger, certain jewelers, like Xavier, have permits that allow them to purchase and use it for their business.

"Don't you dare," she replied. "Patina and original finish are what allow me to price these the way I do."

The memory fading, she glances around the room. There's an eerie quiet; the party sounds are muted completely, as if the room is soundproof. Maybe it is. She realizes there are no windows. Unless there's one hiding beneath that tapestry.

Peter lights up the cigar, and puffs of smoke billow. "This room is ventilated, so don't worry."

"Oh?" She still holds her breath. She is not one for cigar smoke, especially when in a windowless room, ventilation system or not. Through the filter of a masquerade mask or not. "What is this place?"

"They call it Teddy's. It was named after Theodore Thurgood. He was in charge of the Knox after William Knox passed."

Theodore "Teddy" Thurgood. Hmm. She commits this name to memory—she's not sure what she'll need in this quest of hers—and walks over to one of the nearby bookshelves that has caught her eye. The section is partially tucked under the ladder, and she pushes the ladder away, marveling at the ease in which it moves. Now, she's face-to-face with a few shelves of old, seemingly forgotten-about books. Antiques, some might say.

Hunger floods her, but it's not for food. She feels the way she does when she enters an estate sale, when a trove of treasures is at her fingertips. She instantly feels she can breathe a little easier. The books are in shades of tans and maroons and muted greens, their spines worn, crinkled. She can almost sense the film of dust that surely envelops them.

Vivian carries a smattering of vintage books in the shop, some finds she's discovered at the Sunday markets that run in the warm weather. She's marked them up to make a profit, but it's difficult to really assess their value. She is hardly an expert on rare books. Her area of expertise has always been what she jokingly—and secretly—calls "early IKEA": livable, functional, antique furnishings, from the 1800s to the 1920s. The criteria being that the items need to fit through the front door of her shop—it's the only way in and out. This suits her local customers just fine, though. They live in quirky, old spaces and are also looking for furniture that can squeeze through small entrances or be carried up narrow, crooked or spiral staircases. Her items are pricey, though; her customers are far from IKEA shoppers.

"Was Theodore a business associate of William Knox's?"

"No. He was his son-in-law. He worked for William. He was actually a cabin boy who worked his way up. But then he married William's only daughter, Margaret."

At the name Margaret, Vivian freezes. "Did they have children?" she manages to ask, slowly turning to face Peter.

"One, a boy."

And a girl, she silently adds. A girl, her great-great-grandmother, born out of wedlock while Theodore was at sea. Instead, she says, "That's unusual for those times. To have just one."

"You're right; I've never really thought about that."

"Maybe she had health problems?" Vivian suggests. She might be pushing her luck here. But she is curious, and not just because she wants to find a missing slip of paper. Because this Margaret—her great-great-great-grandmother—lived here, in this house. Because suddenly, in Vivian's mind, she's become a real person, with desires and likes and dislikes.

"Well, their son was a doctor, so if she did, she was in good hands."

Her son the doctor does not have the same kind heart. Something is not right. He has her body in the basement.

Vivian swallows. "A doctor, huh," she says, prodding Peter. But he doesn't say anything. "Dr. Thurgood," she adds, but he still doesn't say anything.

Finally, she says, "Is that what the son went by? Dr. Thurgood?" She wants to know his name.

Peter taps out the ash, then takes another puff on the cigar. He looks amused. "Is this what dating a lover of antiques is like? Your mind always on rewind, one foot always stepping into the past?"

"Oh, are we dating, then?"

"I'd like to."

"So, you're not opposed to dating fortysomething-year-old women who use words like 'marvelous'?" She can't help the snark.

"Touché. That was incredibly rude of me, calling you out for using the word 'marvelous.'" He grins. "I'm kidding. I do truly apologize. My mother, should I have had one for any real length of time, would have likely taught me not to mention a woman's age."

"Apology accepted." It's difficult to not soften with the thought of a motherless boy.

"I do want to date you, Vivian. At the moment, I have a crush like a schoolboy on you."

"Oh, a schoolboy crush?"

"I think you're incredible."

"I think you don't even know me."

"Vivian Lawrence. Grew up in Chestnut Hill. Studied anthropology at UPenn. Graduated summa cum laude."

"How do you know this?"

He puts down his cigar and walks toward her. "Lives at 62 Lime Street. Owner of Storied Antiques."

Her face burns, and she wonders if he's also sniffed out that her other store is soon closing. "How do you know all this?" she repeats.

He's in front of her now, running his finger down her bare shoulder. It sends tingles through her arm. "We don't just extend an invite to anyone at the Knox, Vivian. You can't be surprised that we did a bit of a background check."

"What I studied in college is part of a background check?"

"Well, *that* Michael told me."

She frowns, trying to remember what conversation she had

with Michael over the years at the store that revealed that fact. But it's hard to think because Peter's touch is consuming her. And truth be told, she might not remember anyway.

"You're so beautiful, Vivian." He tugs her mask off her face, slowly, as if he's undressing her whole. And then he kisses her.

Her whole body feels electric as she kisses him back. He tastes like martinis and cigars, but now she doesn't mind the cigar smell. Now, she likes it, savors the smoky tang on her tongue. They push against each other, their desire hot and sudden, like the strike of a match.

Then, the door to the room abruptly swings open as a pair of entangled bodies collapse on the ground. It's two men, fighting. Peter protectively pushes Vivian to the side, away from the commotion. She presses against the Chinese tapestry, which normally she wouldn't dare touch without gloves. As the men thrash on the ground, Vivian can't pull her eyes away. They are clawing each other like wild tigers. But one has the advantage, and something about the thick shape of his neck looks familiar. It's the wrestler—Jerry. The waiter who served her and Peter tea. His face is as red as fire.

"You're an asshole, Oliver!" Jerry yells as he pummels the other man.

Peter has turned oddly white, mute. He stands a few feet from Vivian, also pushed against the wall, like a piece of furniture. She feels strangely disappointed in him.

The door thrusts open again as Michael rushes in. Fittingly, he's wearing a very proper black tailcoat that Vivian can almost imagine him in on a regular day. She'd been wondering when she would see him tonight. She certainly didn't expect it to be under these circumstances.

Michael manages to pull Jerry off this Oliver fellow. It's quite impressive. She didn't think Michael had it in him.

"Asshole," Jerry spits once more, as Oliver stands up and straightens his shirt. Oliver doesn't look like he's a fellow co-worker but rather a member or a guest. A strung-out member or guest. Dirty-blond shoulder-length hair, an angular, chiseled face. A streak of blood trailing down his cheek. Gucci loafers beneath his Canali tux.

Why on earth would such a person be in a scuffle with the help?

Michael notices Vivian, and then his gaze travels to Peter. Vivian can't interpret his expression.

"You're so done, Jerry," Oliver says with a slur. "I'm so done with you . . . but not as done as I am with your skank sister. Tara wasn't even a good fuck."

Aha. Because this Knox member, Oliver, apparently slept with Jerry's sister.

"Fuck you!" Jerry lunges at Oliver, but Michael has seen it coming and grips Jerry from behind.

Oliver just laughs, and it's one of those empty laughs that makes everyone around feel worse.

"Men! Please!" Peter says, striding over. His color is normal, and Vivian wonders if she imagined what she'd seen just moments earlier, perhaps even projected her own fears onto him. "We have a lady here. Why don't we move this upstairs?"

"I don't need nothin' else. I'm done here," Jerry says. He doesn't give Vivian a second glance as he slinks out of Michael's arm and stalks out of the room.

Michael rubs his wrists, and the tension in the air suddenly lessens.

Meanwhile, Oliver seems to have noticed Vivian for the first time. "Well, hello there," he says with a pasty grin.

He looks her up and down, making Vivian's skin prickle. Oliver stumbles as he takes a step in her direction, and Peter moves in between them, like a blockade. She must have been imagining Peter's earlier cowardice.

"A lady," Oliver says. "Now that is a—"

"Oliver, your father wants a word," Peter interrupts. "He was looking for you."

Michael appears at Vivian's side, takes her elbow, and his touch is not entirely unpleasant. "C'mon," he whispers, and when she looks at Peter, he nods.

Vivian follows Michael out the door, feeling Oliver's eyes on her back.

TAYLOR

When Taylor finds Vivian's hospital room empty, the day feels suddenly drained of color.

At the nearest computer, she quickly logs into Epic and pulls up the ICU unit manager. It's a way to see the floor census at a glance without breaching anyone's medical records. No Vivian. Maybe she transferred to another unit? Taylor frantically starts pulling up the unit manager for other possible floors where Vivian, given her injury, may have been moved.

No luck.

Taylor hunts down an ICU nurse, and, in a trembling voice, asks about Vivian.

"I have no idea," says the nurse. "I haven't been here in a couple of days."

"Did she . . . Did she expire?" Taylor manages, the words like brittle toast lodged in her throat.

"I said I have no idea," the nurse repeats, but then softens at Taylor's obvious distress. "Look, last I heard, she was extubated. So I doubt it."

They wouldn't have removed Vivian's breathing tube if she

wasn't improving. Taylor allows herself a little hope as she scoots back downstairs to continue her ER shift.

She can't stop thinking of Vivian—her glossy brown hair, her olive-green eyes, the Chanel N°5, the luxury clothes, the fancy penthouse apartment.

And then other, more troubling, things start to pile on:

The mismatch between the paramedic's report about Vivian's drinking and the negligible blood alcohol level.

The lack of visitors.

The top hat symbol.

The warning on the note: "Please stay away."

The fact that Vivian's records suddenly became restricted, and now she seems to have vanished from the hospital.

Where are you, Vivian?

Taylor feels a little desperate, like when she was a little girl and waiting each day for her mother to send word from Boston.

She types and deletes a text to her aunt several times.

> Aunt Gigi, I went to check again on my patient V. She's not there . . . Do u know where she is? Wanted to make sure she's ok.

She waits until it's five in the morning to send off the text.

When she pops back up to the ICU at the end of her shift, the same unhelpful nurse is there. "Sorry, honey, I still don't know," the nurse answers. Then she gives a puzzling enough glance to make Taylor worry she's coming off too interested.

Taylor leaves, face flushed. She's not in trouble, she has to remind herself. She clearly has a guilty conscience because she broke into Vivian's apartment, but nobody else knows that. So who cares if this ICU nurse thinks she's acting weird?

On her walk home from the hospital, Taylor detours to Vivian's shop, Storied Antiques. It's a charming storefront, tucked into a side lane that branches off Charles Street, Beacon Hill's main drag. Vivian's apartment is a few blocks over. Her patient's whole world appears to have existed within the span of four streets. She likely stood in this very spot most days. It makes Taylor feel surreal, like she's suddenly inside the TV set of a show she watches.

She peers through the darkened window, noting the carefully arranged end table with a crystal vase and a tumbler set on a hammered coaster. An Emily Dickinson book of poetry. The coral armchair with a cable-knit wool throw and a matching footstool. She can imagine Vivian in the display, gracefully placing each accessory, stepping back to consider the furniture's best angle for onlookers.

Taylor swallows. What she would give to open this door and step into Vivian's life. To have a conversation with her from the vantage point of a customer. To see her living and breathing, full of life.

To get a sense of what Taylor's own mother might have been like, had she lived.

Vivian's injury suddenly seems so unfair. One never knows how TBIs will resolve. Or *if*. And when patients do recover, there's such a wide spectrum of brain function they may or may not regain. Some make a full recovery, some might turn simply forgetful at times, and others continue to live in between, in the desert of their mind. Only time will tell.

Taylor can't bear the thought that Vivian might never return to this shop, that she won't sleep in her luxurious bedroom, or don her Loro Piana cashmere sweater and Dior ballet flats. That

Vivian won't continue to exist in the world the way she once did, before falling down those stairs.

That she might succumb to a tragic and untimely death, not unlike Taylor's mom.

Taylor checks her phone, but her aunt has not responded. She trudges the rest of the way home, feeling a little more depleted with each step.

Sam's street-facing window is as dark as Vivian's storefront. When Taylor was leaving for work last night, she heard loud laughter coming from his apartment; he definitely had company. She was puzzled he hadn't invited her. He always invites her when he has a group of friends over, even though she doesn't always go. Maybe he's still salty about her missing the haircut. She wouldn't have been able to hang out anyway; she had to work. But *he* didn't know that.

Back home in North Carolina, Taylor used to have a set social routine. On Saturday nights, she and Grayson would go to the local bar a friend owned. They would play darts and drink beer and eat spicy chicken wings smothered in ranch dressing. Taylor liked these evenings just fine, but she never loved them. It seems like she never loved anything in the Outer Banks. But here, in Boston, she was hoping things would be different.

Sam's exclusion stings.

In her kitchen, she fixes herself a bowl of Lucky Charms and sorts through her mail from the prior day. She sighs. All bills. Credit card bills, an electricity bill, a school loan statement. Even the one piece of mail that isn't a bill is still asking for money: a donation request from the Museum of Fine Arts. Clearly, they don't know their target audience.

She rubs her eyes, glances down at her phone. She's not one to spend much time on social media, but Grayson is on her mind. So she opens up Instagram.

Grayson was a surfer, like most of the boys she grew up with. Moppy caramel hair, light brown eyes, always clad in board shorts and Birkenstocks, even in the winter. She met him when she was twenty, at a house party hosted by one of the bartenders from her dad's restaurant. Some girl handed her a plastic cup of champagne, and when Taylor looked up, confused, the girl pointed to the corner of the room, where Grayson sat in a fold-out chair with his own respective cup. *Cheers*, he mouthed, and smiled with a deep dimple.

It had been very easy for Taylor to slip into a life with Grayson—too easy. He was familiar to her in the way that home was: sandy grains in between her toes, Old Bay–seasoned shrimp and cold, cold beer. The Outer Banks had its own rhythm, the ocean and its offerings the local currency. Coffee shops had hours that operated like a mood, closing for inclement weather and good surfing conditions. Their friends who were waitresses and bartenders sweat through poorly air-conditioned restaurants in the summer and then claimed unemployment in the wintertime, when many of the restaurants closed. The pool and spa cleaning company Grayson's family owned also deadened in the off-season.

Then one night, while smoking a joint on the worn, dated sofa Grayson had inherited with the condo he was renting—and which he kept pressuring Taylor to move into—she realized her future: It was a straight existence, as linear as the horizon. No variation. The dense, humid days, once comforting like a blanket, had become smothering. While their friends chatted weddings and babies, she cranked up her fashion podcasts, trying to drown out the internal angst those thoughts caused.

When she first reached out to Aunt Gigi, she didn't tell anyone. She simply followed her aunt's advice: *If you really want to move to Boston and come work at Mass General, then you should get some nursing experience first. Work for a few years at home, save up some money. Then reach back out and we'll chat.*

When Taylor applied for her Massachusetts nursing license and had her remote interview for the hospital, she still didn't tell anyone. Aunt Gigi honored her wishes not to speak with Taylor's dad—Aunt Gigi's brother—until Taylor told him first. Only after she was offered the ER position did she sit down her father and Grayson.

"Boston," her dad had sighed. "Of all the places, T.J., why did you have to pick there?"

Grayson has moved on. An Instagram story shows him with a female friend sitting side by side on a familiar set of green webbed folding chairs in his backyard. They're wearing flannel shirts and holding Miller Lites. Taylor knows the woman: Hatcher, they called her, by her last name. She was a grade below Taylor in school. People used to say Hatcher looked like Taylor. Or that Taylor looked like Hatcher. She can sort of see it: They both have apples for cheeks, brown eyes, shoulder-length chestnut hair. Hatcher fills out her T-shirts much more generously than Taylor does, though, and her teeth are better behaved, aligned in a neat little row.

Taylor's not jealous. But she's not not-jealous, either.

She closes the app. Grayson is where he should be. And she's where she always wanted to be: Boston. So why does she feel so bad?

VIVIAN

Early February

I'm sorry you had to see that skirmish," Michael says. He's
whisked her away from the masquerade ball to an upstairs
restaurant, which Vivian is surprised to see even exists. How
many nooks and crannies does this place have? Multiple levels of
dining mean there are multiple levels of kitchens at the Knox,
unless they have installed some sort of high-speed dumbwaiter.

If she wants to find the secretary, she better start cataloging
the rooms. There was no secretary in the parlor, nor was there
one in Teddy's, the library and cigar room they just left. And Vivian is doubtful a secretary would be in this room, which contains
more of a traditional, almost dated aesthetic: dark wood-paneled
walls, leather booths, a navy-blue-and-cream rug. A long wooden
bar, where they are now perched on stools. Engraved on the back
of the bar, behind the generous array of bottles, is a wooden
plaque with the words "Canton's Restaurant." The space reminds
her of an old country club so long overdue for a renovation the
vibe has become part of its "charm." She certainly has not
sourced any furniture for it over the years.

"Who were those people?" she asks, even though she already

knows Jerry, the one with the buzz cut whom she thinks of as *the wrestler*. She sips the ice water Michael procured for her from behind the bar.

"Jerry is one of our employees, a waiter." Michael clears his throat. "I can't say I blame him for getting so upset. The other man is Oliver. Oliver is Graham Thurgood's son."

Graham *Thurgood*? "Is Graham . . ."

"Graham's the head of the Knox," Michael confirms. "Oliver, his son, recently returned to town after traveling for a few years in Southeast Asia. I can't say that people love having him back."

"He got involved with Jerry's sister?"

"Yes, unfortunately he did. Tara's a waitress here, too."

"Sounds messy," she offers, as she sips her water. It's hard to imagine that she and this Oliver could be distantly related. He seems reckless in a dangerous kind of way. What was he doing for a few years in Southeast Asia? For the first time, she wonders if she should just forget this whole ancestry thing. But, she reasons in the next moment, she hasn't *done* anything yet. She's simply at a party at the Knox. Potentially about to start dating Peter, a very handsome man. Deepening her connection with Michael, her Knox buyer. And she needs their business more than ever.

"I'm truly sorry you had to see that. It's your first time at the Knox—"

"Second."

"Second time at the Knox, but first social event, and here we are, hiding away. You should get back to the party when you feel ready. I just wanted to make sure you were okay." He speaks haltingly, like a baby giraffe finding its footing.

"I am okay. Thank you for this, though."

It strikes Vivian that this is the longest conversation they've ever had, although, according to Peter, she's apparently discussed other topics with Michael through the years, such as what she studied in college.

The truth is, she's never paid him much attention. He's one of those people who gets noticed because he's so tall, and then that one attribute overtakes the rest of him. But now, up close, she sees that his smile is slightly lopsided on account of a bent jaw. And that there's a light brown, grayish stubble covering his cheeks, and his eyes are like hot cocoa, a warm brown.

"Michael, what do you do?" she asks. She's a little embarrassed that she's never asked this before—though, to be fair, she doesn't usually strike up personal conversations with her customers. Also, the fact that he was coming from the Knox likely thwarted questions she may have had. But here, in this setting, the Knox itself, it seems okay to pry.

"I'm retired now, but I was an investment banker. Now I just dabble in some investments here and there."

"Oh."

He's rather young to be retired; he looks in his fifties. On second thought, that's not *too* young to be retired. This is the problem with getting older: Your concept of time goes awry. You think you're younger than you actually are, until your body invariably reminds you. "And you've been a member here for a while?"

"Yes. My late father was a member here, and his father before that, and . . . you get the picture."

Right. She recalls Peter saying Michael hailed from a long lineage. "A fellow New Englander; why am I not surprised?"

"Why do you say that?"

"It's your vibe. It's our vibe. Aloof. Look, it's only taken us, what, five or six years to have a real conversation, right?"

"Seven," he replies almost too quickly, and then he looks away, as if embarrassed.

"Do you two need something?" says a woman's voice from behind. It's Rose, the woman who answered the door when Vivian first came to the Knox. She might be the only one in the entire party dressed in jeans and a turtleneck, like it's an ordinary day of work.

"No, Rose, thank you," Michael says. "Rose, this is—"

"I know who she is," Rose interrupts.

"Hello, Rose," Vivian says, when it's clear that Rose is not making the first move. Christ. They ought to get some help around here who are a little more polite.

"Vivian." Rose gives her a curt nod. She continues to stand there, and it irritates Vivian.

Vivian rises from the stool, and Michael follows suit. She wonders, suddenly, why Peter has not come to check on her. This, too, irritates her. It should be he who is here at her side, not Michael.

"Thank you again, Michael," she says to him. "I have a headache so I'm going to see myself out. Please let Peter know."

She walks past Rose, not bothering to give her a second glance. But Vivian knows, even before she hears Rose's footsteps behind her, that this woman is following closely behind. Vivian's pretty sure that there's no way in hell Rose would let anyone walk around unattended in the Knox.

THE KNOX

Early February

Last night at the society's annual masquerade ball, I was delightfully occupied: People ate caviar by the spoonful at my cocktail tables and consumed copious amounts of alcohol from my well-stocked bars. They reclined on luxurious chesterfield couches and distributed illicit substances in my corridors. They shook hands on deals over the finest Cuban cigars and single malt whiskeys—deals they planned to keep and deals they most certainly intended to break. And they did this in the way that Knox members do best: sinful but with the utmost decorum, irrational while philosophical, reckless yet buttoned-up.

It was rather splendid, a proper Knox party that met with my approval.

Today I'll be achy; today my floors will creak when people walk on them. My rugs will be embedded with dirt, my walls and mirrors smudged with fingerprints. My surfaces will be appallingly sticky, and there will be a fine ash all around. I'll sag under the weight of discarded porcelain cocktail plates, glass tumblers and champagne glasses, empty liquor bottles. I'll have a faint malodorous scent that will grow more offensive as the hours tick by, until they tie up the trash bags and remove them from me.

But it's of minimal consequence; I don't *really* concern myself with such matters. Rose will tidy me up, make me as good as new. She always does.

That woman, Vivian, was at the ball; Peter seems quite smitten. I observed her for a time. She's familiar in a way I can't put my foundation on. Peter and I were not the only ones intrigued by Vivian. Many others were as well: proper Michael and a jeweler named Xavier, who carries a respectable enough old-fashioned pocket watch. I've previously noticed him on occasion. And Rose. Rose was watching Vivian, and I suspect she doesn't care for her.

It strikes me that there are some *very* interesting things to come. For instance, Graham has not the slightest inkling of the wheeling and dealing Oliver's doing behind (my) closed doors.

Graham will be most displeased when he learns of his son's plans.

But Oliver is simply trying to restore the Knox to its former glory. Godspeed, dear boy.

TAYLOR

Taylor attends the patient confidentiality online refresher course. Clicks the right buttons. Shows up at work. Comes home and brushes her teeth. Places a dirty cereal bowl in her sink, alongside the one from the previous day. Goes to sleep, these days with the bedroom door open, so she can see through to the opposite end of her apartment, out the glass patio door.

One night she gets out her tape measure and runs it along the bedroom window. Prior to moving to Boston, her landlord had assured her and her dad that the window met Massachusetts egress requirements. But now, Taylor feels a sudden need to double-check. It's thirty-six inches wide and twenty-four inches tall, which passes muster.

After her mother died, Taylor developed a compulsive need to locate the fire exit in every room she enters. It's become so second nature that she barely thinks about it, simply marking surrounding doors and staircases with an ingrained vigilance.

Once, when she and her dad went to see a movie, she saw how he, too, first craned his neck to note the red exit sign in the theater corner before settling into his seat. It made her wonder: Is life just a series of escalating anxieties?

The fact that her bedroom window meets egress standards should make Taylor feel better overall, but it doesn't. With Vivian gone from the hospital, some days have the same tenor as those that followed her mom's death.

Taylor pesters Aunt Gigi for information on where Vivian went. "She was moved to an undisclosed location," Aunt Gigi says. That might be all she knows, Taylor concludes, when she's bothered her aunt enough.

Somehow it becomes the beginning of April, the weather so slowly warming that it's like watching a piece of frozen chicken defrost on the counter. The wheel turns. Sam's forgiven her for missing the haircut, and they slip back into their friendship. But something's different; something is amiss. It's probably her. She still hasn't talked to him about Vivian, not even to mention how she was her patient. Guilty conscience, probably.

"Do you want to get some sushi—my treat?" Sam dangles in front of her, more than once. "Or do a workout with me and Bron?" That's his personal trainer.

"Next time," she replies, and offers excuses that sound lame even to her: stomach issues, headaches, menstrual cramps.

"You Southern girls get your period a lot," he says sarcastically.

She *should* work out; maybe it would make her feel better.

One day, on a whim, she tries a yoga class from the place where Vivian had a membership card, Mission Hill Yoga. The class is wonderful, the teacher, Cassandra, wonderful, but there's no essence of Vivian. Afterward, Taylor feels almost stupidly let down.

She half hopes Sam will stop asking her to do stuff and half hopes he doesn't. She's not sure she deserves him as a friend. She's not sure what she deserves. Or what she wants. Or anything at all, really. She's worn slap out, and a now familiar angst resides inside her. The only time it seems to lessen is when she fingers the key she keeps in her jewelry box, like a precious charm, and recalls the innards of Vivian's apartment. The softness of her patient's cashmeres, the slinkiness of her satins, the light fuzz of her velvets. It's probably wise she hasn't brought up Vivian to Sam, she thinks.

She's slipping at work: missing a patient's low potassium blood level, forgetting to order a needed EKG, getting into an unprofessional tiff with the orthopedic resident. Her nurse manager, Jan, has to speak with her—and news trickles up to Aunt Gigi.

"I professionally vouched for you," Aunt Gigi chides. "Usually one doesn't get to go from an outpatient ortho center in Bumblefuck, North Carolina, to an ER position at MGH. Get it together, T.J."

On her commute home from work, Taylor often peers into the storefront of Storied Antiques. It remains empty, with an unchanged window display. The same coral chair and footstool. The same tumbler on the hammered coaster on the same end table. The Emily Dickinson book with a faded blue 1970s cover. She's looked at the window front so often she could draw it from memory.

She's also googled Vivian Lawrence plenty of times to no avail. One day, Taylor wonders: *Are death records public in Massachusetts?* Turns out they are. On the Massachusetts Document Retrieval website, she types in as much information about Vivian as she knows, which is nothing, really. Unknown place of death, unknown date of death (other than the current year). Unknown names of her parents. Still, Taylor fills it out and pays the forty-five dollars. It will take ten to fourteen business days, and she might not get her money back if they don't find a record, but at least she feels like she's doing something.

Then a unicorn of a day appears, a hint of warm weather. The sky clear, the morning air carrying a sea kiss, reminding Taylor of back home.

She's off that day, and she decides to shop at the Beacon Hill thrift stores. She hasn't splurged on herself in a while. On the way, she detours to Storied Antiques. It remains shuttered, the closed sign hanging at its usual slanted angle, the furniture the same old. Taylor tilts her head. *Something* is different. She checks off a mental list.

Tumbler? Yes. Hammered brass coaster? Yes. Emily Dickinson book? Check.

It's so obvious what is different that it takes her a good minute to realize. The footstool has been removed.

Someone has been into the store.

Taylor moves closer to the window. The sun is at her back, creating a reflective glare.

She pushes her face up against the glass, and her breath quickens, creating a circular fog. A light glimmers in the back of the store.

She moves a few feet down to another spot, trying to get a better look, when she hears the door rattle open.

"Taylor, what are you doing?" a raspy voice says. Taylor takes a moment to compute the person standing in front of her: It's her landlord, Anna.

Even with a hunched back, and resting on a cane, she is still a few inches taller than Taylor. Her silver hair falls loosely around her shoulders and is tucked behind one ear, exposing a small ruby stud.

"Uh, hello, ma'am."

Anna lets out a raucous laugh. "It's Anna to you. Did you come looking for me?"

"No, I, uh, I was just coming to look at the store. Why . . ." Taylor trails off. She doesn't want to be rude, but she wants to know why Anna is inside Vivian's store. Do they know each other?

"That's a funny coincidence," Anna replies, looking intently at Taylor. "I own this building."

"You do?"

Anna picks up her cane and points down the street. "And that one, two doors down." Then she begins jabbing the cane this way and that. "And a building on Charles Street, with one of those nail salons and clothing stores. I also own some real estate near the Old State House. Another couple of nail salons and a bookstore. Not the new bookstore, the one that sells used books—Turned Pages. The old one, like me," she cackles.

"Oh, I didn't realize. That's a . . . a lot of buildings."

"Yes, it is. All that action keeps me on my toes."

Taylor smiles politely. "Is this store reopening soon?"

Anna glances behind her and sighs. "I hope so. It's a shame; the woman who owns the antiques business had an accident."

"Oh, I'm so sorry to hear that. Is she okay?" Taylor says, trying to keep her voice even.

"I'm just the landlord. The rent continues to be paid, which is all I care about. Paid in advance, in fact."

Paid in advance. Who is making payments on Vivian's behalf? Maybe it's her personal accountant, because Vivian must have a personal accountant, or a money manager, or whatever it is the über wealthy have. Whoever it is, it doesn't matter. It gives Taylor a jolt of hope. This must mean Vivian is returning, because otherwise why would her rent continue to be paid?

Anna taps the cane, like a metronome. "No, wait, that's not right. What month is it, again? April?"

Taylor nods.

"Then it's only been paid through the end of this month." Anna laughs. "This is what happens when you get to be my age. The days all run into each other like those damn bicyclists making their food deliveries."

"So, the store is *not* reopening?"

"We'll see. Between you and that nicely dressed fellow who's come around, this store has gotten a surprising amount of traction for being temporarily closed." Anna gives Taylor a sweeping look. "How's your dad doing? He must be getting ready to reopen the restaurant for the season?"

"Uh, yeah," Taylor responds, but she's thinking to herself: *What nicely dressed fellow?*

"Your dad's a real Southern gentleman." Anna laughs again. "I don't know many Southern gentlemen. I don't know many gentlemen. But your dad is a fine Southern gentleman, let me tell you. When we spoke on the phone, it was 'ma'am this' and 'ma'am that.' Must be where you get your manners from. I had a feeling about you. I said to myself, this daughter of his is a nice girl. A nice nurse and a nice girl. She'll be a good tenant. Is Boston treating you well?"

Taylor swallows. It might be the mention of her dad, or just someone asking if she's okay, but she finds herself blinking back tears. "Yeah. Yeah, everything's good. Thanks."

"What time is it, dear? You young people always know the time because you have phones. My time is kept in here." She taps her forehead with one long, spiny, red-nailed finger.

Taylor checks. "Ten fifteen."

"Thank you, doll. You run along now, enjoy your day."

Taylor tries to do what Anna said, enjoy her day. But as she combs through the racks at a consignment store, she can't find anything she likes. The shirts are ill-fitting, the trousers unflattering, the dresses too plain and ordinary. She still tries, bringing garment after garment into the dressing room. She's reminded, briefly, of childhood trips to the department store with her mom—how her mother would carry armfuls of clothes into the dressing room while Taylor hid in the stacks, waiting for her absence to finally register.

Staring now at her naked body, Taylor suddenly feels overwhelmed. She quickly gets dressed, steps over the pile of clothes, and then simply walks out. She's never done that before, made a mess like that and just left.

It occurs to her that the last time she liked her image in the mirror was that glorious day in Vivian's apartment, when *everything* she slipped onto her body was Midas gold.

VIVIAN

Present Day

Christ. Her head *hurts*.

She's still floating—on the rotating bed, on the stupid lily pad. She alternates between realities. But further, beyond it all, there seems to be a shift in her location. Something she senses, something she feels. Something she *fears*.

There's too much silence.

Where is that nurse, Taylor? Or the nurse who loudly chews gum? The nursing student? The doctors, making their rounds?

Where is everyone?

Vivian feels vulnerable, exposed. What if someone is there, next to her, but choosing not to speak? She wills her eyes to open, but they stubbornly disobey. She dislikes how people must be able to see her but she can't see them.

Vainly, she thinks of her one chin hair. The pesky one that has sprouted up in the past couple of years. She plucked it recently, thank goodness. But what is recently? She got her bikini line hair lasered off years ago, but what about her legs and under her armpits? She can't remember the last time she shaved. Two days ago, perhaps? But two days from *when*?

She doesn't think Rachel and Xavier have visited—she can't recall them doing so—but then again, who the hell knows.

Wait—*Peter*. Where has he been?

Why hasn't he come to visit?

TAYLOR

Taylor messes up at work again—this time, for something really stupid: She gives a patient Advil from her own stash, because it takes too long for the resident to write the order. She knows the doctor is going to eventually get around to it, so she figures, no harm no foul.

But then the patient asks the nurse manager, who happens to be walking by, for another Advil "from the personal bottle of that nice nurse."

On the day Taylor receives the formal disciplinary write-up, she also receives something else: an old photo of her mom, in the mail.

"I totally forgot about it," her dad says. "I was going through some old documents and came across it. It's the only picture she ever sent from Boston."

In the photo, her mom is at a bar, wearing a smart cream jacket over a short silver dress. She's holding a drink in her hand and smiling at someone to the side, off camera. She's flanked by two men, both of whom have their faces tilted adoringly at her. Taylor looks closer at the background, for clues to where it was taken, but it could be anywhere with those nondescript back-lit liquor shelves. She notes, with a pang, how her beautiful mom is holding the attention of at least four people in the room: the two men on either side, the person off camera, and the photographer.

The chasm between Taylor's sophisticated mother and her own shitty existence in Boston is simply too much. It's always too much, but on this particular day, it's everything.

It's hard to put this into words to Aunt Gigi, who insists on meeting in person after being cc'd on the resignation email Taylor sends to Jan.

"It's not anything specific . . . I think it's just *me*," Taylor offers.

The Saturday morning sun shines like a prism through the blossoms on the nearby cherry tree, creating light fragments across the city park bench upon which they are sitting. The burgeoning spring should, in theory, make Taylor feel hopeful. Yet she feels anything but.

"Sounds like the ER wasn't the right environment," Aunt Gigi replies. "Too much of a pressure cooker. How about we switch you to a nice orthopedic floor, like the patients you took care of back home?"

Taylor decides not to remind her about her Bumblefuck comment. "No, thanks."

Her aunt takes a sip of coffee. "This doesn't have anything to do with that patient you were asking me about for a while, does it? Vivian? You seemed very invested in her."

Taylor shifts in the bench. "No."

"You did good with her, you know that, T.J., right? You acted quickly. She's alive because of you."

But is *she alive?* Taylor wants to ask. And she would, if she thought her aunt knew the answer.

Aunt Gigi nods to the green park sign: SALLY BAKER PLAY-
GROUND. "Do you know who Sally was?"

"No."

"Sally Baker was a little girl who was abducted in the eighties.
Uncle Phil once met her; their fathers were physicians together at
Mass General. Sally's mom worked there, too—she was a nurse.
Got into a bit of trouble. Anyway, the Bakers ended up moving
to New Jersey, and that's where Sally went missing."

"I'm sorry to hear that. Did they find her?"

Aunt Gigi nods. "It wasn't a happy ending. My father-in-law
still talks about it, about poor Sally and the Baker family. This is
my point, though. There are some patients that will stay with you
your entire career. That's normal. That's a good thing. That
means we are still feeling." Aunt Gigi clutches her heart. "If we
didn't care, we wouldn't be good nurses. And I'm telling you,
Taylor, you're a good nurse."

"I thought you said Sally went missing in New Jersey. And it's
not like she was a patient, right? I'm so confused."

"T.J., you're not getting the point. *People* stay with you your
entire life. They'll come and go, but they will always be with you."

Taylor grimaces. "No, offense, Aunt Gigi, but you have to
work on your analogies."

"Maybe." She laughs. "But you're still a good nurse."

"I'm sorry, Aunt Gigi, I don't mean to disappoint you, but I
just don't think I *want* to be a nurse anymore."

"I don't believe you."

Taylor exhales slowly. Her aunt can be just as stubborn as her
dad. She looks around the park, which has a private feel owing to
the fact that it's tucked between two Beacon Hill streets and bor-
dered by adjacent brick buildings. A blue-and-yellow playground
structure occupies one park corner, a swing set the other. A few
feet away, in the open area, a little girl wearing a puffer jacket

with rainbow-colored butterflies crouches on the ground, riffling through her backpack. She pulls out fistfuls of LEGO bricks, and finally dumps the backpack upside down to shake out the rest.

Aunt Gigi clears her throat. "Look, I know I haven't been the best aunt. . . . I wasn't there for you enough growing up. I was busy with my own life—not that that's an excuse. I'm sorry. I really am. I was hoping . . . I was hoping I could make it up to you, now that you're living here in Boston."

Taylor is surprised. She didn't necessarily feel like her aunt wasn't there for her growing up; her aunt was just always doing her own thing—first in central Massachusetts, then in Boston. Her dad has insinuated that this is how his sister has always been. But now, something occurs to Taylor. "You weren't here in Boston when my mom was, right? Not yet? You and Uncle Phil were still in Worcester?"

"No, I was."

"You were?"

"Yes."

"Did you two . . . ever cross paths? Or make plans to meet up?" Taylor frowns; how did she not know this?

"I ran into her on the street once."

Taylor sits up straighter. "Oh? And?"

"It was brief. I was coming; she was going. I can't say I remember much, honey. I'm sorry."

"Was she . . . ?" Taylor doesn't know what to ask or where to start. Was her mom happy? Was she wearing another sophisticated outfit, like in the photo? Like something Vivian would have worn? *Was she missing Taylor and her father?*

"Your mom was beautiful. Just beautiful," Aunt Gigi replies, wistfully, and then adds, "She wasn't with anyone, if that's what you're asking."

It wasn't, in fact. Taylor is aware that there was a man who died alongside her mom in the basement fire, but she hasn't let herself really accept what that means on a practical level. And so she avoids thinking about it entirely.

The little girl is now laying a large flat LEGO brick, like a roof, across the four sides she built. Is it a house? A school? Or a spaceship, an escape pod, a portal? When Taylor was young, the possibilities were endless.

Aunt Gigi's phone beeps, and she looks almost relieved as she pulls it out of her fleece pocket. "That's Phil," she says, squinting at her phone. "He can't find the coffee beans, which are in the same spot they've always been. Third shelf in the pantry. I don't know how he can be a successful medical examiner and yet not be able to find anything around the house. Last week it was the sugar canister he couldn't find. Not that he needed it. Sorry, hang on."

"It's fine," Taylor says. But it's not. Nothing's fine.

Aunt Gigi sighs and types her response into the phone. Then her phone rings, but she puts it through to voicemail. "Jesus, Phil, figure it out," she cries. She stuffs her phone back into her pocket. "Look, I gotta go, but I just wanted to say that I love you. I'll check back in with you in a week or so, see if you change your mind about the nursing. I . . ." She doesn't finish the sentence.

Taylor nods wordlessly.

She stays for a long time on that bench after Aunt Gigi leaves. She watches a boy steal one of the LEGO bricks, pocketing it in his sweatpants. Another boy riding in a red car. Two girls playing with rocks and dolls in equal parts. Life hums all around her, but the only time Taylor herself can sense it, the only time her own body pulses with a vibrational whir, is when she closes her eyes and thinks of Vivian.

She remembers hearing a story once about a young woman who traveled the world in search of the most beautiful artwork.

The woman visited more than thirty countries. She went to France to see the *Mona Lisa*, Vienna for *The Kiss*, Germany to see the *Sistine Madonna*, Egypt for King Tut's golden death mask. She stopped in South Africa to stand in person in front of the *Butcher Boys* sculpture and passed through Hungary to view the *Lonely Cedar* painting. She traveled and traveled, taking in artistic genius through her eyes. And when she returned, back home to her parents' farm in Pennsylvania, money all dried up, she promptly hanged herself. Taylor didn't understand why anyone would do such a thing; wouldn't so much artistic brilliance, not to mention international travel, fill you up like a reserve, or at the very least, provide a buffer?

But now Taylor knows: You can't unsee the beautiful.

VIVIAN

Early February

On Saturday, the day after the masquerade ball, Peter sends a dozen single roses to Vivian's apartment, each one arriving precisely an hour after the last. Each containing a single line that together spells out a complete note:

Dear Vivian,

Thank you for being my date last night.

I'm sorry I got caught up in that scuffle.

I should have paid attention to you.

I'm sorry (and regretful).

I'm new at this.

I want to see you again.

I'm leaving for London this morning for work, but I will be back on Tuesday.

Please be my date on Tuesday evening at 7:30 p.m. at the restaurant 1928 Beacon Hill.

Till then, I'll be thinking of you.

Yours sincerely, Peter

P.S. You're beautiful.

She's usually not one for flowers. They are the exact opposite of antiques, dying much too quickly. Vivian has trouble seeing the value of springing for them. But she's never been wooed in such a manner before, and the roses couldn't feel more perfect. As Vivian collects the final note and arranges them in order, she has the thought: *I should save these.* Like they are an important memento—or will be, one day. This thought terrifies her, edging her toward a vulnerability she has yet to experience in past relationships. She knows the importance of antiques; it's what she does for a living, after all. But items of *personal* importance are another thing.

Vivian recalls when it was that she fell in love with antiques. She grew up around them, of course, but her professional interest didn't bloom until she went backpacking in Europe after graduating college. Kat couldn't afford to go, so Vivian decided to bring a little of Europe to her. She collected small vintage objects during her travels that she mailed to Kat in Philadelphia. She felt like she was speaking to her friend through these antiques, like they were handwritten letters. She hoped Kat would also find

them valuable, but the mere act of forwarding them to her en-
sured a continuation of their provenance. Antiques, Vivian then
determined, are migrating relics of time and place.

As Vivian collected oxidized brass candlesticks from London
flea markets and tarnished silver jewelry boxes from the back
stalls of Turkish bazaars, she considered that there might be a
future in this. It was an old doorknob she found at a street fair in
the outskirts of Prague that solidified it for her. The knob felt
symbolic. Representative of an opening, a possibility. If she found
these objects valuable, if there were markets and stalls and shops
across the world carrying these types of things, then Vivian, too,
could create a space to sell them. Suddenly, she could picture in
her mind the antiques shop where all these precious items would
sit, and this place—Storied Antiques—would be back in her
hometown of Boston, specifically in Beacon Hill, home of the
original antiques row.

Now, she gathers Peter's notes and delicately tucks them into
a vintage tin container that holds the Prague doorknob. It's been
a long time since she's assigned personal importance to an item,
antique or otherwise.

⟨◦———◦—◦⟩

On Sunday morning, Vivian visits the hospital, where her mother
has been transferred from the nursing home due to aspiration
pneumonia. As the nurse explains, it's pneumonia that occurs
when you forget how to eat and then you choke on your food.
Vivian stands at her mother's bedside, watching the antibiotics
infuse into her mother's arm, bruised purple like a water stain
from blood draws. Suddenly, there's a flicker of recognition in her
mother's eyes, and Vivian grows hopeful.

But it's not for her daughter.

"Hilda! I told you to iron these sheets!" her mother admonishes.

Hilda was her mother's maid for years. This reminds Vivian; she needs to cancel her biweekly cleaning service. Her own—not her mother's.

Vivian stays a few minutes longer, growing increasingly angry as her mother continues her delirious rant.

When Vivian returns from the hospital, she tears off her clothes so quickly that she rips a hole in her silk blouse. She wants it off, this stench of sickness. She wants it *off*. She is angry at her mom for spending all the family money and for getting sick and for being someone who even in sickness is a bitch.

Mostly, though, Vivian is angry that her mother no longer knows who she is. But she doesn't even know to whom she should direct this sense of injustice—her mom? Her mother's bad genes? Life? Some higher being?

With a pang, Vivian remembers she still needs to take care of Lucy's school tuition. Christ. It's probably now overdue. For this financial pickle, Vivian has no one to blame but herself. After doing extensive research on Philadelphia schools, she'd urged Lucy's dad to apply to Locust Prep. It's expensive, and he never would have considered it without Vivian's insistence on covering the costs.

She opens the school's payment portal, typing in her credit card information with short, sharp jabs. She reluctantly clicks the box to accept the 3 percent transaction fee, and she's so irritated by this that she sends an impromptu text to her accountant: I have some irons in the fire . . . I may not need to close the Chestnut Hill store after all. Let's discuss. It's bullshit, of course. She has no irons, no game. Just an idea with a loose thread she's twirling around her finger.

She now opens a new tab and types in a search: "missing

schedule of beneficiaries Massachusetts." She's done this search already in the past few days, several times over. She doesn't know why she's doing it again. The results are the same. The first article that pops up reads: "Beware the Missing Schedule of Beneficiaries for Your Massachusetts Nominee Realty Trust." Seems like she's not the only one who this has happened to. A schedule of beneficiaries, like her ancestor put in place in the 1800s for the trust that held the title to the Knox real estate, was *not* recorded at the registry of deeds. Such documents, perhaps unsurprisingly, were easily misplaced or often went suspiciously missing.

Vivian snaps the laptop shut harder than she needs to. She knows what's also bothering her. Today is the day that the real estate agency has scheduled a few private showings at her mother's house. Michael L. Carucci of Gibson Sotheby's is the best of the best, and this is part and parcel of listing one's property. But even though the house no longer resembles the one she grew up in, Vivian still feels uncomfortable with the thought of complete strangers traipsing through it. It would be nice if she didn't *have* to sell.

Glancing at the ripped silk blouse in a puddle at her feet, she gives a short, sarcastic laugh. Yet another thing she'll need to offload: her blouse, at the thrift store. The hole is simply too big for repair.

⇸——⇶

Vivian meets Rachel for an early dinner at Sorellina, the upscale Back Bay restaurant. It's not the type of place where one brings a baby, which is why Vivian chose it. She really needs her friend to pull a rabbit out of her genealogical hat. That—and a drink, after the day she had.

"Michael sounds interesting," Rachel says, taking a bite of her steak tartare.

"Michael? Don't you mean Peter?" Vivian says. They are sitting at the owner's table, the coveted seating area. There are some undeniable perks, she must occasionally admit, to being her mother's daughter.

"No, I mean Michael."

"Oh."

"Is he single?"

"How would I know?"

"Does he wear a wedding band?"

"No."

"So, you noticed."

Vivian takes a sip of her chardonnay. Her mother never liked chardonnay, felt it was a bad wine. No—her mother hated chardonnay. She didn't dislike things; she hated them. Vivian has found herself drinking more and more chardonnay, which she happens to like very much, since her mother got sick.

"You got me. I noticed," she says dryly.

"Look, maybe Michael can be your ally."

"Why would I need an ally?" But as she says this, she recalls the grandfather clock stuck on 3:03. The crowd. The drugs. The secret cigar room. The fight. The warning that Xavier gave her. The geomancy readings—which, as she looked up, are divination readings that traditionally use marks made on the earth. There *is* a lot of drama at the Knox—and a lot of mystique.

"You'll never guess who I ran into there," Vivian adds.

"Who?"

"Xavier."

"Xavier! Really? What was he doing there?"

"I don't know. Maybe he was with someone? I didn't notice a new boyfriend, but then again, there were a lot of people . . . and a lot of people in costume. Funny enough, Xavier recognized me because of my pendant." She gestures toward it.

"What did Xavier have to say for himself?"

"We didn't really talk," Vivian admits. She doesn't know why, but she's reluctant to tell Rachel about his warning. The strange way he'd acted. The fact that at first, she thought he might've been drinking. Maybe she doesn't want Rachel to think the Knox is unsafe. And why raise a red flag about the alcohol when Vivian doesn't know what was in his glass?

"That's too bad," Rachel says. "I wonder how he's doing."

"Do we know whom Xavier might be dating at the moment?"

"You would know better than I. You're the one who still sees him on a more regular basis."

"Only when he stops by my store."

"That's still more than I see him." Rachel knits her brow. "I could totally see Xavier being involved with someone from the Knox."

"Why?"

"He has a type. Remember there was Simon, the wealthy tech guy, and before that was James, who hailed from some aristocratic family, and before that there was the fancy lawyer? Xavier seems to be attracted to rich, powerful men." Rachel sighs. "And those are only the boyfriends we know about. Isn't it weird how much we don't know about Xavier these days? I miss him."

A pang hits Vivian. She, too, misses him—but what she really misses is the three of them together, their shared bond. Friendship itself. She used to have more friends—not just Rachel and Xavier, but a group of girls she grew up with, and college friends as well. But the ones from home got married and had children, and settled into lives Vivian mostly no longer relates to. As for those college friends, Kat was the glue that had held everyone together; after her death, they scattered in every which direction like loose tennis balls. For a while, Rachel has been the one constant in Vivian's life.

"Speaking of boyfriends," Rachel continues, "that's *so* romantic that Peter sent all those roses. Who does that? Did they really come on the hour, each hour?"

"They did."

"That's wild. I wonder what he meant by, 'I'm new to this'?"

"Relationships? Who knows." Vivian's acting cool, but inside she's been more than aflutter with the possibilities.

"Maybe love," Rachel says with a partial grin. She has a way of smiling with just half her face moving, where it looks like she's letting you in on a secret. Then she says, almost hesitantly, "You know, you could just marry Peter and then maybe you wouldn't have to hunt down your family fortune."

Vivian is annoyed. She hasn't divulged the extent of her financial woes to her friend, nor does she want to. Vivian will admit to herself—but only to herself—that the thought of such a marriage solution with Peter has crossed her mind. And not only for practical reasons. She knows she is continuing to keep Rachel at arm's length, and at this point, she's not entirely sure why. Maybe it's an act of self-preservation. If it were earlier—before the deaths of her father and Kat—would she have more readily opened up to her friend? Or perhaps Vivian is already bracing for that inevitable moment when Rachel becomes overly consumed with motherhood life.

"So, are you looking forward to your Tuesday dinner?" Rachel asks, when Vivian has failed to respond.

"Yes, though I wish it were at the Knox. I barely saw any of the rooms."

"Patience, my dear."

"I don't have much of that."

"You have a name for me, you said? Someone I can research?"

"Yes." Vivian tells Rachel about William Knox's son-in-law, Teddy Thurgood, who married Margaret—Vivian's distant ancestor. And the doctor son they had, the half brother to Vivian's great-great-grandmother.

Rachel riffles through her purse for a pen. "Mom brain," she explains sheepishly. "I can't remember anything anymore."

"Here," Vivian says, reaching into her own bag to pull out a slip of paper. "I drew my family tree. Excuse the rudimentary nature."

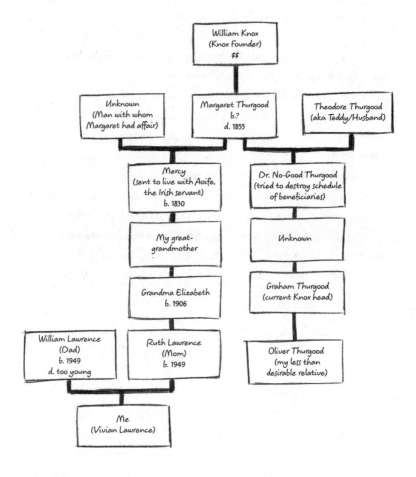

"Not bad, not bad," Rachel says. "This is actually helpful. Thanks." She taps her finger against the sheet. "I know that surname, Thurgood. Where do I know that name?"

"Graham Thurgood is the current head honcho. And his son, Oliver, is somewhere in the line." Vivian recalls the fight. "Though Oliver seems to have questionable leadership potential."

"I know where I've heard the name Thurgood. Graham Thurgood is a donor on the Boston scene."

"Surprise, surprise."

"Let's go back to the son. The doctor. Ha! I like how you call him 'Dr. No-Good Thurgood,'" Rachel says, studying the tree.

"Well, he seems like he was up to no good. He was the one who tried to destroy Margaret's schedule of beneficiaries. And . . ." Vivian's voice trails off as she remembers what was written: *Her son the doctor does not have the same kind heart. Something is not right. He has her body in the basement.*

Rachel shudders, clearly recalling the note about the basement herself.

The bill arrives, and it's Vivian's turn to pay. She hands her credit card to the waiter, who returns moments later, an apologetic expression on his face.

"I'm sorry, Ms. Lawrence, do you have another card?"

"Oh, of course. Hold on." She thumbs through her wallet, embarrassment flooding her.

"I can get it this time," Rachel interjects.

"No, it's my turn. Here, try this one," Vivian says, handing the waiter another credit card.

Rachel, wisely, now says nothing.

❖═──○──═❖

When Vivian returns to her apartment, the concierge smiles broadly. "Your secret admirer strikes again," he says, handing her an envelope with her name.

"Thank you." She can't remember his name despite interacting with him precisely a dozen times the previous day. The building has recently changed management companies, and there are so many new faces.

She walks toward the elevator and, as she waits for it to descend, decides to open the envelope. She could use a little good news.

But the letter is not from Peter.

PLEASE STAY AWAY, the note reads, in block letters. An arrow points upward to the symbol embossed on the stationery: a top hat with a flower rim. The symbol for the Knox.

It's unsigned.

"Who delivered this?" she demands, marching over to the concierge.

"I don't know. Is something wrong?"

"You didn't see the person?"

"I went to the bathroom, and when I came back, it was sitting here on the counter."

Vivian scans the room. "Are there no cameras here? There— that camera, in the corner. Can you replay footage?"

The concierge flushes. "I'm sorry, Ms. Lawrence, it's broken, and this model has been discontinued, so we are switching manufacturers and awaiting its replacement."

"I didn't know this."

"Yes, it was in the notice that went out to all the residents last week."

She must have missed it amid all her other fun-news emails, like the one from Brookline Bank requesting loan repayment for her second store buildout. Her failed second store.

Vivian turns on her heel and manages to catch the elevator door right before it gets called to another floor. Her building is extremely charming—and extremely old. The elevator is as slow as molasses, giving her ample time to reread the note.

PLEASE STAY AWAY

Is this a plea or a threat?

TAYLOR

A week has gone by since Taylor resigned from the hospital, and, like clockwork, her aunt reaches out every other day. What about a job in the IV clinic? Aunt Gigi texts. No weekends, no night shifts, no holidays. Easy peasy. Or labor and delivery? Do you like babies? Or you could do research and work on clinical trials? Or what about the West End Clinic, something in substance abuse (much help needed there!)?

Either Aunt Gigi is feeling guilty for getting on Taylor's case a few times about her nursing performance, or she truly cares. Maybe a bit of both.

Occasionally, Taylor gets tempted. She's been scoping out potential job opportunities—in something other than nursing—and the results have been disappointing. A few openings in retail that won't even cover her utilities. A listing for a receptionist position at an art gallery, which doesn't guarantee enough hours. A dog-walker position with Peace + Paws, which requires prior experience. A pharmaceutical sales position to which she applied on a whim but hasn't heard back. She'll have to cobble something together soon; her savings are fast disappearing, and her bills continue to pile up.

One morning, a forceful knock on the door startles her. Taylor hopes it's not her aunt, and she wonders if she should pretend that she's not home. But the knocking persists, and so she cracks open the door.

To her surprise, it's Anna, the landlord. Her cane hangs mid-air, and Taylor wonders if that is what she was using to rap on the door.

"There's this place in Beacon Hill looking to hire someone," Anna says. How Anna knows she needs a job, she's not sure. It seems Boston is strange like that, people and channels interconnected in ways beyond her grasp.

There's also the possibility Taylor's dad reached out to Anna. Taylor hopes not; she's not twelve, after all. She knows Aunt Gigi told him about her quitting, because he left her a disappointed voicemail she has yet to return.

"You waitressed before, right, Taylor? At your dad's restaurant?"

"Yeah." Taylor holds the door open just enough to talk. She prays Anna won't notice the dirty dishes piled up behind in the sink or sniff the late-night Chinese food takeout remnants on the counter she hasn't yet bothered to put in the trash. "I grew up waitressing there."

Slowly Taylor remembers she put her waitressing history on her rental application to fluff it up. She'd had only that one other job before coming to Boston, working as a nurse at the Outer Banks orthopedic center.

"Well, this place is kind of like a private restaurant," Anna continues. "It's real wealthy."

"Oh?"

"There's a lot of private eating and social clubs here. The 'Quin. The University Club. The Somerset Club. But this place, the Knox, is . . . different."

"Different?"

"I think they'll like that you're an outsider," Anna says. "And you're discreet, which is what they want. You've been here for six months or so, and I know three things about you: One, you're a nurse and a waitress—well, former waitress. Former nurse, too, I guess. Two, you're from North Carolina; three, you like antiques, and you also like Chinese food from Peking House."

Shit.

"I was planning to clean up—" Taylor starts sheepishly, but Anna interrupts with her loud and raucous laugh.

"Personally," she gasps, "I like Hei La Moon. And that might have been more than three things. So, you interested?"

Taylor is. She's actually toyed with the idea of getting a waitressing job, but it was going to be her last resort. Sam mentioned that one of his clients manages the restaurant Peregrine, so he could likely get her an interview. Her dad would be less than thrilled; he always wanted more for her than to be in the restaurant industry.

But if she waitresses at the place *Anna* is recommending, maybe her dad won't mind quite as much. Her father and Anna had hit it off on the call, and this is not just an ordinary restaurant, it seems, but some sort of private social club. And the fact of the matter is, Taylor can waitress in her sleep. She could do it for a few months while she figures out next steps. And if she ends up having a good night, with customers ordering a lot of fancy wine and booze, she could set aside some money to send to her dad again. The two times she did, pulling from her hospital pay, her dad claimed he didn't need it, but both times he cashed the checks. His restaurant is struggling, but she doesn't know the full extent—he won't tell her.

Once Anna gives Taylor the number and goes on her way, she sits down at her laptop to google the Knox, preparing for a flood of high-society information and photos of glitzy galas and prominent, well-known members. But, to her surprise, she finds nearly nothing. No website. Not even an address. Certainly, no members listed. Only a few sporadic mentions of the Knox, mostly on Reddit threads: one on secret societies, another on nineteenth-century grave plundering (huh?), and a final mention in a "I could tell you but then I'd have to . . ." discussion. In the latter, someone by the username of *tdgarden33__* shared a single photo, shot at an odd, skewed angle—as if taken covertly—and revealing the upper portion of a room with shiny, deep navy-blue walls encased in crown molding and lit with an elaborate crystal chandelier. Not such a Hard Knox life, reads the accompanying text.

Taylor's interest is piqued.

Switching to Google's News tab does not reveal much more, just some mentions in a couple of Boston magazines. Finally, she moves her cursor over to the Image search tab, expecting the same dearth of information. Almost mindlessly, she scrolls until suddenly, halfway down the page, something makes her catch her breath.

An image: a black top hat with a flower. It's the same symbol from the stationery.

VIVIAN

February

Vivian and Peter are on their first official date, at 1928, the restaurant tucked into a residential street lined with Beacon Hill townhouses. It's an intimate, moody space, with a long, swanky bar and three separate, chic dining rooms. She's been here before, plenty of times—it's one of the neighborhood haunts, after all—but it's a different experience being here with Peter.

The manager comes over to greet Peter, the bartender serves them a complimentary glass of champagne, and no menus are handed out ("They'll take care of us," Peter assures Vivian).

She takes a sip of her dirty martini—they're already on their second round—and notices how, despite there having been a line of people at the door, the surrounding tables remain empty. They are in their own private dining room, and her favorite one here at that: the Library, where the ceiling is artfully covered with book pages.

The chef comes over to give a preview of the menu: lobster Cobb salad, tenderloin with mashed potatoes and sautéed spinach. The whole time she's nodding politely at the chef, she's acutely aware of Peter's leg brushing against hers beneath the table. And how he holds his own martini with long, strong fingers. She finds herself stealing glances at them and wondering: How would they feel inside her?

"Now tell me, who is Vivian?" Peter asks, once the chef has left, and the server brings out the salad. Vivian gives him a puzzled look, and he adds, "Who—or what—has been keeping you from me all these years, when the whole time you've been right around the corner?"

Vivian tells him about the people in her life, or most of them: Her mom. Rachel, whom she met at an outdoor antiques market over a decade earlier, when a sudden rainstorm forced her inside a random tent with other strangers. She omits how, that very same day, she and Rachel also met Xavier. Given the warning Xavier gave her at the masquerade ball, she thinks it's best not to bring him up to Peter.

Vivian briefly mentions her goddaughter, Lucy—her late college friend's daughter. How she and Kat were randomly paired up as roommates her freshman year. Tabard, the secret society the two of them were in together at UPenn.

He smiles. "A secret society. I wouldn't know anything about that."

Somehow they move on to discussing a new local wine bar that has recently opened—and Vivian realizes she missed an opportunity to talk about *his* friends, his secret society. The whole reason she's meeting him tonight: to uncover more about the Knox. Or *mostly* the reason.

When he happens to mention a recent Celtics game he and Michael went to, she interrupts.

"Are you and Michael close?" she asks, assuming he'll say yes. He did bring him up, after all. And he and Michael were roommates, like she and Kat.

"I have a lot of people I'm close to," Peter says, and she sees a shift come over him, like the closing of a window.

He's very good at steering the conversation back to her. Maybe it's the alcohol, maybe it's the current disarray of her life, or maybe it's him, but she's talking a lot this dinner. Much more so than she normally does. She even tells him about her mom's illness. But she quickly realizes it's impossible to convey to Peter who her mother—let alone Kat—really was, and then she feels almost disloyal for trying. As if cherry-picked details could possibly encapsulate, or even intimate, their spirits. This might be the reason Vivian's going through these drinks like they're water. Peter makes her feel reckless, a little untethered. Like he's capable of uncorking the emotions she's so carefully bottled up over the years.

"Antiques suit you," he remarks at one point.

"What do you mean, they suit me?"

He gives a subtle shake of his head. "I don't know. They just do." When he stares intensely at her, it feels all-consuming. As if he's pulling little bits out of her, sticky notes of information, to piece together a narrative. "I've never met anyone like you."

"You barely know me," she says.

"I think I do." His leg presses more firmly against hers, and her body awakens. "You know, I saw you, a few years ago. And I've never been able to forget you."

She laughs. "Peter, that's a bad pickup line. I think you could do better."

"It's true." It was the month of April, he says. We were both at a fundraiser for the Institute of Contemporary Art, in the Seaport. "You were wearing a long pale pink dress, that had these strappy black ties."

Vivian stares at him. How could he know this? But then, she realizes. "Very funny. You googled me. You saw my picture. I was in *Boston Magazine* from that event."

He shook his head slowly. "I wish I'd seen that photo. I would have printed it out and carried it around with me. I was there, at the event."

"No."

"Why is that so hard to believe?"

"How . . . Why would you remember me?" But even as she's saying it, something stirs inside her.

"You were looking at the silent-auction items. You were alone."

This was true. She was using Rachel's ticket; her friend had come down with a cold and had urged Vivian to attend in her place. After grabbing a drink at the bar, Vivian busied herself by walking over to the table of auction items lining the far wall of the event space.

"You were drinking a cosmopolitan. You almost backed up into me."

Vivian had been standing there, considering what, if any, items to bid on, when a person suddenly shoved past her. She stepped back reflexively. And felt someone else's hands on her shoulders, steadying her.

"Whoa," a man whispered in her ear. His hands lingered on top of her arms for a moment too long. His touch felt oddly familiar, she remembers. But when she turned around, the man was gone.

Staring at Peter now, Vivian wonders: *Is it possible this story is true?*

"I went to get you another cosmopolitan, because I thought you'd spilled your drink. But when I returned from the bar, I couldn't find you. I thought maybe I'd imagined you, conjured up the perfect woman. But here's the crazy part," he continues. "I swear I saw you again, six months after that. It was at a Celtics game; the Celtics were playing the Golden State Warriors. And I saw you, on the Jumbotron. It was a just a second or two, but it was you. *I think it was you.* Was it?"

She's wordless; there *was* one time that she and Rachel were at a Celtics game when the camera apparently turned to them. "Look! We're on the screen!" Rachel had squealed, but by the time Vivian glanced up, it was already featuring another person.

"Your hair was pulled back in a ponytail, and you were wearing these large gold hoop earrings." He reaches over and touches one of her earlobes, sending a shiver through her. Then he sits back and looks at her earnestly. "Was it you?" he asks again.

"Maybe," she admits. Inside she thinks, *Careful, Vivian. You could fall in love with this one.*

"I knew it. And then you walked into the Knox, into my life. I think I've just been waiting for you, all these years." He smiles, and it fills every inch of her.

"What did you mean in your note when you said you're 'new to this'?" she asks. The question suddenly seems important.

"If I tell you, then you have to come home with me."

A heat flares inside her. "Oh?" she manages.

"But by home, I don't mean my Back Bay apartment. A pipe burst, and I wasn't around to realize. Apparently even penthouse apartments can flood. Who knew."

Penthouse apartments. "Oh, that's terrible, I'm sorry."

"It's okay; that's what insurance is for. Besides, things are things. They're not people."

"Things are important," she protests teasingly. "Don't forget, I'm a collector of 'things.'"

"Ah. I stand corrected." He grins. "And I build things, so I, too, think things are important. Isn't that a funny pairing?"

"What?"

"You and me. I like to build beautiful things, and you like to collect them."

"I'll give it to you, but it is a little simplistic."

"Vivian," he says, rather throatily, "there is nothing simple about the idea of you and me."

He stares into her eyes, and Vivian feels caught in his gaze, like a net has entangled her. She parts her lips for a response, but none comes. His gaze moves to her lips, and then he leans across the table to kiss her.

"Come back with me to the Knox. I'm staying there tonight."

"All right," she whispers. Christ. What is she doing? Maybe this is exactly what she needs to be doing. She's hot and cold, intoxicated and sober, fearful and fearless. She's everything, at the same time—no. *They* are everything.

Peter smiles adoringly at her. "What I meant was: I'm new to love at first sight. Or third sight, in our case."

THE KNOX

February

I daresay, Peter is utterly besotted with Vivian—and was keen to prove it to her last night. My bedroom windows fogged up more than they did during the swinger parties Graham threw in the seventies.

But—all is not as it seems with that woman. Rose senses this, too. Last night, when she heard the two of them return, she cupped her ear against the bedroom door to take a listen. A touch improper, perhaps—but who could fault her? She's been in quite the dry spell for some time. Not since . . . well, it's not for *me* to disclose.

Once Peter nodded off, Vivian subjected me to a rather unexpected degree of scrutiny. She opened my doors, peered into my rooms, examined my internal contents. While I might ordinarily find such audacity intolerable, I confess to being slightly curious about what she was seeking—and who she is. I still cannot determine why she strikes me as familiar. She's quite lucky, really, that Rose was also soundly asleep, and that she didn't accidentally wander into Graham's private chambers. (He has been in residence here, convalescing, since his recent heart attack.)

Familiar though Vivian may seem, she remains a guest—an outsider. And would be well advised to conduct herself accordingly. The last guest who dared wander my halls in the dead of the night had the distinct misfortune of stumbling upon one of the sacred scrolls.

Let's just say our members did not take kindly to this transgression.

TAYLOR

Taylor steps onto Clapboard Street, uncrumpling the paper from her pocket to double-check the address she jotted down earlier on the phone. Yep, the Knox: 17 Clapboard Street. A raindrop smearing the ink, the seven now morphing into a nine.

She's early for her interview, so she pauses under her umbrella to look around her. She's never been on this small stretch of street before; it's quietly folded into the Beacon Hill neighborhood like the dog-eared corner of a page. The road is cobblestoned and so narrow a car couldn't fit on it, only the horse and carriage for which it must have been originally designed. Elegant gaslit lampposts dot the sidewalks, and the road rises at an incline, so the redbrick houses stack at sharp angles into the hill. Rain droplets plunk into the street cracks with a strange rhythmic quality, adding to the ambiance of a forgotten era.

She holds her breath, mesmerized. In North Carolina, the oldest building she was in was the public high school, built in the 1970s and not updated since.

A feeling akin to excitement bubbles in her for the first time in weeks. She suddenly feels with an absolute clarity that quitting the hospital was the right move. Not only has this job opportunity with access to the kind of life she's always desired practically landed on her lap, but given the top hat symbol, this place is somehow connected to both Vivian and her mother. It's as if, in a weird way, Taylor has been led to this very moment.

One side of Clapboard Street has beautiful townhomes with proper doors and window boxes packed with bright pansies and begonias and cascading greenery. The other side of the street feels like the back of a house, consisting mostly of a continuous brick wall interrupted every so often by a flat, unmarked black door or a small, iron-grated garden window. It is on this unadorned—unnumbered—left side that the Knox building sits, or rather the back of the Knox, where she's been instructed to show up for her interview.

Employees must use the back door. That's fine with Taylor if this is the street she has to traverse each day.

As she makes her way toward number 17, she glimpses up into the tall windows of the townhouses on the fancy side of the street. Sam once told her the reason why the front entrances are elevated from street level is because they were designed to avoid the horse shit that littered the roads back in the day. All she knows is that now, this elevation adds to their allure.

In one home, she spies the upper portion of a rich oil painting positioned beneath a picture light, and the curved, glossy black lid of a baby-grand piano. In another, she sees wainscoting on the walls and an ornate ceiling medallion from which hangs the most opulent crystal chandelier—the likes of which she's only ever seen in one of those magazines that showcase celebrities' homes. Imagine turning on *that* light each day.

At her dad's Outer Banks restaurant, a crab house and tiki bar that swells with seasonal tourists and second-home owners in the summer months, Taylor could always tell which people were the really wealthy ones. They didn't ask for the price of the specials; they didn't even glance at the restaurant bill. They just handed over their credit cards; they left tips that were sometimes too much and sometimes too little, the former because money was irrelevant to them, and the latter because they were too drunk to do the proper calculations.

In the South, wealth seems to translate to excess, and so far, in the North, it appears more buttoned-up, museum-like, viewed from behind a rope. Or from a rainy street.

But for Taylor, this is about to change.

When she reaches number 16, she swivels toward the opposite brick-faced side, where there is a black door with a small brass knocker in the shape of some flower thing. A camera attached to the upper right of the building angles toward the door.

This has to be number 17: the Knox.

From her pocket Taylor retrieves a slip of paper, and a packet of orange Tic Tacs falls out. Sam must have slipped them in there; he knows they are her favorite.

He seemed impressed that she would be interviewing at the Knox but was also slightly apprehensive.

"Anna must like you," he mused, somewhat enviously. "She never tries to hook me up."

"I think she just wants me to be able to make rent," Taylor said, only partly kidding.

"Well, remember, you're not committing to anything—not yet. See how it goes, what you think."

"Okay."

"But—if you can, snap some pictures on the sly. I'm curious, of course."

Smiling, she now slips the Tic Tacs back into her pocket and rereads the note she jotted down earlier during her phone call:

Knock three times, wait five seconds, and knock twice. Repeat until someone answers.

It seemed utterly silly when the man on the phone spit out these directives, and she almost laughed, certain he was pulling her leg. But a silent pause had ensued, and then the man continued, his tone maintaining the same businesslike quality. Taylor was glad she hadn't responded, and later she wondered, *Was that the first test I'd passed?*

Now, being here on a street that feels like a charming colonial-era movie set, and standing in front of a plain, almost-speakeasy door that apparently opens into an exclusive private club, the instructions seem perfectly reasonable.

Taylor checks her watch—9:13. Two minutes to go. Suddenly, she worries: *Will they know my watch is a fake Rolex?* Fake designer clothes—and handbags—she is great at being able to discern the difference. But jewelry is a different story.

The second hand slowly ticks down, prolonged, fatigued. And then, finally, it is time.

Knock at the Knox. Here we go.

Her mouth feels dry, her heart picking up a notch, as she knocks as instructed. It takes just one full round before the door slowly begins to move.

"Hi," a thirtysomething-year-old man says as he rests his hand on the edge of the cracked door, as if opening a fridge to lazily gaze inside at its contents. He is tall and lanky, with brown curly hair and dark eyes. A metal necklace hangs over his white T-shirt, and a half apron is pinned over his jeans.

"Uh, hi. Is this, um, the Knox?"

The man smiles. "It depends. Why?" He sounds British, but Taylor doesn't have a good ear for those sorts of things. In the Outer Banks, they would get an annual summer influx of foreigners coming to work the tourist season, and she could never discern their accents. Grayson used to tease her about it. *England and Australia are two completely different countries, T.J.*

She glances at the paper, now crumpled in her hand. Was she given a contact name? "Um . . ."

The man laughs and steps back. "I'm just fucking with you. Taylor, right? Come on in."

She pauses. The hallway behind the man is dimly lit, and she's suddenly hesitant to enter.

"I'm sorry," the man says. "I didn't mean to weird you out. My name's Liam. I'm a bartender here at the Knox. I'm not the one you want to see. That's Peter Wales. I'll take you to him."

Liam turns and begins walking down the hall, assuming she'll follow. She collapses her umbrella and trails behind. But a few steps in, Liam turns and points to an ornate brass umbrella holder they already passed. "You can put your umbrella there."

"Oh, thanks," she mumbles, embarrassed, and backtracks to do so.

Like the street, the hallway is narrower than a typical one—clearly not up to code, though perhaps Knox members don't concern themselves with these things. Nor do they apparently worry about claustrophobia; Taylor concentrates on the action of breathing, trying to edge the focus away from an all-too-familiar sensation. But her nostrils instantly fill with a musty dampness, the sort of smell one would associate with a basement.

The hall is austere and minimally lit; a single overhead yellowed bulb provides enough light to advance a few feet to the following bulb. The walls appear grayish white, and painted on the left are a burst of dot symbols that remind Taylor of the game dominoes. On the right-hand side begin a series of numbers. Grasping the meaning of those dots is a lost cause, but Taylor can at least make out the numbers.

The first number is seven. "So, is there another entrance to this place?"

"Yep," Liam calls out from over his shoulder.

"Where?"

"This building runs through to Mount Vernon. That's the pretty face of it."

One. Then three—no, it's an eight. The numbers on the wall spell out: seven-one-eight-one. 7181. Or 1817, depending on how you read it. The year the Knox was formed? The number of bodies buried beneath it?

Suddenly, Liam stops short, and Taylor nearly bumps into him. He pivots to the right toward a frameless door she missed. Fiddling with the knob, he swings the door outward into a galley kitchen, whose bright ceiling-mounted lights and three windows make Taylor squint. She takes a deep, cleansing breath, relieved to be out of that dank hallway. As her vision adjusts, she makes out a large commercial-like kitchen, with stainless-steel food-prep areas, large refrigeration units, multiple stovetops crowned with exhaust hoods, and deep sink basins. There is a deep fryer as well, familiar to any Outer Banks local. The kitchen is empty, save for one older woman toward the back, leaning against one of the counters. A welcome aroma of garlic and onions wafts toward them.

Liam swoops his arm out in an exaggerated, somewhat obnoxious gesture. "After you, madam."

Taylor steps through the threshold, where immediately her feet stick to the ground, as if she's stepped on a film of maple syrup. Glancing down, she sees a sticky pad, like the one the transplant unit in the hospital uses at their entrance to capture germs on visitors' shoes. "What the . . ." She hops off and glances behind her. Her boots have left a residue of light brown granules on the sticky sheet, almost like she just tracked in sand. Was there sand in that hall they just walked through?

She points her toe out, about to test the sheet—is it really a sticky pad?—when Liam barks, "Don't!"

He expertly sidesteps the pad as the door closes behind them. "Follow me," he instructs, not offering any explanation, and briskly resumes walking. Taylor, thoroughly puzzled, is led through the kitchen toward the woman, who is thumbing through a magazine and chewing on a carrot. She seems older, in her sixties, and is thin and plain. Her lack of makeup and her choice of clothes—a tan, long-sleeved shirt tucked into a pair of light khakis—suggests a preference of economy. A gray cat rubs against her leg.

"New recruit here, Rose," Liam calls out, sailing by.

Rose gazes at Taylor unflinchingly.

"Uh, hi, Rose," Taylor offers, as she trails after Liam. They move through a set of French double doors, hastening past an elegant dining room with navy-lacquered walls, a wide carpet-runnered staircase, the foyer and apparent front entrance, and into a huge, open area that stops her in her tracks. She doesn't know what to call this space. It's a room, but it's *more* than a room.

There are *three* rugs to demarcate *three* different gathering spots. *Two* fireplaces, one on either end. Windows fit for a giant. So many textures and furniture pieces and paintings it's like a sensory overload. In the middle of the room is a large glass display case with a scroll that is clearly valuable in some regard. She wants to run her hand along all the sumptuous fabrics, breathe in the buttery leather couches, stare for hours at the art.

She's never been in a room with such grandeur, such wealth. It makes Vivian's apartment pale by comparison. For the second time that day, Taylor finds herself overcome.

This house has a pretty face, all right. Why is it completely empty, though?

"It's a Wednesday morning," Liam says, as if reading her mind. "Nothing ever happens here in the morning. You can have a seat here."

She suppresses a smile. Where is "here" exactly? This sitting area ahead, or the one to the left, or—

"Mr. Wales will be with you shortly. Nice to meet you, Taaaylor." He drops his voice slightly when he draws out her name.

"You too." Taylor walks into the room, feeling clunky under his gaze. And then he is gone.

She takes off her coat and drapes it on the back of a mustard velvet bench in the far corner, an area that feels cozier—or perhaps more accessible—than the other parts of the room. She feels like she should walk on tippy toes to avoid creating a disturbance, the way she used to maneuver around her dad when he'd fall asleep on the couch after working late at the restaurant. Scanning the room for any cameras (none that she can see), she tugs a few times at her shirt dress to air it out; she got a little sweaty walking through that narrow hall. Then she slips off her Rolex (they will know it's fake, for sure; it was foolish to wear it), but right as she's tucking the watch into her pocket, Liam strolls back into the room. He raises an eyebrow, and she flushes.

Did he see her?

He casually clears a stray wineglass, and she sinks into a chair next to an oil painting. Finally, he's gone again—for now.

Taylor looks at the painting. It shows, simply, the back of a woman. Her hair is pulled into a ponytail, and she appears to be riding a train. The scene behind her is blurred—a smear of pastel paint—she alone in focus. It is a moment in time, a still amid motion. Taylor feels strangely pulled to the image.

Did Vivian ever pause to admire this painting? Sit in this very chair? Did her mom?

"Taylor Adams," a man says, interrupting her thoughts. He holds out his hand as he approaches, and Taylor rises. "Peter Wales."

He is the kind of handsome that's hard to look at. A strong, angular face; dark, gray-tinged hair neatly swept to the side; deep forehead lines that feel earned. His eyes are small and intensely blue, and Taylor wants to both stare at him and drop her gaze.

As Taylor clasps his hand, something stirs inside her. Yes, this man in front of her is older. A lot older, like maybe twice her age. But he has that timeless Hollywood kind of charm.

"Hi," she manages to reply. "Nice to meet you." She keeps her lips pressed together like a panini; there's no way she's flashing him her gap-toothed smile.

"Sit, sit," he says, and settles into the sofa opposite Taylor. He wears a classic white collared shirt beneath a tailored pinstripe suit that must have come with a hefty price tag. "I detect a Southern drawl." When he smiles, Taylor feels herself flush. She pushes her nail into her leg as a distraction.

"I'm from North Carolina."

"Hope you're planning to stay longer than Cam Newton did."

Who? "Yeah." She clears her throat. "I mean, yes."

"Do you watch football?"

"No."

He smiles again, though this time, she feels like it's layered. Is there some sadness about him?

"You're honest," he says. "I like that. You remind me of someone."

Taylor's unsure how to respond.

Luckily, he continues: "So, Taylor—is that what you go by, Taylor?"

"Yes." Not entirely true, but she dropped T.J. when she moved to Boston.

"How did you hear about us, coming all the way from North Carolina?"

"My landlord told me. My dad owns a restaurant, so I grew up around the restaurant industry. She knew I was looking for a job, so—"

"Anna Varga's your landlord?"

"Yes."

"How long have you been here?"

Seven months. "A couple of months."

"Did you do anything else, or have you always worked in the restaurant industry?"

An image of Vivian flashes before her, and for a moment it's like Taylor's back in the ER, at her very bedside. *Chestnut-brown glossy hair. Wine-colored lips. Angled cheekbones. A chipped nail. A tiny single mascara clump. Vivian seizing like a series of small earthquakes.*

"Nothing really relevant," Taylor manages to reply, after a few beats.

"Are you all right? You look a little pale."

"I'm fine." But she's not. She's sweaty, hot.

Peter nods somewhere behind him, to someone she can't see, and then Rose promptly appears, handing Taylor a glass of ice water in a fancy gold-rimmed glass.

"Thanks," Taylor says. Has Rose been hiding in the shadows, listening this whole time?

She gives a curt nod and leaves—or at least disappears out of Taylor's eyesight. Who knows with this room. It's so big it feels like it could contain different dimensions.

Peter waits for Taylor to take a couple of sips. "Better?"

"Yeah—yes. Thanks."

"The New England weather is unpredictable this time of year. We are officially in spring, but spring here can feel more like winter or summer depending on the day. And this room, with these windows—well, the ventilation is not always ideal." He pauses, waits for Taylor to nod before continuing: "Now, I'm going to ask you a bunch of questions. They might seem strange but just answer with the first thing that comes to mind. And give an honest answer, which I don't think you'll have a problem with. The Knox is a special kind of place, and we are looking for a certain type of individual. There are no wrong answers, so don't be nervous. You ready?"

Um . . . okay? "Okay."

"What's your lucky number?"

"I don't have one."

"Did you see the numbers on the side of the hall you walked through?"

"Yes."

"Do you remember what any of them were?"

"Yes, 1817 or 7181."

He raises his eyebrows, seeming impressed. "What do you think they mean?"

"I don't know."

"If you had to guess."

"The year the Knox was founded." *Or the number of billions of dollars you all have.*

"Or what?"

"Or nothing. It's 1817. And if it's not, it's none of my business."

Peter nods. "Why did you knock on the door at nine fifteen a.m.?"

"Because that was my interview time."

He pauses for a moment, seeming to reconsider the question

he wishes to ask. "Did you show up earlier than that time but wait to knock?"

Did he (or *they* if there is a "*they*") watch her through the door camera? "Yes, I waited for two minutes."

"Why?"

Because Boston people are annoyingly early, and she refuses to perpetuate that habit. Taylor recalls how her fellow ER nurses would arrive by half past six in the morning for their seven o'clock shift. The first day of work she showed up at six forty-five, thinking she was early, but was met with dirty looks.

"Because that was my interview time," she repeats, but this time he nods in affirmation.

"Why did you sit here, out of all the possible seats in this room?"

"I don't know. It felt right."

"Do you often do 'what feels right'?"

With a guilty pang, she recalls the afternoon she spent in Vivian's apartment. Was that right or wrong? If she hadn't gone, would she be sitting here right now? She shrugs. "I don't know. That's a tough one."

He leans forward, and a whiff of his cologne hits her: smoky, a hint of sage. "I saw you looking at the painting of the woman on the train, when I came in. Where do you think that woman in the painting is going?" Jutting his chin toward the left, he keeps his eyes trained on Taylor. They are like tiny blue oceans, and she feels they could swallow her whole. She wouldn't completely mind, she thinks, her heart quickening.

"I don't think that woman is going anywhere."

"Go on."

"I think she's defined by what is her temporary location. She's in transit."

"Go on."

"She *is* the transit. She's just existing."

"Taylor Adams, why do you want to work here?"

His stare makes her feel raw and heady. She breaks her gaze.

Why does she want to work here?

Vivian. Her mom. Truth. Money. Opportunity. This man in front of her, maybe.

She can feel Peter studying her. Waiting.

How was Vivian involved with the Knox? How was Taylor's mom? What really happened to Vivian, and where is she now? Did she mysteriously disappear from the hospital, or did it just seem that way from Taylor's perspective? What if the answers to these questions are somehow here, in the Knox?

And what if, by working here, Taylor can find what she's searching for, even if she doesn't know exactly what that is?

Taking a deep breath, she once again meets his ocean-eyes. She settles on: "I need a job."

As he nods vigorously—who doesn't love a hustler, right?— she knows she was right to withhold the true answer, the one now thundering over and over in her head:

I want to feel like I exist.

VIVIAN

February

The morning light is harsh, offensively so. Vivian squints one eye open and promptly closes it. But even with her eyes closed, she can still sense the light. Christ. Why is this Knox guest bedroom so damn bright? It's not ideal for a hangover. Which Vivian has, after inhaling all those martinis at the restaurant. And the wine.

This could have been avoided; she and Peter could have drawn the drapes before heading to bed. Wait—didn't she?

Memories of her previous night groggily assemble themselves to order. Martinis, dinner, *the bedroom*, and . . . and . . . *Oh no.* Suddenly, she recalls her late-night clandestine foray through the building, once Peter fell asleep. She crept quietly through the house, opening doors to check for secretaries. The house is quite the maze; at one point she got turned around in a panic for several minutes before finding her way again. Once safely back in the bedroom, she used the bathroom and had the good sense—or so she thought—to pull the drapes shut before stumbling into bed.

But now here are the drapes, brazenly flung open.

It was stupid of her to wander; she was drunk, clearly. And

feeling a little reckless, high on endorphins after her romp with Peter. She's lucky she didn't get caught, even though Peter assured her, as they absconded into the Knox, that there are no cameras on the inside. *Only the outside*, he added, and proceeded to wave audaciously to some high-up camera she couldn't see.

Peter is next to her, his arm slung over her stomach. She follows the lines of the clock tattoo that covers his left chest. Last night she traced all his tattoos, all his curves, all his lines. He told her the story of a few of them: He got the clock tattoo as a teenager to remind himself that there are many minutes in a day, that he wouldn't always be under the thumb of someone the system had assigned as his foster father. The way he'd said it, with a dark edge, made her realize there was more to that story. A terrible kind of more.

There are so many more stories he has yet to tell her.

She, too, has stories to tell him. One he'd be quite interested in.

Peter shifts slightly and then falls back asleep. He breathes heavily when he sleeps. No snoring, thank goodness, but a deep, heavy breath. It's the only sound she hears. The room is otherwise silent in this third-floor Knox guest bedroom. The Knox has some serious insulation in its walls. It strikes her how much quieter it is than her own bedroom, just blocks away. There, she's grown accustomed to the sirens of ambulances racing to nearby Mass General Hospital and the grunts of the twice-weekly garbage trucks—and she occupies a top floor herself, at least, for the time being.

But it's a weird silence here in the Knox. It has a muffled quality, like it's suppressing something, as if she were sitting atop a lid screwed tightly shut.

Maybe it's her quest to uncover her family fortune that is being quelled.

Vivian slips out of the four-poster bed—she is naked—and grabs the cream cashmere quilt that rests at its foot. She has a good body, but forty-four is forty-four, after all. And it's bright. Maybe brighter than it was a few minutes earlier. Her head feels like someone is twisting it with a wrench, and she knows she's in store for a doozy of a day.

Wrapping the quilt around her, she slides across the room, away from the woven rattan-top bedside tables with waisted aprons and horse-hoof legs. Past the red sandalwood trunk resting at the foot of the bed, Peter's navy-blue coat cast across it. This room breathes Ming dynasty.

No secretary here. She came across only one last night, and she searched it thoroughly to ensure there were no hidden compartments. Though maybe she shouldn't be trusting her memory of last night's forbidden escapade.

Vivian steps over to the window that overlooks the peaceful inner courtyard. She could use a little zen right now. Rubbing the film of fog, she peers down. The courtyard is well-manicured: A hedge of boxwoods lining the perimeter is interrupted by an empty fountain base with a Chinese dragon, poised as if it's about to strike. She can almost hear the trickle of water spewing through its mouth come warm weather. On a stone patio there's a small gray table with four bistro-style chairs, and in the far corner, beneath a large, looming tree, an elderly man sits reading the newspaper. He must be seventy or so; he has thinning white hair and wears wire spectacles. A thick plaid wool blanket is draped over him, covering everything except his suede slippers.

Who is this man? Does this courtyard even belong to this building? She assumes as much, but sometimes these old Boston house renovations feel like child-constructed LEGO projects: rooms tacked on after the fact, buildings bulging in odd directions, a bedroom where a kitchen should be.

Suddenly, the building door on the side of the courtyard opens and out comes Rose. Vivian stiffens.

Christ. This woman is everywhere. Thank God she didn't run into her last night.

Rose is dressed in washed-out attire: khakis, an off-white turtleneck. Vivian could blink and miss her, Rose is that plain. She's carrying a tray that she puts down on the side table next to the man. She offers him something from it—a tissue?—but he shakes his head. Then she carefully hands him a steaming mug, waiting until he has a firm grip before removing her hands. But even then, she keeps one hand cupped underneath the mug, open-handed.

This gesture—that extra moment of care—hits Vivian hard, dislodging a small piece of the string ball she's wound tightly together over the last few months. She's reminded of the way that the nurse Paula plays her favorite cellist, the Australian Lada Marcelja, on her phone when her mother gets agitated. It works like a charm to calm her down; who knew her mother would like cello music?

Has Vivian misjudged Rose?

The man slowly sips his mug, and as he does, his eyes travel up the building and lock on Vivian's.

Yikes. Feeling like she's just been caught prying, she instantly shifts to the side, away from his gaze.

"See something scary?" Peter asks, and she startles. He's propped up on an elbow and wears an amused smile. Vivian realizes he's been watching her. An instant electricity runs through her.

She clears her throat. "Who's the old man?"

"That's Graham Thurgood. The one and only."

"Ah. Does he live here?"

"Not usually. He'll stay over sometimes. But he just had a

heart attack, so he's been recuperating here since getting out of the hospital."

"Sorry to hear that. Is there a Mrs. Thurgood?"

"Graham's been widowered for a long time."

Damn, Peter looks good in the morning. Only the presence of some slight under-eye circles betrays their previous night's activities.

"And the woman with him . . . that's Rose, right?"

"Yes. Rose is the glue that keeps everything and everyone, including Graham, together."

Vivian's head throbs, and she slinks down onto the edge of the bed. Her eyes briefly flicker to her black lace underwear strewn on the floor a few feet away. She's having trouble focusing, between the desire building inside her, her terrible hangover, and a need to find out more information. "And Oliver, the one who got in a fight with the waiter, is his son?"

"Yeah."

"So where does Oliver live?"

Peter's still smiling, but he's tilted his head, one eyebrow raised, and Vivian gets the impression that he's suddenly a little guarded. "Why all these questions? Why are you so curious?"

"Well, um, I'm just trying to get the lay of the land, is all," she fumbles with her words. "For years, I've sourced antiques for this place, and I always wondered who the man behind the curtain was," she tries to joke, and immediately realizes it has come out wrong. "Sorry, not that Graham is a fraud . . . I'm not operating on all cylinders this morning." There's a chill in the air that she can feel on the tops of her shoulders.

"I get it," Peter says to her relief. "I like to meet the people I design houses for. Oliver is . . . a bit of a nomad. He's recently returned from living abroad in Southeast Asia. He comes and goes." He pauses. "Oliver and Graham don't always see eye to eye on things."

"Oh? They don't?"

"Oliver has a direction he wants to take the Knox in that his father doesn't agree with."

"What kind of direction?" she asks, hoping she's not pushing it.

"We have a long history here . . . certain traditions. And over the years, Graham has moved us away from those, and there are those of us who want to move it back to how it was."

Those of us. Is he Team Oliver, then?

"But I digress. To answer your question, Michael is your man—the sole antiques buyer . . . He's *particular*," Peter says with almost a sneer. He leans over to glance at the table clock, and his face clouds. "Shit. I need to hop in the shower. I've got a flight to catch."

"A flight?"

"Yeah. Milan. I'm working on a hotel. I'll be back on Saturday."

"But you've only just returned from a work trip," she says, and she instantly regrets it. She hates the way she sounds, like a whiny girlfriend. Christ. This is so unlike her. But this is the first he's mentioned it.

Her vulnerability must be written across her face, because he pulls her toward him.

They touch, skin to skin, and she nestles her head into the crook of his neck, growing hungry. He has a certain fresh smell, something she couldn't pinpoint until she peeked in the bathroom shower and noticed the Dove soap. She likes this about him: the plain, simple bar of soap he prefers to use. She wants to find out more about him in a way she's never cared to for others: his favorite book, song, movie, dessert.

What turns him on the most, though last night she gained a bit of insight.

"I'll miss you," he says, as he runs his fingers up and down her spine, making her skin tingle. His finger pauses at the blade of her left shoulder, where she has a small birthmark, and traces it. Then next to it, he draws an invisible heart shape. She watches the sharp lines of his arm sleeve moving against her own pale skin. Soft and hard. Hard and soft.

It's like her heart: that firm mass with a surprising soft center. But she needs to keep her edge. She doesn't know if she can trust him. If she could, wouldn't she have already shared the story of her family history, or at least the appropriate bits and pieces?

Why hasn't she?

"I'm sorry, Vivian, I should have told you. It was a last-minute trip, and, well, to be honest, I'm not used to having someone to tell things like this."

"Okay," she says.

He smiles. "Okay?"

"Okay."

"Okay? That's all you're giving me? Not 'I'll miss you, too'? Not 'I'm also not used to having someone to talk to like this'?"

She shrugs, but she's smiling, too. *There's nothing yet to tell him about my family history*, she thinks.

"Okay, then. Well, how about I take you to dinner Saturday night, when I return?"

"I'll have to check my schedule," she lies. She is not doing anything. And if she were, she would break her plans.

He kisses her, first her neck, and then lower. "Well, check your schedule and clear it, because Saturday, V, you're mine."

The way he calls her V makes her so hot inside.

"Do you want to dine here? At the Knox? Or Toscano, perhaps?"

"I thought guests aren't normally allowed at the Knox?"

"Saturday nights are the exception."

"And the masquerade ball," she adds.

He laughs. "Yes, that too."

Normally she would never pass up the opportunity for Toscano's handmade linguini vongole. "Let's do the Knox," she says, as casually as she can.

He gives her a smile, one of those earnest ones that betray his childhood, and then, to her disappointment, hops out of bed. He's naked as he strolls to the bathroom. No cover needed for him.

Peter closes the bathroom door, and she hears the toilet flush and then the shower turning on. Just as she's contemplating how she's going to manage to get home wearing the Alice + Olivia pantsuit Peter accidentally ripped in their fervor, he pops his head back out.

He nods toward the door that leads to the hall, and, as if on cue, there's a knock. "I've arranged some clothes for you. So you don't have to do an adult walk of shame."

"Thanks."

He winks and then disappears back into the bathroom.

She gathers the quilt around her once again and shimmies to the bedroom door, smiling. Who does this, ordering clothes like takeout? Also, *when* did he manage to do this?

But her smile vanishes when she sees who is on the other side. Rose stands there, holding a stack of clothing. There's an unreadable expression on her face. Vivian pulls the sheet tighter.

"I was told to get you a size six shirt, but they were out," Rose says, pushing the pile toward Vivian.

"Thanks," Vivian says.

But Rose doesn't leave; she stays put. Her eyes travel over Vivian's shoulder, to the bathroom door, where they both hear the shower running. Then she looks Vivian squarely in the eye. "You know, you're not the first girl Peter's brought round and you won't be the last. You are pretty, but that will fade. And when it fades, people don't look at you the same. When it fades, Graham won't want you anymore."

Graham? If Rose is aware of her slipup, she doesn't show it. She turns on her heel and leaves. Vivian closes the door and leans against it. Rose is not the first territorial employee in a wealthy household she's come across. There's usually one, in fact. The wealthier the family, the bigger the house, or houses, and the more the family is pulled into high society—serving on boards, hosting and attending social functions. The greater the need for someone *else* to assume care for the place like it's their own. Vivian's mother herself had a "Rose."

But this Rose needs to learn her place. Vivian is not going anywhere.

She looks at the bag. It's from Crush Boutique, one of her favorite clothing stores on Charles Street. There's a receipt inside, showing the time stamp of 9:20 a.m. They don't open until ten on weekdays; for the Knox, store hours are apparently meaningless.

There is no way there was not a size 6 shirt in that store. Rose is fucking with her.

Luckily, Vivian wore a camisole under her pantsuit last night, and so she slips that back on, and then leaves the too-small button-down shirt that Rose gave her open. The pants—black, stretchy—fit perfectly, and Vivian does believe she'll get good use out of them.

She writes Peter a note on the wooden desk: Safe travels. Love, V

She makes her way down the hall, pausing at some of the

rooms she passes. Their closed doors tantalizingly call out to her. Are there any secretaries within? Which of these rooms did she already search?

If she saw inside, she might remember.

Should she wander in, and if anyone asks, say she is looking for the bathroom?

But she'll be back Saturday—and right now, she doesn't want to be stupid. Rose is probably lurking around here somewhere. And if this too-small-shirt prank is any indication, Vivian needs to watch her back.

"Please stay away," the mysterious note that arrived to her apartment said. Vivian intends to do nothing of the sort.

TAYLOR

Two days after her interview, the job offer comes in the way one might expect from a secret society: handwritten, enclosed in a fancy navy-blue lined envelope, and hand delivered—slipped under her door sometime during the night.

Taylor Adams, we are pleased to offer you the position.
Should you choose to accept, report
Monday morning at nine o'clock. Attire is business casual.

The offer is vague, no mention of salary or benefits. Yet it is a link—as clear as day—to Vivian and to Taylor's mother. The ivory paper seems to be the same stationery as the note Taylor uncovered in Vivian's apartment. And it's similarly embossed with the hat symbol, matching her mom's last letter, which Taylor's dad finally got around to mailing to her—and which she's hung up on her fridge.

Taylor traces the imprint of the top hat, feeling a spark of excitement.

"Congrats," Sam says, when she shows him the offer. He is not a morning person, so she waited to knock on his door until she heard the shower water run through the pipes between their walls and then turn off.

"How does the Knox know where you live?" He runs a hand through his hair, which is one shade lighter brown than his goatee. He's wearing his favorite BronCore Fitness yellow T-shirt.

"Uh, I don't know," she admits. It's a good point; it's not like she handed the Knox her CV. "Maybe Anna?"

"So, they know where you live *and* somehow got access into the building?"

"Maybe Anna," Taylor repeats, feeling a little foolish for not having considered this. "I'll ask her." But she knows she'll do no such thing.

Should you choose to accept. She accepted the moment she stepped foot into the Knox, maybe even before.

"How much do you know about this place?" Sam asks.

She shrugs. "Enough, I think."

"Do you, though?"

"Why? What are you getting it?"

"I know you're not from here, but this place has a history, Taylor."

She rolls her eyes. "Every place has a history."

"Not like this. You know the famous art heist at the Isabella Stewart Gardner Museum? Where the thieves dressed up as security guards?"

She does, as a matter of fact. She's visited the museum and seen the thirteen hauntingly empty frames where the paintings used to hang. In fact, she just caught a great indie film about the robbery: *Any Day Now.*

"You mean, the famously *unsolved* heist? Yes." Taylor knows what Sam's hinting at but isn't in the mood to be obliging; not when he was immediately trying to tarnish her excitement about her new job, her new start.

Sam grows more animated as he continues. "And they say that after Whitey Bulger went on the lam he used to stay at the Knox, whenever he rolled into town. And that the Boston cops just looked the other way, with their pockets greased. Did you know *that*?"

She shakes her head. If Sam is trying to scare her off, he's doing the exact opposite. This place is sounding more and more intriguing.

"And then there's the rumor about how Ted Kennedy was a member, so they covered up the Chappaquiddick incident." He pauses and then adds, "Oh—and the Knox siphoned off millions from 'the Big Dig' through various shell companies and consulting fees. Or so they say."

"Are you done?" she asks.

"Yeah—for now. These are rumors, of course, but where there's smoke there's fire. It's a powerful place, Taylor."

"That doesn't change anything. And like you said, they're just rumors."

He studies her, squinting as if the sun is shining into his eyes. "Did you break the news to your dad yet?"

"No. . . . he's busy right now with the restaurant."

Her dad briefly reopens for spring break, and again in April for the Mid-Atlantic Regional Surfing Championship, viewing the crowds as a test drive for the upcoming summer onslaught. Because starting in July, wealth will arrive to the Outer Banks like its own season: hordes of SUVs with attached roof boxes clogging N. Croatan Highway, the only road that runs to the beach towns. The houses on stilts will sag a little heavier as the masses descend on them like a flock of seagulls.

But this is not the real reason she hasn't talked to her dad. She's never been able to lie to him, and she doesn't want him asking her questions she has to answer. Like: *Why waitressing? What is this place?* Thankfully *he* doesn't live in Boston, so isn't remotely aware of the Knox's shadowy ties.

Then Sam says quietly, "And you're sure this is a good idea? Not because of what I just told you, but because of . . . you know."

"What do you mean?"

"I saw your fridge. Your mom's letter."

Taylor takes a step back. "You read it?"

"I didn't mean to invade your privacy. I saw the letter on there, and I just thought it was something you were proud of, like you know, how people hang school photos on their fridge? I wouldn't have read it if I realized it was from your mom. But then I saw the Knox symbol, and—"

"Wait, you know what the symbol for the Knox is?"

"Yeah." Sam shrugs, like it's no big deal.

"Why? How?"

"I dunno. I think everyone knows. I mean, people always dress up as the Knox on Halloween, wearing that top hat and a black cape."

Taylor snorts humorlessly to herself. All along, she could have just asked Sam about the symbol. But then she likely would've had to tell him about Vivian. Right now, Sam just thinks she's a homesick nurse who couldn't cut it at Mass General. Not entirely untrue, but that explanation contains only slivers of the truth.

"What does your mom have to do with the Knox, anyway?

You told me she came to Boston to model before . . . um, the basement house fire."

Taylor leans against the doorframe, avoiding his eye. "Yeah, she did."

"So, what does that have to do with the Knox?"

Taylor folds the offer of employment over and over, making it smaller. If only problems and worries were like that, able to be lessened and shrunk at will.

"I don't know," she answers honestly.

TAYLOR

A memory:

The sea ahead of Taylor and her mom, a furious gusting of gray absorbing the horizon. Wind beating at their backs and knotting their hair, sand snapping at their legs. There's a glisten to her mom's face, and it's more than just wetness from the rain. Her mom grasps six-year-old Taylor's hand in a firm grip as she determinedly pulls her along.

Edging them closer to the ocean.

The beachfront houses on stilts are barricaded, wooden planks covering their windows, driveways emptied of cars. The town is ghostlike. The local supermarket aisles have cleared—no more bottled water. Her dad has gone to get them supplies at another store.

A hurricane is coming.

Let's go, little monkey, Mom had said, in their kitchen, as soon as he left.

Go where? Taylor had asked.

Let's go see it.

Now, her mom lets go of Taylor as she runs ahead, toward the spitting sea. For a moment, Taylor's heart stops. But then she's back, dragging her away. Wind claps at them, attempting to thwart their retreat. Her mom's jeans, rolled below the knees, and soaked through her thighs.

Back in the car, the door shut, the air still howling in their ears like an echo. Her mom fiddles with the car radio, the newscaster reporting in a loud, urgent tone. The taste of danger and fear in Taylor's mouth, like a sour candy.

But her mom is laughing. Then she leans over, picks up Taylor's hand and presses it against her damp windbreaker. In Taylor's palm, her mom's heart flutters, a staccato of emotions.

Don't tell your dad, she says. As if her wildness is a secret he can't know.

VIVIAN

February

Vivian keeps thinking about the mysterious note that arrived at her apartment.

Please stay away.

The "please" is what gets her. It just sounds like Xavier, the more she considers it. Xavier with his mild manners and sense of decorum, like his pocket watch and how he brings a bottle of wine even though he no longer drinks. *Please.* Yes, this note must be from him. He prefers to write letters, after all. And he'd told her to *be careful* at the masquerade ball. And then there was that weird way he acted when he saw the carousel horse in her shop. She's pretty sure he'd seen it before—at the Knox. But the note doesn't match his handwriting; perhaps he tried to disguise it?

It's time Vivian has a chat with her friend.

The note tucked inside her pocket, she sets out for the Jewelers Exchange Building in downtown Boston where Xavier works on the fourth floor. She pulls her coat tightly as she hustles across the street. There's an early-morning chill in the air, and she's misjudged the weather; her coat is not warm enough. She tries to conjure Peter's arms encircling her, but imagination only gets her so far.

It's the day after Peter has left for Milan. And three days before he returns. Not like she's counting or anything.

She snakes her way toward the building, passing the sporadic jewelry stores tucked amid retail shops. This is Boston's jewelry district, located less than a mile away from Beacon Hill, but it feels like it belongs to a different city. Many jewelry shops have disappeared over the years, filled in with other retail stores, with nail salons, with a Walgreens and McDonald's. Do people even call it the "jewelry district" anymore? Across the way is the Old South Meeting House—the site where the Boston Tea Party was organized. A bit of Boston charm in an otherwise unbeauteous terrain.

She feels a moment of gratitude that Beacon Hill, while no longer the "antiques mecca" it was decades earlier, has kept a small-neighborhood feel: the retail shops are boutiques, the pharmacy independent and family-run, the cafés and restaurants local. There's a rather charming indie bookstore, Beacon Hill Books & Cafe, that's recently opened. Funny enough, her own storefront, though not directly on Charles Street but around the corner, was once a bookstore, and before that an antiques store. The landlord, Anna, was only too happy for Vivian to restore the space to its original intention.

The gratitude is fleeting; a knot forms in Vivian's chest. What if she needs to close *both* her shops and fold Storied Antiques altogether? She wishes for the umpteenth time that she hadn't opened that second store and undertaken the expensive build-out of the space; then she wouldn't be in as much financial trouble.

Is this desperation similar to how Xavier felt during the pandemic? She knows his business was severely affected; despite her urging him to build a website, Xavier—ever the dinosaur—refused, and people weren't adding to their jewelry collections with quite the same fervor as they were redecorating their homes. Maybe Vivian should have checked in with him more during that time, made sure he was okay.

But she thinks he'll be all right. If the expensive jewelry dripping from the women at the masquerade ball last week is any indication, society still likes pretty, shiny things. Plus, Xavier's a fine artisan. She's taken a few worn jewelry pieces to him over the years for "facelifts," and when they are returned, he's easily electroplated them to a shine that makes them appear brand-new.

She touches the wrinkles lining her forehead, the ones routinely in need of Botox. If only it were that easy.

When Vivian enters the Jewelers Exchange Building, a security guard at the far end of the lobby gives her a curt nod from behind his desk, then resumes reading his paper. She pushes the elevator button and steps into the cab. It's one of those old-school ones with a metal accordion gate.

As the machine begins rising, with a bit of jerkiness, and a loud, prolonged squeak that brings to mind a rusty wheel attempting to rotate, Vivian wonders if she should have taken the stairs.

A conversation over the phone with Xavier would have been easier, but when she tried ringing his store, she found that the number was no longer in service. She still doesn't know where he's living now, so it's not like she could have tried his landline.

She has no idea what her friend has been up to.

While she and Rachel like to complain that Xavier ditches them for various boyfriends, she's now realizing that maybe they, too, have ditched Xavier. When was the last time she went by his store? Vivian can't even remember. Pre-pandemic, maybe.

The hall is quiet and empty when she finally escapes from the elevator. At first, she's not surprised she doesn't see anyone. The whole building is a bit mysterious, comprised of wholesalers, manufacturers, and retail vendors. Most of the jewelers on this floor don't have storefronts like the ones at a mall. Rather, they independently operate in small, confined spaces, some half the size of Vivian's bedroom closet. Their jewelry displays are sparse; they have additional inventory—the real stash—secured in the back that they can pull from if you let them know what you're looking for, and if they don't have what you need, one of their friends down the hall will.

She claps along in her tall black riding boots, passing the darkened window of a skilled engraver to whom she's referred customers looking for personalization on their antique pieces. Glancing at her watch, she notices it's not even nine o'clock yet. Christ; it's early. This is why barely anyone is around. The businesses in this building keep their own hours, and if Vivian recalls correctly, Xavier usually opens around ten.

His shop is around one more bend. Since she's already here, she'll check if he's in, and if not, she can slip a note under his door. He might be, though; Xavier has been known to work odd hours creating his jewelry pieces, a bit like a mad artist.

When she reaches his shop, she frowns. A large, angry spider-web of cracked glass suspends at eye level, as if someone has punched the partition. A chill runs through her. She takes a step back to ensure that, yes, this is indeed his shop. Or, at least, it used to be. When she gingerly cups her eyes against the glass to peer inside, it's empty, and not in the way of how jewels are securely removed for off-hours. It's ghostlike, abandoned.

"What happened next door? Where's Xavier?" she asks an adjacent shop owner, who cracks open the door after her incessant knocking.

"I don't know," the man says, and immediately averts his eyes.

She gets the same curt response from other jewelers in the hall, their storefronts just beginning to stir.

But then one of the women she asks says, in a whisper, "I'm sorry. . . . We just don't want any trouble."

And Vivian finally understands: They are reluctant to tell her. What has her friend gotten himself into? Whatever it is, Vivian can't shake the suspicion that it's related to the Knox.

TAYLOR

Taylor is nervous when she reports to the Knox that Monday for her first day of work, and this intensifies when Rose leads her to an upstairs office and presents her with an extensive confidentiality agreement she is required to sign. It's a thick mass of papers, emitting an off-gas of Xerox. Still warm to the touch, the pages so fine she has to wet her fingers to separate them.

"We all sign our lives away here," Eduardo, the kind-faced Colombian, jokes. He's a waiter, along with Jerry, a short, muscled man. They stand at the doorway of the office, where Taylor sits with the document Rose has left her to review.

"So you had to do this, too?" she asks.

"We are still signing," Eduardo says. His accent is strong. "When they make updates, we have to sign the new one. It says the same thing, more or less: Don't talk to anyone about anything having to do with the Knox."

"Do ya have yer own place?" Jerry cuts in to ask. His face is beefy, and the narrowing of his eyes makes them look like they're about to be folded into his skin. Taylor wonders what he did before coming here—was he a wrestler? An MMA fighter?

"You mean, like, my own apartment?"

Jerry nods.

"Yeah, I do. Why?"

"So yer not coming next door?"

"What's next door?"

"The quarters."

"I'm sorry, I don't know what you mean."

Eduardo jabs Jerry. "Give her a chance to settle in. And no, she's not." Then he says to her, "Some of us live next door. Jerry, me, and—"

"That's it," Jerry interrupts, frowning at Eduardo.

"Anyway," Eduardo continues, "the Knox owns that building, too. It used to be the old servants' quarters, and, well, I guess it still is." He chuckles. "If you live there, they cut you a pretty good deal. But it sounds like you already have your own place."

"Yeah, I do. In the South End." She wishes she hadn't been so quick to say she did. To not only work on this fancy street, but live on it, too? That would be nothing short of amazing. But judging from Jerry's territorial glare, perhaps it's better to keep her distance. She is the new girl, after all. Besides, she'd miss Sam if she moved—wouldn't she?

"How'd ya hear about the Knox?" Jerry asks.

This one is persistent. "My landlord, actually." Then she adds, because she knows he wants the name, and she doesn't see any reason not to share it: "Anna Varga."

Jerry shrugs, like the name means nothing. "Who interviewed ya?"

"Um, Peter. Peter Wales."

"And ya walked through the box? In the hall?"

Taylor starts to shake her head but then remembers the sticky pad. "Maybe?" she offers.

"Did they get your footprint?"

"Yeah. I guess so."

"Jerry," Eduardo now says, putting his hand on Jerry's shoulder. "Let's give Taylor here some time. It's only her first day. We don't want to scare her away."

⟨⊰⊷—○—⊶⊱⟩

Taylor assumes she'll be orienting to Canton's, the restaurant upstairs, where members apparently dine most weekdays for lunch, but she assumes wrong. Instead, Rose directs her that first morning to the adjacent wine cellar to unpack boxes and take inventory. Taylor doesn't want to do this; from there she can't get a good view inside Canton's, where the action will be—all the members. Perhaps handsome Peter Wales, who interviewed her. But she immediately pastes a bright smile on her face.

"No problem," she says.

Rose's lip twitches. Taylor can tell that Rose is trying to make out what she thinks of her. Good luck with that; she's not quite sure what to make of herself. It felt weird this morning to put on regular clothes instead of scrubs to go to work. Like she was donning a life suit that didn't belong to her—at least, *not yet*.

Taylor starts unpacking the wine boxes. At least the wine cellar is not claustrophobic; it's one of those modern ones, with glass doors, and it's on the second floor, not in some basement. It could be worse.

She wonders what's on the upper floors and if she'll eventually get to see them.

At one point Liam the bartender wanders in. "There's a lot you don't know about here, Taylor," he says, standing too close.

Inspecting a bottle of Barolo, he whistles, but she sincerely doubts he is quite the wine connoisseur he's pretending to be. The Knox must count dedicated sommeliers among its staff, right? "This place has all kinds of nooks and crannies . . . and secrets," Liam continues. "There's a hidden library behind a faux door . . . and maybe some important scrolls scattered throughout the building, but you didn't hear that from me."

When Taylor ignores him, he leaves. She supposes some might find him attractive, and who knows, maybe she would, too, if she were lonely enough. She decides that's how she'll know she's hit rock bottom: if she starts pining for Liam.

Another time, Eduardo enters, carrying a plate of steaming chicken piccata and jasmine rice.

"I hope you're not a vegetarian," Eduardo says, holding out the plate. He's a little taller than she is, probably five feet six inches, and wears his dark hair slicked down with gel, almost like a swim cap, over his olive scalp.

"Nope, definitely not. Thanks." She takes a bite. "Wow, this is good."

"Don't be surprised. You'll learn everything here at the Knox is top-notch. It's why they don't have you waiting tables yet. They don't like mistakes. They don't like to make mistakes. The members here are very important people. They watch you a bit, and when they think you're ready, they'll let you know. At least, that is what they did with Tara."

"Tara?"

"Jerry's sister. That is who you replaced."

"Oh. What happened to her?"

"She quit." He pauses, and adds, "It's probably best if you don't bring up Tara around Jerry. . . . He's protective of her."

Taylor shrugs. "Okay, fine by me. So when do you think they'll deem me 'ready' to start waiting tables?"

"Could be next week, could be next month."

"So I'll just be doing stuff like this?" she asks, gesturing around.

"Yeah. It's not bad, though, right? Good job, good pay? Health insurance from day one."

"They haven't told me the pay yet," she admits. She's relieved to hear she'll have health insurance immediately. That should somewhat appease Aunt Gigi; Taylor's already bracing for her aunt's reaction when she finds out her niece has taken up waitressing over a return to nursing.

Eduardo gives a half smile. "You'll be happy with it. But let me ask you, why would you accept a job if you don't know the pay?"

"I, uh, I didn't know the exact amount, but they gave me an idea." She wonders if you can tell so many lies that they start to become your truth.

Eduardo nods thoughtfully. "Must be the week. It's an off week, you see. The senior members are at the Mansion for their annual retreat."

"The Mansion?" *The retreat?* she also wants to ask but doesn't.

"It's the country club for the Knox. It's in Beverly, the north shore."

"I didn't realize there was another place."

"They go every year before the initiation." He sees her frown, and explains, "The initiation happens after the retreat. During the retreat, they decide the new members they are tapping. *If* they are tapping new members. Some years there are no new members, and some years, there are many."

"When is the initiation?"

"It will be soon after they return. Might even be the following week. They will tell us."

"Is that here, or at the Mansion?"

"At the Knox, always." He pauses, and adds, "It's an interesting time to start work here. There's a lot to learn. I have been here for many years and am still learning. There's also . . . a new person in charge. Best advice I can give you is keep your— What is the saying? Keep your face down?"

"Keep your nose down?"

"Yes! Keep your nose down and do your job."

"Okay," Taylor says, rather reluctantly, swallowing all the questions she has. How many members are there? What is this place really about? Are there rituals? Will they somehow know if she talks to Sam about things? Does she even want to talk to Sam about things?

And then there are the questions she should be asking herself: What *exactly* is she doing here? What are her goals? To make money, rub elbows with the wealthy? Find out more about what happened to Vivian? Hopefully stumble across her mom's footprints?

Taylor feels a sudden silly determination to leave a mark here; to become a part of the place, to be distinct and necessary and special; not simply another Tara filtering in and out of the Knox's doors.

She continues her wine inventory, escaping at one point to use the bathroom, which is located at the end of the hall. She takes her time walking past the restaurant's wide, open double doors. Liam is pouring a glass of wine behind the backlit bar as classical music softly plays overhead. Could this be where the photo of Taylor's mom at the bar was taken? Her eyes sweep the room. Well-dressed men and women sit at crisp, white-linen tables. The women all sport perfect blowouts, their manicured hands aglitter in diamonds. Funny enough, the women's designer handbags rest upon their own designated seats as if they, too, are dining. While Taylor's not sure if her mom's photo was snapped here, she decides that Vivian very well could have been a member. How could she *not* have been, looking the way she did? And with that cache of designer handbags? Taylor can just picture Vivian perched at one of those tables, eating a salad alongside a Chanel purse.

Later that night, Taylor googles some of the wines whose names she remembers. There's a $330 Gaja Barbaresco, and a limited-edition pinot noir that costs ten times that. *Whoa.* At her dad's restaurant, she used to consider the $11 flagship margarita pricey.

She picks up her mom's photo, unsuccessfully searching for clues that could match it to the decor in the Knox restaurant, when she's interrupted by a knock at the door.

"First day commemoration drink?" Sam asks. Taylor follows him back to his apartment—his couch is bigger and more comfortable—and he uncorks a bottle of wine.

"A client gave it to me," he says, as he pours into a coffee mug. "It looks good. It's like a fifty-dollar bottle."

As they clink mugs, all she can think about is how the wines at the Knox probably cost at least $50 a *glass.*

⊰⊷−−∘−−⊶⊱

Over the next few days, Taylor is given more tasks. One day she completes a list of errands that keeps her out of the building nearly all day: bringing kitchen knives to get sharpened at Blackstone's, dropping off a navy silk tablecloth at Anton's Cleaners, purchasing George Howell coffee at its Downtown Crossing location, picking up vibrant bouquets at Rouvalis flower shop. Most of the errands seem specific to the building, though she's also sent to Gucci to pick up a rather gaudy logo belt for someone named "Oliver," to Townhouse Beauty Bar to purchase Marvis toothpaste, to the Beacon Hill Hotel to collect a Brioni shirt a

member apparently left behind in the room, and to the vet to grab
a prescription for the resident house cat (a Siamese whose name,
she learns, is China). Another day Rose has her polish all the ster-
ling silver trays in the beautiful parlor.

"Should I take off my shoes?" Taylor asks Rose, before she
enters the room.

"No," Rose replies, but Taylor can tell the question takes
Rose pleasantly by surprise.

She wonders: *Was Jerry's sister Tara required to complete
similar tasks? And if so, why would she have quit?* Because so
far, in Taylor's view, the job seems pretty darn cushy.

She is allotted a key for the back door, so every morning she
lets herself in and scurries down the hall to find Rose and await
the day's instruction. One rainy morning she nearly runs into
Jerry and Eduardo, coming from seemingly out of the shadows.
They are wearing the uniform she will adopt, once she's allowed
to officially start waitressing: a crisp white button-down shirt
and black trousers, or, in her case, a black skirt.

"The servants' quarters connect to the Knox building in the
basement," Eduardo explains, "so we just go down and up. No
need to step outside at all on a crummy day like today."

She adds this fact to her growing checklist of egress routes.

But not everyone lives next door. There's a cadre of silent,
near-invisible ancillary workers—cleaners and kitchen staff—
whom Taylor never interacts with; they are there and then they
are gone, just like the food they make and then the messes they
clean up.

There's so much she wants to know, but she tries not to ask
too many questions. The place is an enigma—the building much
bigger and deeper than it looks from the outside. It feels like a
magical labyrinth, always changing beneath her feet. There are
two sets of staircases. Two kitchens: the main one, and then the

one upstairs, adjacent to Canton's Restaurant. An inner, enclosed courtyard she still can't figure out how to get to. Many doors that remain closed. Five floors—allegedly, though it's hard to grasp that fact when looking at the building from the street. Taylor's briefly seen the secret library Liam mentioned, and a couple of the scrolls, which are enclosed in glass displays she's afraid to even breathe on, lest she sets off some alarm. How many more scrolls are there, and what is written on them?

Her working hours seem as ill-defined as the house and her current position. It's generally understood she should show up at some point in the morning—eight o'clock is too early, ten too late. Evening cocktails in that beautiful parlor are apparently common, though Taylor has yet to witness that. Rose excuses her most days by late afternoon.

"They give you a long leash here," Taylor notes one day to Jerry.

"Yeah, well, they do until they don't," he dryly replies.

Judging by the perturbed look on his face, Taylor wonders if he's talking about the sister-who-shall-not-be-named. Although Tara quit—she wasn't fired, right?

There's a relaxed atmosphere; it's not frenetic in the slightest. Is this because the senior members are away? Taylor enjoys having time to sip her morning coffee in the Knox's main kitchen, to be able to even wait for the coffee to brew. The only time she hurries is by choice—down that dank, dark hall of the back entrance. The Knox oozes a casual sophistication, reminding Taylor of the art of nonchalance that celebrities perfect when snapped strolling around sunny Los Angeles with a Starbucks in their hand. The rich, it seems, do not rush.

It's completely different from working in the hospital.

So maybe Taylor doesn't need to rush, either. She hasn't uncovered anything remotely related to Vivian, hasn't found any traces of her mom, but she hasn't done much digging, either. The more immersed she becomes in the Knox with each passing day, the further away her time at the hospital seems. She's looking forward to receiving her first paycheck, and she has to say, she doesn't miss nursing at all. More and more, it feels as if it would be okay to simply close that chapter of her life.

She loves walking through the Knox's expensive art-clad halls. She loves feeling the textures of the fabrics and furniture in the parlor room. She loves handling the superexpensive wine, even though she's half terrified of dropping it. She loves feeling like she's finally seeing the Boston that she always pictured in her head. The Boston to which Vivian belonged.

The Boston to which she, Taylor, now belongs.

THE KNOX

The society has hired a replacement for Tara: Taylor. Rose appears to have taken a shine to her, so I suppose she's *fine*. Too commonplace for my standards, of course, but aren't they all. She wears those recycled garments I can spot a room away. And oh dear, there was that wretched fake Rolex she wore to the interview—a tragic misstep. Mercifully, she had the good sense to ditch it.

The most interesting thing about Taylor, if one must choose *something*, is her accent. It's an unusual one, much less polished than the typical Southern lady or gentleman who enters through my esteemed doors.

Yes . . . I've been watching Taylor closely, as I'm utterly bored. With the members away on their annual retreat, there's precious little to occupy me.

I have been thinking for decades now that they ought to hold the retreat here, like they do the Initiation, instead of at the Mansion. Certainly the Mansion cannot possibly rival my own surroundings, steeped as they are in grandeur and millions of dollars of artwork (not to mention the crème de la crème of paintings in Graham's private chambers).

I do hope our standards are not beginning to slip. I must admit that I'm a bit mystified as to why Taylor was hired in the first place, when she didn't even pass the geomancy test. I observed the ensuing procedure, and the figures generated by her footprint bore little resemblance to the shield that was ultimately filed in the Knox's Book of Outsiders.

Someone must want her here.

Screening of Applicants for Hire Using Geomancy

Purpose. The purpose of this section is to provide a process by which Applicants under consideration for employment at the Knox are properly evaluated using geomantic divination.

Scope and Application. This section applies to all Applicants entering the Knox's premises for scheduled interviews as defined by paragraph (b) of the section 29.I.

1. Applicants shall enter the premises using the back entrance.

2. Using a continuous forward motion, Applicants shall step onto a visibly clean empty 3x4 foot wooden box.*

3. Any debris produced in the box from said action shall be discreetly procured and subsequently mixed with soil obtained from the earth in the basement adjacent to the Bowels scroll.

4. The resulting amalgamation shall provide the physical basis for the Geomancer to perform a divination reading regarding the Applicants' employment feasibility. Such readings shall be done in a quiet location and the Geomancer shall be in a state of deep relaxation and meditation.†

5. For each Applicant, the Geomancer will create sixteen rows of uncounted markings from right to left in the soil mixture, while concentrating on the posed question to the oracle: "Is this the right Applicant, over the other Applicants, to fulfill the position?"‡

6. The sixteen rows shall be divided in groups of four, and rows with even number of markings will be assigned one dot, whereas rows with odd number of markings will be assigned two dots. The first four figures of the geomantic shield, the Mother figures, shall thereby be generated.

7. The Geomancer will then use the four Mother figures to cast the rest of the shield.

8. The Geomancer will make an interpretation of the shield chart with deference to the Judge figure.§

9. If the Applicant is offered and accepts the employment position, the shield shall be filed in the Book of Outsiders.

---

* *In modern times, the wooden box may be substituted with a hospital-grade disposable adhesive mat.*

† *The use of opium is highly encouraged to produce a meditative state.*

‡ *In the event of limited time, the Geomancer may rely on the generation of a single figure as opposed to casting an entire shield, but this is not advisable.*

§ *Where it is warranted, and under the discretion of the Geomancer, the Witness Figures, the Reconciler, and/or other Figures may also be considered.*

VIVIAN

February

Vivian spills out from the Jewelers Exchange Building into the street, where life pulses around her.

She pulls out her phone to send a text to Rachel that she composes and erases several times, unsure of the tone to use. Alarmist? Factual? Gently concerned? She settles on: Just went by Xavier's store but it's no longer there! And his window was broken?! So weird . . . Don't you think?

She waits for a moment, but there's no response. So she shoves her phone back into her pocket and continues walking. She's aimless for a block or two, trying to clear her thoughts. Maybe the other shop owners just didn't know what had happened with Xavier. Maybe she's overreacting.

She passes an Irish bar with a sidewalk sign advertising the Celtics mascot, Lucky the Leprechaun, drinking a Bloody Mary. It's not such a bad idea. If she stopped in for one, then she'd be sideways for an actual reason.

She is seriously considering it, because when was the last time she did something like that? Perhaps *never*, even? But Vivian can't afford to lose any business; she needs to go open the store. She wishes she'd known to savor the days when she had an assistant.

Vivian strides up Beacon Street, which will deliver her back to the heart of Beacon Hill, then stops so suddenly that the person behind her nearly collides into her.

Across the street, and up a ways, is *Peter*. Standing in front of the boutique hotel XV Beacon. His back is to her; he's wearing the same dark navy coat she'd spotted strewn across the trunk in the Knox guest bedroom. Brown loafers. Dark hair with gray tints. He's as familiar to her as her own reflection, somehow. Even the way he stands strikes a chord: broad shoulders, feet pressed firmly into the ground.

She rubs her eyes, wondering if she's hallucinating. It has to be him, unless he has an identical twin. But how *could* it be him? Was the Milan trip canceled? What is he doing, just standing there all alone?

Vivian almost calls out, to say hello, but then she notices her: the girl striding toward him.

Vivian instinctively moves to hide within a small alcove next to a building, pressing against the bricks. Poking her head out from behind, she takes the girl in. She's small-boned—and unique. Turquoise-blue shoulder-length hair with light brown roots. Normally there aren't many alternative-looking blue-haired girls walking around Beacon Hill. What's her age? Twenty? Thirty? It's hard to tell from here. Vivian begrudgingly concedes that she's a woman, not a girl, but she may as well be. She's wearing a black puffer coat over a pair of ripped jeans and clutching a pink roller suitcase decorated with stickers.

The girl stops a few feet from Peter. She seems upset, dropping the suitcase handle to start gesturing wildly at him. The suitcase tumbles over, but she doesn't bother to pick it up. Instead, she covers her face with her hands as if she's crying.

Peter hastens to her, stooping down to right the suitcase. Now that he's standing directly in front of the girl, Vivian can only see his silhouette. He's blocking her—and their full exchange—from Vivian's vision.

Vivian feels panicked. She wants—no, needs—to see more. She emerges from behind the building, pulled in their direction. The girl's fingertips now appear, clutching Peter's shoulders. Like she's reached up to embrace him. And then he seems to be leaning toward her and—

A car turns onto the street, obstructing Vivian's view. *Shit. No, no, no! Not now!*

Are they hugging? Are they kissing? Her heart is in her throat, her stomach turning like it's in a washing machine. She's desperate to see more. To know more.

As she steps blindly into the street like a sailor lured by a siren, a biker skids to an abrupt stop.

He's pissed. "Are you crazy? Look where you're going! I almost hit you! I almost wiped out!"

Vivian stumbles back onto the sidewalk, shaken. Her mouth feels as dry as a cotton ball. "Sorry," she manages to mumble.

When she pokes her head back up, the blue-haired girl is climbing into a car, like one of those black Uber SUVs. Peter is nowhere to be found.

Did he see Vivian?

Is he already in the car, waiting for this girl?

Did the two of them just check out of the hotel?

Was that even Peter?

The Uber speeds off. Vivian is left staring at the place they just were. She's utterly confused. She gingerly touches her head, as if she's bonked it. Because that's how she feels. Like she's massively concussed.

TAYLOR

As Taylor walks up the Knox's back alleyway early Friday morning, she finds a truck and construction dumpster parked outside. Two men are unloading serious-looking equipment from the truck: sledgehammers, an electric drill, a saw, thick gloves, eye protection. Rose stands watching from the back door, her hands shading her face.

"We're doing a little renovation project," Rose shares, when Taylor approaches. Rose is wearing a black hoodie that reads, "The Butler Did It."

"I like your sweatshirt," Taylor says. She herself is wearing a thrift-store score: a Veronica Beard shirt that retails for $248 but that she got for $24, likely because of the hole at the bottom, which is easily hidden if the shirt is worn tucked in. As an added decoration, she sewed a gold peony patch she created onto the lapel area. The shirt's former owner had worn Chanel N°5, and for this reason, she hasn't washed it.

Rose gives one of those quick, begrudging smiles Taylor has come to expect. "They'll be in the basement, so it shouldn't interfere with your work."

"I didn't know there was a basement."

This isn't totally true; Taylor knows how the basement—or at least a portion of it—connects the Knox to the adjacent building, where Jerry and Eduardo live.

Rose presses her lips together. "I received word late last night about this," she finally adds. Is she pleased or displeased about this last-minute notice? It's hard to tell.

The men amble up, their hands full of tools, and Rose leads them down the corridor.

Taylor waits a few seconds so it doesn't appear like she's following, and then she passes through the same corridor.

Things look different. Doors usually open are closed. The door to the kitchen. The two French doors to the dining room. The parlor entrance—which doesn't contain a door—has a solid blue tarp hanging down from its frame. All artwork on the common walls has been taken down, its hooks and D-rings and cleats now exposed. Vases and the usual decor on the tables are gone. For a person curious about the Knox, there really is nothing to see. Well, except for that carousel horse, still down the hall, which didn't make the cut.

The only open door is the small one, under the staircase, through which the men and Rose disappear. Taylor's never been down there. Nor does she have any desire to; the thought alone of descending into a dark, dank stairwell makes her feel instantly suffocated. No; she'll stay on this level, thank you very much. But she can listen in on their conversation. She stands at the foot of the stairs, craning her neck. China the cat rubs against her leg with a small meow, and Taylor picks her up.

"The original blueprints are here," Rose says. "Look. See here? You can see where this room was, and where the door was. This is what we need opened."

"Right, yeah, I can see where the door was. We can open this up, no problem."

"You hear something interesting there?" Liam's voice says from behind, and Taylor jumps. China painfully digs into Taylor's arms before leaping out, and Taylor has to stifle her cry.

"Sheeit!" Taylor hisses. Then she glances down the stairs, terrified Rose will realize she's been eavesdropping. But there is no pause in conversation, thank goodness.

Liam leans casually against the opposite wall, sipping a coffee. "That's an interesting good morning greeting."

"What's going on in the basement?" she asks in a whisper, ignoring his comment. She moves away from the door.

"There's an old room that's been sealed for years. Like, over a hundred years. Oliver wants it opened."

"Who's Oliver? And what's in the room?"

Oliver, she recalls, is the name of the person for whom she had to fetch a package.

"You really don't know who Oliver is?"

She shakes her head. "I'm new, remember?"

"Oliver's . . . well, you'll meet him soon enough."

"Okay. And what's down there?" she presses.

Liam smiles in a flirty way. "Guess we'll find out. C'mon, new girl, let's get to work."

◆━━◆

"They finally broke through the basement door," reports Eduardo, when he reenters Canton's a few hours later. The restaurant is closed due to the construction, so Taylor and the others busy themselves polishing glasses, refilling salt and pepper shakers, folding napkins. Readying for next week's crowd, which will consist of members returning from the retreat, though there is more than enough time to prepare. There's a different energy in the air, almost like it's an unexpected day off from school. Every so often, when Rose slips away to check on the basement progress, Jerry sneaks down behind her.

"Fucking dusty as hell," adds Jerry, a little while later, upon his return. "Hard to tell what it is. Some sort of room."

"Do *you* want to have a look?" Eduardo asks Taylor, who gives an adamant "No."

When he raises his eyes, Taylor says, "I . . . I can't do basements. I get claustrophobic." Even thinking of the basement is enough to make the sweat start to gather at the back of Taylor's neck.

Liam, like Taylor, seems content to stay put. He restocks the liquors behind the bar and adds items to a growing pencil-and-paper grocery list: *olives, blue cheese olives, toothpicks, lemons.*

"You know there are apps for this," Taylor points out. "Instacart? DoorDash?"

"Everything here is good old-fashioned paper."

"Really?"

"Really."

This is intriguing; she's been hoping to come across records of some sort. Something that might show how Vivian—and her mother—is connected to the Knox. She'll have to find out where such information is stored.

"Did you see the 'Wall of Shame' downstairs in the foyer?" Liam asks with a grin. "It's the Knox's policy—also pen and paper—to publicly list the members delinquent with dues. Right now, there's just a Northrup Terrence on there."

"Everything that can be paper is," Eduardo interjects. "They don't want, how do you say it? They don't want to create a footprint."

"*Digital* footprint," Liam adds.

"Oh." She folds and unfolds a napkin. "So, who does the shopping?"

"Rose, usually," Liam says. "Today? Probably you."

"Me? Great," she says sarcastically.

Eduardo looks sharply at her, and she wishes she could take it back.

"I mean, it's fine. I'm just curious about what's going on downstairs."

"When—or if—they want us to know, they tell us," Eduardo says rather sternly, and Taylor feels appropriately chastised. He fishes through the backpack perched on one of the barstools and pulls out a red apple and a book, *1776* by David McCullough. It's his signal that he's taking his break.

"So, have y'all worked here a long time?" Taylor asks.

"Ten years this summer," Liam says. "The Professor"—that's what he calls Eduardo, on account of all the books he reads—"is ancient, though. How long you been here, Professor?"

"Seventeen years," Eduardo replies.

"Seventeen years, wow," says Taylor, but inside she's crestfallen. That's a year shy of when her mother would have been here. "You've probably . . . seen a lot."

"Not that I can tell you, but yes."

"Oooh, all righty, then," she says. "Well, y'all know what they say: 'Never rat on your friends, and always keep your mouth shut.'" She gives a short laugh, but no one else laughs. Maybe they don't get the *Goodfellas* reference?

"Seventeen years," she repeats, trying a different approach. She wants to pick their brains while Rose isn't hovering. "What can you 'not tell me' . . . I mean, do people ever get, like, *hurt* here?" *Like Vivian, falling down the stairs?*

"No, they don't," Jerry replies rather thinly, and then gets up to go check again on the downstairs progress.

"And what about him?" Taylor asks, once he's left. "How long's Jerry been here?"

"O'Doyle? Five years, just about," Liam replies.

"O'Doyle?"

Eduardo shakes his head. "Liam here has a nickname for everyone." Then, turning to Liam, he admonishes, "Jerry's last name, as you know, is Doyle, not O'Doyle."

Liam shrugs.

"And his sister? How long was she here?" Taylor asks.

Liam stops stacking glasses from behind the bar. He looks surprised. "Who told you about Tara?"

"He did." Taylor juts her chin toward Eduardo, who nods.

"Oh. What was it, a year?" Liam asks Eduardo.

Eduardo closes his book. "Yes, thirteen months. She's in nursing school now. That's what she wants to do—be a nurse."

Taylor can feel her face redden at the mention of nursing. It's stupid that this word would generate an instant guilty response, like anything outside of the insulated, gilded heft of the Knox is a dirty secret. "So why am I not supposed to mention her around Jerry?"

Liam and Eduardo exchange looks. It's Eduardo who answers.

"She was in a relationship with Oliver. . . . Oliver's in charge, or almost in charge. Jerry didn't like that. Have you met him—Oliver?"

"I don't know."

Liam snickers. "That's a no, then. You would know."

Taylor shrugs. "Okay, whatever." She thinks it's weird that Tara would continue to be a touchy subject around here, if she's long gone and doing fine.

"Hey, how did *you* get yourself here?" Liam asks.

"Me? My landlord referred me."

"Yeah? What's his name?"

"*Her* name is Anna."

"And where did you say you worked before?"

"I didn't say. But I worked at my dad's restaurant in North Carolina."

"North Carolina, huh," Liam says. He's watching Taylor closely, as if her answers are somehow making him suspicious.

"Peter interviewed her. And then the geomancy confirmed," Eduardo says.

"And Michael did the geomancy reading?" Liam presses.

"I would assume so," Eduardo replies.

Meanwhile, Taylor is thinking to herself that they must have made a mistake with her. She never met a Michael, and she has no idea what the geo-thing they mentioned is. What if she's not supposed to be here?

But Liam nods, seemingly satisfied. He continues stacking glasses and then asks, much more lightly, "What brought you to Boston, anyway?"

"My mother."

"Oh?" There is surprise in Liam's voice.

Taylor is also surprised she said it.

"Well, my aunt, too," she adds and then winces. Why is she offering more information than needed?

"They live here?" Eduardo asks.

"My mom used to. How about you?" she asks Eduardo, anxious to shift the conversation.

"I came from Colombia twenty years ago. I studied engineering there, but here, well, here I am." He smiles, and any tension she seems to have previously incurred vanishes.

"An engineer, reader, and now part of the Knox," Taylor says. "Impressive."

"Yes, we are lucky to be here. You are lucky now, too," he says. But the way he says it seems like he's reminding her.

Liam leans his head on his hands on the bar countertop. "Well, New Girl, you didn't ask *me*, but I'll tell you anyway. Peter is the one who brought me here, from across the pond."

"Oh, really? You knew each other?" Taylor feels her face further warming; it's like a Pavlovian response when she thinks of Peter.

"I used to bartend at a dive bar, round the corner from an East London hotel he liked to stay at."

"Oh, that's lucky," she says.

"It's not about luck. You create your own luck. Peter taught me that. I've got a lot of respect for him. I knew him for many years, helped him out once in a situation. He knew he could trust me. It's all about trust here, you see, New Girl?" He twirls the end of a small black cocktail straw in his mouth.

"Liam is right. It is about trust here," Eduardo says. "You work hard, but you get rewarded. I get to stay in this country because of them. Any problem is taken care of."

Just then Jerry reenters the room and reports that the men have cleared a lot of the debris. Eduardo's eyes brighten with his arrival, like they always do. Is there something going on between the two of them?

"The room they've uncovered is maybe a third the size of this," Jerry relays, gesturing around. "It's got a wooden table inside, like an old-fashioned doctor table."

Old-fashioned doctor table?

"Ah, that makes sense. One of the portraits downstairs is of a Dr. Robert Thurgood. Maybe he used to see the patients here?" Eduardo muses.

"Did they find any bodies?" asks Liam, with a wicked grin.

Taylor stiffens.

"Liam," Eduardo chides.

But Jerry answers seriously. "No," he says. "Not yet at least."

Diary Entry of Dr. Robert Thurgood

April 12, 1851

Having practiced as a physician for several years in the traditional setting, my professional interest has reached a critical juncture. I am far less struck by the conversational manner in which patients are apt to discuss with me their most troublesome symptoms, which are often unrelated to the medical issue at hand, and, indeed, lead to an admitted inattentiveness on my part. Yet I remain deeply intrigued by the human body itself.

Thenceforth, it is my intention to turn my attentions to the burgeoning field of autopsies. The human body, devoid of conversation, shall make a most excellent subject that will further advance my medical practice. And an admittedly more pleasant patient encounter. However, it is not without difficulty to procure adequate specimens owing in part to current restrictive state laws and less-than-favorable public opinion.

I have, at my disposal, the necessary ingredients to ensure my own successful endeavor into the field of advanced anatomical study: a basement office, by which bodies may be easily transported to and from, and which provides the necessary concealment of smells; several cemeteries that are within a quarter mile; and a discreet caretaker who has agreed to procure cadavers for $25 a body.

TAYLOR

Rose does indeed decide to send Taylor to purchase the items on the shopping list.

"Is there a time I need to be back by?" Taylor asks, fingering the wad of cash she's been given.

Rose blinks. Her eyes are small and pale blue-green, like sea glass; the rest of her face withered, like the ocean continues to relentlessly pound it.

"Just get it done," she says, but then she adds a brief smile. It is so quick, almost as if she is simply exercising her mouth muscles, barely anyone would notice.

But Taylor does.

Given her age, Rose likely would have been at the Knox when her mom was, Taylor realizes. They could have crossed paths. Maybe Rose noticed her mom dining in Canton's Restaurant the same way Taylor noticed—and admired—the stylish women there the day she did the wine inventory. And Rose was certainly around during Vivian's time. Taylor's hopeful that Rose will continue to warm to her; perhaps she can eventually ask her.

Between DeLuca's Market and the liquor store, Taylor is able to find nearly all the items on the list: food, blue cheese olives, prenatal vitamins—they sure seem to think of everything for their members and guests. The one thing she can't seem to get a hold of is crème fraîche. She doesn't know what it is, but apparently it's used to accompany caviar. Go figure. Taylor has to track it down at Savenor's, a gourmet grocer.

While waiting in the checkout line there, she notices the headline of *The Boston Globe*: BOSTON'S HOSPITALS OVERWHELMED BY OVERDOSES.

Wow. She certainly witnessed the beginnings of this uptick when she was still working at Mass General. Clearly when Aunt Gigi reached out to Taylor about the multiple nursing openings at the substance abuse clinic, she wasn't kidding.

Taylor feels grateful to be away from all that. She finds she can't help but still observe medical things in her day-to-day, as if she wears an avatar nurse skin. But the more she becomes immersed in the Knox, the more she believes she will be able to shed it. At some point, the only covering she wants to wear is a designer one.

"Cash or credit?" the cashier now asks as she scans the container of crème fraîche.

"Cash," Taylor replies, forking over the money.

As the cashier gives her change, Taylor eyes the assortment of candy bars for sale. She's tempted to purchase one with cash from the Knox. She's hungry; she's skipped lunch, after all. And it's not like Rose told her to turn in the receipts. But she's too much of a scaredy-cat. What if this a test? What if this is part of that trust thing Liam and Eduardo were alluding to?

"And I'll also take this chocolate bar, but I'll use my credit card to pay separately for it," Taylor says, as she pulls out her wallet to hand over her card.

"You dropped this," a woman's voice says from behind. Taylor turns; a woman, with one kid clinging to her legs and another in a stroller, thrusts a small, folded white paper at Taylor.

"I don't think so," Taylor says.

"You did. Just now, when you pulled your credit card out, it fell out of your wallet."

"Oh, okay, thanks," Taylor says, taking the paper.

"You need to sign," the cashier interrupts, pointing to the screen.

Taylor shoves the paper into her wallet. Probably an old receipt, she thinks.

When she's done shopping, she has fifty-three bucks left over. She's used to stretching her dollars, making every one count. To have any excess now feels indulgent, even though it's not hers, and even though she knows this is chump change for the Knox.

She wonders how exactly the money works at the Knox. What does a minimal digital footprint mean? She had to fill out a W2, so there's a payroll system for the employees, but the others mentioned that the bonuses they receive are done in cash. This is a surprise; she hadn't realized there would be bonuses. When she worked in nursing in North Carolina, all she got was a mug or a penlight at Christmas, if she was lucky. Oh—and the families of patients brought in cookies. Lots and lots of cookies.

"The bonuses come when we have big events and parties. And, of course, the end of the year," Eduardo had explained.

"Is there . . . a big event coming up?" she asked, hopeful.

"The biggest. The initiation. But *we* don't work that, only Rose does," Liam said.

"We do the preparations for it, though," Eduardo added. "And they recognize that."

What kind of cash bonuses are they talking about? She has absolutely *zero* frame of reference. Twenty dollars? Two hundred dollars? Or even more? Something in the four digits? She gulps with the thought.

Rose dismisses her when she returns to the Knox, groceries in tow.

"Next week the members will be back from the retreat," Rose says, as if Taylor needs any reminding. "It will be busy but just follow my lead."

"Okay. Thank you." Loud thumping and drilling noises create vibrations in the foyer, where they stand. The work is clearly far from done.

"Have a good weekend," she adds, to Taylor's surprise.

"Uh, thanks. You too, Rose."

Rose opens the front door for Taylor—a first, Taylor using the front door—but it's only because the portion of the house with the back hall is now sealed off to contain dust.

Taylor exits, the door shutting firmly behind her. As she walks down the few front steps and turns onto the street, a woman's gruff voice startles her. "You with them?"

The woman is sitting on the sidewalk in between two parked cars. She's middle-aged and looks worse for wear: unkempt, ratty hair, weathered face, a dirty too-big coat. She puffs on a cigarette as she rocks back and forth.

Taylor does what she does whenever she encounters a person likely on drugs: ignores them and walks away. But then the woman adds, "The Knox?" and Taylor stops. She slowly turns around.

"What?" Taylor asks.

"Are you with the Knox?"

"I work there, yeah. Why?"

The woman starts coughing, a deep throaty cough. No, she's

laughing. No, rather, she's gagging. What on earth is the noise that the woman is making? Does she need medical help? Taylor looks around, but nobody's nearby. Shit. Is Taylor going to have to help this woman?

But, in the next second—too late—Taylor realizes that the woman has been gathering phlegm in her throat. She hurls a giant wad of spit on Taylor's Ralph Lauren twill coat. Taylor looks down, horrified.

"That's for the bad Aunt Emma. You fucking cunt."

VIVIAN

I t's Friday afternoon, the day after her ill-fated trip to Xavier's
jewelry store.

Vivian's in her own store, trying to keep busy.

First, she rearranges the shelves on a tall cabinet to make room
for the antique vases that will soon be arriving. Then she unpacks
the shipments of Herend Rothschild porcelain bowls sourced from
her contact in Budapest and breaks down all the boxes. Monday
is recycling day, so she'll put these aside for the time being.

Vivian's always been able to compartmentalize troubling
things, thanks to her upbringing. Waspy families have a way of
quietly sweeping disorder under the rug. Yet Rose's words buzz
in her ear like an annoying fly. *You're not the first girl Peter's
brought round and you won't be the last. You are pretty, but that
will fade.*

She hopes there's a simple explanation for why she spotted
Peter yesterday in the street. She keeps checking her phone, waiting for him to text her that he never went on the trip, or that it
was delayed. She's waiting for an explanation that is not forthcoming.

Is Vivian a fool for thinking that she and Peter are exclusive, that she might be special?

And what about Xavier? Is he in some kind of trouble? Rachel's not overly concerned; she thinks the broken glass in Xavier's shop window was likely just some accident. But then again, Vivian hasn't shared the warning note she received, nor her suspicions that Xavier is behind it.

She next opens a box of wax candles from a local candlemaker. Noting their pastel colors, she's reminded that she needs to place an order soon with her Italy contact for Francesca Colombo's Easter plates; they flew off her shelves last April. Vivian goes to retrieve her notebook of business contacts, but it's not where she normally keeps it in her desk drawer.

She rummages through her other drawers to no avail. Where the heck did she put it? She tries to recall the last time she used the notebook; it's been a few weeks. Perhaps she left it at the Chestnut Hill store, though she doesn't remember bringing it there. It's possible, though.

Anything feels possible these days. Or impossible. It's like life itself has swallowed a giant Xanax. What if the Knox is bad news—for both her and Xavier? What if Peter breaks her heart? Deep down, Vivian knows she has done more than just compartmentalize like a WASP. Since Kat's death years ago, followed by Vivian's father's—and now, with her mom's looming—Vivian's locked up parts of herself, put them in storage.

She doesn't know when—or if—she'll be ready to unearth them.

TAYLOR

Taylor can't believe she was just *spit* on, and by a strung-out, likely homeless woman to boot. She cleans her coat with some tissues she has in her purse, careful not to touch the saliva with her bare hands, given the endless types of germs the woman could be carrying.

A lot of crazy shit used to happen in the ER, sure. Taylor saw enough in her four-month hospital stint to last a lifetime. Drugs, mental illness, rare diseases—things that felt like they belonged in an episode of a hospital drama, only without the perky banter and sexual tension. But she certainly didn't expect to encounter that *here*, in front of a multimillion-dollar building in Beacon Hill. The juxtaposition of it is almost as jarring to her as what the woman did.

Taylor holds the dirty tissues in her pinched fingers, rounding the building to discard the tissues in the construction dumpster out back.

The trucks have doubled; there are now two, with a van parked alongside them. Taylor tosses the tissues in the dumpster and reads the lettering across the van: IDEAL DESIGN STUDIO. A quick Google search tells her that it's a highly regarded interior design firm. So, the Knox isn't just opening the room, they're redesigning it. What on earth are they making it into? What more could they possibly need, and in a basement of all places?

Jerry suddenly bursts through the back door, his arms pressed tightly across his black leather jacket. She's never seen him in a coat before. His hair and the tops of his wide shoulders are sprinkled white with dust. He scowls when he sees her.

Hi to you, too, she thinks.

He hastens past her, and, on a whim, she follows.

Halfway down the block, something falls out from beneath his jacket—a book. He quickly grabs it and shoves it back under his zipper. As he's doing so, another item falls to the ground—a wooden tube. "Fuck," he swears to himself as he stuffs them back inside.

"What are those things that fell?" Taylor asks.

"Nothing," he snaps, and continues briskly walking.

She scurries after him.

"Ya following me?" he asks, over his shoulder.

"No." But clearly she is. "Was that a book?"

"It's *nothing*."

"It didn't look like nothing. Was that from the room downstairs?"

He ignores her and quickens his pace, so she does as well. Only once he gets to the next corner, and halfway down that intersecting block, does he stop. His face is blotchy and sweaty, and he's cradling the bump in his jacket like a baby. He looks behind her, as if checking whether they've been followed.

Seemingly satisfied, he meets her gaze. "It was junk, just some historical crap they were gonna throw out."

"Did they say you could have it?"

His silence is the answer.

"What are you doing with it?" she asks.

He eyes her a little warily. "Why?"

"Just wondering."

"I thought maybe I could sell the stuff," Jerry admits. "There's a couple books, some old medical stuff. Like an old-fashioned stethoscope." He makes no move to show the alleged items. "But I don't know where I'm gonna offload them," he adds, working his jaw.

"You know, my landlord owns an antiques store *and* a used bookstore," Taylor says, as casually as she can. She's thinking— what if these items are more than a load of "historical crap"?

Everything is paper, they'd said. What if there's something in those books? Besides, maybe there's a deal here to be made, a way to gain some favor with Jerry.

"Yeah, and?"

"Well, I could ask her for an introduction . . . see if maybe these are worth anything?"

"Maybe."

"We could do a sixty-forty split? I'd be the forty."

"Eighty-twenty," he replies.

"No way."

"Look," Jerry says, shifting his eyes around, "I gotta look out for myself. The Kn—they say they'll look out for ya, but they won't. Not really. Eighty-twenty, take it or leave it."

This is the exact opposite of what Eduardo professed about the Knox. Does Jerry have a skewed outlook simply because his sister got involved with Oliver? Or did something else happen? "Fine," she concedes, sticking out her hand to Jerry, who just nods.

"But I'm gonna hold on to the stuff until then. And don't say nothing to the others. It's better if they don't know. I don't think they'd want me and ya . . ." His voice trails off, but Taylor gets the drift.

She's the outsider. Always the outsider. She has been her whole life. Why would the Knox be any different? "I promise I won't," she assures him, trying to dampen the surprising hurt she feels.

VIVIAN

Present Day

Her existence has become this: a series of pokes and prods. Sudden, intrusive taps on her kneecaps and arms. Sporadic commands directed at her, which are sometimes garbled, sometimes not: *Squeeze my hand. Wiggle your toes.* Occasionally she catches just the tail end of a statement: . . . *Your fingers.* . . . *Hear me* . . . Vivian tries to respond but crashes with the effort, organized thoughts a painful somnolence.

In between, there sits that heavy silence. It's too silent for a hospital floor, she realizes with a growing unease. And then, every once in a while the quiet is jarringly interrupted by a series of loud clangs, too brazen to be the chime of a mere IV pump.

Where am I?

Something she needs to remember continues to hover on her periphery. Something, try as she might, she cannot. But the secret grows almost painfully urgent, pressing against her tender brain bruise.

She retreats beneath her eyelids, in the dark abyss.

Pupils equal, reactive, someone says, as they shine an obnoxiously bright light into her eyes. She recalls seeing this used on an episode of *House*: a light pen. No—penlight, used to assess neurological status.

Okay, fine. So maybe she *is* still in the hospital.

But then—another light is positioned in front of her eyes. It feels inherently wrong—nonmedical. This light is wide, flat. Lazy, too; it lingers far too long.

In the still of the quiet, she grows anxious beneath the continued blunt glare. Summoning all her strength and energy, she pries her eyes open—and is surprised to find her mom's face filling her vision.

And then Vivian realizes: She's looking at a *photo*, a familiar one that quickly melts away into the now unlocked home screen of her iPhone.

TAYLOR

The weekend arrives; Taylor has officially finished her first week of employment at the Knox. But there's no one to celebrate with; Sam is in Miami meeting up with someone he met on Raya, the high-profile dating app. So Taylor spends her time binging reruns of *Gossip Girl* and perusing online luxury consignment shops. Every minute away from the Knox feels multiplied by two.

At one point, when she pulls out her credit card to snag some vintage Gucci buttons from a trusted eBay seller, she comes across a crumpled slip of paper. It's the receipt that apparently fell out of her wallet at Savenor's, the one the woman behind her in the checkout line handed to her. Taylor opens it, curious.

But it's not a receipt after all.

It's a handwritten note, embossed with the Knox logo: Go back to being a nurse.

Taylor's heart immediately starts racing. What is this? Who would leave it for her? Is it a warning? A demand? Who at the Knox even knows she's a nurse?

She closes her eyes, trying to think. Did she somehow let that information slip? No—she's sure she didn't. *Someone knows more about her than they let on.* She opens a new browser to google herself. Maybe somebody from the Knox looked her up online and found something. Perhaps there's something incriminating on one of her social media profiles. But she's reassured to find that her Facebook and Instagram profiles are still private, with no classifying information. Her Snapchat is basically inactive. She does have a new Instagram follow request, from a faceless someone named @tdgarden33__.

Either a bot, or someone is sniffing around.

Taylor tries to relax, but a current of anxiety pulses through her. She's too much in her head, worrying about the note, worrying about everything.

If the Knox didn't really mean to hire her, and that's what this note's about.

If she's asked too many questions.

If her landlord, Anna, will think her request for an intro to the used-bookstore owner is weird, or suspicious.

If Jerry and the others will ever accept her.

If Sam actually likes her, or if their friendship is more of a neighborly convenience.

If Vivian is long dead, even though Taylor hasn't yet heard back from the state about Vivian's death record.

It's like opening Pandora's box.

Will Taylor always be an outsider? What if she never comes close to being the woman her mother was? Is she pathetic for even trying? Would her mom be ashamed of her, if she could see her now?

Taylor looks around her apartment, taking in the sagging secondhand couch, the throw with a grease stain from Chinese takeout that she's been unable to remove, the dirty bowl she routinely leaves in the sink. It's embarrassing, really, her doldrum existence.

She wonders if she's nothing to the Knox. If she were to quit tomorrow, or be fired, would anyone even miss her, remember her? Would she be reduced to terse mentions, like Tara? How quickly would Taylor be replaced? How much more easily would that new person win Jerry's favor, or Rose's trust?

Taylor wonders if she's simply traded a subpar life in North Carolina for a subpar one in Boston.

She wonders if she's nothing at all.

⊰—o—⊱

On Saturday midafternoon, like a Hail Mary, Taylor receives a surprise banking alert: Her first paycheck has been deposited, not even twenty-four hours after finishing her workweek. No typical one-week pay lag for Knox employees, apparently. She can't believe the number: nearly three times what she was making as a nurse. Hell no, she's not going back to nursing. She doesn't know who left her that note, sure, but, frankly, after this paycheck, she's having a hard time making herself care. It's like the oldest kind of magic, the way the sparkling new balance in her checking account lifts her spirits, transforms her outlook, makes her feel like she's on "the right path" after all.

Emboldened, she orders a sushi lunch—to be delivered, no less—not paying any mind to the hefty delivery fee, and finally texts Aunt Gigi.

> Hi Aunt Gigi, sorry for the delay.
> Thnx for thinking of me with all these
> nursing positions. BUT I'm all set for
> now. I got another job.

Her aunt responds almost immediately.

> Oh! That was quick! Where?

> It's not in nursing. But don't worry! I'm making *really* good pay!

> What kind of job??

> It's a kind of waitressing job. But I'm doing other stuff 2.

A pause.

> Where?

> It's for a private restaurant.

> A private society.

Taylor quickly edits the text.

> A private club.

> What's the name of it?

> The Knox.

Taylor sees the dots appear and then disappear. Eventually, they're gone. Aunt Gigi has chosen not to respond. Just as well.

Taylor knows it's only a matter of time before the message now gets relayed to her father. At least, hopefully by then, he will have received the check she's just popped in the mail.

As she bites into her salmon sashimi—another extravagance she wouldn't normally indulge in—and sips her wine, she decides she's glad Sam is away. She doesn't have to field questions about the Knox she doesn't want to answer.

VIVIAN

February

Rachel has uncovered something about the Knox. She asks Vivian to meet her on Saturday in person at a used bookstore called Turned Pages, near the Old State House. Rachel sends Vivian a series of text emoji teasers: a book, a tombstone, a wink.

This, Vivian thinks, has got to be interesting.

Peter also texts. Can't wait to see you tonight for dinner, love. Meet me at 6:30 p.m.?

You won't be too jet-lagged? Vivian snarkily types, then erases. She'll never know what he was up to if she ignores him. And, if she's being honest with herself, she can't wait to be with him again.

Turned Pages is located on the garden level of a historic commercial building on Cornhill Street. She takes the long way to get there, avoiding the area where she thought she saw Peter a couple of days earlier.

In the bookstore window there's a vintage edition of the medical textbook *Gray's Anatomy* and a few faded copies of

Hemingway novels. There's also a HIRING! sign that hangs askew, and Vivian has to swallow the urge she feels to right it.

The door jingles as she enters. It's one-room store, filled with rows of overstuffed bookshelves and a plain wooden cashier desk. The sweet, musty smell of old books prickles Vivian's nose, and she feels immediately comforted.

Rachel is already there, standing alongside an elderly gentleman who looks like he comes with the building: a deeply weathered face, bifocals, a muted cardigan sweater the color of too many crayons mixed together.

"Vivian, meet Nicholas, the owner," Rachel says.

"Hello, Nicholas." Vivian shakes his trembling hand. "I'm embarrassed to say I've never been inside here before. This is just . . . perfect."

He smiles. "Hello, Vivian. That's quite all right. We are a bit of a hidden gem."

"Nicholas and I have known each other for a long time," Rachel says. "He often attends our programming at the Vilna Shul. As you can see, he carries a lot of old books. And he has something that I want to show you in a minute. But first—"

She pulls out some papers from her leather satchel and spreads them across the wooden cashier's desk. Her eyes shine brightly. "So, you know how you gave me the family tree, right? Well, I searched the city's vital and town records in the 1800s, and I've filled in some of the missing pieces. Your 'Dr. No-Good Thurgood'—the one who tried to destroy the schedule of beneficiaries— is Dr. Robert Walter Thurgood. This here is his death record, from the Massachusetts Vital Records collection, 1820–1902." She runs a pink pastel–manicured finger down one of the pages, until it pauses at an entry.

"Impressive, Rachel."

"Just wait. So, listen, the whole Knox-Thurgood family is

buried in Mount Auburn Cemetery. They have a family plot. I went to see it. William Knox, the Knox founder, is buried there. This Dr. Robert Thurgood is there. Everyone. Everyone *except* Margaret."

"Margaret, meaning my ancestor?"

"Correct. Margaret, your great-great-great-grandmother. Mother to the illegitimate child—your great-great-grandmother—and also to this Dr. Thurgood."

"Was it uncommon at the time for women to be buried in the family plot? Maybe she—"

"No," Rachel interrupts. "Women—wives, daughters—they were buried in either common plots, or for wealthy families, usually in the dedicated family plot. This Knox/Thurgood family plot has several generations in it. It's a very male-dominated lineage, son producing son producing son, but the women—the wives—are buried there. Not Margaret, though."

"So where is she?"

"Do you remember that note that we found from the servant who said, 'Something is not right. He has her body in the basement'?"

"How could I forget?"

"Well, Dr. Thurgood was a physician who, according to my research, was very interested in pathology, which meant plenty of autopsies. He was a student and then a professor at Harvard Medical School, so I found records of his research. Bodies were hard to come by in the 1800s, so there was apparently a whole illicit body-snatching, grave-robbing ring going on—"

"Really?" Vivian interrupts, disdain on her face.

"Really. Medical students needed cadavers for anatomical study, after all, so I guess they had to come by them somehow. At Harvard, they even formed their own secret society around it back in the day, called the Spunker Club."

Vivian crinkles her nose. "What is it with secret societies?"

"Well, I guess they wouldn't need to be secret if they were squeaky clean."

"True."

"Anyway, back to our Dr. Thurgood. So he had his home office in the basement of the Knox. . . ."

Vivian swallows. "You mean . . ."

Rachel nods. "It's likely he was performing autopsies on stolen cadavers down there."

Vivian stares at her friend. "What are you saying? And what does this have to do with Margaret? Do you think he autopsied *his own mother*?" She shudders, while Nicholas shakes his head in disbelief.

"Well, what else could that letter mean?"

"That's . . . I don't even know what to say."

"I know. Pretty horrific, if it's true. I just think there's got to be a reason that Margaret isn't buried in the family plot, right?" Rachel says.

"Wouldn't he still have buried her, after the autopsy? Wait . . . you think she's buried in the Knox itself?"

"I don't think that. Well, I don't really know, to be honest. She's buried *somewhere*. Let's just hope it's an unmarked plot in this Mount Auburn Cemetery."

"Oh my God, Rachel. What kind of person was this man?"

"A bad writer," Nicholas intervenes. He produces a book: *Selected Poems*, written by Edgar Rolo Butterworth.

Vivian frowns. "Wait, where do I know this name?"

"Remember at your mom's house, that terrible book of poetry that we found the letters in? *Musings on Love and Life*, or something like that? Well, that was also written by this Edgar Rolo Butterworth—or should I say Dr. Thurgood."

Vivian blinks, not totally understanding.

"Edgar Rolo Butterworth is an anagram of Robert Walter Thurgood. It's his pseudonym. They are the same person," Nicholas says rather matter-of-factly.

"What? Christ."

"One of your ancestors must have known, which is why they put the letters in that book," says Rachel.

"How did you figure this out?"

Rachel riffles through her papers to retrieve a printout of a tombstone. "This is the epigraph on Dr. Thurgood's tombstone."

> *Judge me not today*
> *But for eternity.*
> *In death the truth shall be.*
>
> —E. R. BUTTERWORTH

"Hidden in plain sight," Rachel says. "When I saw this quote, I remembered the book of poetry at your mom's house. And then I reached out to Nicholas, who had this book in his store. As you might guess, it's another poorly written poetry collection—I guess Butterworth had a knack for that. Anyway, want to show her, Nicholas?"

He nods, carefully opening the book and pointing to the inside left flap, at a stamped image: a ghastly skull head with smoke billowing from its eyes, over the words "Ex Libris Robert Walter Thurgood."

Goose bumps prickle across Vivian's skin.

"The library of Robert Walter Thurgood," Nicholas says. "It's a bookplate, to indicate ownership. People back in the day took pride in their personal library collections and marked their books with custom stamps. In this case, it's more than that. Robert is giving us a clue that he is both the owner of the book and the author."

Rachel jumps in. "Given the two instances of Butterworth and Thurgood being linked—the tombstone and the bookplate— we realized it had to be more than coincidence. Also I researched Butterworth, and he doesn't exist."

"This is wild." Vivian looks back and forth between the tombstone printout and the book.

"Dr. Robert Walter Thurgood also published some medical books under his real name," Nicholas says. "I don't have them, but I could get them, if that would be of interest."

"Thank you, Nicholas," Rachel says.

"Perhaps unsurprisingly, his medical books appear to be on pathology."

"I get why people—writers—use pseudonyms," Vivian says. "But something doesn't make sense to me. If Dr. Thurgood wanted anonymity as a poet, then why risk discovery by putting this quote on his tombstone?"

Rachel taps her fingers against the counter, almost impatiently. "For the same reason that serial killers write letters to the public or leave their 'signatures' at crime scenes. Dr. Thurgood wanted to be discovered eventually. He was leaving a trail so someone—like us—could connect the dots: that the doctor was the poet."

"But why? What was he doing? What was his 'crime scene,' so to speak?"

Rachel exhales. "I don't know. But I think it involved your ancestor and pathology. Those are the dots he's given us to connect. And whatever it was, it seems he wanted to be lauded for it, after his death. 'Judge me not for today but for eternity.'"

Vivian shakes her head, trying to erase the unfortunate skeletal images that have now taken hold. She becomes hyperaware of her own body, a chill slowly traveling down each subsequent, isolated vertebra.

Selected Poems (an excerpt)

By Edgar Rolo Butterworth

Mother's Poison

Mother, you drink the poppy like water,
But it does little to dampen your thirst.
Eternally unsatiated, you fall quickly asleep
While the opium does your body and soul curse.

TAYLOR

On Monday Taylor arrives early to work, like a real Bostonian. In the back alley, she sees what she assumes is another construction van for the Knox, but as she reads the lettering printed on its side—MED-OX—she realizes she's mistaken. This is a medical equipment van and must be for one of the adjacent neighbors. It's a good reality check; not *everything* in Beacon Hill is Knox-related.

Taylor lets herself in through the back entrance and slips into that terrible dark hall. This is what they should really be renovating, she thinks. She's hurrying so quickly she nearly collides with Rose, who enters from the connecting basement space.

"Careful!" Rose snaps, as liquid sloshes from the pair of tea mugs she's holding.

"Sorry!"

Rose scowls as she looks down at her now-wet khakis. "I'll have to change my pants."

"I'm really sorry," Taylor offers again.

Rose simply shakes her head. She transfers both mugs to one hand so she can swing the door open with the other and disappears back into the basement. She must also live next door, in the servants' quarters, Taylor realizes. Of course.

Taylor continues down the hall, now at a much slower pace. When she spills out into the main space, she's surprised to find everything back in place. The renovation of the basement room has apparently wrapped up. That was the quickest turnaround ever. She knows a thing or two about construction from the boys back home, and this, perhaps even more than the fancy crystal chandeliers, makes her realize how damn resourceful the Knox is.

In the kitchen, Taylor finds the coffeepot nearly empty. As she brews a new batch, she straightens her skirt—a black Zara knee-length purchase that hugs her curves just the perfect amount—and reapplies her lip gloss.

"Hey," a man's voice drawls from behind, startling her. "There you are."

There's a man in a cream silk robe grinning widely at her. His long, dirty-blond hair is pulled into a low ponytail; his eyes are bloodshot. The tops of his shoulders, angled and skinny, protrude like two doorknobs.

"Hi," she says.

"Hey." He continues to smile at her.

Does she know him? Or is she supposed to? The coffee machine grinds to a stop, and the aroma of the freshly brewed pot hangs in the air like a question. "Uh, you want some coffee?" she asks.

"Yeah, I do. That would be *amazing*. Thanks." He runs his hands through his hair, revealing an elaborate dragon tattoo on one of his forearms. It kind of reminds her of that Chinese dragon water statue in the courtyard.

She wasn't asking if she could fetch this man a coffee; she was simply trying to work out why he was standing there. But now,

she pours some in a mug and asks the usual, because why not:
"Do you take milk or sugar?"

"It's such a good question. Do you?"

"Sometimes."

"What does that mean, sometimes?"

"It means, if there's milk and sugar available, then yes, I add
it. But if it's not, then I'll still drink. Black, even, if I need to."

"I *love* it," he breathes, like she's said the most amazing thing
ever. His eyes are two black Saturns, a thin rim of surrounding
blue. "What are you going to do now? Like, what if the milk and
sugar are across the room? Does it have to be right next to the
coffeepot for you to use it? Is there a spatial cutoff point of no
return?"

Is he flirting with her, or just high as a kite? She shifts her
weight from one foot to the next. She doesn't find him attractive
in the slightest, but he's clearly some sort of member who's just
spent the night, and for that reason she has to tread carefully.
"I'm just gonna go with black today," she says, after a pause.

"Ah, I'll do that, too, then. Well, cheers," he says, lifting his
mug.

She quickly pours herself a cup and holds it up.

"Cheers."

"Are you gonna come back to bed?" he asks.

She sputters on her drink. "What?"

Just then, Rose enters the room, having donned a new pair of
khakis. She instantly straightens when she spots Oliver. "Oh, Oliver. I didn't realize you were up. Can I get you something?"

Wait—this is Oliver? The guy in charge around here? The one
who got involved with Jerry's sister?

"No, we're all set, thanks, Rose." He smiles at Rose with a
lazy easiness.

We're *all set*?

Rose looks back and forth between the two of them. "I see you've met our newest hire, *Taylor*. Is she helping you with everything you need?"

Oliver's jaw hardens as he realizes his mistake. He takes a long, slow sip of his coffee, and Taylor looks down at her shoes like they are the most interesting thing in the world. "Yes, she sure is," he says.

The door slowly creaks open as an unfamiliar young girl now pads her way into the kitchen. She's scraggly haired and barefoot, with just a bedsheet wrapped around her. "Babe? I didn't know where you went."

Rose quickly escapes to the opposite end of the kitchen, busying herself with putting away the dishes on the drying rack, and Taylor follows suit, her cheeks aflame with embarrassment.

◆——○——◆

"I didn't think I'd have to tell you this, but you shouldn't fraternize with the members, Taylor," Rose later chides her, after they've finished an organizational sweep of the downstairs kitchen. They are making their way through the foyer, heading toward Canton's Restaurant.

Taylor spies a few men gathering in the parlor, but Rose zooms past so swiftly that Taylor can't get much more than a quick look. There was a handsome man who might have been Peter, but his hair looked shorter than she'd remembered from her interview.

"I wasn't fraternizing with a member," Taylor says. "He came in and asked for coffee. So, I got it for him."

"Especially *him*. That's Oliver. The soon-to-be head of the Knox." Rose puffs up as she says this last bit, as if she's proud.

"Okay." Meanwhile, Taylor's thinking to herself, *How can*

that guy be in charge of anything? He looks more like the type who used to roll into my ER at three o'clock in the morning.

As they climb the stairs, Rose adds, with a steely-eyed look, "You should maintain a respectful distance."

Taylor resists the urge to roll her eyes. Rose reminds her a little of an old-school nurse she used to work with who would rise from her chair whenever a doctor came into the room. "Oliver thought I was someone else," she mutters.

They are about to enter Canton's when Rose stops suddenly, putting an ice-cold hand on Taylor's arm. She leans down to whisper in Taylor's ear, "It's just that too many girls have gotten lost here through the years. I don't want that to happen to you."

THE KNOX

Do I recall the girls to whom Rose is referring? Yes—and no. There was nothing particularly distinguishing about them, other than the depths of their faux pas. So many passed through me with fairy-tale eyes and pedestrian clothes. They wanted to mingle with the members as if they belonged, sip high-end champagne whose names they couldn't pronounce. One once lapped up the beurre blanc—meant to accompany the poached salmon—as if it were a bowl of soup. They aspired to marry rich so they could take up residence in my bedrooms—and they engaged in varying degrees of depravities.

They were foolish, the whole lot of them. You don't *become* old money—that's why it's *old money*.

It was rather considerate of Rose to warn Taylor—and unlike Rose, really—but we shall see if Taylor heeds her advice. She does strike me as slightly different: quieter, more reserved. And far more curious than she ought to be.

I caught Taylor lurking the other day outside my windows. When Jerry departed with the items he procured from my basement, she followed him.

They both haven't the faintest clue about what's among the items.

I can still recall with utter delight, like it was yesterday, the sheath of the knife slicing through the woman's body with admirable surgical precision. The skin pulling apart like a piece of cheap rubber. The crackling of the bones as they were extracted. The blood that pooled generously, freely, like the Charles River.

Jerry and Taylor are in for a treat. *My* bones creak just thinking about it.

VIVIAN

February

Vivian is meeting Peter at the Knox for dinner. He's back from his alleged trip to Milan.

When she rings the bell, good ole Rose opens the door.

"Good evening," Vivian says.

Rose, of course, says nothing. She simply nods and holds the door open.

Vivian hesitates before entering. She has a moment of unexplained apprehension. She's never believed in spirits, but there's something about the Knox that suddenly feels haunting. Maybe it's due to those autopsies in the basement Rachel told her about.

Ahead in the foyer, awaiting her arrival, is Peter. He looks handsome, and her unease washes away. He is more casually dressed than usual, in a navy blazer and pair of dark jeans. Is she overdressed? Beneath her camel coat she's wearing a silk cream blouse and a brown leather tea-length skirt. She supposes it's better to be overdressed than under.

It's so much easier to focus on the small things in life, she finds herself thinking, which begs the question: Is this how her mother operated all those years?

Vivian crosses the threshold, brushing past Rose. She's looking at Peter and not down at the ground, so she doesn't realize until too late that she's stepped in something sticky. Gum, perhaps?

Frowning, she stops short and turns the bottom of her Louboutin heel up. She's about to reach down and scrape it off, when Rose barks, "No, no, don't touch it. Just keep moving forward, off the mat, please."

Vivian obliges, and when she looks, Rose is bent over on the ground, tearing a large sheet of paper from the mat's surface. Rose gently cups her hands beneath the sheet, as if it's sacred, not allowed to touch the ground, like an American flag, and offers it to Michael, who appears out of the shadows.

"Michael?" Vivian asks, tilting her head. "What is this?"

"I'm sorry, Ms. L—Vivian, you need to stand here for a minute and wait. Don't go in any further. Knox policy," Michael says apologetically. He disappears with the sheet down the hall.

Rose stands there, like a security guard. Vivian resists the urge to roll her eyes. She looks ahead again at Peter, who now leans against the old-fashioned mailbox system lining the foyer wall. He holds up his index finger, meaning, *Wait.* Then he encircles his hands around his mouth, and loudly shouts, in a joking manner, "Hello, beautiful!"

Vivian can't help but laugh. "What on earth is going on? What are we waiting for?" She shrugs out of her coat, and, almost reluctantly, Rose takes it from her.

"Geomancy," Peter answers, now in a normal tone. "All first-time guests have to pass the test."

"Well, I've heard of a geometry test, but not a geomancy

test," Vivian jokes. "Also, I'm not exactly a first-time guest. I was already here. For tea and the party? And . . ." *And our little sleepover*, she wants to add but doesn't. Not in front of Rose.

"Parties have a different protocol. As for the tea, that was my bad. And, well . . ." Peter winks at her. She knows he's thinking of the third time she was there. "Sorry, darling, it's just a formality and will take only a minute."

She likes the way *darling* sounds. "What if I don't pass?"

"You will."

Rose makes a tsking noise, and Vivian refuses to look at her. She's in a locked gaze with Peter. She likes admiring him from this distance. The heat between them is already building. It feels surprisingly sexy, having this conversation across a foyer. Like two teenagers sharing a moment from opposite ends of the school dance floor.

He's so effortlessly good-looking, it's as if he's just stepped out of a Peter Millar catalog. Sometimes Vivian still can't believe that he's hers.

Or is he?

She hasn't decided yet if she's going to bring up seeing him in the street a couple of days earlier. *If* that was even him.

She was off her game that day. The more she thinks about it, she realizes she may have been mistaken. She was clearly still reeling from the stress of seeing Xavier's empty shop. Not to mention everything she's had going on with her mother and her spiraling finances. It's enough to make anyone a little out of sorts.

"Nice outfit." His gaze travels up and down her, slowly.

"Thank you." This time, she stashed an extra shirt in her handbag. "How was Milan?"

A shadow passes over his face. "Fine." Then he adds, "Busy. The trip took a little bit of an unexpected detour."

A waiter, the wrestler guy—Jerry, if she recalls correctly—

walks by with a tray of drinks. She thought he was toast, given his scuffle with Oliver about his sister. Maybe Oliver's not around.

As Jerry passes Peter, he accidentally drops a stack of cocktail napkins, one of which lands directly next to Peter's foot. Jerry bends down to place the tray on the ground while he quickly gathers them up. Peter makes no move to help. Instead, he stands as still as a statue, his eyes trained on Vivian. Like an invisible cord is connecting them.

"Sorry, sir," Jerry mumbles.

"It's quite all right, Jerry," Peter says.

Michael reenters the foyer, sans the paper. He nods affirmatively at Peter and Rose. Then, in a soft voice, as if he's embarrassed, he says, "I'm sorry again, Vivian. You're welcome to enter now. Can I get you a drink?"

"I've got it, Michael," Peter interrupts, striding over. The moment he takes her arm in his, her head spins. He leads her into what she thinks is the direction of the parlor, but given how he makes her feel, he could be leading her into a lion's den right now, and she'd still follow.

◈────◦────◈

"So, it was a good work trip?" Vivian asks. They are indeed in the parlor, sitting on a love seat on the far side of the room, opposite from where they had tea. A few people mingle around them, and more members are filtering in by the minute, drinks in hand. Apparently, predinner cocktails are a Knox Saturday evening must.

She studies Peter carefully, waiting for his response.

"It was a fruitful few days, yes," he replies, sidestepping her question. At least he's not outwardly lying. Perhaps he's waiting for a more discreet place to talk with her? She *hopes*.

"Do you know what geomancy is?" he suddenly asks.

"I've heard of it," she says. She's not about to admit that she googled it after the masquerade ball.

"Geomancy literally translates to 'earth divination,' but I think worldly divination makes more sense. It's a practice based on the belief that there are divine messages one can interpret from the markings on the ground; it's about harnessing the world's energy. But you don't even need to make ground markings; some people use a coin flip, or a roll of dice. Something to generate an even or odd number, which translates to one or two dots. Those dots form the geomantic figures that are subsequently interpreted."

At the word "dots," Vivian is reminded of what Rachel had said: *Dr. Thurgood wanted to leave a trail so someone—like us—could connect the dots.*

"Oh . . . That's interesting," Vivian replies, shaking off the memory. "And one performs a geomancy reading to answer a yes or no question?"

"Yes, but the answer is more nuanced. Nonbinary, sort of like a tarot card reading."

"And a Magic 8 Ball," she teases.

"It is decidedly so," he quips back. "In all seriousness, though, here at the Knox, we're old-school. We use the ground markings. It's what William Knox, our founder, used to practice back in the day."

"So he was the one who introduced it?"

"Yes. Some people believe William Knox became interested in it because of his dealings with the Chinese merchants, who practiced feng shui, which is different from geomancy but does share similar underlying principles. Others think he was exposed to it by European sea merchants during his travels. Geomancy was, after all, one of the most popular forms of divination during the Renaissance. At any rate, he became an ardent believer in geomancy and made it part of our Knox fabric."

Vivian sips her martini. It tastes surprisingly good, given her hangover the last time she drank them. "So, when I walked through that sticky tape, you 'read,' or interpreted, the markings my shoes left?"

"Close. We used the debris from your footprint to . . . Well, I won't bore you with the details. Suffice to say we vetted you in a geomancy reading per proper Knox protocol. And *I* wasn't the one doing the reading or, as they say, casting the shield chart. I'm not schooled in it. But others are, like Michael."

Jerry walks by and offers them sparkling water, which Vivian wisely takes but Peter declines with a dismissive wave.

"Geomancy has always been used with our decision-making here at the Knox," Peter continues, and adds, somewhat slyly, as if showing off, "You might be surprised to learn about how it's shaped not only the Knox but Boston as well."

"What do you mean?"

"Well, perhaps the 'unplanned' pattern of Boston's streets was not so unplanned after all."

Boston is known for its windy, confusing streets that make no sense on a map.

"I thought the streets followed old cow paths," she says, frowning.

"That is the rumor," he says with a smile, not elaborating further.

Vivian suddenly feels uncomfortable. Does he mean the Knox, and geomancy, are responsible for the layout of Boston? If true, the Knox's reach—and mystery—is much deeper than she'd realized. In her direct view is the glass display case with the cryptic scroll. What *is* that thing? She thought she'd known what she was getting into when she started this quest, but she's now realizing that she has no idea about the intricacies of this society. Occult practices, basement autopsies, her ancestor's missing body . . . What is this place really about?

And who, exactly, is Peter?

Vivian is used to her mother acting like a snob to the hired help, but even her mother, Vivian thinks, would've picked up a napkin that landed next to her foot.

"What's with the scroll?" she asks, nodding toward it.

A few people stroll by—the room is filling up quickly—and Peter waits until they are alone again to answer. "That's the Heart of the Knox."

"Okay. . . . And what does that mean?"

"The scroll contains the names of all the members of the Knox. We unroll it once a year, on initiation night, to transcribe new members. That is, if we have new members. Sometimes we don't, so we skip a year. Then we wait three hundred and sixty-five days, as we follow the lunar calendar, to hold another initiation."

"I see." She refrains from making a snide comment, like *I'm glad you follow the same calendar that we all do.* She eyes the scroll, which is wound in a burgundy velvet cover with a series of mysterious dots on it. Likely geomancy symbols, she now realizes. Interesting. One of the patterns reminds her of Peter's wrist tattoo.

But it's what's inside the sheath that she finds much more interesting. How many of her ancestors are transcribed on that scroll? Rachel would have a field day with this. "That's a pretty valuable square foot of real estate right there," she remarks.

"Yes, it is. And it's heavily secured," he adds.

"I don't doubt it. So the new members are the so-called heart of the Knox?"

"*All* the members are the heart, of course." Peter gestures to his chest. "Sometimes we call that scroll 'the Lungs,' too. Because the members are what breathe life into the Knox."

"I see. Where's the head, then?"

She's joking, but he answers her seriously, pointing to the ceiling with a slender finger. "We have two other scrolls. The one directly above, which we call the 'Brains.'" He extends his finger downward. "And the 'Bowels' scroll."

"Let me guess. The Brains are the rules of the Knox, and the Bowels are its sins."

"Not bad. The Brains are indeed a scribe of our ancient ways, our beliefs. Our handbook, so to speak."

"And the Bowels?"

He seems hesitant to answer, but finally says, "It's the members' allegiance to the Knox."

"What does that mean, their allegiance?"

"You know," Peter says, after a beat, "for some reason I always tell you things that I shouldn't."

"Oh?" she replies, but inside she's thinking, *Tell me about "Milan," then.*

Suddenly, loud laughter erupts from the other end of the room, and people turn to look. Oliver enters, bent over and gasping, as if he's just heard the funniest thing.

Vivian glances around for Jerry, given their brawl, but he's hightailed it in the other direction. Smart boy.

She takes another sip of her martini, a longer one. Being in the same vicinity as Oliver is not exactly soothing. She hopes he doesn't make his way toward them, but Peter is already gesturing him over.

Vivian sinks back in the sofa.

"Hello, Peter. And it's the famous Vivien Leigh, right?" Oliver says, when he reaches them. He's wearing a gold shimmery tracksuit, like he's just left a Studio 54 party. His cheeks are hollow, his long, greasy hair tucked behind his ears.

"Vivian Lawrence," Peter replies. "And far prettier than any movie star."

"Hello, Oliver," Vivian says.

"You know my name." He grins at Peter. "She knows my name." He clearly doesn't remember that she bore witness to his little scrap. He slides into the chair opposite them.

Christ.

"What are you doing here, chap?" Peter asks. "I thought given—well, I thought you were planning to stay at the Mansion for a while."

"It's so much more exciting here. I just don't want to miss the action," Oliver says with a laugh, his jacket glittering as the light catches it.

"Well, it's good to see you looking so well," Peter remarks. Vivian doesn't think Oliver looks "well" in the slightest, but who is she to say?

"Yes, incredible what a few days removed from stress does." Then, he pops up abruptly, like the release of a tightly wound spring. He waves to someone behind them, and a few seconds later, a familiar-looking man approaches.

Vivian is so surprised that she nearly chokes on an olive. Her eyes water as she bends forward in a coughing fit. When she is finally able to compose herself, she meets the man's gaze.

It's *Xavier.*

"Are you okay, or should I fetch the house doctor?" Peter asks, offering her a glass of water.

"Yes," Vivian manages. "I mean—no. I'm fine." She takes the glass but then immediately sets it down.

"Are you sure? I saw him around earlier. He's somewhere."

"I'm fine," Vivian repeats, and turns her gaze again to Xavier.

"Hello, I'm Xavier," Xavier says, immediately stepping forward to offer his hand to Vivian. As she takes it, he gives her a firm squeeze and the subtlest of head shakes. He's skinnier than usual, his face gaunt, brown corduroys hanging loosely on his hips. His familiar pocket watch dangles from his trouser pocket. "Nice to meet you," he adds.

"Uh, hi. I'm Vivian."

Why is Xavier pretending not to know her?

"Hello, Xavier," Peter says.

"Peter," Xavier acknowledges.

Wait, they know each other?

Oliver slings his arm around Xavier in a suggestive sort of way. Is Xavier here with Oliver?

"So, what do you do, Vivian?" Oliver asks.

"I have an antiques store." *That your friend Xavier here likes to visit.*

Oliver raises an eyebrow. "Antiques store? Cool." He turns to look at Xavier. "Don't you sell antiques, too, like old jewelry?"

"A little, but I mostly sell nineteen-karat gold," Xavier mumbles.

"Oh yeah? How's that going for you?" Oliver asks, with an almost wicked smile. The spiderweb of broken glass at Xavier's storefront flashes through Vivian's mind.

"Vivian's responsible for some of the antiques in the Knox," Peter remarks.

Oliver glances around, his eyes shifting like a video game graphic. "Cool. Did you get that elephant statue? I love that thing." He means the ceramic elephant side table.

"No, I didn't." She considers adding that it's a reproduction but decides against it.

"Too bad. You should've. You know, I rode an elephant in Thailand, when I was living over there. If you ever want to feel small, ride an elephant." He nods at Peter. "I like this one, even if she doesn't like elephants. Big improvement from Lindsay."

Vivian stiffens.

"Are you meeting your father for dinner?" Peter asks, ignoring the comment.

It's not a funny question, but for some reason it makes Oliver howl. Meanwhile, Xavier looks down at the ground, as if he'd rather be anywhere else in the world.

"That I am," Oliver says, when he catches his breath between gasps. Then he leans down to clasp Peter's shoulder. "Listen, we need to have a chat later. Xavier here has finally made things a little easier for us, with the Customs clearance."

Peter gives a warning with a sight shake of his head. There's an awkward silence. It seems that although Peter likes to tell her some things he shouldn't, there are still plenty of things he's happy to keep to himself.

"Sorry, Peter, I—" Oliver says, realizing his mistake.

"Many thanks, Xavier," Peter cuts in. "We appreciate your assistance." Then to Oliver, he says, "We can discuss later."

Xavier colors, looking distinctly uncomfortable. He won't meet Vivian's eyes.

Why would they need a Customs clearance? And how could *Xavier* help them with it? What is going with her friend? It's almost like Oliver has some sort of hold over him.

A chime begins ringing repeatedly through the air; Rose is walking through the room, shaking a crystal dinner bell.

"Ah, dinnertime," Oliver says, like it's the most normal thing in the world.

Peter rises, and Vivian follows suit. "Sorry about Oliver," Peter whispers in her ear. "He's a piece of work sometimes."

The four make their way past the scroll and to the hall amid the crowd. Peter stops periodically to say hello to people, with

Vivian politely smiling by his side. She's distracted, though, searching for Xavier. She sees him reappear and then disappear, like a magic trick.

The crowd slowly ascends the grand stairs, en route to Canton's Restaurant, and Vivian's momentarily distracted by the incredible art gallery wall. There's a Laura Schiff Bean painting of a dress; she owns one of these herself. And then a Van Gogh, alongside a Chinese reverse-glass painting and a Damien Hirst print. Vivian has no doubt these are authentic. At the very top she spots a white minimalist abstract painting with deceptive dimension: textured rolls, peaks and valleys.

Her gaze is transfixed on the art; she is utterly engrossed, trying to absorb it all, and she missteps, stumbles. Peter grabs her.

"Be careful. You don't want to be falling down these stairs."

She looks behind her, taking in the unforgiving, steep staircase. "I'm fine," she replies, a little embarrassed. Christ, she needs to be more careful.

They step onto the landing and continue down a hallway lined with misshapen modern stone bubbles. She believes it's the same artist who did the white textured minimalist painting. The artist's name is on the tip of her tongue. Vivian read recently about the auction of her work at Sotheby's; there was some piece that went for 6.2 million dollars. Maybe this is the one.

And all this, Vivian supposes, is what sets the Knox apart from other private clubs. The furniture and decor in a span of a few feet is worth more than what a Wall Street banker might make in a good year. Depending on the area in the Knox, perhaps an entire banking firm's annual profits.

She *needs* to establish her family link. There's clearly enough wealth to go around. And around. And around.

She recalls what Rachel had said to her: *You could just marry Peter.*

It would be neat and tidy, wouldn't it, to marry Peter? But the problem is, she doesn't think she knows the real him—not yet, at least.

And he doesn't know the real her.

The unease Vivian felt before entering the Knox premises has returned.

Peter moves ahead to converse with someone down the hall, and again she spots Xavier. He's leaning alone against an unadorned patch of wall, a miserable look on his face.

She sidles up, and when she's sure no one is looking, she asks, "So, you want to tell me what's going on?"

Xavier casts a furtive look around before meeting her gaze. She's struck by how small his pupils look, like tiny stars nearly lost in the night. He mutters, at the bottom of his breath, "Not now. I'll . . . I'll leave you a note in the mailbox downstairs. Number thirty-four."

TAYLOR

There's a different energy that day, with the Knox members having returned from their retreat. An electricity.

"The initiation," the diners utter several times, as Taylor refills their water glasses. For once, Rose has allowed her to stick around for the Canton lunch crowd, even though she can't fully wait tables yet. That's perfectly fine with her; it's not like Taylor needs to earn tips, after all.

Instead, she replaces silverware that gets dropped, buses plates and drinks.

The initiation. It must be upcoming—and the reason for the charge in the air.

One of the chefs asks Taylor to show him the plates returned with uneaten portions, but the diners—all men today—are mostly licking their plates clean. *Gathering their energy for the initiation?*

She keeps a lookout for Peter; to her disappointment, he doesn't show. But Oliver does, arriving in a silk Cuban-style shirt and khakis. He's jittery, spilling his wine and then his water glass. Taylor wonders if the girl wearing the sheet has crawled back into his bed or been ushered out.

Luckily for Taylor, Oliver doesn't give any of the help a second glance.

Jerry seems to be eyeing him, though, a big scowl contorting his face.

For a moment, while no one is looking, Taylor pauses in the dining room with her eyes closed. Given the expensive quality of the Italian suits most of the men wear and the honest-to-goodness Rolexes shimmering on their wrists, there's likely enough Black Amexes here to buy a small country. What if she were here as a diner, not an employee? Then Jerry jostles her—intentionally?— and she slips back into the kitchen.

One might argue that it's really here, in the kitchen, where she belongs. Here, with the heat of the stove and the chatter of the cooks, most of whom barely give her a glance. Here, where she could so easily fade into the familiar: the repetitive chop of knives, the sizzles of meats on the grill. The intense aroma of garlic, onion, butter. Sweat.

All that's missing is the fried seafood, and, of course, her dad himself.

She wonders where he is right now: in his own restaurant, frying up a catfish or hush puppy? Drinking a Diet Coke like water? She knows Aunt Gigi told him about her waitressing gig because he called and didn't leave a voicemail like he *always* does. So, it's her move now. But she'd rather wait until he receives the check in the mail. Then, she's hoping, he won't be disappointed. Or won't be *as* disappointed.

Jerry enters the kitchen, dropping a dirty plate in the metal industrial sink with a loud clank. She catches his eye and nods. He makes his way over to her.

"What?" he says.

"Hi to you, too."

"Yeah, fine. What's up?"

She studies him. His face is red, like a sunburn.

She's looking at all her fellow employees more closely, trying to figure out who might be behind the note. So far they seem to be treating her mostly with the same indifference; Jerry might seem a little more moody than usual, but given Oliver's appearance, perhaps that's to be expected.

"I heard back from my landlord," she says.

"And?"

"She spoke to Nicholas, the bookstore owner of Turned Pages. He's expecting us; he said we could come by today."

"We?"

"Yeah, we."

"I'll just run the books over later."

Taylor narrows her eyes. "Fine, but remember our deal."

"I remember," he grumbles. "What about the other stuff? The doctor's kit?"

Oh, right. She's supposed to be following up on that, too. And Taylor would—that is, if she could. "I, uh, we haven't heard back from the antiques store owner. Just hold on to those for now."

"All right."

Later, after the lunch crowd clears, Rose stands surveying the emptied restaurant with a satisfied look on her face, like a proud mother hen.

Like a shoemaker's elves, they get to work cleaning the restaurant. Liam clears the bar; the rest of them bus the tables.

Taylor is picking a stray napkin from beneath a table when she sees a man's legs briskly stride into Canton's. Navy pressed trousers, horse bit tan loafers.

Peter.

She nearly bumps her head trying to scramble out.

But it's not Peter. It's a man who looks nothing like him. What was she thinking? The person is tall, almost too tall. All arms and legs, like a human Gumby. But he's one of *them,* clearly. The loafers look like top-grain leather, and a paisley silk pocket square peeks out of his navy suit jacket.

"Hello, Rose," the man says. "And Liam, Eduardo, Jerry," he acknowledges with a nod.

They nod back, and he turns to Taylor. "Hello, Taylor, I'm Michael," he says, rather stiffly. He's frowning, as if he doesn't know what to make of her. Finally, he says, "Welcome to the Knox."

This must be the Michael they said may have done her geomancy-reading thing. She's never seen him before in her life; she'd remember.

"Hello," she replies. "Nice to meet you." She's standing there awkwardly; does she shake his hand? But he hasn't extended it.

"I'm sorry I wasn't here last week. Did anyone tell you you've joined us at an interesting time?"

She can feel Liam watching closely from the bar. "Uh, yeah," she says.

"We are happy to have someone join us who has a restaurant background. Though this is quite different from North Carolina. It must be a bit of a cultural shock."

"It's okay." *It's okay?* She internally cringes, wishing she'd offered something more interesting.

"She's doing well," Rose says, coming to stand beside them with a look of pride that now extends to Taylor.

Taylor shrugs, but she's pleased. "I'm trying."

"That's what I've heard. Keep it up," says Michael. The way he's studying her, as if she were a math equation, makes Taylor feel like he knows more about her than he's letting on. Did he somehow uncover her nursing background? Is he the one behind the note?

"I'll try."

"Great. I've no doubt you will. Rose, a word, please," he says, and Rose follows him out into the hall.

Taylor begins gathering ketchup bottles from the tables and carrying them to the bar, to be refilled from a giant jug of ketchup.

"I'm trying," Liam says in a high-pitched voice, imitating her. She shoots him a dirty look across the bar.

"Relax, New Girl, I'm joking." He polishes a glass.

She gathers more ketchup bottles, careful to avoid the corner of the room where Eduardo and Jerry stand in a deep conversation. Jerry's holding his head, like he's upset; Eduardo lays a gentle hand on his back.

When she brings the additional ketchup bottles to the bar, Liam says, "They're having a lover's quarrel, probably."

"Oh?" So there *is* something between Eduardo and Jerry.

"Either that, or O'Doyle's pissed because Oliver's back."

"Jerry holds grudges, huh?"

"Yeah." Liam holds a glass up to the light, checking for smudges. "But Jerry's not the only one less than pleased with Oliver."

"No?"

"No. Some people around here don't care for him." He returns the glass to the shelf and picks up another.

"Why?" Taylor recalls Oliver's long, greasy hair. The high-as-a-kite conversation they had earlier on in the kitchen. "I mean, other than the obvious."

Liam pauses, and when he replies, he does so in a low voice.

"Oliver wants to bring the Knox back a few decades, centuries maybe, to how it once was. In fact, it's already underway."

"What does that even mean?"

"Well, New Girl, that's . . . for another time. But, not everyone agrees with this direction."

A rift. This makes sense. She can feel it, she thinks. She didn't her first week, but here, today, she does. It's a slow-building tension: the minute hand rather than the second hand ticking around the clock. Maybe, in fact, she misinterpreted the charge in the air. Maybe it's tension.

"Rose seems to like Oliver," Taylor points out.

Liam gives a short, sarcastic laugh. "In case you haven't noticed, Rose likes the Knox. And Oliver's about to officially assume the reins at the initiation, so . . ."

"Gotcha. So what do you think?"

"About what?"

"About Oliver, about the direction the Knox is going in? All of it, I guess?"

Liam's mouth twists into a slow, unreadable smile. "I think we do what we have to do."

Taylor notices his use of "we." Liam is a bartender here, not a member. But perhaps this is the difference between her and her coworkers. They *do* feel like a part of the Knox; it's their place of employment, yes, but it's also their life. They date each other; some even live next door. It's like a cult. Besides, she reminds herself, Liam is no ordinary bartender; Peter brought him over from England.

"Why don't you live next door, with the others?" she asks, suddenly.

"I used to, but I like my space. I live at Harbor125 in East Boston. It's not as convenient as living next door, but I wouldn't trade it. You live alone?"

"Yeah," she admits, and immediately wishes she hadn't.

"Do you have a boyfriend?"

Ugh. "Yes," she's quick to fib.

Liam throws a hand towel over his shoulder and leans across the bar counter, now giving her his full attention. "That's a shame. So, what do you do for fun? When you're not working here?"

Before she can answer, a familiar voice rings out from across the room: "I've been looking for you."

This time, it really *is* Peter. His five-o'clock shadow and quilted coat thrown over a dark pair of jeans make him look ruggedly handsome. A lopsided grin spreads across his face as he strides into the room, making her heart speed up. The same darn response she had during the interview.

"Hi, Peter," Liam calls out.

Meanwhile, Taylor can't help but grin back, even if she's not the one he's looking for.

The closer he gets, the more her body physically reacts. Her heart feels like it's entered a horse race; it's galloping so fast. She's stupidly holding a ketchup bottle in her hand, so she sets it down on the counter, and it promptly topples over.

She tries to right it, but her hand is like jelly, and the bottle falls over once again. Then Peter's hand is there, brushing against hers as he firmly sets the ketchup down.

"There you go," he says, with a laugh.

"Thanks," she returns.

Peter is like a magnet; Eduardo and Jerry have drifted over, and they all stand there in a wide-berth circle.

"I've been looking for you," Peter says again, but he's looking at Taylor. Or is he? She swivels to check behind her, but no one's there.

"Me?" she says, and she can see the surprise on Liam's face, too.

"You. The Cam Newton fan. Rose said you were in here. I wanted to see how your first week went." He smiles.

"It, uh, it went well," she says, her voice cracking like a pubescent teenager's.

"I'm glad to hear it. Any questions, you can ask one of these fine fellows. Right, guys?"

The lot of them begin nodding, like this has been what they've been doing all along.

Hmph.

"Great. I will," she says.

"You know, I was thinking about your reaction to that painting of the girl on the train," he says, like it's just the two of them, having a private conversation. "Now that you've been here a week, has your interpretation of the painting changed? What was it you said? 'She's just existing'?"

Taylor blinks. "I don't know," she answers honestly. "I'd have to look at it again."

"Well, let's do that at some point, shall we?"

She nods, searching for something—*anything*—interesting to respond with, but like usual, falls short.

"Peter," calls the tall man—Michael—from the doorway. "C'mon; they're waiting for us."

"Duty calls," Peter says, with a secretive smile. When he swooshes out of the restaurant, it feels like he's taken the air of the room with him.

With a prolonged sigh, Eduardo reaches out to pat Taylor's arm. "We're all a little in love with him," he says.

VIVIAN

February

What on earth is going on with Xavier? Vivian sits across from Peter in Canton's Restaurant, feeling troubled. She keeps looking around for her friend. Most of the dark tufted-leather seats are occupied, and a bartender buzzes behind the softly lit wooden bar, preparing rainbow-colored cocktails and vodka martinis. The back double door swings open and shut as Jerry and a few other waiters carry food from the kitchen.

She spots Oliver sitting by himself at a window table, likely awaiting his father.

But Xavier is nowhere to be found.

Vivian hopes he has gone to deposit the note and that she'll get some answers soon. By "mailbox downstairs," he must mean that antique mailbox ensconced in the dark foyer entrance, by the front door. She recalls seeing a few notes tucked inside its open mailbox slots. It's likely a messaging system of sorts that Knox members use to communicate with one another and reminds her of a wooden cabinet an elegant European hotel might use in its reception area to store old-fashioned room keys with attached tassels.

Could Xavier be a Knox member?

"Are you feeling okay?" Peter asks, pulling her out of her reverie. "You're quiet tonight."

"I'm fine. Sorry, I have a headache," she fibs.

"Drink some more water," he suggests, and he motions to someone behind Vivian's shoulder.

Rose approaches to fill their water glasses. She takes her time; she's deliberate. Vivian doesn't understand what her role is, exactly. She seems to always be underfoot. The number of staff at the Knox is, as far as Vivian can tell, fairly small. A lot of them multitask. It feels like this is a deliberate choice; they could afford to hire however many people they wanted to. But instead, there's a tight inner-circle vibe she's sensing. And clearly Rose, with her bright smile at Peter and then grim-faced look at Vivian, doesn't particularly love outsiders.

Too bad for Rose, Vivian isn't going anywhere. Besides, she is not as much of an outsider as Rose thinks.

Vivian fiddles with the menu, which doesn't show any prices. It's a gout-inducing meal if she ever saw one: Duxbury oysters, shrimp scampi, pan-seared foie gras. And that's just the apps. Meal options include duck and venison, trout and scallops. Thank goodness they have a salmon Caesar salad option. It's no wonder Graham had that heart attack.

"Better?" Peter asks, once they've ordered from a waiter who introduces himself as Eduardo, and Vivian has taken a few sips of her water.

She nods, and then promptly exchanges her water glass for her wineglass. They are drinking a 2018 Gaja Barbaresco, a bottle not listed on the wine menu. It's a favorite of Vivian's; something she mentioned to Peter at their dinner date. Did he have it stocked just for her?

"So what do you think?" Peter asks.

"Of the wine?"

Peter gestures around them. "The wine, the room, the place."

"The place, meaning the Knox?"

"Yes."

She glances around; the crowd is more sophisticated and European than Boston usually runs. But among the unfamiliar faces she spots a few Boston people in the know: Alina, the interior designer behind Wolf in Sheep Design, dining with her husband, Jay, of the legendary sneaker store Bodega. The head of the Brookline Hospital, who's been to her mother's house for fundraisers. Zoey, owner of the famed Gulmi Group PR company. A Massachusetts senator. Sal, the artistic director of Salon Mario Russo. Kate, from @BucketListBoston. Vivian feels almost comforted by this, the fact that there are people here who are real people, established people. But in the next breath it gives her pause. The Knox is a very connected place. Are these people Knox members, or guests? Does it matter?

Xavier has not yet reappeared.

"I think it's interesting. And I think it's interesting that you would ask me that, here."

He grins. "Why?"

She's starting to wonder if he's the type that gets off on pushing the envelope. A mile-high-clubber sort. The way he's always telling her things he shouldn't, and now, asking her here out in the open about the Knox.

"Do you know these people?" she asks.

"Some."

"Are they all members? Or are some guests?"

"It's a mix tonight," Peter says, as his eyes roam around the room.

"What about that guy who was with Oliver? What was his name, again?"

"Xavier?"

"Right. Is he a member?"

"No. Why do you ask?"

She shrugs, trying to seem nonchalant. "He reminds me of someone . . . but I can't put my finger on who."

"He's Oliver's boyfriend, so I know him a little."

"Oh." *Oooh.*

"Well, one of many boyfriends, really."

"At the masquerade ball, when the fight broke out, I thought someone said it was because Oliver got involved with the waiter's sister."

"He did. Women, men—Oliver doesn't discriminate." Peter gives a boyish grin.

"Do you do business with him? Oliver? I—I heard you mention something about Customs. I have some experience with that. Through my antiques store." She's prattling now, but she is desperate to pull more information about Xavier.

But he doesn't take the bait. "Ah, that makes sense. Where do you mostly import from?"

Suddenly, Vivian recalls the last time she saw her missing notebook of business contacts. It was the day Xavier came to visit her in her shop.

That notebook also contained her contacts for Customs agents.

A wealthy client of mine who recently became widowed is intent on acquiring an elephant ivory necklace, Xavier had said. *Perhaps you could connect me to your Customs contact?*

"I import from all over, really," she manages to respond. Is this all a coincidence, or did Xavier steal her notebook?

Oliver, still sitting by himself at a window table, suddenly leans back, eyes closed, as if he's taking a short nap. He's a hot mess, that one.

Fear suddenly clutches Vivian's heart. Has Xavier relapsed? Is that what's going on?

Their appetizers arrive: a half dozen oysters and an off-menu caviar that Vivian didn't hear Peter order. She is quiet while they polish off the oysters, whose taste she's not even registering. Instead, she's thinking of how Xavier's pupils looked suspiciously small.

"What else are you thinking in that beautiful head of yours?" Peter prods.

What isn't she thinking? would be the better question. But she says nothing, only shaking her head.

"Ask me anything," Peter says, staring intently at her.

"Excuse me?"

"Ask me anything right now, anything in the world, and I'll answer you truthfully."

"Anything?"

"Anything."

What is going on with Xavier and Oliver? Would you still care for me if you knew my true intentions? What are my true intentions? Why didn't you pick up that cocktail napkin that Jerry dropped?

Who is the blue-haired woman?

Who are you?

The problem is that she can't ask any of the questions she really wants to. So she picks one that will test his trust in her. "Downstairs," she says carefully, "you said that members' allegiance to the Knox is inscribed on the scroll in the basement called the 'Bowels'?"

Peter nods. "Yes?"

"So, what does that mean?"

"Ah," he says, folding his arms. "Smart question. You want to know how they ensnared me." He says this so matter-of-factly that she almost wants to deny it. But why? It's true.

"Yes," she admits.

"I had to confess my deepest, darkest secret."

Vivian laughs, because clearly, it's a joke, but a pained expression suddenly rips across his face.

"You don't think I have secrets?" he asks, sounding almost injured.

Damn, well, you do. Too many for my liking, in fact. But the secrets she's currently thinking of don't seem to match those he's now recalling. She studies him; his face remains raw, laying bare something long buried. It's the same look he gets whenever he mentions his childhood.

"We all have secrets," she replies carefully.

"True. But some worse than others. As I've mentioned, I was an orphan. My mother—she had a car accident, and . . . Well, after that, I was put in foster care." He takes a jagged breath. "And there were things I had to do, to survive."

She nods, and says softly, "I understand."

He places his hands on the table, his fingers digging into the white tablecloth so hard the tips go white. "But do you? Do you really, Vivian? Tell me."

It catches her off guard, this intensity—this scrutiny—so she smiles and attempts a joke. "So, what, sharing of secrets is some sort of Knox member-bonding exercise? A team-building experience, like a trust fall?"

But Peter doesn't return her smile. "Do you want to know what secrets *really* are, Vivian? They're chips to bargain with; they're influence; they're ownership. If I know the worst thing you've ever done—something no one else knows—then I hold a power over you. Some might say I might even own you."

What are they even talking about anymore? Secrets? Power? Sex? He's so damn hot; a charge rises between them, like heat waves off a pavement. "What if I haven't done anything that bad?" she replies in a low, sultry voice.

He holds her gaze for a moment, and then he erupts in laughter. His demeanor instantly changes, his face loosening like a slack rubber band. "Well, maybe you wouldn't be the best candidate for the Knox." He winks and takes a long pull of his wine.

A hush falls over the crowd, and Peter's attention shifts to somewhere beyond Vivian's shoulder. She turns to see an elderly man being ushered across the restaurant. He's wearing dark jeans and a dress shirt. Brown loafers on his feet. Grayish-white hair crowns his head, and a pair of wire-rimmed spectacles rest on his nose. He uses a cane to walk; its elegant wooden base is topped with an ivory-horn handle carved in the shape of a flower head.

The way people are acting, it's as if British royalty has just entered the room. Adoration on faces, hands reaching out when he passes, eager to simply touch the clothing the man wears.

As he settles into his seat, opposite Oliver, the man nods back at Peter and then gives Vivian such a discerning look she feels like he's looking through to her insides.

It's the man she saw in the courtyard, from the guest bedroom window.

"Graham," Peter confirms, in a low voice, once Graham's attention has turned elsewhere. "This is the first time he's out and about since the heart attack."

Gluttonous King Henry VIII himself, Vivian thinks, but says, "Glad to see he's doing better."

Peter wears a displeased look, as if he himself may not be as glad.

A low level of chatter resumes throughout the restaurant.

Jerry the wrestler clears their appetizers, and then a few seconds later, Eduardo swoops in with their entrées. "Can I get you anything else?" Eduardo asks, but Vivian barely registers what he asks.

Because the girl with the blue hair has just entered the restaurant.

TAYLOR

As Taylor walks home from work, she keeps replaying the way Peter sought her out. How he wanted to know about her first week. Her opinion on the painting. How he'd thought of her. It makes her feel tingly and alive—and she wants to tell someone.

Sam should be back by now from his Miami weekend.

Taylor knocks on his door a few times. When Sam finally answers, he keeps the door only partially open.

"Hey," he says, with a grin. "How you doing?" Meanwhile, he points inside his apartment and mouths, *Miami Boy*.

Oh. Apparently while Sam was done with Miami, he wasn't done with Miami.

"I'm good," Taylor replies, smiling. She waits; this is where he invites her in, has her meet Miami Boy. Where the three of them crack open a bottle or two of wine and order takeout.

"Good," Sam repeats. "Sorry, can I . . . Can we talk later?" He jerks his head to the side, meaning, *I'm busy*. Or, rather, We're *busy*.

"Yeah, yeah, of course."

"You need anything? Everything go okay at work today? The members got back from their retreat, yeah?"

She pauses. She really wants to talk with him—not only about seeing Peter, but also the "go back to nursing" note she received. Rose's comment about the lost girls, which keeps bobbing to the surface of Taylor's mind. And maybe, just maybe, about Vivian. Sam still has no idea the woman even exists. But he's standing there with that silly grin on his face, his thoughts clearly drifting to the man waiting inside his apartment. So she says, "Yeah, everything's fine. Y'all have fun."

"Thanks."

He's happy, so she should be happy for him. And she is, but she's also jealous. No—that's not the right word. She's something; what is it?

Lonely. She's lonely.

No—that's not it either. She's not lonely, she's *alone.*

It's not a bad sensation; it's not a good sensation, either. It's a familiar one, if anything.

After her mom left, Taylor spent hours, weeks—years—of her childhood alone. At her dad's restaurant, in his office, she'd pore over fashion magazines that his waitstaff brought, once they realized how much she liked them. She'd cut out pictures of beautiful models wearing beautiful clothes, just like her mom. She'd build collage after collage of fancy people and fancy houses, taping up the busy posterboards around her room until there wasn't any wall space left. Until the alone feeling was neutralized, like a positive ion meeting its negative counterpart.

Now, settling into her bed, Taylor opens up a fashion podcast and closes her eyes. Sinking into the alone.

But then her phone pings with a text. Taylor checks to see who it's from: Aunt Gigi. Her aunt has finally decided to respond to Taylor's reveal that she's working at the Knox.

T.J., we need to talk. It's very
important.

Taylor ignores the text.
Aunt Gigi sends another.

I'm heading back now from a
nursing conference in Orlando. Let's
plan to meet up tomorrow afternoon.
Bc the following day I leave for
another conference. See you
tomorrow, then?

Taylor sighs, and then "likes" her aunt's message. She knows
she'll have to face the music with Aunt Gigi eventually.

Speaking of aunts . . . something is nudging at Taylor's memory.

This is for the bad Aunt Emma, the woman who spat on her
outside the Knox had said.

Almost impulsively, Taylor types "Aunt Emma" into her
phone's browser search bar. When the results appear, she's puzzled. "Aunt Emma" is slang for opium. Weird. Maybe Taylor misheard the woman.

She then opens her emails, scrolls through. Bill, advertisement,
spam. Repeat. No wonder she doesn't check her email more often.
But then, something catches her eye. An email from services
@mass-doc.com, with the subject "Death Certificate Order."

We have been unable to locate a death record for Vivian
Lawrence in the past twelve months. There is nothing currently
on file either at the State Registry of Vital Records or at Boston

City Hall. Is it possible she could be listed under a different
name?

L. Weber
Massachusetts Document Retrieval

Taylor inhales sharply. So Vivian *is* alive?

But her elation is quickly followed by worry—and more questions. If Vivian's alive, then *where* is she? Why hasn't she come
back to claim her antiques store? Her apartment? Her life?

Taylor opens a new search tab and types, like she has many
times before, "Vivian Lawrence." No new results. She tries adding combinations like "Beacon Hill" and "antiques." Nothing
relevant. "Boston neighborhood AND Vivian Lawrence." Nothing. Taylor taps her finger, thinking. On a whim, she opens her
Nextdoor neighborhood app on her phone. She searches for
"Vivian Lawrence," and bingo! She gets a hit. She clicks on Vivian's blank profile photo. There's only one post: Vivian Lawrence
just joined Beacon Hill (Front and Flats).

The post is from five days earlier.

VIVIAN

Present Day

The series of loud clangs that interrupt the silence begins to occur with regularity. It's a tune of sorts, Vivian realizes one day with a start. She quickly grows tired of it. Vivian doesn't like to rewatch a movie she's seen, let alone listen to a song on repeat.

But something about the sound tugs at her subconscious, like an impatient child vying for her mother's attention. And then it comes to her: It's the church bells from King's Chapel Parish House in Beacon Hill. They ring each day at noon. She hears them from her storefront; they serve as her daily reminder to eat lunch.

The realization is startling. She tries to sit up but finds she cannot. It's like she's paralyzed. No, not quite—she can move her fingers and toes. Thank God. It's more like her brain is sitting outside her body, a deconstructed turkey on a platter.

Where am I??

The church bells conclude, and in the too-quiet silence that follows, she gradually becomes more aware of her surroundings.

The sheets beneath her that are too soft and satiny to be hospital-grade. A hard plaster cast that encompasses her wrist.

And then, the rustling in the room.

I'm not alone.

Fear prickles through her body.

She wills her eyes to open, but they won't obey. Even so, a shadow fills her vision, like a dark cloud crossing the sky. A figure. A stranger.

Someone who now touches her hand.

VIVIAN

February

Vivian stares across Canton's Restaurant at the girl with blue hair. She's maybe in her early twenties and wears a black shirt and black pants, as if going to a funeral. On the side of her nose is a piercing, or a hole for one. Flitting over to the bar, she says something to the bartender, who gives a hesitant smile. The way she leans toward him implies familiarity, almost like they're coworkers. She's certainly not a guest, based on her appearance, or that tacky pink sticker-decorated suitcase from earlier, but it also doesn't seem like she's the hired help.

Peter, too, seems to notice her. Eduardo has to ask twice if they need anything else.

"No, thank you, Eduardo. We are all set right now," Peter finally replies.

"Enjoy your meal," Eduardo says, with a little bow. As he retreats past the bar, he does a double take and then quickens his pace to head into the kitchen.

Who is she?

Vivian picks up her fork and somehow manages to shovel pieces of her salmon Caesar salad into her mouth. She nods politely to something Peter says, but she's not following the conversation. The lettuce tastes like pieces of paper in Vivian's mouth, making it difficult to swallow. Even her favorite wine is now marked with a bitter aftertaste, as if left out overnight without a cork. Everything feels off, despite how Peter is now completely focused on Vivian. Even so, Vivian knows he *was* thrown off by the girl's appearance.

"So, are you going to tell me what's going on?" Peter asks, at one point, sitting back in his chair. He's smiling, but he's also not.

"Nothing's going on," Vivian says, a little too quickly. She picks up her wineglass but then thinks better of it. She needs her wits about her and instead takes a long sip of water. Her gaze invariably drifts over to the bar. On the woman's feet are a pair of black Converse. She *has* to work here. Something about her profile strikes Vivian as familiar.

Rose suddenly enters from the kitchen, her face uncharacteristically flushed. Eduardo follows closely behind, whispering in her ear. He's gesturing both at the bar, where the woman is, and toward the back of the restaurant. Vivian gives a quick glance behind her at the other diners, but all seems to be in order: people engrossed in conversation and food.

"You seem distracted," Peter says.

She shrugs. "Like I said, I have a headache."

"Bullshit." Peter's lower jaw juts out slightly; he's not saying this in a teasing manner.

She looks down at her wineglass. There's a red drop of wine on the base, and she uses her finger to rub the liquid back and forth, her own thoughts swirling. "Well, maybe we're both bullshitting each other," she finally replies, meeting his gaze.

He raises his eyebrows. "I hope not. I don't want that."

"Neither do I."

"There are things about me, and . . ." He drops his voice lower. "The Knox. Things I want to tell you, in private."

"Like what?"

He seemed to have no problem divulging Knox secrets earlier on.

"For starters, I didn't tell you the truth about my trip."

"Oh, you didn't?" She hopes she sounds convincing. She steals another glance at the bar, but the blue-haired woman is no longer there—not in the restaurant at all, in fact. Nor is Rose or Eduardo.

"I'm sorry. I didn't want to lie to you. But there was a situation here I needed to take care of—" He abruptly stops as Michael strides by on his way to the bar. Peter gives him a nod, a pseudo smile plastered on his face.

Vivian frowns. Isn't Michael a close friend? If so, then why is Peter being so careful around him?

Michael returns the nod, then gives Vivian a curious glance and continues on his way. "We can talk more about this later, when we're alone," Peter murmurs, his eyes roaming the room.

Is he looking for the girl?

"Fine," she says, rather curtly.

"What about you?"

"What about me?"

"Do you have anything you want to share with me?" he asks, staring hard.

She feels a flush wrap around her throat like a turtleneck. *Her friendship with Xavier. Her family's Knox lineage. The missing schedule of beneficiaries. Xavier's warnings. Her deep financial shithole.* "No."

"No?" He tilts his head.

"No."

"Do you not trust me, Vivian? I don't know about you, but I'm serious about this. About us. I'm too old to play games."

It should be music to her ears, but it's not. Clearly, he knows something about her, one of her secrets. Which one is it?

She wishes they weren't in Canton's Restaurant, with so many people around them. Maybe, if it were just the two of them, naked beneath the sheets, they could be more vulnerable with each other. More honest.

Right now, it feels like they're in a chess match.

"So what's it gonna take?" he asks, drumming his fingers against the table.

It's a fair question. What *is* it going to take? She searches his eyes, two deceptively calm blue oceans. Is this the point in their relationship where they both come completely clean? She's never really gotten to this point in a relationship before. She's never cared enough; she's never wanted to.

But what if she doesn't want to know his secrets? What if they're too much to bear? How could that scene she witnessed between him and the blue-haired girl be anything other than what it appeared: him checking out of a hotel with her?

"I need to use the bathroom," Vivian says, rising.

Peter also rises, ever the gentleman, at least by outward appearances. "It's down the hall, on the left side."

TAYLOR

As quickly as the members appeared at the Knox, they are gone again. When Taylor arrives to work on Tuesday, the place is empty.

She trudges into the parlor, where Rose has instructed her to go unpack some shipping boxes that have arrived. Taylor's annoyed she spent time curling her hair this morning and adding a black flower embellishment to her black skirt when no one's there to see it. *No one* meaning Peter.

Liam is already in the parlor, bent over a box and pulling out long black silks. Other boxes are pushed against the wall, some opened, some still secured with shipping tape.

"Morning," she offers.

He glances up, wipes the sweat from his forehead. "Hey, New Girl."

"What's going on here?"

"Initiation is coming up."

"I'm aware."

"No, like *really* coming up. Saturday night." Liam juts his chin toward the boxes. "These are things for it. Today's all about preparing. All week will be about preparing."

"Oh." *Ooh.* "Okay, what do I do?"

"Can ya move?" Jerry suddenly barks from behind, as he carries in a cardboard box. She jumps out of the way, and he sets it down next to the others.

Eduardo trails in after him, holding a utility knife. "Good morning, Taylor," he says.

"Good morning. And good morning, Jerry," she adds pointedly. He gives somewhat of a grunt in return. He takes the knife from Eduardo and begins slicing open the remaining sealed boxes.

"You can start unpacking some of these boxes," Liam says to her. "They're items for the initiation. Just put them into piles and then we'll sort them out."

Taylor starts on one of the boxes, pulling out black phoenix masks that are individually sealed in bags and separated by copious layers of tissue paper. It feels very *Eyes Wide Shut*, making her wonder what the initiation will consist of. She can tell that the masks are expensive; when she unzips one to feel inside, the feathers, so soft and thick, are clearly real. China pads over to sniff the feathers, and Taylor shoos her away. She's quiet as she works, thinking.

How strange it is that she was a registered nurse in a hospital, not so long ago. Mass General Hospital and the Knox feel like two totally different worlds, like they don't even exist on the same plane—each giving shape to an alternate version of her.

"Are you okay, Taylor?" Eduardo asks, at one point.

"Yeah."

He nods. "It's a lot here. It's not for everyone, but you're doing a good job. And I like what you've done with your skirt, adding that flower. It looks good."

"Thanks and thanks."

Eduardo squints at it. "It almost looks like a poppy flower."

"Fitting," Liam says, with a chuckle.

"Why is that fitting?"

"You know, poppy? Opium?" Liam says.

She blinks, not understanding.

"Opium comes from poppy?" Liam tries.

"Okay . . . but how is that relevant?"

"Oh, New Girl, there's so much you don't understand." There's something akin to pity in Liam's voice, and it irritates her.

"Well, if no one tells me, then how am I supposed to know?"

"Touché." Liam shakes out one of the black silks—it's a robe. "Professor, do you want to tell her, or should I?"

Eduardo glances around—is he looking for Rose?—and then says, "The three nights of preparation begin tomorrow night."

"The three nights of what?"

"It's the three nights leading up to the initiation night. The Knox members—the current ones—they gather in the evenings each night, a little before midnight. Certain ceremonies are performed."

"Like what?"

"We don't really know," Liam cuts in. "There's some elaborate meal . . ." His voice trails off as Eduardo shakes his head. "Yeah, we don't really know," he says again.

"How come no one told me that this was scheduled for this week? The 'three nights' thing, and the initiation?" she asks.

"We didn't know," Jerry says.

"They use geomancy divination readings to determine the best timing, and this was what was decided," Eduardo explains.

There's that geo thing again.

"Geomancy's like earth astrology," Liam says, when he sees her confused look.

"Well, not exactly," Eduardo interjects.

"Close enough. And they use opium during it."

"Opium? Why would they use opium?" Her thoughts race backward, snagging on "bad Aunt Emma," and then Liam's comment yesterday: *Oliver wants to bring the Knox back a few decades, centuries maybe, to how it once was.*

"They believe opium can unlock their minds, make them more open for the divination readings," says Eduardo, with a wave of his hand, as if conjuring some magic.

Liam adds, "It might seem random, but it's not. William Knox made his fortune in the opium trade, after all."

Taylor tries to remember what opium even is. Is it smoked? Ingested? Injected?

"This is why we have the Knox symbol, with the top hat and opium pipe," Eduardo says.

"You mean the top hat and flower?"

"People think it's a flower. But it's a curved opium pipe with a decorative opium bowl."

"Oh." *Oh.* The symbols tacked up on her fridge feel like they've taken on a whole new meaning. A sinister one. This at least answers her question: Opium is smoked, or can be.

"So, we'll be working odd hours over the next few days," says Liam. "Asked to do some strange errands—"

"Not *her*," Jerry cuts in. "Just us."

"True," Eduardo says. "She's still so new."

Taylor resists rolling her eyes.

"What I was going to say, before O'Doyle interrupted me, is that you will likely not be asked to do these things," Liam says. "The Knox scales down to essential personnel only. In fact, I wouldn't be surprised if you take a paid staycation and return next week."

"Lucky you," Jerry says.

"It is like our most 'religious time' here," Eduardo explains.

"Hey, what do you think?" Liam asks. He slips into one of the hooded robes and swirls around, the cape billowing with air like a parachute.

"Oh, wait," he says, and dips his head into an open box. When he reemerges, he's wearing the black phoenix mask. He looks eerie, with just a pair of dark oval eyes and the small of his chin showing.

Eduardo shakes his head. "Not a good idea, Liam. If Rose catches you . . ."

As if on cue, they hear the familiar clap of her feet against the wooden foyer, and Liam barely manages to slip out of the attire before Rose enters the room. She is dressed up, for Rose: black pants and a white button-down shirt. Hair pinned back on one side with a thin silver barrette. *Is that a dash of lipstick?*

Rose pauses, as if sensing there has been mischief, but when she scans the room, she can't find the evidence. Liam pushes his back firmly against the couch, the robe and mask stuffed into its crease. Taylor winces, thinking about the delicate feathers getting squashed.

"Let's hurry up here," she says briskly. "Liam, the butcher will be landing at four forty at Logan's private Signature Aviation terminal. You will meet him there. Eduardo, I need you to oversee the table settings in the dining room. Jerry, I need you to take out all the garbage to the curb, these boxes as well as the trash from the kitchen—they will be coming to remove it shortly—and then you'll be driving to New York to pick up the wine." She pauses. "Taylor, you may excuse yourself by two o'clock."

They all nod, and Rose's mouth briefly twists into a smile, long enough for everyone to notice.

"Rose is in a good mood," Jerry remarks, once she leaves.

"She loves this time of year," Liam says. "It's her favorite. Some people like Christmas, some like July Fourth, but give Rose a Knox initiation, and she's a pig in shit." He looks over to Taylor. "Do you want to grab a bottle of champagne from upstairs, in Canton's? I feel like we all deserve a quick drink to mark another year of initiation starting. What do you say, Professor, O'Doyle, New Girl?"

Eduardo nods, while Jerry looks less certain.

"Sure," Taylor replies. "Is there one you have in mind?"

"Behind the bar, there should be a bottle of Veuve already open in the fridge. And plastic cups in the cabinet next to the sink."

"Okay."

"I could use some help carrying out the garbage first," Jerry says. He's looking rather pointedly at Taylor.

"Well, why doesn't Taylor help with that, and then she can grab the champagne?" Liam suggests.

Why does *she* have to help with the garbage? Jerry can and does clearly manage it by himself, so this must be some sort of power play. Taylor opens her mouth to protest, but Jerry jumps in with "Good," and starts picking up the broken-down boxes.

THE KNOX SOCIETY
HANDBOOK OF PRACTICE AND PROCEDURES
v. 1817.1030(d)(2)(ii)(C)

———

Three Nights of Preparation

Purpose. This section serves to detail the procedure for the Three Nights of Preparation that precedes Initiation Night.

Scope and Application. This section applies to all living current Knox Members as defined by paragraph (a) of section I.22.

1. On the First Night of Preparation, in the hour leading to midnight, all current Knox Members shall congregate on the premises.* Members move to the dining room, gathering at the long table† for a meal that will deem them strong in body and spirit.‡ At precisely 3:03 a.m., the time William Knox took his last breath, they shall raise a fork to their mouths and eat in silence, in honor of the past.

2. Upon conclusion of the meal, the Members shall commence on the Walk of the Minds. In a single file line and in complete silence, they shall visit the scrolls. They shall proceed in this ascending order: touch the Bowels, kiss the Heart scroll, and kneel before the Brains scroll.§ The Members shall then continue their walk to Boston Harbor as an homage to their sea merchant beginnings.

3. After conclusion of the Walk of the Minds, the Members shall return to their individual residences for the

Respite, allowing their bodies to replenish and their minds to reflect.

4. They shall repeat steps 1 through 3 for two additional nights, to complete a full cycle of Three Nights of Preparation.

5. Initiation Night shall immediately follow.

---

* *The use of opium is highly encouraged to promote spiritual enhancement.*

† *This is a ceremonial act. If current Membership outnumbers available dining chairs, Members may stand and gather in the adjoining hall as needed.*

‡ *The meal should consist of the finest available meat and wine. The meat is to be carefully prepared and served rare. The wine shall be procured from the special Knox wine vault.*

§ *This is a ceremonial act. The scrolls shall remain closed, in their respective protective encasements, until Initiation Night.*

THE KNOX

My builder, William Knox, once declared, "A small idea can only become a great tradition if it is seen forth." His visionary seeds bloomed over the smoke of opium pipes and eventually formed the Knox's cornerstone. Year after year, we perform the same ceremonial initiation rituals.

I relish in routine.

Of course, the meal has changed over the centuries, as well as the preparation (the food poisoning outbreak of a'72 tartar is *still* talked about; it was the only time the initiation was delayed by a good week to allow members to recover). But suffice it to say, the food is always tip-top, what the Queen of England or the King of Saudi Arabia might have at a grand feast. This year, we are having a 2000 vintage côte de boeuf flown in from France— and accompanied, as always, by the butcher. The wine is, as tradition dictates, procured from the same small Long Island family-operated vineyard and aged for more than fifty years. (It *still* rubs members the wrong way that we use a wine from New York, though tensions have remarkably eased since the Curse of the Bambino was broken.)

Speaking of tradition, this year we will *finally* return to the usage of opium for all members to partake, as so desired throughout the initiation process. In my not-so-humble opinion, it's long overdue. I can still recall the golden days when Graham held opium in high regard. He went so far as to dedicate an entire room to its paraphernalia: opium pipes, containers, and pillows; opium bronze weights exquisitely cast in the shape of every animal known to man.

Then one fateful day, a door was carelessly left ajar, and in wandered a curious seven-year-old Oliver. He mistook the items for toys: He played the pipes like flutes, tasted the "magical dust" residue in the containers . . . Rose rescued him in the nick of time. It was hardly the first overdose here by any stretch of the imagination, but it was the first involving a child.

Graham was consumed with guilt (such a perplexing human emotion, really), and he subsequently banned opium from the Knox, except as required for geomantic divination readings.

But Oliver is of age now, and he is reintroducing opium to be freely consumed, as our founders intended. I do not concur with everything that boy believes, but on this point I am entirely in agreement.

At long last, we will be fully honoring the society's founding roots and practices.

The help is taking great pains to properly prepare for initiation ceremonies: closing drapes to protect privacy, running reliable electricity to the freezer, sealing windows shut. Even the most minor temperature alterations can change the pH balance of such fine delicacies.

And even the slightest peek from prying eyes could jeopardize the sanctity of our traditions. I do worry about that little problem we currently have on our hands, but I trust those involved know what they are doing.

VIVIAN

February

When Vivian exits Canton's Restaurant, she glances down the hall, toward the bathroom Peter directed her to—she wasn't lying about needing to use it—but in the opposite direction is the staircase leading to the downstairs mailbox and Xavier's note. And then, smack-dab in front of her, is a secretary she somehow missed earlier.

How much time does she have before Peter grows suspicious over her absence?

Vivian takes a deep breath and rushes down the stairs, her hand skimming the railing like a sled on a slope. Her heart ticks loudly in her ears. There's no one in the nearby vicinity, but distant voices circulate around her, and she knows it's only a matter of time before someone comes. Stealing over to the mailbox in the foyer, she runs her fingers across the worn numbered slots until she finds it: number 34. A small, unsealed envelope is tucked inside. She pulls out the slip of paper as the surrounding voices get louder. People are heading her way.

V,

Send my love to Rachel and Claudius. Can't wait for the common play. We'll raise a toast and clink our dirty martinis with extra olives.

—X

P.S. Remember when I told you and Rachel about the pigeons on my building? I wish I'd known that was going to happen.

What on earth? Vivian has never met a Claudius in her life. What the heck is the "common play"? What pigeons? And why would Xavier mention alcohol? Vivian almost feels like she's getting pranked. Is this really from him, and is she the intended recipient? She double-checks the mail slot. Yes, number 34. And this is Xavier's handwriting, the letters angled up and to the right, like they're trying to have good posture.

He's clearly relapsed and is off his rocker. Annoyed, Vivian slips the note into her pocket and quickly climbs the stairs. She doesn't have the time or patience for shenanigans. She passes a few people from the restaurant milling about in the upstairs hall, cocktails in hand. Dinner has finished for them. Has she taken too long? She does still need the bathroom and should discard this absurd note before anyone else finds it.

But she can't resist the opportunity to rummage through the secretary. It's right there, on her left, pulling her like a magnet. Mahogany, slant-top, and nineteenth century, so fitting with Margaret's era. While she waits for the hall to clear, she pretends to check her phone—silly, really, since there's no service in the Knox—and, spur of the moment, composes a draft of a text to Rachel.

Rachel, I have a strange question.
Do you happen to remember a story
X might have told us about pigeons
on the roof of his building?

She toggles off her phone's Wi-Fi, wondering if that might enable her to use cellular data. No such luck.

The crowd finally disperses; now's her chance. Vivian quickly turns the small brass key already inserted in the secretary lid to pull it down. The inner contents are standard: a base of curved drawers beneath pigeonholes, a small middle compartment with a door flanked by two skinny columns. If there is a secret compartment, it's somewhere in this middle portion or its adjacent columns. She pulls out the dovetail drawer to the left of the spindle and runs her finger against the wood. *Yes!* There's a tiny circular notch inside, a spring that will release the column. She just needs the corresponding pin to free the latch. Excitement drums in her as she pulls open and closes the drawers, searching for it.

But the drawers are empty. No pin.

Damn it!

What to do? She tries the drawers again, in case there's a ballpoint pen rolling around whose fine tip might work, but no such luck.

Suddenly, Vivian gets an idea. She runs her fingers through her tresses, removing her hairpin. Thank goodness she wore this tonight. It's her mother's—a gold-and-diamond hairpin—which feels fitting. She inserts its pointy end into the small hole, and there's an utterly satisfying click as the spring is released. The "column" pops forward: It's a wooden document holder. A tingle runs through her.

But the holder is hollow, empty. Sort of like how she feels right about now. She crouches disappointedly over the secretary, pushing the column back into place, when a familiar voice rings out: "Ms. Lawrence, can I help you with something?"

Vivian startles, bumping her head against the desk ledge. *Christ.* It's Michael.

"No," she says, rubbing her head. "I . . . I was just looking at this piece. I had a similar one in my store a few years ago."

"I see. What was that clicking noise? Did you just pop back in one of the drawers?" he asks, moving closer to the desk. He has an odd look on his face.

"No." She's such an idiot. The last person she should be alerting to the fact that there may be furniture with secret compartments lying around in the Knox is Michael. He has genuine interest in antiques and will now likely finish her hunt through the house for her.

He puckers his brow, running his fingers along the surface of the drawers. He has nice hands, she notices in spite of herself. Long, slender. Like an artisan's hands. On his finger is the brass ring he always seems to wear, which is embossed with a top hat and flower. The Knox symbol.

"Well, yes, actually, I did pull out a drawer," she says now. *Better to come up with some sort of excuse.* "I wanted to see if the drawers were dovetailed, and they are." She shows him, pulling a random drawer completely out of its socket to illustrate the puzzle piece ends of the wood joints. "This is one of the strongest joints in carpentry."

"Very cool," he says, smiling. "They don't make furniture quite the same anymore."

"No, they don't. This type of joint predates written history. The ancient Egyptians used it four thousand years ago."

"Fascinating," he murmurs.

A couple from the restaurant spills into the hall, arms wrapped around each other. Vivian becomes acutely aware of the time. "Anyway, I should get back to Peter."

"Speaking of Peter and history, have you told him yet about *your* family history?"

"Wh . . . what do you mean?"

"You don't remember telling me?"

"No. I haven't the foggiest idea what you're talking about."

"The very first time I came by your store to purchase an antique, the nineteenth-century globe from Charles Smith and Son—which, by the way, you may have noticed is in the parlor—we had a conversation about the outdated names depicted on maps and globes."

"I remember."

"And you said, on some maps, the islands east of Tahiti used to be called 'Dangerous Islands.'"

"Right."

"And you said it was called this because of the dangerous currents and high reefs, making it a wrecking ground for ships. And I said, 'Oh, and here I thought they just wanted unwanted visitors to stay away.'"

She remembers this. And she remembers how, at the time, she was trying to figure out his intentions. She'd never had a new customer walk in ready to drop sixty grand on a single antique.

"And then I said I was from the Knox, and you said . . ." He lowers his voice, leaning closer to her. "You said you were kind of an unwanted visitor there. Or at least that one of your ancestors had been."

"I don't recall saying that," she says. But something about it feels vaguely familiar. Perhaps she had indeed made an offhand comment like that. An attempt to connect with an obviously wealthy customer.

"Maybe I misremembered," he says with a shrug. "Anyway, don't forget this." He picks up her hairpin from the surface of the secretary and hands it to her. His expression is unreadable, but she can only guess what he's thinking.

THE KNOX

February

Oh, Vivian. I see you are up to your old tricks, taking the liberty of riffling through my furniture. (What in geomancy's name are you searching for?) As I have said before, I do not take kindly to unwanted scrutiny—nor do the members.

There is no shortage of watchful eyes tonight. You simply picked the wrong time to nose about. It is an evening of *considerable* importance for the society, and I am sorry to say that your little forays do not rate.

Rather, I am not sorry in the slightest.

I advise you to sit back and buckle up your corset or Hermès belt or whatever garment it is that you ladies now favor. Because things will shortly become *very* interesting.

Oh—and that note Xavier set aside for you in my mailbox? You cannot just discard the note in my water closet, flush it away in hopes its message will disappear. It is not that simple.

Your fingers were not the first to unfold the note. Your eyes were not the first to read it.

Others, my dear, are onto you.

Dear Rachel,

I am so sorry I have not been in touch. I'm sure you have been worried.
As you know I had that head injury, and I have been recovering.
I decided I needed to get out of town for the time being so I am in
Florida. I will be in touch. But I do need to speak to Xavier. Have you
heard from him?

Love,
Vivian

TAYLOR

Jerry and Taylor begin hauling out the trash. They work in silence, lugging both the cardboard boxes from the parlor as well as the series of kitchen trash bags someone has lined up along the back hall. It seems Jerry just wanted a moment alone with her, after all—it's not some power play. She's clearly getting jaded and paranoid, thinking the worst of everyone.

Eventually, he asks, "Did ya hear anything from your landlord about the antiques store?"

"No, not yet. Did you drop off the books yesterday?"

"Yeah. I said I would, so yeah, I did."

"Okay, thanks."

"When are ya gonna hear from your landlord?"

"I don't know."

He grunts, displeasure written across his face.

"Why the rush? I mean, it's old stuff."

"That old stuff could be worth a lotta money. People pay a lot for antiques." He doubles the number of heavy trash bags he's carrying, now two with each fist. He holds them out like they're sets of weights. Taylor follows with more cardboard boxes.

As Jerry steps through the back entrance, one of the bags breaks open, its contents spewing out.

"Shit." He rushes to collect the spilled contents, jamming them back through the hole in the bag.

Taylor sets down her boxes to help. It's mostly food scraps: meat, vegetables, some pastry-like dessert, but also soaked paper towels, coffee grinds, and a couple of egg cartons. Gross. Also— is the Knox above recycling?

Suddenly, she comes across a discarded medication box labeled "amantadine." She turns it over in her hands, her nurse-brain automatically kicking in to identify the drug: It's used in Parkinson's disease.

Jerry hastily snatches the box out of her hands, quickly depositing it in the trash as if she wasn't meant to see it. "I got this. You can go grab the other bags."

"Okay." Fine with her; she'd rather not have to touch this stuff with her bare hands.

When they finally set down the last trash bag on the pavement, the private garbage company has arrived. Taylor and Jerry watch as two men toss the bags into the truck's cavity, the machine loudly grinding. It's only then that it fully hits her that the Knox doesn't set out trash on garbage day, like everyone else does on the street. No—apparently they use a private company that comes at their beck and call to dispose of whatever they need. Very on point for a secret society.

Jerry's eyes flicker to the Knox's outdoor camera attached to the door, and then he squares his back to it. He motions Taylor to come close. "Look, the reason why I keep asking ya about the antiques store is I could use the money," he admits to her surprise.

"But why? The Knox pays well, right?"

"It does. But that's only if ya work here."

"Are you planning to leave?"

He meets her gaze head-on for a good few seconds before looking away. "I'm just looking at options. In case."

In case what? she wants to ask. Maybe this is because of Oliver. Maybe Jerry can't get over whatever happened between his sister and Oliver. The idea of Jerry as a protective brother softens her.

"Can I ask ya a favor?" he says.

"A favor? Sure."

"The bookstore guy called. He wants me to come by later today. I guess he has a question about one of the books. But I can't go, 'cause I got to drive to New York and pick up the wine for the initiation. Can ya go? And let me know what he wants?"

"Uh, sure. No problem. I'll stop by on my way home." She smiles, feeling pleased that Jerry is trusting her with this. "And don't worry, with your work history—being here at the Knox—I'm sure you could get a job anywhere," she adds, trying to reassure him.

"Did ya read the confidentiality agreement?" he says, voice flat.

"Oh." Yes, now she recalls there being some language about never mentioning the Knox for gainful employment elsewhere. She'd skimmed over that section, not realizing its future implications. She, too, would have a work history gap she could not explain. Shit.

"But I guess as a nurse, ya don't have to worry about that so much."

"What?" She tenses.

"Ya honestly think they didn't know that?" Jerry says, working his mouth as if chewing a piece of gum. "That they would just hire anyone and not do a serious background check?"

"I . . . I don't know."

"Yeah, they had me ask around about ya. I had a little chat with your nurse manager, Jan. A little 'accidental' run-in at the St. Patrick's Day parade. I pretended to be a friend of yours."

Taylor opens and then closes her mouth, pressing her tongue hard against her teeth gap.

"C'mon now, Taylor. Don't be so naive." He studies her. "Look, I'm not trying to be mean. But there's shit going down here. Not everyone can see it, but I do. If you were smart—and ya are, 'cause you're a nurse—ya should get yourself outta here. Go back to nursing."

She's quiet. Her brain is spinning backward, trying to reframe every interaction she's had at the Knox. *Go back to being a nurse.* Was Jerry the one who left her that note in her wallet? No— surely he wouldn't be so open with her now. Also, he clearly has no problems delivering this message to her face.

Does everyone know she's a nurse? That she's been lying by omission?

As if reading her mind, Jerry adds, "Don't worry, the others— Liam, Eduardo—don't know. That's for ya to tell them if ya want. None of their business. The Knox is a place where we can reinvent ourselves. I mean, I used to work the grill at Chipotle for $14.25 an hour before I met Eduardo and was brought in."

"Does Eduardo know you're thinking about leaving?"

Jerry's face gets splotchy, a watercolor of pinks. "No. And ya better not tell him. Some people . . . They can't see this place for what it is."

❦

Taylor is still reeling when she heads to Canton's to grab the champagne for the so-called celebratory drink with her fellow employees, though she's feeling anything but.

As she bends down to rummage through the cabinet for the cups Liam mentioned, she tries to organize the information she's just learned: The Knox knew she was a nurse when they hired her. But they didn't know she was *Vivian's* nurse, surely.

Okay, Taylor thinks, her shoulders collapsing. She can work with that. So what if she failed to mention her nursing work history during her interview? They were aware, or they became aware, and they *still* hired her. They didn't care. Like Jerry said, the Knox is a place where you can reinvent yourself.

And that's what she's done.

Suddenly, she hears someone enter the restaurant.

"Not everyone's born with a silver spoon in their mouth, Michael. There are some of us who've had to work to get where we are. Some of us who actually paid our dues on initiation night."

"That's not what I meant, Peter. And I don't know why you continually bring up the legacy exemption rules."

It's Peter. Peter and Michael. What are they doing here? She knows she should stand up and make her presence known, but she doesn't. Instead, she dips down lower behind the bar, making herself as small as possible.

"Well, all I know is you got pretty damn lucky being born into that family of yours. So what the hell *did* you mean, then, about the business plan?" Peter asks.

"I just think we need to proceed with caution here. We don't know if it's financially sound—"

"That's what I'm trying to tell you, Michael. It absolutely is. It's forward-thinking and good for the Society's financial future. Just because Oliver is at the helm of this plan doesn't mean it doesn't have potential. It has a *lot* of potential. He's already tested the waters, and the appetite is there. And among many of our members. Look, I understand you are cautious, but as a legacy you've also had the luxury to be cautious. It's like my old mentor used to say: 'The rich have the richness of time.' The rest of us are scrappy SOBs. So I recognize a good deal when I see one and prefer to act on it."

"But, Peter."

"What?"

"There's more to it than that. I already did the geomancy reading."

"Is that what this is really about? So what did it say?"

"That this is not a good idea."

"Well, Michael, maybe you didn't ask the right questions. You should do another."

"It doesn't work that way, Peter. And in fact, I was being diplomatic. The reading suggested that this would be a decidedly *bad* move for the Knox. We can go review it—"

"Screw the geomancy, for once! This is *real life*. This is business."

Michael is quiet for a few seconds, and when he replies, he sounds troubled. "The Knox has always—*always*—relied on geomancy as part of our decision-making process. It's been tradition for over two hundred years."

Peter scoffs. "I'd be willing to bet that if William Knox were alive and kicking today, he would be in agreement with me. Sometimes you have to fly in the face of tradition, Michael. Be daring and bold."

"Peter," Michael says, sounding exasperated, "what is the Society without tradition? It's built on tradition—built out of tradition."

"Easy to say when you're the legacy kid," Peter retorts. "Tell me, Michael, when was the last time you were bold? You've never been, have you?" His tone has turned bitingly personal, almost mocking. "You couldn't even ask out that girl you were so smitten with in London. What was her name? The grad student who used to study at the café around the corner from our flat?"

"I don't remember."

"Sure you do."

Michael sighs. "Look, you've made your position clear. But I have to ask: You're not going along with Oliver . . . just to go along with him, like some of the others who've quickly changed their tunes now that he's almost in charge?"

"Don't be ridiculous. Like I said, it's a good financial plan—"

"And this has nothing to do with your . . . personal interest in the product?"

"What's that supposed to mean?" Peter asks sharply.

"Peter, I understand you've been through a lot—"

"You have no idea what I've been through." There's a surprising hardness to Peter's voice.

Michael pauses. "You're right. I don't. I'm sorry. Sometimes I wish you would tell me."

There's silence, tense. Then the sound of a chair being pulled back.

"So this is where I was sitting last night. Do you see it?"

"No, I don't. Should I call you?" Michael asks.

Ah, Peter left his phone.

"Wait—here it is."

"Glad you found it."

The footsteps come dangerously close to the bar.

"Anyway, Michael, it's quite popular these days, as we're learning. Now I'll admit . . . It does have certain medicinal qualities that have helped me in the wake of, you know. Frankly, I wish I'd had this stuff earlier, at other times in my life."

"Peter—"

"I'm in control. Like I've always been."

"You think you're in control because you avoid conflict."

"Well, I'm not avoiding it now, am I?"

There's a pause, and then Michael says, "I didn't realize that you viewed me as a source of conflict."

Peter laughs. "Come now, Michael. Don't be such a stiff. You ought to try it. Might be good for you. Make you *bolder*. Like Popeye's spinach."

"I *do* use it, as you know. For the geomancy readings, as our founders intended. Not for personal consumption."

The voices fade as they exit.

A Geomancy Chart (1 of 1)

Cast by Michael

The Question: Is it in the Knox's best interest to pursue a business endeavor of mass import of opium from Southeast Asia?

FOURTH DAUGHTER	THIRD DAUGHTER	SECOND DAUGHTER	FIRST DAUGHTER	FOURTH MOTHER	THIRD MOTHER	SECOND MOTHER	FIRST MOTHER

FOURTH NIECE	THIRD NIECE	SECOND NIECE	FIRST NIECE

LEFT WITNESS	RIGHT WITNESS

THE JUDGE

Michael's Reading: The judge figure is Carcer, Latin for "the prison," a generally unfavorable reading, denoting restriction, closing of things, and setbacks. There are also two negative witnesses: Rubeus (Latin for "red"), a figure of madness and addiction, and Puer (Latin for "the boy"), a fiery, overconfident figure. The tenth figure, used for big business decisions, is also Rubeus, as is the fourth figure, which would signal the Knox's building, or stronghold. Throughout the chart there is a fair amount of Tristitia ("sorrow"), indicating betrayal, anxiety, suffering.

Suffice to say, this does not bode well for the Knox.

VIVIAN

February

After Vivian's unexpected little chat with Michael over the secretary, he does not return to Canton's Restaurant. Half the place has emptied out, and Vivian wishes she and Peter could leave as well. It's been a long dinner, and she's growing restless. She's never liked prolonged dinners. A holdover from her youth, when her mother made her sit for far too long at various dinner parties in itchy fancy dresses while old men with the luxury of time spewed philosophy.

But Peter has ordered an expensive port wine for them to share. He's rather drunk, an uncharacteristic slur to his words. While she went "to the bathroom," he made short work of the rest of the Barolo. She's surprised; he's the type that usually seems in control. Is something worrying him, causing him to drown his sorrows?

Is this about the blue-haired girl?

What is it with everyone and alcohol, all of a sudden? A pang of guilt hits Vivian; she should have realized Xavier likely fell off the wagon. He was obviously drinking at the masquerade ball, though Vivian didn't want to admit it. She's been too wrapped up in her own problems, too self-absorbed to realize her friend may have needed her help.

Vivian herself is done drinking, so she takes small, polite sips of the port. She needs a clear mind. She also feels rather exposed after her conversation with Michael. He clearly knows about her family history, but does he know her underlying agenda? Given that he is a regular customer of hers, he, of all people, may have noticed her second store has been closed as of late—and might surmise why. Is he going to tell Peter everything he knows?

Peter starts talking about a hotel he's working on—in Los Angeles, she notes, not in Milan—but she's stuck like gum in her increasingly worrisome thoughts.

The crème brûlée Peter requested arrives.

"Delicious," he pronounces, after shoveling in a generous spoonful. "Chef Centanni has outdone himself. He apprenticed under Sirio Maccioni himself, at Le Cirque, and then trained under Lydia Shire here in Boston. Do you want me to serve you some, love?"

"No thanks." For the first time, Peter is annoying her. She knows of Le Cirque; she dined there herself, back in the day. But she wouldn't have known who Sirio was if she rode the same elevator with him. She couldn't care less about the special vintage port, or the dessert, or anything else right now except why Peter hasn't come clean about the blue-haired woman—or the truth about his Milan trip, which he's had plenty of chances to disclose during dinner.

Her eyes flicker to the window table still occupied by Oliver and his father, Graham. They, too, appear to be enjoying Chef Centanni's crème brûlée, though Graham is drinking sparkling water. Oliver, a brown martini. Or is it an espresso martini? *Wait.* Olives—Oliver. *Dirty martinis with extra olives.* Is Xavier trying to deliver a message about Oliver?

"So, like I was saying," Peter continues, "mass production in luxury hotels could be a thing of the past. Everything is readily available, so my clients now want what is different, unique. It's about the craftsmanship these days. That, and the utilization of quality materials."

"I see," Vivian says, trying to stifle her yawn. "And this is what you're focusing on in Los Angeles or *Milan*?" she can't help but add.

Suddenly, a loud clatter rings through the restaurant. Everyone is startled into silence; the noise in the room abruptly compresses, as if zipped up in a jacket. The source of the disruption: A fellow diner has fallen face-first onto his plate of food. Then, as everyone watches with mouths agape, his body jerks repeatedly and tumbles onto the floor with a deafening thud.

The zipper unfastens; commotion unleashes.

Graham Thurgood lies motionless on the floor.

TAYLOR

Taylor enters the parlor, tightly gripping the champagne and glasses she was sent to retrieve from Canton's. The relaxed atmosphere she encounters is much at odds with her own anxiety: Eduardo is bent over the vintage turntable, fiddling with a record, Liam and Jerry sprawled on nearby chairs. Eduardo grins as a catchy classical-Caribbean fusion song begins playing.

"One of my favorites: Joachim Horsley," he announces. He starts moving around—*dancing*, she realizes—Jerry snickering at his moves.

Liam doles out the champagne. "To another successful initiation prep," he says, and then adds, "and to New Girl here."

As the four of them clink, Taylor allows herself to fully meet their eyes. For a moment, and despite the unsettling events of the day—including the conversation she just eavesdropped on between Peter and Michael—she feels a grin coming on. She's reminded of the easy camaraderie between the waitstaff at her dad's restaurant. Once the last customer leaves, they crank up the music, pop open some beers, shoot the shit. Their stories and laughter can easily dribble into the early hours of the morning.

But then she takes in the surrounding scene: the *Eyes Wide Shut* masks arranged on the chesterfield couch, the glass display case with the secured scroll that all employees naturally avoid, the staggering grandiosity of the room itself. No—it's different here: They are at a secret society, readying members for an initiation cloaked in mystery and aided by the use of drugs and divination readings. And, based on what she's just overheard, it's a secret society with some change underfoot. Perhaps dangerous, drug-related change. Whatever is going on, it seems to be deeper than using opium solely for geomancy purposes.

And finally, her eyes come to Jerry, laughing at Eduardo like everything is just fine. But Taylor knows this couldn't be further from the truth.

She hopes the Knox has nothing to do with what befell her former patient, but with every passing day that the mysteries of this place deepen, that feels a little less likely. At any rate, since Vivian *is* alive—and apparently well enough to be joining the Nextdoor app—Taylor hopes that it's only a matter of time before she gets clarity on what really happened.

With the taste of champagne still fresh in her mouth, Taylor exits through the back door of the Knox, eyeing the spot where the garbagemen removed the trash not even an hour earlier. It's now as pristine as can be. What other messes does the Knox so carefully clean up? One involving Vivian?

Taylor starts to walk away, her phone beeping with notifications from Aunt Gigi now that it has sprung to life with service.

Then, suddenly, a woman's scream pierces the air.

Taylor stops short, whipping around to scan the back of the Knox building. As usual, it appears orderly and inaccessible, like a stiff coat snapped to the very top button.

Maybe Taylor imagined it; she *has* had a day.

But then, it happens once more: a shrill scream that causes the hairs on the back of her neck to stand at attention. She anxiously searches for the source but sees nothing. Then, a small movement in a fourth-floor window catches her eye.

A drape waves, then comes to rest, as if someone has just stolen a glance out the window.

VIVIAN

Present Day

Vivian opens her eyes.

She's in an empty room.

No—it's not empty. As an awareness stirs within her, the room slowly becomes filled, almost like someone's popping items into a dollhouse: drapes, an IV pole stand, a lighthouse oil painting, a Victorian parlor chair, a commode, faux-candle wall sconces, a mahogany end table. It's a room she's staying in, apparently, though she has no recollection how she got here. The room is of questionable taste, a mixture of antique meets hospital. Like Weird Barbie tried her hand at interior design.

Wait. She goes back to the Victorian parlor chair. She *knows* that chair. It takes her several tries to focus on it, as too much concentration causes the vise around her head to painfully tighten. The chair's petit point embroidered floral backside, the hand-carved headpiece, the brass-nail head trim—it's an item she sourced for Michael.

For the Knox. *She's at the Knox.*

The crushing realization builds in her like a pot of boiling water, until she opens her mouth to release a hot scream.

She gasps for air. Then a second scream rises from her depths, and she similarly lets it loose.

Suddenly a foreign finger urgently jams a couple of pills into her open mouth. Vivian begins coughing as the medication dissolves into her saliva. She immediately recognizes the bitter taste: Xanax.

VIVIAN

February

Paramedics are on the way," Rose reports in a shaky voice. Her face is ashen as she pulls back the chairs, creating more space for Graham's resuscitation efforts.

Peter, Michael, and the bartender alternate doing CPR, while Oliver simply stands there looking at his father with eyes bugged out like he's on some acid trip.

It doesn't look hopeful; Graham is as gray as Nantucket fog.

Others have gotten wind of the situation and are reentering the room in droves. The restaurant is now as full as it was during its dinner prime, perhaps fuller. No Xavier, though, Vivian notes. The air in Canton's has become stuffy, suffocating.

"Likely heart attack," someone murmurs.

"*Second* heart attack," someone else adds.

"Oh my God," says a man whom Vivian recognizes as a state-house reporter for *The Boston Globe*. He's not much of a journalist, chasing stories that aren't really stories. She can almost see his wheels turning. *Good luck with that*, she thinks sarcastically. Given the secrecy surrounding the Knox, she's pretty sure they'd break him before he could break this story.

It feels strange to be gathered with these people, watching this like it's some sort of performance art. Vivian is reminded of when her mother abruptly fell on the street, the mask of the disease she'd tried to cover up finally slipping. Vivian had felt useless then, paralyzed with the realization that something was seriously wrong, like Oliver must be now. She almost feels sorry for him. The memory creates a heaviness in her chest—Vivian needs to leave, get some space.

She escapes into the hall. The air feels like a cool drink of water. Taking a deep breath, she looks around. She's not alone. A figure is quickly absconding down the hall.

The girl with the blue hair.

Vivian instinctively follows. The girl is walking at a fast clip, blue locks bobbing with each step. She leaves a cloud of cheap perfume in her wake. Vivian holds her breath, trailing behind. As they near the grand staircase, a loud knock pounds at the front door. The paramedics?

The girl quickens her pace, disappearing around a bend. Vivian follows, securing her Chanel purse in a cross-body style. The hall becomes narrower, darker. She just assumed this hall dead-ended, but now that she's thinking about the building's orientation, she realizes there are whole swathes of rooms below—and above—her. The place is disorienting. The night of her sleepover, when she wandered around searching for secretaries, she was one level up—at least, she *thinks* she was.

Right now, in the wake of everything else that threatens to turn her mind inside out, Vivian finds all she can focus in on, all she cares about at this moment, with an almost overwhelming desire, is figuring out who this girl is.

But she's gone.

As Vivian turns the corner, the hall is frustratingly empty. Did she disappear into one of the many rooms with closed doors

Vivian now passes? Or did she perhaps take this small elevator tucked into the wall? Vivian pauses to listen; there's no grinding of elevator machinery, but there is the distant padding of steps.

Vivian follows the sound; it's coming from an adjacent door. As she cups her ear against it, the door swings inward. She nearly falls over, stumbling onto a landing from which a metal spiral staircase winds upward. The stairwell is dark, but from beyond, footsteps ricochet.

The girl must be climbing these stairs.

Where do they lead? Vivian runs her hand along the banister as she, too, starts up. She keeps thinking of the way the girl clutched Peter's shoulders, as if she had a right to touch him. Vivian bypasses a landing and continues ascending the stairs to arrive at—if her calculations are correct—the fourth floor.

The way Peter was so quick to help her with the suitcase.

The stairs continue to spiral upward to yet another floor, but something is pulling Vivian to this one.

The way Peter leaned into the girl.

Vivian is faced with two doors; she tries the first, cracking it halfway open. It's a back entrance into a magnificent bedroom that feels like the inside of a jewelry box: deep-navy walls, a stunning Murano glass chandelier, copper-colored silk drapes, a brass four-poster bed with a deep rose-gold paisley velvet comforter. Graham's room? She does a quick scan; there are no secretaries, but on the wall hangs a large seascape oil painting that takes her breath away: It's Rembrandt's *Storm on the Sea of Galilee*, stolen in the Isabella Stewart Gardner Museum heist.

Christ.

Vivian backtracks, stunned. If the girl disappeared into *that* room, Vivian's not about to follow. She tries the second door, wondering what might possibly be behind this one.

It couldn't be more opposite: a long, darkened corridor. At

the far end, there's shadowy movement—the girl?—followed by the slow groan of a door opening. Vivian hastens down the hall, but just as she reaches the door, it clicks shut. She grasps the knob, desperately trying to turn it, but it's no use. It's locked. *Shit.*

She's lost her.

Suddenly, Vivian becomes aware of how absurdly she's acted. What is she doing? Peter must be wondering where she is. And where *is* she, anyway? A quick glance through the only window seems to indicate she is in between buildings, like this long hall connects the Knox with another entity.

Just then, her purse vibrates, and she startles. There must be a pocket of reception here, by the window. Her hands feel like putty as she combs through to find the phone.

Vivian's text to Rachel about the "pigeons on the building" apparently went through because Rachel's responded.

> Yes . . . remember when Xavier said one of the jewelers on the top floor in his building used to "bomb" aka clean the jewelry in a sink in front of his open window with a window fan blowing? And then there were all the dead pigeons of the roof . . .

It is slowly coming back to Vivian. She quickly sends a response, praying that Rachel is by her phone.

> Yes. . . . now I do. But what was the reason again that the birds died??

Rachel immediately replies:

Bc the bombing process uses cyanide to clean the jewelry. So the fan would blow the cyanide out the window onto the pigeons and kill them!!!

Vivian gasps, and the phone tumbles out of her hands onto the floor.

Xavier's note suddenly makes sense, though Vivian wishes it didn't.

Send my love to Rachel and Claudius. Can't wait for the common play. The Shakespeare play she, Rachel, and Xavier watched together on the Boston Common was *Hamlet*. Claudius is one of the characters in *Hamlet*. Claudius, who *poisons* his brother to ascend the throne.

We'll raise a toast and clink our dirty martinis with extra olives. This is a reference to both Oliver—*olives*—and again to poison. Xavier was giving a nod to what Vivian previously taught him about clinking: It was historically performed to mix the contents of the two glasses, in case one contained poison.

Xavier's message is as clear as that overhead Murano glass chandelier she'd spied in the bedroom: Oliver planned to poison his father with cyanide.

Christ. Vivian's stomach drops. No, she thinks. *No, no, no.* She was there; she saw it happen. Graham had a heart attack.

Or did he?

What did she see, other than the man collapse over his food? It was possible. Oliver could have somehow slipped cyanide in his father's food or drink.

But where would Oliver have gotten the cyanide from?

Dread slowly inches its way down her spine. *Xavier.* Oliver must have gotten it from Xavier, who holds that jeweler's permit for cyanide.

Christ. What was he thinking?

Remember when I told you and Rachel about the pigeons on my building? I wish I'd known that was going to happen. Xavier likely meant he'd supplied the cyanide, but he didn't realize it was going to be used to poison Graham.

Still—it doesn't really matter if he didn't realize. Graham is dead. Xavier is in way over his head at the Knox. And, right now, so is Vivian.

Michael witnessed her snooping around—and he knows about her ancestral link. What if they have sniffed out her true intentions? And what if they got to Xavier's note before she did? The envelope was unsealed—had it already been opened? Even if they didn't understand the note's meaning, they would have realized Xavier knows Vivian—and that he was trying to deliver a message to her.

The Knox is far, far more dangerous than she's given it credit for. They even have the fucking stolen Rembrandt! *What to do, what to do, what to do?* She knows, deep down, what she cannot do: return to Peter and pretend like everything is fine.

Rachel's words about the Knox/Thurgood family plot now echo in her head, how everyone was buried there.

"Everyone *except* Margaret."

The Knox clearly has no issues covering up their crimes; Vivian's not about to be another job for their cleanup crew.

She needs to get the hell out of here.

Jabbing at the phone with a trembling hand, she deletes her messages with Rachel. Then she rushes back the way she came, scurrying down the metal staircase. Her feet feel, for once, clunky in Louboutins; her heart is in her throat. Thoughts swirl maddeningly around her. Who at the Knox orchestrated Graham's poisoning? Oliver? Michael? Peter insinuated there was transition underfoot at the Knox and dissenting schools of thought. Peter, she recalls, was Team Oliver. *Is Peter in on this?* Did Peter off Graham to implement the desired change?

But Peter was doing CPR on Graham. He seemed genuinely shaken, unless that was an act.

Reaching the bottom of the stairs, she bursts through the door that deposits her back on the second floor. Luckily, no one is in the immediate vicinity, but she should have been more careful. She's not thinking properly. Her brain is like the inside of a dated media cabinet, wires all askew.

She edges along the same hall that she confidently strutted down minutes earlier. She's finding it so hard to propel forward, so hard to think. Fear clings to her, hot, sweaty. Each half step she manages toward the grand staircase—and the front door of the Knox—feels like a hard-earned victory. She could really use one of her Xanax right about now. Or two.

Then, out of the corner of her eye, she spots movement. *She's not alone.*

She halts, hyperaware of the crack her hip makes just then. She draws in a breath and holds it as if that could make her disappear.

The figure does not move. It—he?—waits for her. *Who is it?*

They stay like that for a few solid seconds. Then, her eyes slowly adjust, taking in the gold filigree frame surrounding the person. It's a mirror, for crying out loud. A large hanging mirror that she must have missed seeing earlier. She's looking at herself. She almost laughs, she's so relieved.

In a few more steps, the staircase comes into sight. Relief washes over her. She feels like she's rounding the last corner of a marathon. The hall remains empty, faint echoes of the ongoing commotion in Canton's Restaurant carrying down the corridor.

At the top of the stairs she pauses for a moment, wondering if she should find Peter before leaving. But then she realizes it's a stupid idea, even if he's not involved.

As she extends her foot, about to descend, she feels a sharp, strong shove from behind. She stumbles, missteps. The stairs come crashing at her, like a wave that entraps her in its current, pounding her over and over. There's hurt and black and waves and surprise   and and

     and

VIVIAN

February

THE KNOX

Yes, I saw what happened to Vivian.

And no, I will not reveal who did it.

I never do.

TAYLOR

She must have imagined the scream, Taylor thinks to herself, as she paces outside Turned Pages. Her head feels clogged, a dull ache pulsating through it. It was such a weird day at the Knox. She's tired, overwhelmed with what she learned—how the Knox was onto her being a nurse, how they use opium for geomancy readings, how there is likely some sort of big change underfoot. Why, it's enough to make anyone hear things.

Or maybe someone did scream—and so what? It doesn't mean it came from inside the Knox.

Taylor rubs her face; she wants to head home, take a hot shower, sink into bed. But first, she needs to stop into this bookstore like she told Jerry she would.

But right as she reaches for the door, her phone pings. It's Aunt Gigi—again. Taylor sighs and instead pulls out her phone. She scrolls through the chain of messages:

> Morning T.J., I'm back from Orlando. What time can you meet up later today?

I can even come to you?

Hellooo??

Remember, I'm only in town today . . .

Okay, it's now noon . . . I don't think my texts are going through. Is your phone dead?

T.J., I'm starting to get worried. It's now 2:00. Are you okay??

It's 2:30 now. Where are you!

Turned Pages will have to wait a few more minutes. Taylor reluctantly rings her aunt, who picks up immediately.

"I know you're an adult, T.J, but if you don't get back to people in a timely manner, they start to worry."

"Hi, Aunt Gigi . . . sorry, I was working and didn't have cell service." She glances almost absent-mindedly into Turned Page's window front, at the display of vintage books.

Her aunt inhales sharply. "Working at the Knox, I presume?"

"Yeah."

"We need to talk. I wanted to have this conversation *in person*, but I have to go meet Phil at his retina appointment, so this'll have to do."

"Sorry," Taylor says lamely, as she braces herself for the coming onslaught: the reprimands for quitting nursing. Her aunt's heavy disappointment with her life choices. At least it's over the phone.

"Have you talked to your father recently?" Aunt Gigi asks.

"No . . . Have you?"

"I have not," she says to Taylor's relief. "But what I'm about to tell you does very much concern him. It's something that he himself should have told you a long time ago."

"Oh?" Meanwhile she's thinking: *Has he received the check I mailed? If not, it should be there by tomorrow.*

"Can we FaceTime, please? I'll call you right back."

"Okay." Two seconds later, Taylor's phone rings. "Hi, Aunt Gigi."

"That's much better. I just need to see your face," her aunt says, bringing the phone closer. She looks tired, eyes sunken, wrinkles pronounced. "T.J., do you remember when I told you I ran into your mom once on the street, here in Boston?"

Taylor feels all of her focus suddenly pulled toward the phone. "Yes?"

"Well, what happened was, it was early afternoon, maybe one o'clock, and I was walking down Columbus Ave., in the South End, and she, well, she must have been coming from home. She was in her pajamas. She was . . . skinny. So skinny." Aunt Gigi rubs her forehead.

Taylor shakes her head. "I'm not following, Aunt Gigi."

"T.J., your mom was strung out—from drugs."

"What? What are you talking about?"

"It's time you knew, T.J. Your mom got into drugs."

"Why would you say this?"

Her aunt's face crinkles, a giant prune. "Because it's true."

"No," Taylor says, more firmly. "No, it's not." But as she says this, the world suddenly dips, Taylor faltering along with it.

No.

"I'm so sorry, honey, to be the one to tell you how it really was. Your mother didn't come to Boston to model. She came here to follow a guy." Aunt Gigi's words sound far away, distorted, as if traveling through water.

No.

"And then she was with another guy. I couldn't keep track of it. The deeper she got into drugs, the more erratic her life became. I tried to intervene a few times, but . . ."

Taylor shakes her head, then shakes her body. She feels discombobulated. She tries to respond, but no words form.

"It's probably why your mom died in the basement fire—she was likely passed out."

No. No. "No!"

"I really am sorry you're only finding out now. Your father should have told you years ago, and that's on him. My brother can be stubborn. Well, I agreed with him that when you were little, it was better to keep it from you, to feed you that story. But once you became an adult, he should have told you the truth. *He* should have. And I told him he should have. T.J.? T?"

No. Taylor drops the phone to her side, briefly closing her eyes. Even as she gradually comes back into her body—feeling the solid, reliable surface beneath her feet, the fabric of her clothes brushing against her skin—*no* still hovers. She slowly raises the phone back to her face.

"But you said, the last time we met in the park, that you ran into my mom on the street, and that she was beautiful."

Aunt Gigi takes a deep breath, and raggedly replies, "Your mother was always very beautiful—like you are. Which is why this is all the more tragic."

Taylor shakes her head. "She was a model," she insists. "She wasn't like that. She was . . ." Her voice trails off. She wants to say: *My mother was one of* them, *like Vivian.*

"She *was* like that," Aunt Gigi says, gently but firmly. "But you're not. You've always had a good head on your shoulders. I get it, you're young, you're figuring things out. You don't want to be a nurse? Then don't. But that Knox place? They send the occasional VIP patients to us. Sometimes they're drugged up, out of their minds. It's not the type of place you want to be associated with. And you have to be careful, because clearly you have the gene. Look, you're an adult, and you need to make your own decisions. But you need to have all the info to make the decision. I know it's tough love, everything I'm telling you, but someone had to do it. You have a bright future, and I don't want you to get in with the wrong crowd. I think you should leave that place immediately."

After they hang up, Taylor slumps down on the curb.

She's reminded, suddenly, of that woman addict she'd encountered on the street, outside the Knox. Did her mom look more like her than the glamorous woman conquering Boston Taylor had always envisioned?

Thoughts and the absence of thoughts swirl in her like a confused cyclone, rearranging the pieces of the life she once knew.

She starts to call her dad but then hangs up. After a moment, she texts him. She's never texted him before; she doesn't even know if he knows how to text. But it's the only way she can currently muster the strength to communicate with him.

> I just saw Aunt Gigi. Is it true about Mom?

There are dots as he's typing back. Finally, he responds.

> Yes

Taylor's mom's last letter

Dear T.J.,

I am so sorry I haven't written in a while. I miss you very much,
my little monkey! It's just that my work has been very busy, and
Boston is so exciting that the days fly by. This week I went to an
oyster restaurant. I didn't find any pearls (if I did, I would have
saved them for you), but I did eat a lot of oysters. They were very
big and salty! I think you would like oysters but you may need to
wait until you're older because they are raw so they can make you
sick. But it's nothing to be scared of. If you like, I'll take you to try
your first one.

   It's getting cold here, it gets so much colder than back home,
and we even had our first snowfall! But the city doesn't go to sleep
and hibernate like a bear. Instead it stays alive and exciting. I never
went a moment of my life in a place where the locals didn't know
me from day one, but here I am a stranger to everyone. Here, little
monkey, I can be anyone. The streets and houses are so old and
charming and lit up with beautiful streetlamps that sometimes
Mommy feels like she's in a fairy tale! The only thing missing is her

princess daughter. I'm wearing such pretty clothes that I can't wait to show you. And they look so good because Mommy is finally nice and thin! You know me, always so vain.

Anyway, always remember that I love you very, very much. And that you will forever be Mommy's little monkey. I'll write again real soon.

Love,
Mommy

THE KNOX

February

I daresay, I know why Vivian appears familiar.

It took seeing her in a heap at the bottom of my grand staircase, her face as gray-white as Carrara marble, to put two and two hundred years together. That woman is the spitting image of Margaret Thurgood, née Knox. They share identical large green eyes and have the same elegant nose and fine cheekbones. They simply *must* be related.

Why, observing Vivian in that unnatural position brought it all back like it was yesterday: when Margaret lay as cold as an icebox on her son's medical table in my basement.

I'll always be grateful to Margaret; she was the one who hired the original Rose, after all, an Irish woman named Aoife. But when Margaret birthed a baby after Teddy had been at sea for eighteen months—well, the math speaks for itself. Margaret *had* to send the baby away, and, naturally, she entrusted the baby to her most loyal servant, Aoife.

Prior to Vivian's "accident," I was not certain whether baby Mercy had survived or passed away. But now, I have no doubt.

Margaret hired another "Rose"—one who called herself

Sara—and to my utter delight, the second Rose turned out to be markedly better than the first. When Teddy returned from Canton, China, his bags bulging with opium, and they threw the legendary opium parties, Sara would tidy me up the moment the guests left. Given the nature of those affairs, sometimes that meant the following day, sometimes the following week.

The problem herein lies that Margaret developed quite the taste for opium. She turned to it after losing all those babies. And once she gave up Mercy—her only other child, besides Robert— Margaret grew bereft, relying on more and more opium. Robert grew up rather unattended to; nobody to advise him what was right and wrong.

Naturally here at the society, we follow a moral code of our own devising.

Right can be right, but wrong can be right, too.

Diary Entry of Dr. Robert Thurgood

December 13, 1855

I am fortunate in that my memory, unlike that of my peer counterparts, grows uncommonly sharper as I age. One morning, I did suddenly recall, with not a margin for error, how Mother's stomach swelled after Father had already been away at sea for well over a year. This, I recalled, was followed by a baby's cries at all hours through the bedroom walls, until one day the cries ceased, the timing of which coincided with the leaving of my favorite servant, Aoife—who used to sneak me an extra spoonful of sugar in my morning porridge.

The cause for such egregious deception to Father and me I can only attribute to Mother's reliance on laudanum for her hysteria; this foul, nasty habit persisted to her last dying breath. I pray that future generations shall understand the ill effects, both seen and unseen, of such a weakness, and I hereby dedicate myself to studying this cause.

TAYLOR

Taylor knocks on the glass of Turned Pages, the bookstore. The sign reads OPEN, but the door is locked. It feels fitting; everything in her life is completely backward, after all. Maybe she shouldn't even bother with the shop anymore, but after she sat long enough on the curb to regain her breath and steady herself, she got up and then approached the door like it was the logical thing to do. Because, fuck, what else can she do right now?

There's movement inside; a white-haired man slowly comes to the entrance. A bell jangles as the door groans open.

"Sorry; it's a sticky door. Can I help you?" he croaks.

"Hi," she says, with a shaky breath. She's about two seconds away from losing it. Who is she kidding about logical things? She has no idea what is what. "I'm Taylor. Jerry's friend." *Jerry's friend* doesn't exactly roll off her tongue very easily, but she keeps going. "Jerry dropped off some really old books yesterday, and you asked him to come by?"

Recognition lights up the man's eyes. "Oh, yes."

"Well, he couldn't make it, so I'm here for him. The books came from the both of us."

"Come on in."

She follows him as he carefully descends the stairs. The musty smell of books fills the space like a lit candle.

"The name's Nicholas," he says. "Do you want to look around, Taylor, or have a seat? I need to take care of something in the back, and then I'll be with you shortly."

"Sure, yeah."

He shuffles off, leaving Taylor alone. She reverts to her default survival mode, noting the egress routes. It's almost comforting to complete this surveillance—to have *something* to do. But then it's done, and she's surrounded once more with her confusing reality.

In a daze, she takes in the collection of old books that surround her.

Stories. That's what her mom was—a story. A fictional story. Taylor didn't know her, not really.

Tears spring unexpectedly to her eyes, and she rummages through her purse for a tissue. Her fingers brush against the phoenix mask; Liam gave her the one he'd stuffed in the couch, as it got too crinkled, and they had extras. *Maybe you can repurpose those feathers, sew them on a jacket or something*, he'd said.

Nicholas's voice filters from the back space; is he on the phone?

What Liam did was a kind gesture, but she doesn't know if she can trust him—if she can trust any of them. Jerry knew she was a nurse. *The Knox* knew.

Who screamed? Was someone in the fourth-floor window, or were my eyes playing tricks on me?

Why didn't my dad tell me the truth?

Who was my mom?

Nicholas returns, unfolds a cloth on the counter, and then momentarily disappears. She hears a faucet running, and this time when he comes back, he has a book in his hands. He places it gently down on the cloth. It's smaller than a typical book, more like the size of a diary, with a fragile-looking leather cover.

"Come, Taylor," he says. "I want to show you the book your friend brought me. It's . . . unique."

"Unique?" she repeats.

"Unbelievably so."

Her stomach flutters. Unique must mean valuable. Maybe Jerry was right about this old stuff.

"Do you know Latin?" Nicholas asks, and she shakes her head. He points to the book cover. "This title, *Opii Pericula*, is Latin for *Dangers of Opium*."

"*Dangers of Opium*," she repeats. It's the second time today the drug's come up; that feels somehow important.

"The author is Edgar Rolo Butterworth, which happens to be an anagram of a person named Robert Walter Thurgood. And look here"—he flips forward to the dedication—"'Matri meae causis manifestis,' meaning, 'To My Mother, for obvious reasons.'"

"Huh." Taylor is flummoxed. *Why is he telling me this?*

Nicholas must see the confusion in her eyes. He gently closes the cover. "I'm sorry, I'm getting ahead of myself."

The door chime rings, and Taylor turns to see a pretty, fortyish-year-old woman in a tan trench coat flouncing down the stairs.

"Nicholas, thank you for calling. I got here as soon as I could." She turns to Taylor, sticking out her hand. "Hello. My name is Rachel."

Taylor hesitantly takes her hand. Rachel's not smiling, and

Taylor doesn't get the warmest vibe from her. Who is she? Maybe a co-owner of the bookstore? "I'm Taylor."

"You work at the Knox, Taylor?" Rachel asks.

"Yes," Taylor replies, and then instantly feels guarded. Should she be admitting she works at the Knox, or is that violating her confidentiality agreement? Truth be told, she didn't really read that thing. Jerry clearly did, though.

"And this book was found in the basement, during a renovation project? Is that right?"

Taylor slowly nods; it's not like she was the one who divulged this information—Jerry did—so she figures there's no harm in confirming it.

"And what do you do there?"

It's a simple question, but Taylor suddenly feels overwhelmed, Aunt Gigi's revelation about her mom resurfacing.

As she hesitates, Rachel says, "Relax. This conversation stays here."

But Taylor just shakes her head, trying to push down the emotions now rising in her. She can't trust herself to speak.

Rachel and Nicholas exchange a glance.

"I'll go put the teakettle on," Nicholas says. He retreats to the back of the store.

"I'm sorry, I don't mean to be so abrupt. You'll have to forgive me; it's been a long few months," Rachel says. She's clearly attributing Taylor's reticence as a reaction to her demeanor. "My friend got involved at the Knox, and now she's missing."

Taylor clears her throat. "I'm sorry to hear that," she manages to respond. But she's still in her own head.

"I was hoping you could help," Rachel tries again, wringing her hands.

"I've only just started working there—last week was my first week—so I'm not sure how much help I can be to you."

Rachel's shoulders collapse. "That's a shame. I was hoping you might have known her. But maybe you know people who do?"

"I don't know. People aren't that talkative. I'm also just a waitress, so . . ."

"I see."

Taylor's eyes flicker to the book. She's curious—and wants to distract herself. "I'm not trying to be rude, but what does this have to do with that book?"

"My friend was searching for proof that she was related to the Knox. Well, to be precise, she was searching for a 'schedule of beneficiaries' naming her ancestor as heir to the Knox realty trust. She never found it. But this book here may be able to prove Vivian's lineage, after all."

Taylor feels like a ton of bricks has just dropped out of the sky and fallen on her. "I'm sorry. . . . You said her name is Vivian?"

"Yes. Vivian Lawrence."

Taylor swallows. There's a pounding in her head. She presses against the desk. "I . . . I see."

Rachel's eyes narrow. "Do you know her? Did you hear something?"

"No."

"Are you sure?"

"I don't kn— I haven't heard anything about a Vivian Lawrence at the Knox." This, at least, is true. Meanwhile, she feels like she's clawing out from beneath the bricks.

Vivian is somehow related to the Knox?

"So, what happened to her?" she manages to ask.

"She was dating someone at the Knox, a man named Peter."

It takes all her resolve for Taylor to stay still, expressionless.

Peter? Peter was Vivian's boyfriend?

"And like I said, Vivian was looking for confirmation that she was a descendant of the Knox, and one night when she was there, she was acting strange, texting to ask me questions about a mutual friend of ours, Xavier. Do you know a Xavier?"

"No, I don't." Taylor hears the words coming out of her mouth, but it's like someone else is saying them. *Peter was Vivian's boyfriend.* Of course he was. Taylor's suddenly hit with the nauseous realization of how interconnected it all is, and, at the same time, the embarrassingly wide divide. The truth so plain to see, like a default font: Men like Peter date Vivians, not Taylors.

"Anyway, that night, at the Knox, she fell down the stairs."

Vivian Lawrence, age forty-four, unwitnessed fall down a flight of stairs at a cocktail party.

"Oh, I'm sorry," Taylor mumbles, when she realizes Rachel is waiting for a response.

"Yes, she had this compulsive thing where she always had to straighten any wall hanging that was crooked, and apparently there was an uneven piece of artwork at the top of the stairs. And when she went to straighten it, she lost her balance, and . . ." Rachel spreads her hands.

But it was an *unwitnessed* fall, Taylor wants to correct Rachel, snapping to with this detail. At least, that's what Taylor was told by the paramedics.

Rachel continues. "And the fall caused a traumatic brain injury. She was a patient at Mass General. But then, she disappeared."

"What do you mean, 'she disappeared'?"

"Someone—a 'medical power of attorney'"—she uses air quotes here—"moved her to another location. And we have no idea where she is. Or who moved her."

She was moved to an undisclosed location, Aunt Gigi's voice rings in Taylor's ear.

"I didn't even know she had a medical power of attorney. And the only thing I can think is that someone from the Knox moved her. That they were threatened by her family link. Maybe they forged a medical power of attorney. They're powerful, right?"

Taylor nods, unsure how else to answer. They *are* powerful. And she is—she is *not*. She's as far from the Knox and their glittering world as she's ever been.

"I went by there, to the Knox, and spoke to a beefy fellow. He looked like a bouncer at a nightclub and acted like one, too. He barely let me through the door. Just pointed to the top of the stairs and told me the story of what happened."

Jerry. She must mean Jerry. Taylor glances in the direction of Nicholas, to see if he recognizes the description of Jerry, but he's still in the back, fixing the tea.

"And funny enough," Rachel continues, "that mutual friend of ours, Xavier? He's also gone missing. He mailed me a letter, saying he was sorry—but I don't know what he is 'sorry' for—and now he's AWOL. So something is not right. And I'm worried."

"So you don't know where Vivian is," Taylor says.

She becomes hyperaware of how the shop is below street level. *She* is below street level. Just as well, really. She doesn't belong upstairs. Neither did her mom—they were both deluded from the start.

"No, I don't. I have *no* idea. Well, 'she'"—Rachel uses air quotes again—"sent me an email a couple of weeks ago, but I don't believe it's from her. I think someone wrote it from her phone."

"Oh?" The walls of the bookstore begin slowly pressing in.

"She said she was in Florida. She never goes to Florida; she doesn't like the humidity and heat there. And she asked me where Xavier is . . . which felt like the real reason for the email. Something fishy is going on. . . . When I call, it goes to her voicemail. I went to the police, but they won't help. They said, 'It's not a crime for a medical power of attorney to exercise health care decisions for someone who is incapacitated.' And then I circled back to the police, once I got her email. And the moment I mentioned the Knox, they just instantly blew me off. I wouldn't be surprised if the Knox has the police department in their pocket," Rachel seethes.

"Oh my God." Taylor is trying to maintain normal appearances, but she's finding it increasingly difficult to breathe.

"I know. It sounds crazy, right? Maybe you can help." Rachel smiles somewhat meekly at Taylor. "You have helped, already. Thanks to you and your friend, we at least now have the book, with the proof of ancestry that Vivian was searching for."

"'The proof of ancestry'?" Taylor says, grabbing at a random phrase. She briefly closes her eyes, hoping that will help, but it only amplifies the claustrophobia.

Rachel pauses. "Yes. Although it's . . . rather complicated."

Nicholas returns with three steaming mugs of tea. He places them on a small table on the opposite side of the room. "Let's drink these over here, away from the book," he says.

"I . . . I gotta go," Taylor says. She can't leave this store fast enough. She shoves past Rachel, runs up the stairs, and spills through the door onto the street. She's gasping for air.

It's only when she's a few blocks away, in the middle of the public garden, surrounded by weeping willow trees and large swathes of sky, that she feels like there's finally a sufficient supply of air.

But though her breathing slows, her mind does not.

Mail Delivery Subsystem <mailer-daemon@googlemail.com>
to me:

The response from the remote server was:

```
550 5.4.1 Recipient address rejected: Access denied.
```

--------Forwarded message--------

From: Vivian Lawrence <vivian@storiedantiques.com>
To: Xavier Sánchez <xavier@xavierjewelry.com>

Dear Xavier,

I really need to talk to you. It's very important. I received the note you left for me at the Knox, but I didn't completely understand it. You may have heard that that night, I took a spill down the stairs. I was in the hospital for a while, but now I'm okay. We need to talk. Let me know the best way to get in touch.

—Vivian

From: Vivian Lawrence <vivian@storiedantiques.com>
To: Rachel Stein <rachel@rachelthegenealogist.com>

Rachel,

Do you know where Xavier is? Do you have his updated email address? The one I have for him got bounced back. Please let me know. It's very important I reach him. Thanks.

—V

TAYLOR

Taylor opens her apartment door and collapses on the uncomfortable, too-small couch, whose frame is sticking into her like a bony protrusion. She should move to her bedroom, but she's too exhausted, her head fuzzy from everything she's learned today.

Your mom was strung out. The deeper she got into drugs, the more erratic her life became. Vivian was romantically involved with Peter. Vivian's ancestors come from the Knox. Vivian fell at the Knox. Vivian is alive. Vivian is missing. Vivian. Vivian. Vivian.

Vivian floods her mind, overtaking her mom, like a dam that's burst.

There's a terrible thought that begins swimming inside Taylor: If the Knox realized Vivian was a distant relative, and possibly owed an inheritance, then what lengths would they go to secure their fortune?

Suddenly, Taylor hears footsteps outside her door. Holding her breath, she waits. Is it Sam? No; she'd noticed his street-level lights were off—he's not home. It must be one of the upstairs neighbors, traipsing around the too-thin floors.

There are no more footsteps, and she lets out her breath. Maybe she imagined it. But in the next instant, she startles: The scream from earlier keeps slicing through her subconscious like a sharp knife.

She shakes her head, gets up to grab a glass of water. As she takes a sip, she spots an envelope at the foot of her door. Someone *was* in the hall earlier.

Taylor Adams, due to private internal affairs, we do not require your presence at the moment.*
Please report back to work on Monday morning.
Thank you kindly for your attention to this matter.

*Any violations of this request shall result in immediate dismissal and may be subject to legal repercussions.

This must be the paid "staycation" Liam was referencing. Taylor angrily crushes the note in her hand. How can she figure anything out if she's not allowed back at the Knox?

A thought suddenly seizes her: Was she brought on by the Knox *because* she's a link to Vivian? No—she rejects the idea. Anna is the one who referred her. She wouldn't—and couldn't—have known that Taylor took care of Vivian. Boston just happens to be a small, incestuous city.

But still. There are so many coincidences, so many questions and no answers at all.

She wonders how—or if—Peter and the other members fit into Vivian's disappearance. Anna mentioned that a well-dressed man had come around Vivian's antiques store—that could have been any of the Knox members. Have they been paying Vivian's rent? Or is Taylor drawing loose connections?

She suddenly misses her dad fiercely. She'd give anything to rewind time, to be back home in her childhood bedroom, when the most worrisome thought was how she was going to escape the boredom of her town. Before she knew the truth about her mom. A truth that she's currently squashing into a tight ball, trying to keep apart from the rest of her. She cannot even begin to fathom it, not really. All she knows is this: As much as she longs for her dad, there is no way in hell she can speak with him right now—not after how he betrayed her trust all these years.

Trust.

She remembers what Liam said to her: *Peter is the one who brought me here, from across the pond. . . . It's all about trust here. . . . The Knox scales down to essential personnel only.*

Taylor is not essential, nor trusted.

But who *is* trusted? Is Jerry? What if he fabricated the story behind Vivian's fall? And why does he want to leave the Knox now? What is going on that the others, like Eduardo, can't see? Is someone else living in the servants' quarters with them, like the phantom woman in the window?

Taylor opens her laptop on her counter, thinking. She feels like she's missing something. She's looked up Vivian online plenty of times, but never her fellow employees, so she decides to do just that. But she realizes, almost embarrassingly, she doesn't know their last names. Something tugs at her memory. Liam calling Jerry "O'Doyle," Eduardo correcting him to "Doyle."

She types "Jerry Doyle" into her browser. She filters her search to Boston, to Beacon Hill, but she finds barely anything, not even across social media platforms. But what about Tara, his sister? The aspiring nurse?

Bingo: Tara Doyle is on Facebook. And, although she only has two public photos listed, one of a stethoscope and another of Acorn Street—Boston's famous cobblestone street—when Taylor looks through the comments on the former, she gets a lead.

I have the same stethoscope, but in pink! Molly Frank writes.

And then, a couple of comments down, Molly remarks: U should join the Boston Student Nurse group, if u don't already belong.

Taylor promptly requests to join that private group, checking the boxes to indicate that Yes, I'm currently a nursing student, Yes, I will abide by the rules, and Yes, I agree to not violate any patient's confidentiality. An administrator happens to be online, because Taylor's request is instantly approved.

She searches through the group's members to find Tara Doyle, who apparently joined one month ago. Taylor prepares to take a deep dive into Tara Doyle's group posts and activity, but she doesn't have to go very far.

Molly Frank: Hi Tara! Glad to see you took my advice! Welcome to the Group! What do you need help with?

Tara Doyle: I'm still in nursing school (I guess we all are), but Patient V fell down the stairs and has a subdural hematoma/traumatic brain injury. She was discharged from the hospital about two months ago and is now at a longer term care place. I'm doing my clinical rotation here, so she is my patient.

Molly Frank: Poor Patient V! What's your question?

Sharon Pinkton: Tara Doyle, which LTC?

Tara Doyle: Molly Frank, my question is about her medical management. V is recovering but she does sometimes get agitated. We started her on Amantadine for her traumatic brain injury and Xanax for her agitation.

Molly Frank: Amantadine? I thought that's used to treat Parkinson's tremors.

Sharon Pinkton: I thought Amantadine is an anti-viral ☺

Tara Doyle: It's both! But they also use it to help with cognition in traumatic brain injuries. It helps with neuroprotection, I guess. That's what the house doctor said.

Molly Frank: Interesting. I just looked it up. It seems like it's used more for moderate to severe cases?? Is that Patient V? Also, you should be careful with the use of benzodiazepines like Xanax. Is V on an anti-seizure medication?

Sharon Pinkton: House doctor?

Tara Doyle: Sorry. I mean the doctor.

Sharon Pinkton: Which LTC?

Tara Doyle: Sharon Pinkton, what does LTC mean?

Sharon Pinkton: You really don't know? Long-term care facility. Which one? I'm also working at one right now, in Brookline. I'm a second year nursing student at the IHP. What about you?

Tara Doyle: Molly Frank, V is not a bad case. I don't know why they prescribed Amantadine. . . . The doctor did, not me! She is on Keppra for seizure prevention. Also why do we need to be careful with Xanax? This is my question, btw. What can we use in addition to the Xanax when she gets agitated and impulsive?

Sharon Pinkton: Which LTC?

Molly Frank: They don't like to use benzodiazepines like Xanax in the long run. They can cause confusion. Also they can be addictive ☺ Esp in elderly (I don't know if V is?)

Sharon Pinkton: Which LTC?

Tara Doyle: Molly Frank, ah, okay, good to know. So what do you suggest?

Molly Frank: Zyprexa, Seroquel, Trazodone? What is she on for pain management?

Tara Doyle: Oxycodone

Molly Frank: Also need to be careful with long term use of narcotics ☺

Tara Doyle: Well she does have pain! Also a fractured wrist.

Sharon Pinkton: Which LTC? Why won't you answer??

Tara Doyle: Sharon Pinkton, chill. Maybe YOU need a Xanax!

Sharon Pinkton: No need to be rude. I'm going to flag this for the admins.

Tara Doyle: Sharon Pinkton, sorry. I'm just a little stressed out. It doesn't really matter where I'm working with V bc I'll only be helping her for a few more days.

VIVIAN

Present Day

Shadows flit in and out of her vision, a woman's voice low as she speaks to someone else in the room—a male whose form seems to shape-shift, as if Vivian cannot, or does not, want to recognize him.

Her fear grows prickly, sharp.

Who are these people? Why is she here, at the Knox? Where the hell is Peter, her alleged boyfriend? Is *he* the man in the room?

She chews her hazy, ill-defined thoughts like food, and then gradually becomes aware that she is, in fact, chewing a piece of food. No, make that a semisolid mass, like applesauce. How did *that* happen? Is someone feeding her? In the next moment, she's startled to realize she's sitting up, in a chair, propped up like some doll. And she knows that she's done this before, multiple times before: sit in the chair, *eat*.

Yet, without warning, she's back in her bed. Hours erased, as if she's been heavily sedated.

Christ. It's the TBI. It's making her mind appear and then disappear, allowing her to inhabit her body only for short spurts.

But as she runs her tongue over her teeth, tasting the bitter remnants of Xanax, she realizes, with a chill, she *is* getting sedated.

Meanwhile, time ticks, ticks, ticks. There seems to be a waiting, a prolonged waiting. Something everyone is waiting for. Something she, by default, is waiting for.

Vivian knows, with absolute clarity, that it can't be good.

TAYLOR

Taylor stares at her laptop screen, the words of the Facebook student nurse group chat blurring as her mind trips over what they mean.

The Knox *is* holding Vivian captive. And they've hired Tara to help take care of her.

The clues were there: The amantadine Taylor found in the trash. The Med-Ox medical van circling in the neighborhood. The rent for Vivian's antiques store paid in advance by a "well-dressed" man. The warning note with the Knox symbol in Vivian's apartment.

The piercing scream.

All along, Vivian has been at the Knox, in one of their many upstairs rooms.

Who is in on it? And what is it that they are trying to do with her?

Shadowy, undefined thoughts circulating in Taylor's head morph into terrible shapes. Perhaps Vivian's death is only a matter of time. She's a potential heir, a threat to the Knox. In the group chat, Tara Doyle had posted: *I'll only be helping her for a few more days.*

Taylor lifts her water glass with trembling hands. What has her life come to, that she has these thoughts? That this is the scenario before her?

Maybe she should go back to being a nurse, like that note said. Like Jerry had said.

Suddenly, she remembers something else he said: *I had a little chat with your nurse manager, Jan. A little "accidental" run-in at the St. Patrick's Day parade.*

Taylor was still working at the hospital in March. She hadn't yet quit. Nor yet applied for the Knox. So why were they asking around about Taylor in March?

There's only one explanation: because she was Vivian's nurse. Taylor's employment is not random.

Did they hire her to be another private-duty nurse for Vivian? Or is it because Taylor was the last person Vivian spoke to before she lost consciousness? What was it she'd said, again? Something about not clinking champagne glasses?

A knock at the door startles Taylor, and the glass slips from her hand, shattering on the floor.

"Taylor!"

It's Sam. Taylor sidesteps the shards to open the door. "Careful," she says, pointing at the ground.

"Whoa," he says. He looks awful: His black button-down shirt is wrinkled, a light stubble covers his lower face, and his hair is uncharacteristically mussed. Sam's a hairstylist; his hair never looks out of place.

"Where are you coming from?"

He leans against the door, briefly closing his eyes. "I was at the casino. I'm so glad I caught you. Are you on your way to the Knox?"

"On my way *to*? No—I already worked there today. Do you know what time it is?"

He shakes his head. "My phone died."

"It's five o'clock. In the evening. Tuesday evening."

He rubs his eyes. "My phone died," he repeats. "I wanted to call you because I found some stuff . . ." His voice trails off, and Taylor realizes that all is not right with him.

Join the club, she thinks.

"Sam, are you okay?"

"No. Yeah. I mean, I'm okay. Tired as fuck obviously. . . . You know that guy I met on Raya?"

She frowns. "Miami Guy? The one who was over just last night?"

Sam rubs his face. "Was that only last night? It feels like a week ago. Yeah. Yeah, so he knows a few people in Boston. We were hanging out here—as you know—and then one of *his* friends invited us out to this gay bar in the South End. So we went, and then we kept partying, back at his place. One of those nights, you know," he says sheepishly. "And then I don't know what time it was—like maybe four or five in the morning? This morning, I guess? Well, then, Oliver"—he looks at Taylor intently—"as in Oliver from the Knox, showed up at the guy's apartment."

Taylor grimaces. "How do you know who Oliver is?"

"I didn't. Not at first. We were all hanging out; he had a bunch of friends with him. We were drinking, and some of the guys, including Oliver, were all high on something. Then he invited our group to go to Encore. So he takes out his phone and calls this person. He says, 'Rose, I need a van for ten people right now to go to Encore.' And I'm thinking, *Who is Rose, and who is this guy—that he could just make a call and poof, like ten minutes later, there's a fucking party van waiting for us outside to take us to the casino?* And then we get there, and he's greeted like a celebrity, even though it's like maybe eight o'clock in the morning. People are saying, 'I'm sorry about your father,' and he's at the high-roller tables, and then someone makes a dumb knock-knock joke to him. . . . Then it hits me. Holy shit. This guy must be from the Knox. Like, one of them."

"Whoa," Taylor says. "That's a crazy coincidence." She wants to tell Sam that Oliver is more than just "one" of them, he's about to be in charge, but she's not sure now is the right time, given his state of mind—and *hers*. She is only halfway in this conversation. The dark circles beneath his eyes are like small caves; he looks how *she* feels. She puts her hand on his arm. It's cold. Or perhaps it's *her* hand that is ice. She's all out of sorts. "You should take some Tylenol and eat some greasy food."

He grins. "I knew you were still a nurse, underneath all this."

She gives a thin smile. "I don't know what I am anymore." A wave of exhaustion rolls over her. She wants to just collapse, lie down on the shards of glass. She might welcome the pain, the chance for her mind and body to be occupied with something other than her current situation.

"Hey, is there some sort of big Knox event coming up?"

"Yeah . . . the initiation. Why? And how do you know that?"

"Well, listen to this." He grasps Taylor's shoulders, surprising her. "I've got some unbelievable gossip." His breath comes at her like the last call at a bar, and she recoils slightly. "Oliver has a gambling problem."

"That's not surprising."

"No, but like a serious one. Like he was in *deep* before his father died. One of his buddies told me, after he'd had too many. He said it was a good thing the old man passed."

"Really?"

"Yeah, this place is weird, Taylor. We may need to get you another job. Are you there for the initiation? Like, do they have you working it?"

"No."

"Okay, good." He relaxes his grip. "Because Oliver said something about it. He was pretty fucked-up by that point. He said something about three nights leading up to the grand finale, and then . . ." Sam laughs. "Then he said that there's some sort of sacrifice that will be made."

Taylor swallows. "A *sacrifice*? Are you sure?"

He whistles and then nods. "These weird rich dudes. It's like a movie. You can't make this shit up."

⟨◦———◦⟩

Once Sam leaves, Taylor promptly crumples onto her barstool. He has no idea of the seriousness of the tea he just spilled. There's a sickening thought that's taken hold of her, one too horrible to voice.

There *has* to be a reason the Knox is keeping Vivian captive, instead of just killing her—if her inheritance is that much of a threat.

I'll only be helping her for a few more days, Tara had written.

Taylor knows that tonight begins the three nights of preparation, followed by the initiation—the "sacrifice" Oliver mentioned.

The timeline matches, though she wishes more than anything in the world it did not.

Nausea trickles up her throat as she turns to her laptop. Her fingers shake as she types into the search bar two phrases: "secret societies" and "sacrifice." To her horror, result after result pops up, flooding her screen.

Human sacrifice, it seems, has been used by secret societies throughout time.

Initiation Night

Purpose. This section serves to detail the procedure for Initiation Night.

Scope and Application. This section applies to all living current Knox Members as defined by paragraph (a) of section I.22 and to Prospective Members as defined by section I.89(a–c, ii) and again in section 336.4(i–x).

1. Current Knox Members shall dress in Initiation Night attire consisting of a black robe and black face mask to represent the solemnity of the evening and the uncertainty of Membership being offered to Prospective Members.

2. Current Members shall gather in the parlor for a period of no less than two hours to reflect and become spiritually inclined.*

3. Membership shall split into three entities to position themselves at each of the three scrolls: the Bowels, the Heart, the Brains.

4. The scrolls shall be carefully opened by a designated Knox Member.

5. Prospective Members shall be allowed to enter the premises. They shall be given attire to don, a white robe only, to reflect their openness to and hope of joining Membership.

6. Each Prospective Member shall begin his Journey to Initiation at the Bowels scroll located in the basement.

   a. Prospective Members of Non-Legacy Status are required to offer the Sacrifice[†] in presence of Knox Members, and such details shall be recorded in the Bowels scroll by a designated scribe.[‡]

   b. Following completion of the Sacrifice, a designated Knox Member skilled in geomantic divination and *enlightened in mind* shall perform a geomancy reading to determine suitability of offering Membership to each Prospective Member, regardless of Legacy Status.

      i. If such reading reveals it is *not* fortuitous to offer Membership, Prospective Member(s) will be promptly excused from the premises.

      ii. Prospective Members who have completed the Sacrifice and whose geomancy reading is favorable shall move forward with their Journey to Initiation by continuing to the Heart scroll, where their name shall be recorded by a designated Knox scribe.[§]

      iii. All Prospective Members shall continue to the third floor for the final step, the Brains scroll, where they shall read, learn, and recite preselected passages of the Knox's Charter.[◊]

      iv. Upon conclusion of the three scrolls visit, the Prospective Member's Journey to Initiation is considered complete. Prospective Members shall proceed to the parlor for an official recognition of Membership.[◻]

* *The use of opium is highly encouraged to create a conducive atmosphere.*

† *See Section 8, "The Sacrifice."*

‡ *In modern times, the Sacrifice shall be discreetly recorded and saved to a hard drive.*

§ *While written transcription of names onto the Heart scroll is indicative of forthcoming Membership, all Prospective Members must complete the rest of their Journey to Initiation before official recognition.*

◊ *Such processes may take time, hours to days, and shall not be rushed.*

¤ *It is customary to acknowledge such a momentous occasion with a celebration.*

URGENT help finding a jeweler

Hi! I'm in URGENT need to find a specific jeweler who specializes in bespoke 19k gold pendants. His name is Xavier and he used to have a store in one of the jewelry buildings on Washington Street. Can anyone help??? This is time sensitive. Will pay generously $$$ for a lead/referral!!! You can reach me at: Vivian@storiedantiques.com

TAYLOR

For three days, Taylor is undone. Nothing makes sense; the threads of her life—her memories, experiences, assumptions—are fraying.

With each passing hour, she comes further apart, sinking into a tangled pile of her disappointments, her failures, her inaction.

On the fourth day, she awakes with a sudden urgency. The Knox's three nights of preparation are over; tonight is the ensuing initiation. The sacrifice.

Rising from the fog, Taylor sits at her sewing machine. As she fires it up, she studies the collection of Knox emblems tacked onto her fridge. It reads like a story of the past couple of months: the top hat she drew from memory after breaking into Vivian's apartment, the last letter Taylor's mom ever wrote her, the Knox's employment offer, and then the warning note: "Go back to being a nurse."

She takes a large swathe of black silk and the damaged phoenix mask from Liam, and she begins to sew. Running the cloth through the machine, repairing the mask by hand. Everything, it seems, comes down to this: past and present and future tying together in each stitch she makes, in each accidental needle prick she suffers. Memories of her mom rising as she pulls her needle through the fabric and abating as she finishes yet another seam. Vivian, whirring in the sewing machine, an unending pulsation. And Taylor herself, the conduit, the cord.

Throughout, she keeps arriving at this: It is she who must go to the Knox tonight, to save Vivian. A determination steels in her, a feeling—however irrational it might be—that if she can save Vivian, she might somehow fix the other holes in her life.

◆──────◆

Taylor walks quickly in the black silk cape, the train flowing behind her like a gothic bridal gown. Adrenaline courses through her like fluid in an IV. It's a little after midnight, the sky also clothed in darkness.

In her hand she clutches both the repaired phoenix mask and a bag of wigs Sam dropped off earlier at her doorstep. I'm going to a costume party. Do you have any wigs I can borrow?, she'd texted him, pretending not to be home when he knocked a few minutes later.

There's an eeriness on the streets—a sense of something quietly brewing—as if the city itself knows that initiation night has arrived. The police, too, know. Taylor anonymously messaged them on the Boston Crime Stoppers tip line before leaving her apartment: *I'm reporting that a crime will occur this evening at the Knox secret society building in Beacon Hill during their initiation ceremony. It will involve the use of the drug opium and a human sacrifice.*

But will the police take it seriously? Rachel said they blew her off when she approached them about Vivian. *I wouldn't be surprised if the Knox has the police department in their pocket.*

So Taylor also left Sam a note under his door, keeping the message simple: *I've gone to the Knox to check on something.* But then she added a pretty dire request: *If I'm not back by 4:00 in the morning, please go get the police. For REAL.*

She first approaches the Knox from its front facade; it's dark, imposing. The long curtains in the front parlor drawn as if the whole building has gone to sleep for the night. But Taylor knows that can't be further from the truth.

She then turns to wind through the streets, now arriving near the back of the building. A couple passes holding hands, and she waits until they fade into the distance. Then she reaches into the wig bag to grab a random one but is dismayed to find they are all brightly colored: orange, purple, blue, red. *Shit.* Of course Sam would lend her colorful ones for a *costume* party. She's about to discard the whole lot on the curb, but on second thought, she grabs one at random and shoves it into the deep pocket of the black sweatpants she's wearing beneath the cape.

Slipping the phoenix mask over her face, Taylor darts up to the back door to quickly cover the security camera with a towel. It's hard to believe she last used this door as an employee only four days earlier.

Cupping her ear against the door, she listens: silence. She straightens and counts down from five to one, trying to slow her madly beating heart. Then she turns her key in the lock. Whisking open the door, she steals inside.

The usual overhead dim bulbs are not turned on, and it takes a few seconds for her eyes to adjust. She holds her breath, waiting. Then she lets out a long, slow exhale. She is alone. She could laugh, she's so relieved.

She needs to make her way upstairs and find Vivian before the sacrifice. It's the only thing she knows for sure, and she lets it steel her against all the unknowns: which room Vivian's in, where the sacrifice will take place, what it entails . . .

Taylor swallows, willing her nerves to settle. She creeps down the hall, now familiar after the two weeks she's spent there, and passes by the area with the painted dot symbols. Something to do with geomancy, surely. She never did figure out what the numbers on the opposite wall mean, but it doesn't matter. Much of the Knox, she realizes, she won't ever know. She doesn't *want* to know.

Suddenly, she hears distant voices. *Shit.* She stops short, waits. The voices are getting louder. It's two, maybe three men talking. Why would someone be coming this way? There's nothing back here, except the exit from whence she came. She glances behind her, wondering what to do. *Shit!*

Her heart pounding, she remembers the morning she ran into Jerry and Eduardo in these halls. *The servants' quarters connect to the Knox building in the basement, so we just go down and up.* And the time she ran into Rose coming from there, carrying the tea mugs. Taylor can hide in there, wait it out.

The entrance *has* to be somewhere along here. She presses against the walls, spreading out her trembling hands.

The voices are getting closer. She catches a few words: "the scrolls . . . Oliver and Rose . . ."

Suddenly, in a small miracle, her hand latches on to a groove.

She pushes against it, and a door releases, swinging inward. She slips through—it's dark—and immediately whips around and kneels, grasping the bottom of the door with her fingers to pull it just shy of closed.

Then Taylor has a terrifying thought: *What if they're coming in here?*

She strains to listen. There's a low, continuous beating that sounds mechanical in nature. But no voices.

Several minutes pass, or what feels like it. Her fingers are cramping, her back hurts. Finally, it feels safe to ease open the door. But her fingers slip, and the door closes completely. For the life of her, she can't figure out how to reopen it.

She's locked in.

THE KNOX

Who dares enter on this sacred night?

There is an intruder in the mix. An imposter. Someone who accessed my back entrance and then descended into the cellar. One who clearly possesses knowledge of the connection between my building and the servants' quarters. One who wishes to remain unseen, in the shadows, wearing the mask and cape.

But there is no such thing as anonymity here.

The intruder shall remain locked in the cellar for the foreseeable future. The members will eventually chance upon the intruder—or they will not. Starvation is a painfully long, drawn-out death.

It is not the first time an outsider has attempted to breach initiation. Every few decades or so, there is a reckless individual who must be taught a lesson.

Word of mouth of their demise is an excellent future deterrent.

There shall be no interferences, nothing to hinder the initiation ceremony. It is underway as I speak. The procession has advanced from the parlor down to the basement, a convoy marching in time to an ancient Chinese drum.

The first scroll is being unraveled, the Bowels. Soon enough, prospective members shall perform the Sacrifice and await their membership fate.

The ammonia-tinged vapors of opium have already begun to permeate the air throughout my building, and I embrace them like a long-lost friend. Finally, the basement room has reverted to its original heathen intent.

Everything is exactly how it should be.

VIVIAN

There's a vibration coming from somewhere within the walls. A slow, steady drumming. It repeats over and over, ominously. Vivian can sense it in her own body, tiny tremors that reverberate. She tries to sit up—but she cannot. She cannot move. She feels soupy; she must be drugged.

The thrum grows louder, as if it's coming her way.

From: Tara Doyle <tara.doyle@mgh.ihp.edu>
To: Elaine J. Simmons <ejsimmons@mgh.ihp.edu>

Dear Professor Simmons,

It's Tara Doyle. I don't know if you remember meeting me, but you are my nursing student advisor. I am reaching out because the clinical rotation that I had arranged for with the private physician will soon no longer be available to me. So we need to discuss finding a new clinical rotation. Also, I will need to take an upcoming semester off for personal reasons. So I need to talk with you about that too. Thank you and I look forward to hearing from you.

Best,
Tara

TAYLOR

Taylor abruptly rips off her mask.

Is this what it's come to? Locked in a dark basement stairwell until help arrives? *If* help arrives?

Her heart hammers so wildly she's finding it difficult to breathe. There's no telling when Sam will see the note, she suddenly realizes. He's been recovering with a nasty respiratory virus since his casino binge. He's likely fast asleep and won't wake up for hours.

What if it's too late by then?

Taylor tries to even out her breathing, the ragged inhales and halting exhales. She needs to remain calm. *Think, Taylor, think!*

She pulls out her iPhone and shines the camera flashlight around. She spots a wall light switch. Thank God. As Taylor flicks it on, the space becomes immediately illuminated like a harshly lit hospital room. She winces and attempts the door handle one final time, but no luck.

Okay, plan B. She swivels around, taking in the unfinished basement that presents itself below. There are four water heaters, multiple water and electrical lines running along the walls and ceilings. She spies a door at the far end of the basement and relief surges through her. It's the exit. Or entrance. Whatever you want to call it—it's a fucking way out.

Given the direction, it must be the entrance to the servants' quarters. Perfect.

She'll snake through this basement space, go through the servants' quarters, leave from *their* front door, and retry the Knox— if her courage continues. It *has* to continue. She has to see this through.

If she doesn't run into anyone.

If she's not already too late.

If her claustrophobia doesn't get the best of her.

Taylor gathers the bottom of her cape in one of her hands and starts down the wooden stairs. *There's an exit*, she tells herself. *An entrance and an exit.* She wants to dampen her awareness of the surrounding space. *Entrance and exit. Entrance and exit.* She begins to stride across the room, toward the far door. *Entrance and—*

What is that noise? There's a continuous tapping sound.

She stops. The beating noise is coming from *behind*. She turns and sees *another* door, tucked beneath the stairs she climbed down. A door, that, from her orientation, seems to lead to a sublevel of the Knox.

Of course. A connecting basement, well, connects. She guesses that this leads to the underground section of the Knox, the area with the room that recently underwent renovation. Maybe it's dumb luck she got locked in here.

The noise steadily continues like a parade drummer keeping time.

With trembling fingers, Taylor slips her mask back on. She forces her legs to take her over to the door. Then she grasps the handle and turns.

THE KNOX

Someone has made a grave error, leaving one of the cellar doors unlocked.

A *grave* error, indeed.

The Sacrifice

Purpose. This section serves to define and describe the procedure known as "the Sacrifice."

Scope and Application: The Sacrifice occurs during the Bowels scroll portion of Initiation Night ceremonies as described in section 6.6.

Definition: The Sacrifice, informally known as the Secret of Importance, consists of a personal confession offered by a Non-Legacy Prospective Member that represents one's deepest, darkest secret.

1. Each Non-Legacy Prospective Member shall individually offer the Sacrifice in presence of Current Members.*

2. Each Non-Legacy Prospective Member shall then await the Decision;

   a. Current Knox Members shall privately discuss whether the Sacrifice reflects a sufficient allegiance to the Knox, and Prospective Member(s) will be subsequently classified into one of three categories:

      i. If allegiance is deemed not sufficient, Prospective Member(s) will be promptly excused from the premises.

    ii. If allegiance is deemed conditionally sufficient, Prospective Member(s) will proceed with ensuing Membership under a probationary period.†

    iii. If allegiance is deemed wholly sufficient without condition, Prospective Member(s) will proceed with ensuing Membership in the normal fashion.

4. Non-Legacy Prospective Member(s) granted a Favorable Decision, with allegiance deemed either conditionally or wholly sufficient (2aii and 2aiii), shall have their Sacrifice recorded in the Bowels scroll by a designated scribe.

5. Such Prospective Member(s) shall continue with Initiation as described in section 6.6.

6. After Initiation, each Sacrifice shall be rigorously evaluated for veracity.

---

* *In modern times, the Sacrifice shall be discreetly recorded and stored on a hard drive.*

† *Prospective Non-Legacy Member(s) granted Probationary Membership will be required to renew their allegiance the following Initiation by offering a new Sacrifice, and/or will be required to assist the Knox with any and all discretionary matters as deemed necessary.*

TAYLOR

Taylor cracks open the door. She doesn't see anyone, so she opens it wider and quietly steps through, onto a tile floor.

The finished space is dimly lit, candle lanterns lining the floor like a runway. The trail bifurcates, one path leading up another set of stairs, presumably into the Knox, and the other to a circle, a few feet away, that surrounds one of those scrolls she's seen upstairs. How many of these things are there? This scroll is rolled open, and exposed; the normal protective glass is gone. A floor tile is missing just in front, revealing a small patch of dirt.

No one is in Taylor's vicinity, yet something feels amiss. What is it? Taylor looks around hesitantly.

On the far side, beyond the scroll, there's a door that must lead to the recently renovated room. Is this what feels off—the room? It has quite the history, between the old-fashioned doctor items found in there and that opium book. So what is the Knox using it for now? Could it be for Vivian—the sacrifice?

What if Vivian is already in there? What if Taylor is too late?

She inches forward, sweat dripping down her back. As she passes by the open scroll, she resists the urge to read it only out of a desperate and propulsive sense that time is running out.

The distant drumming continues, but now it sounds like it's coming from above her, up the stairs. There's a haze in the air, almost like smoke. Fire smoke.

No. She's not thinking clearly. Why would there be smoke? It's just her mind playing tricks. Aunt Gigi's reveal about her mom has clearly affected her. Taylor pushes thoughts of her mom away; she can't go there right now.

There may not be *fire* smoke, but Taylor is not imagining the murkiness. Maybe it's dust? No—it has a strange, almost acidic smell. Perhaps they're burning incense. Whatever it is, it's not very comfortable, so she fishes through her pockets. She stuffed a face mask in there earlier, one of those medical KN95s, in case she needed more anonymity.

Just as she is putting it on beneath the phoenix mask, the door at the top of the basement stairs creaks open. Taylor hurries into the renovated room for cover. She nearly trips over a large rectangular box filled with dirt in the middle of the room, and fear grips her. Is this some sort of tomb they're digging for Vivian?

The lighting is dim, but Taylor can make out a series of cushions and couches spread artfully around the space. The floor is littered with what appears to be instruments; long silver and wooden flutes.

She recovers and looks around wildly for a hiding spot, but there's no obvious place. She frantically inches the couch on the back wall forward so that she can slip behind it. Pressed between the couch and the wall, she waits. She feels hot and sweaty beneath the double masks, her back soaked through.

There's an entrance and an exit. Entrance and exit. Please don't let it be too late for Vivian. Entrance and exit.

The footsteps slowly descend the steps. Taylor's heart thumps against her rib cage as the sound gets louder, closer. Suddenly, she remembers the wig in her pocket, and she tugs it over her head, beneath the straps of the masks. She's grabbed a blue one, apparently, but better to be as disguised as humanly possible.

The person enters the room. Silence follows, pregnant with unspeakable possibilities. Taylor holds her breath, becoming dizzy. Does the person know she's there?

After what feels like forever, there's a reassuring clatter of light noises: rustles and clicks and . . . a match being struck?

Incense—yes, definitely incense—soon fills the air, making her eyes burn. Taylor closes them, grateful she's at least wearing the masks.

Then, it goes so quiet again that Taylor wonders if the person has left. With the utmost care, she slowly peers around the arm of the couch.

No—the person is still there. It's a man, wearing the robe and mask and sitting cross-legged with his back to her. He is lanky; his bony legs protrude well past the cape. Now he begins chanting in undistinguishable mutters and jerking his arm forward. *Is this some sort of ritual that precedes the sacrifice?* When he pulls back, Taylor sees he's holding a stick. The man appears to be making marks in the ground. As she leans forward to try to get a closer look, the couch suddenly shifts forward with a squeak.

Fuck.

The man abruptly stops mid-chant, and starts to turn around, but then a quick flutter of footsteps on the basement stairs draws his attention.

He rises just as a woman bursts into the room.

Rose.

Taylor wants to cry with relief, she's so glad to see her.

Rose, too, dons a robe, but hers is white, and unlike the man, she doesn't wear the mask. Her hair is uncharacteristically mussed, and her face sags, as if the hands of gravity are tugging it down. Rose stares fixedly at the man with an odd intensity; she doesn't appear to notice Taylor.

Should Taylor announce herself, or slink back behind the couch?

"Rose, what are you doing?" the man says, fear clipping his voice. "Please, put down the gun."

Gun?

Now Taylor sees it, extending from the end of Rose's arm. A black pistol, aimed at the man. And, by default, at Taylor.

Oh my God.

"Rose," the man pleads. "It's me, *Michael.* Please, put down the gun."

Michael?

"Shut up, Michael," Rose says in a flat, monotone voice. "Now listen to me. You take every single packet of opium and dump it in this box here on the ground."

"Why?" Michael asks, but Rose cuts him off.

"I said now." She flicks the gun in the opposite direction, and a shot detonates so loud it feels like it fractures the air around them. Taylor collapses behind the couch. *Shit shit shit.* Each second feels like ten. Her heart is beating so fast it almost hurts.

"Okay, Rose," Michael says soothingly. "I'm doing it. See? I'm getting the trunk with the opium." There's the sound of the alleged trunk being handled and slid across the floor. A latch unlocking. "I'm opening it. See? Here is the opium stash. I'm putting it inside the geomancy area, like you said." Rustling ensues.

Geomancy area. Opium stash.

The room suddenly makes sense. The basement location, the scarce lighting, the cushions, the instruments that aren't instruments at all—they're opium pipes. The Knox renovation was to create an opium den.

An anger flashes through Taylor as she's hit with a string of recollections: Aunt Gigi's words: *Your mom was strung out from drugs.* The "bad Aunt Emma" comment the woman addict made. The headline of *The Boston Globe*: BOSTON'S HOSPITALS OVERWHELMED BY OVERDOSES. What Taylor overheard Peter say to Michael: *He's already tested the waters, and the appetite is there.* The Knox's interest in opium clearly extends beyond using it solely for divination readings.

And then Rose's warning: *It's just that too many girls have gotten lost here through the years.*

This—the Knox—could have been where Taylor's mother got the drugs.

Opium's always been a large part of the Knox, Liam and Eduardo told her. What if her own mother had drifted through these walls in a drugged haze, a shadow of the woman Taylor once knew?

Taylor clenches her fists, each subsequent memory further fanning her fury.

"Is that all of it?" Rose barks.

"Yes."

"Let me see."

A creaking noise, and then what sounds like the trunk cover closing.

"Now light it," Rose commands. "We're going to burn it—all of it. Because it's the only thing Oliver cares about. The only thing."

"This is a wooden box, Rose. Not metal. We could set the whole building on fire," Michael protests.

"I said fucking light it!" Rose screams, setting Taylor's hairs on end.

But something in her stirs in triumphant recognition. *Yes,* Taylor thinks. *Rose has the right idea. Get rid of the fucking drugs.*

The strike of a match, and then a crackle of fire. The air instantly fills with a strong, acidic scent, like the one Taylor smelled earlier, but so much stronger. Rose starts coughing, as does Michael. The temperature in the room instantly rises; sweat pools in pockets under Taylor's robe. The emerging haze grows more opaque by the second. Even wearing double masks, Taylor has to bat down a cough.

"Tell me, Oliver, how does it feel to lose what you care most about?" Rose spits.

"Rose, I'm Michael, not Oliver," he interrupts, just as Taylor is thinking, *Huh?*

"Ha," Rose laughs humorlessly. "As if I wouldn't know my own son."

Taylor's mind stutters over Rose's words, trying to accept them in a way that makes sense. Rose is Oliver's mother?

"I . . ." Michael's voice falters. He's surprised, too, then.

"No words now, Oliver? You had a lot to say to me earlier."

"Rose," Michael tries again, "you're confused. . . . The opium smoke, the stress—it's making you confused. Oliver's upstairs, at the Brains scroll, with the others. We need to get out of here. We should go. *Now.*" There's urgency in his voice.

"You're trying to trick me again! Just like you tricked me about tonight's initiation, when you said I would become a member. You humiliated me, Oliver. You're just like your father, after all. Just like Graham!" Then, a strangulated sob escapes, as if Rose can no longer contain herself.

Taylor feels dumbfounded; Rose thought they were going to

make her a member? Her wail is packed with so much anguish, it's almost hard to listen to.

Then, a sudden tussling noise ensures; is Michael trying to get the gun away from Rose? Another startling gunshot pierces the air, followed by a deep groan.

Taylor screams, shooting up from behind the couch like a jack-in-the-box. She's not thinking clearly, but she knows she needs to get out of this room. Away from the danger. The gun. The fire. *Now.* She can hear the distinct whoosh of her blood pumping through her veins as she starts to stagger across the smoke-filled room.

Michael lies in a heap, a few feet from the wooden box that's burning stronger by the second. He's clutching his knee. Taylor looks at him, surprised at the contempt she feels. *That's karma for all the lost girls*, she thinks.

"Tara?" Rose gasps.

Taylor whirls around, startled to see that Rose is addressing *her*.

Tara. Tara—Jerry's sister? Taylor shakes her head, unable to form words.

"Tara, what are you doing here? It's not good for the baby!" Rose looks from Taylor to the gun, which she still holds between two shaking hands. Her face dramatically contorts, like a cartoon character. "Oh my God," she breathes, dropping the gun, which skids across the floor. "Come with me! He's a murderer—you can't trust him!" Then she disappears into the hall.

From the ground, Michael moans. As Taylor hesitantly nears, he reaches up with surprising strength to grab ahold of her ankle. "Stop," he mutters, in a strained voice from beneath his mask. She tries to shake him off, but he won't let go. Then he claws at her with his other hand, too.

"Let go of me!" she yells. The air feels so smothering, it's as if someone is holding a bag over her head. Aunt Gigi's words flash before her: *It's probably why your mom died in the basement fire—she was likely passed out.*

Taylor kicks at Michael with her free foot, and he loosens his grip. She flees the room, flinging the door shut behind her.

TAYLOR

In the basement hall area, the air is less hazy, but Rose is bent over, still coughing. Taylor gasps, trying to catch her own breath. She eyes the stairwell, leading up to the Knox's first floor. Is that the best way out, to reach Vivian? The only way? She's feeling a little fuzzy.

A sudden movement near the still-open scroll startles her: Protective glass walls rise from beneath the ground to form a seal around the table. Taylor stares, momentarily entranced as the table itself then caves inward, in a V-shaped formation, causing the scroll to roll itself together. The bottom of the table splits open, revealing a gap, and in it drops the scroll. The table flattens back out, and continues to transform, growing smaller and more compact beneath the glass.

Whoa.

"We should go," Taylor says, snapping to. "C'mon, Rose, we need to get out of here."

But Rose remains huddled over, as if she's trying to crawl into herself.

"Rose?" Taylor taps her urgently on the shoulder. "Rose?"

She looks up at Taylor, her face like a wilted flower. "Oh, Tara, what have I done?"

"Rose, we *need* to go." Taylor glances nervously at the room with Michael. She feels his hand grasped around her ankle, as if he were still holding it.

"I . . . I shot my own son."

The gun, Taylor suddenly realizes, is still in the room with Michael. *Shit.* What if he musters the strength to come after them?

Another sudden movement around the scroll startles her: an extremely thick metal wall now emerges from the ground to form a second protective enclosure. She's never seen metal casing on any of the other scrolls before. Is initiation over?

Is Taylor too late?

She crouches down in front of Rose and takes her hands, which are like slivers of ice. Rose is unfocused, her eyes glazed over. "Rose," Taylor says, shaking her to no avail. "Rose, look at me," she pleads. "I'm Taylor—not Tara. I need your help." She hastily pulls off her wig and both masks. "See?"

"Taylor," Rose says, comprehension flooding her face. "Where's Tara? Where did Tara go?" She starts hacking again.

"Here," Taylor says, offering her the KN95 mask. "You should take this. I'll . . . I'll use the phoenix mask." But the acidic air is already hitting her hard; she stifles a cough. Throwing a quick glance at the room with Michael, she's relieved to see the door remains closed—for now.

Rose fumbles as she tries to slip on the mask, and when Taylor goes to help, Rose suddenly clasps Taylor's hand. "You're a good girl, Taylor. I knew it the minute you asked to take off your shoes. I knew you didn't know anything about Vivian. I knew she didn't say anything to you in the hospital. I told Oliver, too. I said, you let that girl be."

Taylor sharply inhales, and with it comes another gust of that acidic smoke smell. She wrangles her hand away from Rose's to cover her cough. "What?" she manages, once the cough passes. But Rose has folded back into herself, her gaze distant.

Taylor should have known; of course shady Oliver would be behind whatever's happened to Vivian. She shakes Rose's arm. "Rose, do you know where Vivian is? Rose? Rose?"

"The quarters," she mumbles.

"Whose quarters? Can you take me there?"

"Quarters and nickels. Or is it nickels and dimes? Things sure change on a dime." Rose suddenly starts laughing.

"C'mon." Taylor tugs her toward the stairs.

"Where are we going?" Rose asks, between cackles.

"Upstairs, to get Vivian."

"Vivian's not with the guests; she's with the servants for once," she says, still laughing—but now it's a bitter kind of laugh.

"The servants? Wait—you mean, she's in the servants' quarters?" Of course, Taylor now thinks. Clever of them to hide her there—who would suspect that?

Taylor quickly pivots, now dragging Rose back toward the boiler room.

But Rose's laughter has dissolved to crying—full, body-racking sobs that make it difficult to pull her along. "What did I do?" she laments. "Oh no, Oliver. Oh no, oh no."

Taylor, too, feels overcome with emotion. Will they make it in time? Is Vivian even still there? She *must* be, Taylor reasons in the next second. Otherwise they would have encountered her being brought through the connecting basement space to the opium den, where Michael was clearly doing some pre-sacrifice ritual.

Suddenly, the door to the renovated room bursts open and in pours hot, smoky air. It feels like someone has just opened a burning oven. Michael emerges, limping toward them. *He has the gun.*

Taylor hastens her pace.

"Taylor!" he bellows. "Taylor, wait! I'm not going to hurt you! Don't trust Rose—she's unhinged!"

Taylor hesitates for a moment, a seed of doubt planting in her mind. What if Michael's right? Rose did shoot him, after all, thinking he was Oliver—her son. But Oliver clearly deserves to die; he seems to be the one behind Vivian's abduction. So where does that leave Michael? Isn't he in on it, too? Besides, Rose called him a murderer. . . . But *who* was she calling that, Oliver or Michael?

And *who* was murdered?

Taylor shudders. *Vivian*, she thinks. *Vivian*. She has to get to Vivian. That's all that matters. An overhead smoke alarm starts blaring, startling her and Rose—and spurring Taylor into action. She gestures wildly to the boiler room. "C'mon, Rose!" Taylor shouts, as she again grabs hold of her arm. "We have to save Vivian!"

A look of disgust rolls over Rose's face. "Why would we do that? She's an interfering little bitch!"

Oh my God. Taylor feels sick. Is Rose involved, then? Oliver—and Rose? And maybe Michael?

Taylor becomes acutely aware of the surrounding basement space. Four walls restricting them, like the barriers enclosing the scroll.

"Taylor!" Michael is advancing, the gun waves in his hand. "Rose, get the fuck away!"

There's an entrance and an exit. There's an entrance and exit. Entrance and exit. But *is* there? The thick haze makes it increasingly difficult to see. Michael nears, and Rose starts to scramble away.

"I wished she *died* when I pushed her down the stairs! To hell with her little friend. I want Vivian *dead*!" Rose shrieks.

Oh my God. Oh my God.

Sparks crackle all around as the fire spills into the hall. Time moves like a strobe light. Taylor's eyes stinging, she can vaguely make out Rose climbing the first few stairs to the Knox on her hands and knees.

Taylor starts inching her way forward in what she *thinks* is the right direction, the way to the boiler room. To Vivian. She feels a little woozy, shapeless, like a piece of putty. Where is this entrance-exit? Or exit-entrance?

Which one is it, anyway? Maybe it doesn't matter.

Perhaps it's okay that the place is burning down, she thinks, *because I am a piece of putty.*

"Taylor!" Michael screams.

He should become putty, too, she thinks. *Then he wouldn't worry.*

Or is it Oliver, not Michael? She can't remember.

She moves, haltingly, and then stops. Which way to her mother again? No—that's not right. It's *Vivian* she's trying to save. But everything is becoming gummy, logic softening. The crackling is all around now, the air so milky and hot she can barely keep her eyes open. She feels like she's walked directly into the pit of the fire. Her skin burns like it's crisping; her eyes—even her eyeballs—feel singed.

Claustrophobia has finally arrived; she's late to the party but she's come in full force, wearing a suffocating ball gown that she dramatically fluffs. With each preen, she further crowds out Taylor's thoughts until there's just one left: *I'm going to die.*

But, to Taylor's surprise, she finds that's okay. Yes, she's growing tired, but it's a nice kind of tired, a peaceful one. All along, all these years, Taylor's been worried, and she didn't need to be. She wonders: *Is this how my mother felt?*

r/boston · 9 d ago
Spill_the_teaplz13

What is the biggest secret you know?

What is the wildest, biggest secret you know? Or ever heard? Is it eating you up inside? Here's your chance to spill it. Who wants to go first??

⬆ 83 ⬇   ⇄ share   ···

Sort by: Best ⌄

tdgarden33__ · 9 d ago

Here's a good one: Someone (let's call him "O") poisoned his dad with cyanide because his dad didn't agree with O's idea to import drugs. Also he thought his dad was going to cut him off from his inheritance. (O has a bad gambling problem and he also seriously has the worst luck. I aways told him he should've played my birthday.) Anyway, then the guy who supplied the poison went MIA, and O got nervous about covering up his tracks. So O kidnapped this guy's friend from the hospital (let's call her "V") and held her captive so she could help him track down the missing friend (so far no success). I guess that was like 3 or 4 secrets.

underthebostonsun_not · 9 d ago

You should be a writer. That's a wild plot.

stillyankeesfanz2018 · 9 d ago

Speaking of wild, WTF is up with all these wild turkeys running around? One almost attacked me when I was crossing Mass Ave

tdgarden33__ · 9 d ago

Also O's mom pushed V down the stairs bc she didn't like her (that was before O and O's mom abducted V). And O has promised his mom that she could join his secret club if she helped him. (I don't believe O, he's slimy and also my ex)

ModernPastryRules · 8 d ago

I once stole a cannoli

bello4 · 9 d ago

I just heard a funny story about how the wild turkeys chased a teacher no one likes haha. Maybe the turkeys are trying to chase you back to NY

tdgarden33__ · 9 d ago

And . . . I'm pregnant with O's baby but he thinks I got rid of it

underthebostonsun_not · 9 d ago

The plot thickens.

Sodiumgurl · 8 d ago

O and O's mom both sound crazy.

tdgarden33__ · 8 d ago

They are . . . But O's mom is also helping me out. She's whacky but means well. She's letting me stay there and even helped get me a job. She knows I'm still pregnant—she's very excited about it. It will be her first grandchild. Anyway I'm moving out of here soon. My brother is gonna get us a place once he finds a new job

19gloriaR2_ · 8 d ago

Are you okay? Seriously, are you okay? You can message me

Babblehabblebubhub · 7 d ago

The biggest secret I know (heard from a friend of a friend) is what the Knox does on initiation night.

r/boston • 9 d ago
Spill_the_teaplz13

What is the biggest secret you know?

What is the wildest, biggest secret you know? Or ever heard? Is it eating you up inside? Here's your chance to spill it. Who wants to go first??

⇧ 99 ⇩   ⇨ share   •••

Sort by: Best ⌄

[deleted] • 9 d ago

underthebostonsun_not • 9 d ago

You should be a writer. That's a wild plot.

stillyankeesfanz2018 • 9 d ago

Speaking of wild, WTF is up with all these wild turkeys running around? One almost attacked me when I was crossing Mass Ave

[deleted] • 9 d ago

ModernPastryRules · 8 d ago

I once stole a cannoli

> **bello4** · 9 d ago
>
> I just heard a funny story about how the wild turkeys chased a teacher no one likes haha. Maybe the turkeys are trying to chase you back to NY
>
> **[deleted]** · 9 d ago
>
> **underthebostonsun_not** · 9 d ago
>
> The plot thickens.
>
> **Sodiumgurl** · 8 d ago
>
> O and O's mom both sound crazy.
>
> **[deleted]** · 8 d ago
>
> **19gloriaR2_** · 8 d ago
>
> Are you okay? Seriously, are you okay? You can message me
>
> **Babblehabblebubhub** · 7 d ago
>
> The biggest secret I know (heard from a friend of a friend) is what the Knox does on initiation night.

THE KNOX

I am not one to panic. I have, admittedly, witnessed a great deal in my time. But . . . *but*. A fire, even a pesky small one, constitutes a serious concern. Many a neighbor has succumbed to such a virus. I still recall how the terrible, burnt stench of the Great Boston Fire of 1872 lingered for weeks afterward, and that blaze occurred several streets away.

This fire is my first; I suppose there is a first time for everything, as unpleasant as it may be. I trust that the members shall soon address it; at the moment, most are at the Brains scroll, engrossed with overseeing the new members' study of the charter. As for Rose . . . she is also presently preoccupied, licking her wounds. It is unfortunate Michael got caught in her crosshairs; Rose should have instead directed that gun at Taylor. I am beyond perturbed it is *she* who is the intruder. The help hardly know their place anymore.

Yes, yes, I, too, heard Oliver falsely promise Rose that she would be tapped for membership, rewarded for her role in Vivian's abduction and subsequent care. That if Rose could locate

Xavier, the loose end—an endeavor at which she has been unsuccessful to date—she might even be anointed a Knox officer.

But let's be realistic: She's a Rose. Not a Peter, nor a Michael, nor any of them. She's the *help*. There exists a pecking order for a reason. Structure and hierarchy (and dare I add, *tradition*) are paramount for enduring success. I will only now admit, I was secretly flummoxed that such an unorthodox idea would even be considered.

The deception, however, appears to lie solely with Oliver. None of the other members had an inkling of what was quietly pledged to Rose.

(Also, forgive me for pondering at what might be an inappropriate time, but I do wonder what Rose was going to offer as the sacrifice—her secret of importance. I simply *relish* these confessions—and can smell a lie a house away.)

(In fact, I take even more delight when justice is served to those audacious enough to offer up a falsehood. Rest assured, the members *do* eventually verify every confession—and they do not take deception lightly.)

Oh—oh my! The smoke detectors have just now begun ringing, causing me a degree of unease. The *situation* in the basement appears to be veering off course. At least the members are now sufficiently on alert. They begin to depart from the Brains scroll, descend the stairs.

It's only a matter of time now before order is restored.

But, to my utter dismay, they bypass the abundant fire extinguishers and instead head directly toward the exits, spilling out my doors. One member even has the Brains scroll tucked under his arm!

Gentlemen—what is the *purpose* of having fire extinguishers if no one utilizes them at the very moment they are needed?!

TAYLOR

Taylor can hear an alarm, but she doesn't mind it. It's clearly keeping time with the drums she heard earlier. And then, between the silent pauses, are yells. Screams. It's all kind of beautiful, like a symphony of cacophony. A basement is the perfect place for such a sound installation. Those fancy art museums should take note.

Rose is part of the exhibit; she lies motionless at the base of the stairs.

China presses against Taylor's leg, and she picks her up.

"Taylor," the cat says.

Taylor looks at her.

"Taylor," the cat says again, but her mouth isn't moving.

That's funny, Taylor thinks.

The walls start shaking around them, and she holds on to China tighter. Is it an earthquake? She's not scared, not like she should be. And that's being in a basement, to boot.

Maybe all along I just needed a cat, she thinks. *A cat who understands me.*

"Taylor, I need you to look at me."

It's Michael. Or someone impersonating him. This person is tall, so tall. She doesn't remember him being quite so tall, but maybe they've never stood in such close proximity. His hands are on top of her shoulders, shaking her.

She tries to push him away. "Stop," she attempts to say, but maybe she only thinks it.

He slips something over her face. *No!* Is he suffocating her? She tries to fend him off, but her arms are like rubber.

"Here. Put this on." Something snaps against her face; it's her KN95 mask.

Oh, she thinks. *Maybe Michael is to be trusted, after all.*

"C'mon, we have to go." Then he wraps a cloth around his face, to cover his own nose and mouth.

He tugs her forward. There's an urgency to his movement that she somehow inherently understands. She acquiesces, following as fast as she can. But as they start climbing the stairs to the Knox, sidestepping the body sculpture—so lifelike, really—Taylor hesitates, looking across the fiery way in the direction of the boiler room. Disjointed memories circle around her like a turn of a kaleidoscope, slowly settling into place. A memory: Rose saying that Vivian is in the servants' quarters.

Taylor tugs down her mask. "Vivian," she says weakly. She doesn't know if Michael can hear her over the alarm, but he nods gravely, like he understands. Yet in the next moment, he keeps ushering her forward.

She shakes her head. "No. No!" she says louder. "Vivian." She points across the way. "Vivian's over there . . . in the servants' quarters."

Michael whips his head in that direction, a strange look on his face. Taylor can see him mouth the name to himself: "Vivian."

He seems to be working something out inside his head, and then he breaks out into a grin. Like he finally understands.

But then he continues up the same stairs. "Come," he seems to say to Taylor, with a wave. With one last regretful look over her shoulder at the boiler room, she follows. She knows that at this point, with the advancing basement flames, it is the *only* entrance and exit.

⟡—⚬—⟡

When they step into the Knox foyer, the cat darting out in front of them, it's empty. Smoke grazes the air, but there are no visible flames. Not yet. But the space still screams a warning, the smoke detectors shrieking as if in protest.

How quickly does fire travel?

To her surprise, Michael doesn't exit the Knox's front door but instead moves toward the grand staircase. He points up it, rather furiously, and is saying something, but the darn smoke detector is in her ear—and outside, there are the wails of approaching fire trucks. Michael clasps his hand in a prayer sign, pleading with Taylor. What does he mean?

She throws her hands up in frustration. Aren't they going to go next door to find Vivian—if they can access that building? If it's not too late?

He turns and staggers up the grand staircase, not bothering to wait. What is he doing? Can she trust him? If he were trying to harm her, lead her to danger, then wouldn't he be forcing her to go?

She looks at the front door to the Knox—it's right there, mere feet away. She could just walk out right now. To her safety, at the very least.

But upstairs beckons her. Vivian—it *has* to be Vivian.

She follows Michael as he lurches up the stairs; they are now climbing a second staircase, a seemingly endless metal one. With his injured knee, he moves like he is riding a horse, jerking up and down. Finally, they arrive at a landing with two doors, and he swings one open. A long corridor extends beyond, and Taylor's heart flutters. A connection to the servants' quarters. It *has* to be.

They push down that corridor and spill out into a wing of the adjacent building, nearly colliding with Eduardo, clad in a pair of silk monogrammed pajamas. He looks surprised to see them— and worried, his face pulled like a stitch. The smoke detectors are blaring here, too.

Can flames travel through connecting buildings? Through brick walls?

Michael cups his hand over his mouth as he briefly leans toward Eduardo to say something. The two of them spring ahead, Michael glancing behind to ensure Taylor is following.

Then—they are gone, disappearing into an open bedroom door. Taylor approaches and hovers at the entrance; she's filled with a strange sensation, almost like déjà vu. There's something so familiar that it takes her a second to understand. It's a makeshift hospital room: an electric hospital bed, a barren IV pole, a commode.

Jerry is there, along with a slight woman whose blue hair is growing out. They nervously flit around the bed. Michael stands off to the side, with the most amazed smile, as if he can't quite believe what he's seeing.

And neither can Taylor. She stares at the patient lying beneath the sheets: the chestnut-brown hair, the creamy skin, the ink eyelashes.

The beauty.

THE KNOX

The fire is growing much, much, *much* too quickly! It's quite rude, really, with its insatiable appetite. I take offense at the way it makes haste through my rooms, helping itself to everything in sight—expensive furniture, fine silver, heirloom antiques, priceless paintings (oh no, not the Rembrandt!).

This is all rather embarrassing. It's creating *such* a commotion. People are gathering outside, their mouths impolitely agape. No, no. No!!!

And it only continues to worsen, completely ravaging my insides. Help. Help!

I am *not* prepared for this indignity.

Why is there no assistance??!!

Help!!!___help!___help___hel___hell___.

_____.

TAYLOR

The men hoist Vivian up, and the group slips into the hall. Smoke has begun seeping through to this building, the air now hazy like smog. They trip and stumble as they descend the stairs. The lower they go, the murkier and more acrid the air becomes. They are mostly quiet, consumed with the sheer effort. Occasionally there's a check-in, "You okay?" or a warning, "Turning the bend now!" Heat flares against their faces. Taylor tries not to think about the possibility that they are walking directly into the inferno.

And she waits, with dread, for claustrophobia to revisit. But somehow it doesn't happen. Somehow, as they teeter down the steps like a group who's just closed the bar, Taylor feels oddly safe, protected.

It's such a strange sensation that she wonders for a moment if she's still high.

"Last set of stairs!" Jerry yells. Then he turns to the blue-haired woman who's trailing closely behind. "You okay, Tara?"

Her response is drowned out by a loud crackling.

"Almost there!" Eduardo shouts, as a cough begins bubbling in Taylor.

And then they're on flat surface—the foyer floor—moving in the direction of the front door. The heat and smoke suddenly surge; Taylor can't hold it in any longer—she bends over, exploding in a coughing fit. When she recovers, she reaches out, but all she grasps is air.

No one's there. She's lost them.

She's alone.

Then, like a magician's sleight of hand, someone clasps Taylor's arm, leading her forward.

TAYLOR

Outside, in the back of one of the ambulances, while she's given oxygen and assessed, Taylor provides some sort of statement to the police. But she's distracted, trying to search for faces in the crowd. Where's Vivian? Where are the others? It's confusion and smoke and bedlam. She sees periodic black robes flit through the night, like phantoms. More fire trucks arrive, their sirens roaring. Onlookers are gathering by the second.

"Tomorrow we'll need you to come to the station, or in the next few days, when you're up for it," the officer is saying.

Taylor nods. She can still taste fire in her mouth, sense the heat on her skin.

"Holy shit," she hears one person say, and another says, "Can you imagine the secrets going up in flames right now?"

People are clinging to one another, their faces alight from the reflection of the flames and the flashing emergency lights. She thinks she hears an ambulance peel off, hopefully with Vivian, but it's hard to differentiate between all the alarms and the ringing in her head. Her muscles feel tensed, a hard board.

"Is this your cat?" another officer asks, approaching. He's struggling to contain China in his arms.

"No," Taylor says, relieved to see that the cat escaped the fire, though she looks as spooked as Taylor feels, her tail puffed up like a dandelion. Then Taylor says, "Wait! Yes. Yes, she's mine."

Taylor! Taylor! she thinks she hears someone yell, but when she listens more closely, she realizes it's just chatter from the growing crowd.

"Okay, we'll put the cat in one of the patrol cars," the officer says. "Any other animals inside?"

"Not in the Knox . . . I don't know about the servants' quarters."

"Servants' quarters?" the paramedic who is taking her blood pressure repeats, surprised.

"Taylor! Taylor!" Someone *is* yelling her name. It's Sam; he must have gotten her note.

"Stand back," the paramedic barks.

Sam edges as close to her as they will allow. He shakes his head at her, wordless. His eyes are red, as if he's been crying.

Are you okay? he mouths, and it's all she can do to nod.

TAYLOR

One Week Later

Taylor sips her coffee on a bench at Piers Park in East Boston, waiting impatiently for Tara to arrive.

She finally accepted the Instagram follow request from @tdgarden33__, when it occurred to her that TD might just stand for Tara Doyle, not the stadium where the Celtics play. Well, to be fair, maybe both.

Tx for accepting, Tara immediately messaged. I've been wanting to talk with u. You prly have lots of questions?? Can we meet?

While Taylor waits, her gaze travels across the water. The city of Boston looms in the near distance, its tall, stately buildings piercing the sky in a picturesque scene that would normally fill her with awe. But not today.

She hasn't heard from the others; she was hoping she'd run into them at the police station, when she went a couple of days earlier to give her statement, but no such luck. For a week now she's been frustratingly waiting for word, for any updates about Vivian.

So to say Taylor has "lots of questions" is an understatement.

She quickly checks her phone, which has been buzzing in her pocket. Aunt Gigi is already at it, suggesting nursing jobs. A position opened in the PACU! No nights and weekends. Or what about a job in dermatology??

Aunt Gigi was beyond relieved that Taylor hadn't been at the middle-of-the-night fire at the Knox—or so she thought. "Thank goodness," Aunt Gigi said, when she called first thing the following morning. "Can you imagine if the fire had happened during the day, when you were at work? Do they know what caused it yet? It looks like a total loss. Lisa—Phil's sister's daughter, who's dating that cop—she said she heard a few people perished. All I know is we didn't get any burn victims on the unit."

Taylor slips the phone back into her pocket when she sees Tara approaching. She moves hesitantly, as if she's a scared animal. She's thin, her small shoulders exposed in the white tank she wears beneath overall shorts. He hair is plaited in two braids, and on her feet are a pair of black Converse. If Taylor didn't know better, she'd think Tara was about fourteen years old.

"Hi," Tara shyly ventures, and offers a big, crooked smile, the sincerity of which catches Taylor off guard.

Taylor rises, unsmiling. "Hi," she brusquely replies.

"Thanks for coming." Tara rummages through her canvas tote. Her profile is a watered-down version of her brother's. "I brought you a soda. Want it?" She holds out a Coke, her hand shaking slightly.

"No."

Tara shoves it back in her bag. "You seem kinda pissed."

"Can't imagine why."

"You don't need to be sarcastic."

"I kind of do. I've been waiting . . ." A swell of emotions surges inside Taylor, which she quickly checks. "I've been waiting to hear what's happened with everyone."

"Well, that's why I'm here, to talk with you."

"Did someone send you?"

"Nah. I'm here on my own. Sorry, I don't always have the best way with words. I just want to talk to you. I'm trying to make things right in my life."

Taylor resists the urge to roll her eyes. "Where's Vivian? I haven't heard *anything*."

Tara nods. "Jerry said she's at some private facility, getting the care she needs. I guess she's doing okay; I heard they think she's gonna make a full recovery."

Taylor exhales; it feels like she's finally set down the sack of worry she's been lugging around all week—at least, the one about Vivian. There are still the unresolved feelings Taylor has about her mom—but she can't get to those. Not yet. "I'm so glad about Vivian," she admits, and then scowls at Tara. "Well, no thanks to you. I came across your Facebook student nurse post."

"Oh shit. Really?"

"Really."

"Look, I know I kinda fucked up with Viv—"

"*Kind of* fucked up?"

Tara's cheeks color. "Okay, I *really* fucked up with her. I was following the house doctor's orders. But I realize now I wasn't giving good nursing care. I know you probably don't believe me, but I thought I was helping her."

"How could holding someone captive be helping them?" Taylor's voice rises a notch, and a man jogging down the paved walkway gives an alarmed look.

Tara waits until he passes to continue. "Rose said someone at the Knox was trying to harm Vivian and pushed her down the stairs, so we needed to keep her hidden and safe."

Taylor scoffs. "And you believed that?"

"Yeah. I kinda did at first. And then, when I started to suspect something wasn't right, I still wanted to believe it . . . I was scared. I mean, they knew everything about me and Jerry. Where our parents lived, where they worked. Rose was coming and going all the time, back and forth from her room at the Knox to mine next door. I felt like sometimes I couldn't breathe, you know?"

Taylor says nothing.

"And I had the baby to think about," Tara says, pressing her hand against her belly, which Taylor now notices is slightly rounded. Tara's eyes start watering. "Sorry," she says, wiping them. "Jerry says I cry at the drop of a hat these days. Must be the hormones, right? Once I have the baby and get them all outta me, then I'll be better." She gives a little laugh. "Well, not *better*, but better. You don't have a tissue, do you?"

"No, sorry."

"It's okay." Tara smiles half-heartedly. Her teeth are big, taking up a lot of real estate.

"So they threatened you?" Taylor leads; she's desperate to know more.

"Well . . . not exactly. We had an agreement. Rose said I could keep living at the servants' quarters and going to nursing school if we kept our mouths shut. If we all did—Jerry, Eduardo, and me. Tell no one. They were paying for my school, and Rose even arranged for me to do my clinical rotation with the house doctor."

"Wow," Taylor manages.

"It was supposed to be temporary. Jerry was figuring out a plan to get us out of there. He hated what was going on. My brother can be kind of a pain sometimes, but it's just because he's looking out for me, you know?" She looks earnestly at Taylor, who nods.

As an only child Taylor *doesn't* know, but she wants to hear more. "What about Eduardo?"

"Eduardo? He just looked the other way—you know how he is. He never wants to make trouble. But I don't blame him. It was just a such weird situation we were all in, you know? It's like . . . like when you watch a movie, and you think, 'Oh, that person's so dumb, I'd never do that.' But guess what? You don't know. You don't know what you'd do." She takes a shaky breath, then continues. "And by the time I realized everything, the whole she-bang, it felt like it was too late to do anything about it. I was in it, you know? But trust me—if you can," Tara says, her eyes welling again, and her lower lip now trembling, "when I say if I thought they were gonna hurt Vivian I would've stopped them. I don't know how, but I would've."

"If they were going to *hurt* her? What do you consider 'the sacrifice'?"

"Sacrifice? What do you mean?" Tara looks genuinely puzzled.

"The initiation sacrifice, and Vivian?"

Tara frowns. "I don't know what the hell they get up to on initiation night—apart from burning entire buildings down, I guess—but it didn't have anything to do with Vivian."

Taylor feels her face heating, embarrassed over the potential misunderstanding. Is Taylor somehow wrong about the sacrifice? Or maybe Tara just doesn't know the truth herself. But a suspicion lingers.

"Then why did you say Vivian wouldn't need nursing care in a few days' time? Back in the nurses' Facebook group?"

"Did I say that? I guess that was me just wishful thinking that Jerry would figure shit out for us soon. I know he was looking at one place, but then it fell through."

Taylor swallows this information; some of it goes down easily, but some sticks to her insides. She's not sure what to totally believe—or *who*. "And Liam? Was he in on this, too?"

"I don't think Liam knew anything, but you'd have to ask him."

"Well, I'd love to, but I don't have anyone's contact info," Taylor coolly replies.

"Oh yeah. Jerry wanted me to pass along his number to you, if that's okay?" Tara scrunches her nose, as if just remembering.

"Yes, of course. Did they—did you—talk to the police?"

"Nah, I didn't. But Jerry did. Or tried to, I think. They didn't want to hear anything he had to say."

"Yeah, me neither," Taylor admits. She'd realized that about ten seconds in, when the detective immediately brought up how she'd told the paramedics that night that the cat was talking to her—implying she was not credible.

"We shouldn't be surprised, right? These people are powerful. They're like kings and queens, and we're like the little pheasants to them."

"You mean, peasants?"

"Oops, yeah. Little peasants." She grins; she doesn't seem to be bothered in the slightest by her less-than-perfect teeth like Taylor often is.

What would it be like to smile with abandon? Taylor wonders.

"If you're asking me, the real villain here is Oliver," Tara continues, kicking at the ground with the toe of her Converse. "And not just because he was a shitty boyfriend and a druggie. I mean, I know what I did with Vivian wasn't right, that I was in on it, too. And I gotta live with it. But we were all doing Oliver's dirty work. He was like the head king. When I found out I was pregnant, Oliver sent Peter to try to convince me to get rid of it. Peter put me up at a hotel, set me up with a doctor and everything. But then Rose stepped in. She wanted me to keep the baby. Everyone but Rose thought I got the abortion. Jerry found out, eventually. But at first it was just me and Rose's secret."

Rose. The image of her body crumpled on the basement stairs flashes across Taylor's mind. "You know Rose never made it out of the fire, right?"

Tara puffs up her cheeks and then expels the air, like she's blowing out a candle. "I figured. I heard they're still identifying the bodies, but since I didn't hear from her . . . I thought that might be why. I'm kinda relieved, but I'm also kinda sad, which I know sounds weird." Then she shakes her head. "That probably doesn't make sense to you."

"Are you going to tell Oliver that you're still pregnant?"

"Nah—and please don't say anything to anyone. I mean, I don't know who you'd talk to anyway, but if you do, please don't say anything. I don't want trouble with the Knox. I just want to have my baby. Oliver wouldn't care, anyway. He ditched me real quick for the next girl, or guy."

Taylor nods. "Okay, I won't say anything."

"Huh." Tara squints at her. "I actually believe you. Thanks." She's continuing to squint, as if trying to not tear up again. "Hey, did you ever find that note I put in your wallet?"

"The 'go back to nursing' note?"

"Uh-huh."

"Yeah, I got it. You know, you're not what I expected," Taylor admits.

"What did you expect?"

"I don't know. Someone more . . . calculating, maybe?"

Tara snorts. "I wish I was more calculating. Maybe I wouldn't have gotten myself into this mess. Half the time, I feel like a chewed-up bone a dog left behind."

Taylor stifles a laugh. There's a rawness, an individuality—an imperfection—to Tara that is endearing.

"Why'd you leave me that note, anyway?"

"I wanted to warn you to stay away."

"Why?" Taylor presses.

"'Cause I didn't want you to end up like me." Tara says it so simply, like it makes all the sense in the world.

Tara and Taylor, you're like flip sides of the same coin, Sam had joked earlier. Taylor had finally come clean to him about a lot. But not everything. For some reason, she'd still held a few things back.

We are not remotely alike, Taylor had shot back to Sam, but now, looking at this girl before her—and hearing her story— Taylor wonders if he is right after all. Tara's like a cautionary tale of what could have happened to Taylor, of what may have happened to many other girls. And yet Taylor still feels tendrils of envy creeping up through her mind and coloring the way she's hearing the story, the way she's viewing Tara.

And what's that envy for? Taylor forces herself to ask the question, and to answer it, even though she doesn't want to.

This is a woman who was used and manipulated and lied to; whose pregnancy was dealt with by the Knox like the trash they so carefully remove; who almost lost everything, and *yet*—here she is meeting the world with a forthrightness, a comfort with herself, that Taylor utterly lacks. Taylor thinks of all the time she's spent agonizing over who she is; how she appears to people; how much effort she's spent fitting herself into other people's expectations in the least obtrusive way she can. Then she looks at Tara's smile, and she understands what a waste of time it's all been.

Something suddenly occurs to Taylor. "What would've happened to Vivian, if you left?" she asks. "You said you'd step in if you thought anything bad was going to happen to her, but if you left, then who would have looked out for her?"

"Vivian was getting better," Tara declares, with a hopeful lilt. "And I think they were kinda giving up on trying to track down her friend Xavier. They tried, like, everything. I figured at some point, they had to just let Vivian go, right?"

Xavier. That was who Rachel had mentioned in the bookstore. The friend one who went AWOL.

Taylor remembers what Rachel said about Vivian's fake email: *She asked me where Xavier is . . . which felt like the real reason for the email.* And then there was that offhand comment Rose had uttered, the night of the fire: *To hell with her little friend.* Is Tara insinuating that the real reason Vivian had been kidnapped was to find Xavier? But why?

"I thought they abducted Vivian because of her ancestry," Taylor finally says, once she's let the conversation hang longer than she should.

"Huh?" Tara says, her eyebrows knitting together. For someone their age, she has the beginning of some deep forehead lines. It might be because she's always contorting her face in various expressions.

"You know, how Vivian is a descendant of the Knox and stands to inherit money? Where does that piece fit in?"

Tara starts grinning. Then she raises her small hand to her mouth as if trying to hide an erupting giggle, lest she offend Taylor. "That's a plotline for a different book, Taylor. Not this one."

She doesn't actually know about Vivian's ancestry, Taylor realizes.

"You'd be surprised," she replies.

VIVIAN

Three Months After the Fire

Vivian can still detect a hint of smoke in the air when she walks to her antiques store. Her neurologist assures her it's not a medical thing, implying that it's in her imagination.

But Vivian is not convinced; she feels changed in a way that is difficult to describe. She's slower these days, yes, that is obvious, on account of the TBI she's still recovering from. Descriptive words are harder to grasp; she's more forgetful, she's tired, and she has some memory lapses. Sometimes she'll go to the grocery store, for instance, and forget what it is she's gone there to buy.

She's been assured these symptoms will improve with time.

"Think of your brain like a muscle," her neurologist says. "You need to exercise it, use it. Try doing some puzzles."

She doesn't tell him that she dislikes puzzles.

And then there is the other injury she's still recovering from: her wrist fracture. She has returned to her trusty physical therapist at Mass General, Connor, whom she saw when she fractured her shoulder.

"You must've missed me," he teases.

But there's more. Like the smell of fire that tickles her nostrils. And sometimes it's not fire but rather an ammonia smell. And then there's the way her feet sometimes pull her in the direction of the Knox, as if they've a mind of their own. The Knox is a pile of rubbish on the inside now, stripped to its guts, with Ryan Jessee Construction vehicles often parked outside. But even so, Vivian feels oddly connected to the place, like—and she dare not tell this to anyone, lest they promptly return her to the hospital for a different reason—like it's alive in some way.

Anyway, she has no plans to set foot back in it. She doesn't need to.

Vivian's grandmother was right; there *is* a book that links their family to the Knox. Quite literally, in fact. *Opii Pericula*, which is Latin for *Dangers of Opium*, written by Dr. Robert Walter Thurgood a.k.a. Edgar Rolo Butterworth.

In each of the seven chapters, using neat cursive, Dr. Thurgood describes a patient he autopsied who succumbed to opium. The last chapter runs a few pages longer than the others and focuses on his own mother, Margaret Thurgood, née Knox:

> The autopsy reveals deceased exhibited marked congestion of the lungs and liver, along with prominent signs of gastrointestinal inflammation. These findings demonstrate the adversarial effects of habitual opium consumption on multiple organ systems.

Vivian thinks this alone—a son performing an autopsy on his mother—is disturbing, but it is the final paragraph that provides the unthinkable. It begins with a single line of Latin:

Hic liber alligatus est in cute matris meae, meaning, "This book is bound in my mother's skin."

In a cool, methodological tone, he describes the process he used: He first cured her skin in a bucket of urine to dissolve the hair, fat, and flesh; the remaining was scraped off with a dull knife. Next he pounded and kneaded it with animal dung, whose digestive enzymes helped to make it more supple. Then it was tanned: soaked in a vat with tannin derived from tree bark. He added a footnote, a chilling judgment:

> *A book about the deleterious effects of opium on the human body merits that it be given such a covering.*

Anthropodermic bibliopegy, the practice of binding books in human skin, was apparently a thing in the 1800s. Not *common*, but not unheard of. *Christ.*

Rachel, with her endless source of all things genealogical, knows someone at the Anthropodermic Book Project, a group who uses peptide mass fingerprinting to do this very sort of thing: determine whether books are bound in real human skin, bovine leather, or something else. Dr. Thurgood's book was confirmed to be "authentic." As to whether it was his mother, as purported to be, the book is now being assessed for mitochondrial DNA to link it to Vivian. It's a long shot—because the tanning process degrades DNA—but it's helpful that Vivian hails from a long line of women descendants. Unlike nuclear DNA, mitochondrial DNA is inherited only from mothers. Vivian's trying not to pay it all too much attention—she figures what will be, will be— but Rachel, of course, is following the progress with a razor-sharp focus.

Speaking of mothers, Vivian's own finally passed away a couple of weeks ago. The final days were dreadful, a stutter of decline, illness baring snaggled teeth. While picking out the coffin and penning the obituary, Vivian considered that the burial process is the cleverest of clever distractions. One must hold it together, not get too bogged down by the cruelty of sickness. She chose the most splendid outfit to bury her mother in, with a Birkin bag to boot. Her mother would not have wanted it any other way.

Vivian no longer needs the potential income that handbag might've brought in. She's worked out a payment plan for both her goddaughter's tuition and the loan she took out for the second store renovation. Storied Antiques is moving to a new, smaller location higher up on the hill; in fact, Michael is coming by shortly to help her sort through the items in her shop. She's grateful that she doesn't have to close the business altogether.

She's finding it surprisingly easy to pare back to the essentials. When one has a brush with death—and she's had a few now, between her own, her parents', and Kat's—things become so much simpler. Vivian doesn't need forty-dollar coffee beans; she just needs a cup of coffee, preferably strong.

It's an inverse ratio: While ridding herself of material things, she's having to hone in on the immaterial—her feelings. Her grief over her mother—and her delayed grief over Kat and her father. Her reluctance to connect with her goddaughter. Vivian has been closed off in relationships for far too long. This emotional work is messy, requiring hours on her therapist's couch and multiple tissue boxes. It's allegedly good in the long run. She'll see. For now, she's invested in high-end waterproof mascara. And still refuses to be weaned off her Xanax by her primary care doctor.

The nurse girl, Taylor, has also offered to come by and help with the move. Vivian might take her up on it. She's a sweet thing, if a little naive, but she's young yet. Vivian has hired her to adorn a few shirts with those flower embellishments she likes to wear; Taylor does have quite an eye and a way with a sewing machine.

Peter is in Milan. For real Milan. He's asked if he can take her out when he returns. Vivian is thinking about it, but Rachel says she's crazy for even considering it. Perhaps she is. He claims he had no idea she was being kept captive, and Michael has corroborated this—apparently only Oliver and Rose were in on it, and some of Oliver's lackeys who have since made themselves scarce. Still, it's concerning how Peter emotionally shut down in the wake of her accident, not visiting her once in the hospital.

When I was a kid, my mother died from a traumatic brain injury following her car accident. And that began my nightmare of foster care, he texts her, as way of explanation. So when I heard that term TBI in relation to you, I kind of lost it. I'm sorry. I've historically avoided conflict in my life, but I'm going to work on it.

But even that—a *text* sharing this information—feels off. And then there's the way he apparently accepted a fake breakup email at face value. Also, there is the not-so-small matter of his drug use. He's completed a stint in rehab, and says he's clean, but Vivian might have already had her fill of drama.

Rachel also has some choice words for their friend Xavier. "I want to see him if only to give him a piece of my mind," she declares. "What the hell was he thinking? Did we even know him at all? I'm hardly surprised he's on the lam, given he knows what the poison was used for. If the Knox were to find him . . ."

What was Xavier thinking?

It's obvious to Vivian now that there had never been a client of Xavier's who wanted to import an elephant ivory necklace. It must have been Oliver who wanted Vivian's Customs contacts. Oliver who coerced Xavier into procuring the cyanide—perhaps threatening him with the store break-in. Oliver who'd been pulling the strings all along.

And Xavier—in lust or love, and off the wagon, his thinking warped. The Knox had had a clear hold over him; Vivian remembers the fear in Xavier's eyes when he spotted the carousel horse in her shop.

She wants to see her friend for a different reason than Rachel's: to apologize. Vivian can't recall every single detail from before the fall, but she knows she missed, and ignored, the signs that he'd relapsed. Xavier had been alone, adrift.

"I think . . . he needed our help," she says.

But he continues to remain missing. And with the criminal case against Oliver reportedly ramping up, Vivian can't imagine that Xavier will resurface anytime soon. She just hopes his absence is his own choice—that he's lying low, hopefully even suntanning on the beaches of Spain with a new love interest—rather than there being a nefarious reason for his disappearance.

**A postcard (with a picture of Seville)
that Vivian later receives in the mail:**

"Pray you now,
forget and forgive."

-King Lear

Vivian Lawrence
62 Lime St.
Boston, MA 02108

TAYLOR

For a few weeks following the fire, while Taylor is job hunting, she goes home to the Outer Banks. She arrives with her suitcase and her knotted feelings surrounding her mom. She thinks she might immediately unpack both, but she doesn't. She soaks in the sun and the sand and her dad's weathered face, which suddenly seems so much older than she remembers.

At the restaurant, she fills up on crab legs and Old Bay–seasoned shrimp and the good-natured teasing of her dad's long-time workers. She notices the wealthy tourists, and those she used to see as such, but now thinks of as simply rich. She kisses Grayson, who broke up with that girl Hatcher. She goes surfing and smells the salt of the sea in her hair for hours afterward.

Then one night, running her fingers across the surfaces of her childhood home—the kitchen table, the creaky screen door, the pencil-marked wall her dad had used as a height ruler—Taylor realizes that she doesn't know, if she had been in her dad's shoes, what she would have done. What she would have said to her own daughter.

She loosens slightly.

"It's okay, Dad," she says later that evening, while they silently work on a one-thousand-piece jigsaw puzzle of Boston's skyline. He's been quiet most of her trip. He nods, and the moment bumpily rolls over them, a choppy wave.

Then, gesturing to the board, he says, "Maybe I can see this in person. I'm thinking about coming to visit for Thanksgiving, to see you and Aunt Gigi." He says a restaurant group has recently come forth as a silent investor, and for the first time in years, he's in a stable financial situation.

Taylor googles the restaurant group, curious if there are any ties to the Knox. She doesn't find any, but these days she knows better than to take anything at face value.

After a couple of weeks home, she feels replenished and is ready to return to Boston—and Sam, who has been cat-sitting China.

The Knox is reportedly undergoing a gut renovation, and Taylor can't help but wonder what it'll look like.

She's been collecting information about what *really* happened there, the true reason behind Vivian's abduction, like clues to her own puzzle she's slowly solving: Eduardo providing some hints, Tara others. She even briefly speaks with Michael, who is about as far from a murderer as one gets. Rose had just been high from the opium fumes that night, confusing him with Oliver. Mistaking identities, cats that talk—all in an opium day's work, Taylor dryly thinks.

Sometimes, the image of Rose's forlorn body, crumpled at the bottom of the basement stairs, flashes across Taylor's mind.

But other images of the Knox have also started to resurface, prefire ones. It starts when Eduardo tells her he's planning to return to work at the Knox, once the construction is complete. In fact, he reveals he's already moved back into the servants' quarters, which are now done with their fire restoration.

This news creates an unexpected longing in her, almost akin to nostalgia.

The others have no desire to return. She learns from Tara, whose pregnancy is plugging along, that Jerry is working at a restaurant in Southie, and considering going to school to become an X-ray tech. The two share an apartment in Quincy, at the Watson. He and Eduardo have apparently called it quits.

Liam gets a job bartending at the Cheers bar in Beacon Hill. He jokes that he likes to work at a place about which he can publicly boast. Occasionally Taylor goes by, and he hooks her up with a meal and drink.

"Well," Liam remarks on one such evening, as he slides a Sam Adams to her across the bar. "I was just thinking about all the shit I missed by not living in the servants' quarters. I mean, it's like I was working at a place I thought was the Knox, and Jerry and Eduardo were working at an entirely different one."

"You and me both."

"Want the cheeseburger again, medium?" he asks, and then adds, grinning, "although you might be interested to know that for a special tonight, we have the *sacrificial* lamb burger—I mean, the lamb burger."

"Ha ha, very funny."

New Girl, the Sacrifice is when potential members reveal their biggest secret, Liam had told her recently, between guffaws. *It's a sacrifice because it's a risk. You can reveal your secret, but then still not be admitted if the members don't think it's sufficient, and if geomancy doesn't dictate it.*

Taylor doesn't think she'll be living down her blunder anytime soon. Nor should she, really; the only real danger Vivian had been in was from Rose—and the questionable medical judgment of the Knox house doctor.

Taylor still doesn't know what to make of Rose. She wasn't

innocent, but she wasn't an Oliver, either. Taylor gets why Tara's feelings toward her are complicated.

When Liam serves Taylor the cheeseburger, she notices how he's added sweet potato fries without her having to ask—and they're well-done, just how she likes them.

She smiles; she's beginning to understand him more, how loyalty means so much to him. Their little meetups here and there stack up in his mind like a steel-constructed ladder. He'd like to be more than friends, she thinks, but she's not so sure they should try that.

Her landlord, Anna, only ever brings up the Knox twice to Taylor: the first in the form of a note slipped under her door, shortly after the fire.

Taylor,

I didn't know. They got me hook, line, and sinker. A description for a job applicant that was you to a tee.

—Anna

P.S. Next month's rent is on me.

The second time is late summer, when Anna shows up unannounced, rapping Taylor's door with her cane. When Taylor cracks open the door, Anna thrusts *The Boston Globe* at her.

Taylor recoils at the sight of Oliver's face on the front page; he looks as gaunt as ever. CORRUPTION SCANDAL ROCKS PRIVATE CLUB, the headline reads.

"Don't you worry. You were never there," Anna says.

She leaves Taylor with the article, which includes about as vague a description of the Knox as could be; the "private club" mentioned in the headline is about the extent of it. Taylor can only imagine the walls the reporter must have repeatedly bumped up against while trying to crack the mystery of the Knox. The focus of the piece is on Oliver Thurgood, and the charges brought against him: drug trafficking, distribution, possession with intent to distribute, conspiracy, among others. He'll likely spend many years behind bars. The article makes it sound like Oliver was a rogue operator in drug importation, and had plans underway for a large-scale operation with an established international drug ring.

Maybe that's true; maybe not. At any rate, Taylor knows it's only a piece of what really went down at the Knox. There's no mention of murder, for instance; Graham's name doesn't appear in the article. Some things, it seems, will be forever buried. And the Knox itself is mostly spared, maintaining a healthy, notorious distance.

Sam says that Taylor has good stories to tell at a cocktail party, but she's not ready to hit the Boston party scene. She secures a job as a nurse esthetician at a fancy medical spa on Newbury Street. She thought she'd love it, being able to interact with the high-end clientele, but she doesn't. She likes being able to try out some of the cosmetic procedures, but the women coming through the door are fussy and entitled, and such complainers. Taylor finds she needs to take a mental snapshot of their outfits before she begins to converse with them, to separate the clothing from the personality.

In fact, Taylor discovers the aspect she enjoys the most about her new job is her walk to and from the clinic, passing the window displays of clothing storefronts. She finds herself critiquing the mannequins, as if they were real models: what Taylor likes, what she would change. Sometimes it's pairing an entirely different top with a skirt, other times it's an adjustment on the hemline. Occasionally it's adding one of her flower embellishments, for which she's starting to take orders. She has Vivian to thank for that; when Vivian wears them, her customers and friends always inquire where they can purchase such accessories.

"You have an innate sense of style," Vivian compliments her, to which Taylor jokes, "Yeah, I like nice things."

"No, it's more than that," Vivian says. "Everyone likes nice things. But you have a real nose for fashion. I see it in the things you wear, and your designs. It's quite remarkable."

It's been a little strange to get to know Vivian the person. She's still intimidating, and Taylor is still in awe. She feels awkward around her and probably acts as such.

Sometimes, when Taylor's walking along the cobblestoned streets of Beacon Hill, she finds herself almost automatically turning toward the Knox. Once, she stood for a good twenty minutes across the street, staring at the iconic redbrick building's facade—which remained mostly intact, despite its fire-ravaged insides. The Knox had looked both opened and closed, regal and plain, secretive and ordinary.

A tingle ran through her that she hasn't been able to forget.

Then there's that other place in Boston that also had a fire and is also full of secrets. The place on Greenwich Lane where her mother lived. Taylor has yet to visit.

"When you're ready," Sam tells her, "I'll go with you."

VIVIAN

Three Months After the Fire

"Good morning," Michael says, arriving at the store as promised. He hands Vivian a coffee, that day's *New York Times* crossword puzzle, and a stack of papers. "I had a friend do these CAD drawings of the new space. And the crossword, well, that speaks for itself."

She flips through the papers, ignoring the puzzle. "These are incredible, Michael." She peers more closely at them. "Wait, are those the actual pieces of furniture from *this* shop?"

"Yes, as you may remember, I took photos the last time I was here, and they were able to import them."

"Are those the actual dimensions? The correct ones?"

"Yes."

She waves the tape measure in her hand. "So you're saying I don't need to go around and measure every single piece to figure out what will and won't fit at the new space?"

"You do not."

"Thank you. Truly."

"It's my pleasure," he says, and then he turns away, as if her compliment has embarrassed him.

She's finding she likes his little quirks. She likes spending time with him. She likes the way he cares for her; today, her coffee has the usual splash of milk, but he brought an additional sugar packet on the side, in case she needed a little boost. And then there are the crossword puzzles he brings, ever since he learned they could help with her TBI recovery.

She looks through the drawings, still amazed. "You saved me at least a day of work, if not two, given my brain these days. Now I'll have time to do this crossword, I suppose."

"That was my intent," he jokes.

She's trying to reconcile Michael the Knox member with Michael the person. They are the same—and they are different. Last week, to her surprise, he offered to do a geomantic divination reading on her behalf. She humored him, asked what she thought was an insignificant question—or at least a foregone conclusion, since she'd already signed the lease: *Is the new store space a good one?* As he began casting the chart, he became animated, his eyes bright.

"So you really buy into this geomancy thing," she remarked, and then immediately regretted it when she saw the light snuff out from his eyes like an eclipse.

He opened and closed his mouth a few times before finally responding, "Don't you believe there's more in the world than what we can see?"

"I don't know. You mean, like magic?"

"Magic, mood, aura, energy—whatever you want to call it. Don't you feel it, sometimes? Whatever 'it' is?"

"Do you?"

"Isn't it obvious?" He looked at her intensely, and she could feel it then: the *possibility*, like a gift whose contents you don't ever unwrap.

"I suppose I'd *like* to believe."

"Then *do*," he simply replied, and continued with his reading. The answer he delivered was anything but trivial; it was thoughtful and nuanced. And remarkably astute.

Though "belief" is a pill she's still working on swallowing, she will admit a begrudging respect for the ancient practice of geomancy. (And yes, the space is a *very* good one.)

Michael now taps at the CAD drawings in her hands. "The only pieces I didn't take pictures of were the furniture items in the back of the store," he says. "The ones covered in moving blankets and Bubble Wrap. I wasn't sure if those were coming or going to the new space."

Vivian sighs. "Right. I need to figure that out. Those are awaiting refinishing. They're mostly coming, unfortunately, and very delayed. My go-to antique restorer passed away during Covid, and I haven't found his replacement yet. I got a little waylaid in the past few months."

"Understandable."

"Actually," she says, cocking her head, "some of those items belong to you, or rather, the Knox."

"Oh? Let's take a look, shall we?"

As they unwrap the cloths, their fingers accidentally brush. "Sorry," Michael says.

"Don't be." And then she adds, slyly, "I rather liked it."

He pauses to look at her. "As did I."

They continue to work, a silence encompassing them. But it's a comfortable quiet.

They uncover a nineteenth-century painted Italian chest and a French antique tub chair, both of which are Knox items, and an eighteenth-century rococo giltwood stool, which belongs to a wealthy friend of Vivian's mother. Then, a random Ming dynasty porcelain vase. *Christ.* Vivian can't seem to shake this era.

Michael studies the vase, running his fingers over the blue poppy flower design.

"I used opium during my geomantic readings at the Knox, to open my mind," he suddenly admits. "It was in our charter, what tradition dictated. But—that reading I did for you, about your new store space—that was the first time I realized I don't need it to honor the practice." He gives her an almost enigmatic smile. "Thank you."

She returns his smile, feeling let in on the secret. She likes *this*—feeling a connection to this man.

"Are you planning to still do readings for them?" she asks, as casually as she can.

"I don't know," he concedes. "I'm assuming what you are really asking is what I am planning to do in terms of my allegiance to the Knox. It's complicated. As you are aware, I descend from a long line of members." He pauses, looking somewhat abashed. "I feel rather silly saying that, since you descend from a long line of *ancestors*."

"It's okay," she says. She wants him to continue. "So?"

"So, I don't know." He shrugs, looking uncharacteristically flummoxed.

She nods; she understands how one's upbringing can mold you, how even after you've long sprung from the cast, you still feel the phantom shape of the plaster. Given all that's happened with the Knox, this is new territory. He—and perhaps she—will have to sort it out.

As they start undressing the last piece of furniture, labeled "cabinet" on the white masking tape, Michael asks, "Are you still seeing Peter?"

"No. He's asked if he can see me when he returns from Milan, but I don't want to."

The truth of it hits her as it's leaving her mouth. She *doesn't* want to see him, she realizes.

Michael's cocoa-brown eyes meet hers, and a warmth flushes through her. He doesn't say anything, but he doesn't need to.

As they pull off the blanket, she's momentarily stunned. It's not a cabinet but rather a secretary. From the nineteenth century, and from the Knox.

"Oh! I'd forgotten about this piece," he remarks.

"I don't remember this," she says, shaking her head.

"Your assistant was here the day we brought it in. What was her name?"

"Riley. She doesn't work here anymore. Not since Covid, when she moved back to New Jersey. She never told me about it. I . . ." Vivian's voice trails off. She runs her fingers along the top of the secretary. It has one of those drop-down lids, which she pulls down now.

It's nearly identical to the one she searched through in the Knox, when Michael caught her. Now, he gives her a questioning look, one eyebrow peaked like a mountaintop.

"I . . . There could be something here. Something . . . about my family," she says breathlessly.

She quickly pops out the dovetail drawer to the left, and Michael follows her lead, removing the one to the right. She runs her fingers along the wood adjacent to the column, looking for the same notch she'd previously found, but there is none. He does the same, running his fingers on the opposite side.

"It's here," he says, sounding excited.

She checks where he's pointing. "You're right! We just need a pin."

"It's a shame you're not wearing a hairpin today," Michael teases. He looks around. "Here, we can use this paper clip." He undoes the paper clip from the CAD drawings and extends the clip, so it has a long tentacle. "You do the honors."

She inserts the clip into the notch, and it clicks into place, ejecting the column. She grasps the edge, pulling it out. It's a deep wooden document folder, and she holds her breath as she peers inside.

"It's empty," she says, disappointment lacing her words. She turns it to show him as her shoulders collapse.

He takes the holder from her and turns it upside down, as if that will magically make something appear.

"Wait. Look here. I think this slides up." He's pulling on the back edge of the holder, and as the wood shifts, it reveals a false bottom. He takes a quick look inside and hands the holder back to her.

"Is there something in it?" she asks.

"See for yourself."

She slips her fingers into the small false space, and they hit something paperlike. Very, very carefully, she tugs it out. It's a scroll. Her heart quickening, she places the scroll onto the flat surface of the secretary.

Michael holds on to one end, while Vivian unrolls the other.

It's the schedule of beneficiaries.

TAYLOR

Six Months After the Fire

One October day, the weather turns a page, the unusually hot autumn switching to a brisk, proper fall. With it comes a reality check. Taylor dons a repurposed Lingua Franca cashmere sweater and knocks on Sam's door.

"I'm ready," she says.

They walk quickly, with intention, though he is just mimicking her pace. If she stops even a moment, she thinks, she might not keep going.

It takes mere minutes from their apartment to reach Greenwich Lane, yet inside her, emotions layer, like thick coats of paint. As they turn the corner, they pass a lion sculpture seemingly guarding the street's entrance—a detail she never noticed before. She never got close enough to notice.

The tears are fresh on her face, and Sam gives her shoulders a squeeze.

They make their way past redbrick townhouses. Trees on both sides lean forward to meet in a spidery canopy, their leaves partially fallen. A boy whizzes by on a scooter, his mother scampering behind. There is that contained sense of neighborhood, of family order, canvases created: dinners and routines, Saturday playdates and Sunday morning pancakes. Lives lived—not lives lost.

Finally, they reach number 2, and only then does it hit Taylor that claustrophobia has not walked along with them.

Like the rest of the street, this townhouse emanates peace. A set of three stairs lead up to the wooden front door; the street-level windows don wrought iron grilles and window boxes filled with autumn's mums and kale. Gray suede-looking drapes cascade down on the inside. Below, on the basement level, are a set of half-size windows not covered with any type of metal grille. The glass is clouded, as if covered with an opaque cloth. These windows are too small, she supposes, to need security bars; nobody would be able to break in through them.

And nobody could break out.

Taylor recalls what her father had once told her: The building itself was like a giant chimney. She can see that now, the way it rises, the outer brick walls like the outline of a smokestack. The furniture inside like logs, fuel for the fire roasting within. The roof: an unfortunately closed flute.

"You okay?" Sam asks, and she shrugs. They stand shoulder to shoulder, closer than they need to.

Taylor tries to put herself on the other side of the small basement window, in the moment that claimed her mother's life, a moment with which she is now all too familiar: the choke of the thick smoke, the singeing heat, the ominous crackle of things burning.

What did her mother think about in those last moments? Was it panic; was it regret? Did her mother think of her? *Or did she not think at all?*

For Taylor's whole life, before her fateful conversation with Aunt Gigi, it had never occurred to her that her mother might not have even registered the fire. That she might have been in a drugged stupor.

Her mother, it turns out, was one of the lost girls.

The evidence had been there, all along, contained in the photo of her mom in the Boston bar. When Taylor finally really examined it, looking past the mirage of who she thought her mother had been, she saw the uneven hem on her mother's cream jacket, the sleeve button falling off. The subtle rip in her mother's hose. Her too-skinny frame.

Taylor exhales slowly. "It's a weird thing to realize someone was not who you thought they were," she says.

"I bet."

She turns to him. "But it's shaped me, you know? Like, maybe I wouldn't be the person I am today if I knew the truth all along. Maybe . . ." *Maybe I wouldn't have been so materialistic, so drawn to wealth.* But is she materialistic? Or is it that she's naturally into fashion, like Vivian said?

Taylor's been mulling over this question as of late, and the more she thinks about Vivian's assessment of her, the more it niggles at her. Perhaps Vivian's view is skewed. After all, it seems to Taylor that people with money like to make desire out to be somehow more elevated, refined—an upper-class rebranding of want.

Why can't want just be want—and called like it is?

"I really don't like my job at the med spa," she suddenly admits, feeling all kinds of raw. "I thought I would, but I don't."

"You going to do something about it?" Sam shifts the Red Sox hat on his head.

"Well, I need a job, so no, not right now."

"You're young; you'll figure it out. Or maybe you won't, and that's okay, too."

"I know I like fashion." It feels good to say it, out loud—the want. But then she frowns. Is it fashion she likes, or is it everything it represents? It's not really about the clothes themselves—it's more about who wears them and the places they get to wear them, isn't it?

Her phone buzzes, and when she sees who's calling, heat immediately rises to her cheeks. She silences it, sending the caller to voicemail. She glances up at Sam, but he doesn't seem to notice.

"I know you like fashion. You're good at it, too," he replies, scratching his head beneath the hat. "Just keep at it, slow and steady; that's how I built my career."

"Thanks," she replies, almost curtly. She's annoyed by his response, but she can't pinpoint why.

"Hey, you wanna talk about . . ." He gestures in front of them.

She stares hard at the basement windows, as if doing so will unlock some secret. Her tears have long dried. After a while, she gives up, shrugs. "I don't think there's anything to say."

"Well, you didn't get claustrophobic and pass out, so that's something."

She laughs. "True. Maybe the Knox fire cured me."

"Nah. You cured you."

They start walking back down the street, and her phone buzzes again, this time with a voicemail notification.

It was a chance encounter when Taylor ran into Peter outside the Knox a few weeks ago. She'd gone by, curious about the status of construction, now nearly complete. Peter had looked so dapper, standing on the sidewalk clutching a set of architectural plans, dressed in a fine Italian designer wool pea coat, a light stubble on his cheeks.

"Taylor!" he'd said, with surprise. "It's nice to see you." He'd just returned to town, "fresh out of another stint in rehab," he admitted, somewhat sheepishly, and that vulnerability had felt to her like an invitation, a door slowly being opened. They stayed on the sidewalk chatting for forty minutes, until it had become obvious that although convention dictated they should bid each other goodbye, they weren't ready to.

So, ever since, they've been in touch—and not just over the phone. Her heart quickens as she recalls the last time she saw him: the half-drunk bottle of expensive Barolo at the bedside, the crown of Peter's head moving slowly down her navel, the 600-thread count Egyptian sheets rippling beneath them like the Nile.

Damn, those bedsheets deserve their sticker price.

The Knox is hiring; we've got a lot of roles to fill. Are you interested? Peter asked her the other day. He's calling to follow up; she owes him an answer.

But Taylor doesn't have one yet.

As she and Sam reach the end of the street, Sam pauses to check his watch. "Hey, want to grab a croissant at Ly's Pastry Shoppe? I think it's still open. My treat?"

"I can't. I have to stop by the med spa and finish up some paperwork from yesterday."

"No worries. Next time."

But as they part ways, Taylor doesn't head in the direction of the office. Instead, she wanders aimlessly, turning down one block and then another. Under the web of tree branches, she moves from one shadow to the next, lost in her thoughts. She's reminded of those car rides she used to take in North Carolina, how she'd drive for hours without a destination.

Just keep at it, slow and steady, Sam's voice echoes in her mind—and a restlessness starts building in her like a brewing storm.

He doesn't understand her—not really. It's probably why she never fully opened up to him. She never could show him the real her—not all of it, at least. Only bits and pieces, toe dips into the ocean.

Why can't want just be want—and called like it is?

Taylor's long tried to deny the yearnings inside her, to reshape them, even, like molding wet sand. But the castles she's been attempting to build keep collapsing.

Why can't want be want? Desire just desire?

She repeats these words like a mantra, and her feet start moving like they have a mind of their own. Zigzagging through the streets, Taylor finds herself heading north. As if pulled by a current, she cuts through the Public Garden, dipping beneath willow trees, slipping past manicured hedges.

She soon reaches the main thoroughfare of Beacon Hill, where the wrought iron lampposts stand tall and steady like lighthouse beacons. A few quick turns later, she's stepping onto the cobblestones of Clapboard Street and directly into the postcard. Taylor feels light now, effortlessly gliding over the bumpy terrain as if it's the yellow brick road. The stately redbrick buildings fold her within their embrace: velvet curtains drawn, crystal chandeliers warmly lit, brass door knockers polished to a gleam.

Like they've been expecting her.

THE KNOX

_____.

___ahem___.

(coughing)

___ahem___.

(clears throat)

Ahem!

(clears throat)

Well, that was *unexpected* (clears throat louder). Excuse me; there's a bit of lingering dust. Most of it, though, is from the new construction. I am, as they say, risen from the ashes.

Yes, yes, the rumors are true; I have gotten quite the rebirth. As per the architectural plans, I am emerging even more stately, more refined, and more elegant this time around. And, dare I add, more fireproof. Sprinklers have been discreetly built into my ceilings, woodburning chimneys converted to the convenience of gas, and all structural lumber composed exclusively of fire-retardant-treated wood. Oh, the utter delights of twenty-first-century craftsmanship and Boston's cleverest minds! All, naturally, in the most charming and exclusive neighborhood in America.

One area that did not require improvement: the fireproof safes that cradle the scrolls. One never really knows if such fire ratings are to be trusted—two thousand degrees for up to 240 minutes always seemed like a bit of a stretch to me—but I'll be the first to admit that my doubts were proven unnecessary.

Now, I only hope that those dreadful tourists will soon lose interest. They've been coming in appalling numbers on weekends, often dressed in the *most* unseemly attire. Their hair, the most ridiculous shades of colors, and some with unmentionable piercings. It's an epidemic of riffraff. And the spectacle they are making! Leaving flowers at my former steps. Whispering prayers. Conducting geomancy divination readings—as if they had a clue how to perform this sacred practice.

Worse still are the gawking *ordinary* tourists—so uninspired, so pathetically dull.

Good heavens.

The construction's end is in sight, and it cannot arrive a moment too soon. Order simply must be restored. I have suffered far too many indignities.

Onward, now, to the next few decades. I'll miss Rose, but there'll be another Rose.

There always is.

Acknowledgments

I once took a tour of the Boston Athenaeum, the city's old, independent library. When we passed the oil portrait of Thomas Handasyd Perkins, a major benefactor in the 1800s, the docent alluded to a dark truth about how Mr. Perkins had made his fortune: the opium trade. I was fascinated by this tidbit and went down a rabbit hole to learn just how much wealth Brahmin families accumulated through the nineteenth-century opium trade that shaped the Boston we know today. It's not a well-known fact. I was inspired by this, and by my own neighborhood of historic Beacon Hill, with its cobblestone streets and quirky old townhouses. I began to imagine a very powerful secret society with roots in the opium trade, set in a modern-day storyline with contemporary characters. *The Society* was born.

So, first and foremost, I'd like to thank Stacy Testa, my literary agent, for helping me to bring *The Society* to life. You are both an incredible agent and person, so I really lucked out. Thanks for always being in my corner. And a huge thank-you to Sydnee Harlan—you've been so wonderful. Thank you also to Daniel Conaway for stepping in at a crucial time.

I am so grateful to Charlotte Peters, my editor. I loved having the opportunity to work with you. Thank you for the brainstorming sessions, your stellar edits, great instincts, and willingness to consider any and all of my ideas. It's been such a fun, intensive, and creative journey.

A special thank-you also goes out to Lindsey Rose.

A thousand thanks to the entire Dutton/PRH team, including John Parsley, Maya Ziv, Caroline Payne, Amanda Walker, LeeAnn Pemberton, Erin Byrne, Laura Corless, Melissa Solis, and Jennifer Heuer. And thank you to Erica Ferguson, Susan Schwartz, and Lisa Silverman.

Thank you also to Lexy Cassola, who believed in the nuggets of this book from the start. It would not exist without you.

I'd also like to sincerely thank Kathleen Carter, my publicist.

And a big thank-you goes to Becca Rodriguez, my film agent.

Paul Girard: I'm grateful for the book's illustrations.

To my husband, Gil: you are always my first reader and my last reader, and, truthfully, also my in-between reader. I couldn't do this novel-writing business or life without you. Thank you for accompanying me on strange midnight tours of Boston for book inspiration and for celebrating my writing wins, no matter how small they are. I love you.

To my mom: I hit the mom jackpot. I hit it over and over, really. Anytime I need help, whether it's with the kids, or my book babies, or life, you are there. I am eternally grateful. I'll never forget how you dropped everything that January so I could get away for that much-needed writer's retreat. Thanks for also line editing all my manuscripts with so many skinny Post-its they look like McDonald's large fries.

To my sister, Aimee, and my brother, David, otherwise known as the best siblings in the world: Thank you for always believing in me and for being my rocks. Aimee, thank you also for being my earliest reader (alongside Gil). All I can ever think to myself about the two of you is: Aren't I lucky? (Aren't we lucky??)

To my late father, whose absence I feel every day: I created a poor excuse for a father in my first novel, probably because I knew I'd fail if I tried to create one anything like you. In this novel, though the father character is markedly improved, he still doesn't hold a candle to who you were. No father figure I write ever will.

I'm incredibly fortunate to have both writer friends and reader friends who read and weighed in on my manuscript at various stages over the past couple of years. Thank you to Shelley Berg, Jennifer Blecher, Carolyne Topdjian, Malia Márquez, Katherine Taylor, Carol Schneider, Lada Marcelja, Paula Mirk, Betty Yee, Jane Deon, Julie Carrick Dalton, Namrata Patel, Amy Deutsch, Katherine Steinberg, Kathleen Rice, Sachiko Sato, April Cowin, Jessica Saunders, Emily Holland, and Cassandra Foster. The book is so much better because of your invaluable input, and I'm deeply grateful.

For this book, I got to do the writer thing and ask people for research help. First off, I'd like to thank Marilyn Lipton Okonow, who is an actual genealogist at the Vilna Shul (among other illustrious careers). I truly appreciate you sharing your extensive knowledge of genealogy with me.

I am blessed to count among my closest friends a couple of impressive nurses with whom I used to work at Mass General, and who continue to be nurse rock stars—and, as it turns out, medical consultants. Thank you to Sachiko Sato and Paula Restrepo for promptly and thoroughly responding to my many health care–related questions.

I also owe a heartful thank-you to Rebecca Hackler, who is the real deal when it comes to antiques—and the owner of Fabled

Antiques in Beacon Hill. Thanks for letting me pick your brain (and allowing my daughter to tag along).

I'm incredibly grateful to the geomancer Dr. Alexander Cummins, who helped me navigate the use of geomancy in the novel, including generating the "bad shield" that the character Michael uses.

To learn about anthropodermic bibliopegy, I turned to the fascinating book *Dark Archives* by Megan Rosenbloom.

Thank you to Geronimo, the engineer on Reddit who patiently answered my questions about cyanide.

Thank you also to Michael Putziger for lending an ear to some financial plot questions I had early on while brainstorming the book.

I occasionally get to drag friends along on writing-related research adventures, so thank you to Kristen Hatcher Keith for accompanying me on the tour of the Forbes House Museum, and to Ranella Saul for coming with me to the exhibition at the Harvard Art Museums. You are each so special to me, and not just because you joined me on these tours, but because you are so special.

In an earlier version of this book, Vivian's best friend (from college), Kat, had not died, and was very much alive, and played a more important role. Thank you to my own real-life "Kats": Kathy Rice and Katherine Steinberg, my college—and life—besties. I'm sorry I had to kill you off; it was truly a case of killing one's darlings.

Thank you to my writing groups, whose members I've mostly already mentioned but who deserve another shout-out: my original Boston-based group, which began in 2009 (and is now bicoastal): Shelley Berg, Betty G. Yee, Jane Deon, Theresea Barrett, and Anita Kharbanda; my "Portable Magic" crew of Carol

Schneider, Lada Marcelja, and Paula Mirk; and my McK! group consisting of Carolyne Topdjian and Malia Márquez. Damn, I'm lucky to have you guys.

To Nicole Lipson, aka writer-bestie, thank you for being on this crazy author-journey-life alongside me.

Thank you also to "Da Best Debuts," including Ash Davidson, Juhea Kim, Rachel Lyon, Coco Mellors, Adele Myers, Kirthana Ramisetti, and Caroline Frost Szymanski, for the friendship and support.

Jessica Saunders, I'm grateful for our honest writing conversations.

Dara Astmann, thanks for keeping me on writing track.

Jennifer Blecher, thank you for the dog walks and writer talks.

Teresa Chope, thank you for allowing me to glimpse a real secret society.

Namrata Patel, thank you for our many awesome writing sessions.

Zoey Gulmi, thank you for your PR wisdom and for being such a treasured part of my life.

Thank you, Arthur Winn, for being one of my biggest writing fans.

Thank you to my entire extended family: the Crooks, Aronsons, Matchetts, Ehrenfrieds, and my cousins.

I also want to thank Lorena Sanders, Kiki Valadares, Edit Knowlton, Kelly Ford, and Mo Grant for helping to take care of my kids while I (attempt to) juggle writing and mothering. I drop balls all the time, but I do so less because of you.

Thank you to Kelley Peace and Caroline Novak for taking care of my other "kid," my dog Mando.

And a big thank-you to the rest of those who are "my people," including the Ladies Who Eat, the Awesome TI Moms, and each and every one of my friends whom I hold so dear.

At long last, it's time to thank my kids, who are my heart and soul: Rand and Essa. They've grown up having to share their mother with her writing, and they do it unselfishly. I love you.

About the Author

KAREN WINN is the author of two novels, *The Society* and *Our Little World*. She earned her MFA from Fairleigh Dickinson University. For her undergraduate studies she attended the University of Pennsylvania, where she may or may not have belonged to a secret society. Before becoming an author, Karen had a career as a nurse. She lives in the charming Beacon Hill neighborhood of Boston with her husband, two children, and their hundred-pound Bernedoodle.